Broken Lion

Devon Hartford

Want to find out about my next book before everyone else and get free novellas not available anywhere else? Then sign up for my mailing list!

Sign up here:

http://eepurl.com/B7crf

DEDICATION

To Anna Lamonica for asking me to write a wounded hero novel. Here it is, Anna. This one's for you. :-)

Broken Lion

SOME SECRETS ARE TOO HARD TO KEEP...

The night the EMTs wheeled Lion Maxwell into my Emergency Room turned my life upside down. Although he was bloody and battered from defending his title as the reigning cruiserweight champion of Mixed Martial Arts, his cocky grin lit up the room.

And every cell in my body.

Our fiery chemistry was off the charts.

The ER staff sensed it.

Lion's entourage and his drooling groupies sensed it too.

If the two of us had been alone, I might have done something entirely unprofessional and completely unethical right there in the exam room. But I was his attending physician. A sexual or romantic relationship with him was grounds for my termination or worse, revoking my medical license. I wouldn't risk my career on a moment of passion. It didn't stop that arrogant caveman from doing everything he could to get me into his hospital bed.

After denying his advances for weeks, the last thing I expected were the wild nights he would be spending in my bed.

It was supposed to be nothing more than a secret fling.

I knew it couldn't last.

He was still my patient.

What we were doing was wrong.

If anyone found out, it could ruin my life.

But we couldn't let go.

We were bound to each other on some primal level that consumed us.

Sometimes love is tragic.

Sometimes two people aren't meant to be together.

But sometimes, two people overcome all adversity and build a love that lasts forever.

Deep in my heart I knew that Lion Maxwell could be my forever love.

As long as we kept our love a secret.

I wish I'd known beforehand that some secrets are too hard to keep...

Chapter 1

BRIGID

I didn't have time for men.

As an attending physician at the busy Los Angeles Central Hospital, I had too many responsibilities. Caring for my patients was always my top priority. For me, dating was an afterthought.

But I wasn't a robot.

I noticed men all the time.

For example, several of the EMTs who wheeled patients into the Emergency Care Unit every night were to die for. The boys in blue were just as yummy, ember-eyed Officer Noah Murdock being the yummiest.

The firemen from the LAFD were even more gorgeous. My favorites were Troy and Rick from Station 10. Both were regulars here in the ECU. Both were also smoking hot and known not only for saving lives and putting out fires, but for starting fires—in women's panties, and not just mine. Ask any of the women on the ECU team (and some of the men). Troy and Rick were also known for appearing topless in the LAFD Firefighter's calendar hanging in our team break room. In it, both men sported oiled-up abs and bulging shoulders while looking rugged and sweaty and deadly sexy in their suspiciously low hanging firemen's pants. Troy was *Mother's Day May* and Rick was *I wish me a Merry Christmas December*. Yes, I skipped ahead to check. Several times a week.

Like I said, I noticed men all the time.

But I was too busy doing my job to date any.

When I wasn't here at the hospital, I was the on call physician and had to come in at the most unexpected times. Not ideal for dating. Most weeks it seemed like I lived here.

After setting a broken arm in exam room 102, I walked out to fill out the relevant paperwork before taking my next patient.

Latisha Brown, the charge nurse, fell into step beside me and said, "Girl, you gonna wet yourself when you get a look at the fine man in 109. Mmm, mmm, mmm." She muttered it in a low voice as we walked toward the nurses station. Latisha and I gossiped about hot men all the time. It helped keep things light when they got too serious. "Man brought a whole entourage with him."

I glanced over at the door to 109. A dozen people crowded the entrance. More were packed inside the room. "Is he somebody famous?"

"Not that I know. But he oughta be a model, the way he looks. Or an actor. Or my next hookup. Mmm, mmm, I'm telling you, girl." Her eyes glimmered with desire. "I had to change my drawers after helping Allison check his vitals."

"Why?" I snickered.

"On account of my lady parts was perspiring." She winked.

"He can't be that hot."

"You ain't seen him yet. The way he looks, that boy must live in a gym. Allison's hands were shaking so bad when she tried to slide the blood pressure cuff up his arm, I had to do it for her."

"I'm sure you hated every second of it."

"Every last one." She chuckled.

"Do you have his medical record?" Now I was curious.

She reached over the counter of the nurses station and grabbed a chart off the rack. "Here you go. Before you go in, I should warn you about the python in his pants."

"Python? An actual python?" From time to time, patients came into the ECU with the strangest things attached to or inserted inside themselves. The obvious: nipple clamps, cock rings, dildos, vibrators, anal beads, condoms, tampons. The not so obvious: fruits, vegetables, latex gloves, flashlights, a toy car, a glass light bulb. Yes, an actual light bulb. When I extracted it, Latisha was on hand. I held it up and said, "This gives me an idea." Latisha struggled not to laugh. The patient was half passed out on muscle relaxants (we were worried about shattering the lightbulb) and he lay face down on the bed. The light bulb was a first for everyone on staff that night. But top of the list for Latisha and me went a step weirder. Two summers ago, we performed a Rectal Foreign Body Removal of a smallish garden gnome, complete with red pointy hat, from a male patient. The man had said he "fell on it" while gardening. By "fell" he meant "sat down." On purpose. Multiple times. After discharging him and sending the man home with his gnome, I warned him to be more careful while "gardening" in the future. In private, I'd asked Latisha if she thought the man did his "gardening" in the nude. She said no, he probably wore assless chaps at the very least, so as to protect him from thorns and thistles. I had said, but not from gnomes? We had both broken into laughter at that point.

"You remembering that nasty ass gnome, ain't you?"

"Sadly." I chuckled.

"Don't worry, the python in 109 is warm blooded. But I'll get you the anti-venom kit, just in case."

"Tisha, pythons aren't warm blooded and they don't have venom."

"This one does." Her eyes flared for a moment before she swallowed a ticking snicker, doing her best to maintain a professional demeanor. It wasn't working. "And it spits like a cobra if you get it all riled up." We both giggled naughtily.

"When was the last time you got any? You sound completely desperate."

"More recently than you. And that ain't saying much."

"Don't remind me." I groaned while flipping through the man's chart. I read his name out loud. "Lion Maxwell? That can't be his real name."

"I think it is."

"Who names their child Lion?"

"Shoulda named him Snake," she said seriously.

I glared at her and struggled not to laugh as I walked toward the crowd outside 109. It consisted of several men wearing matching gold on black T-shirts emblazoned with a roaring lion and the slogan #TeamLion - FEEL THE BEAST.

Why did that sound vaguely sexual?

The other men standing outside wore suits or blazers and slacks. There were also a few women best described as trashy strippers: tight micro skirts, flashy bedazzled tops with too much cleavage, fake boobs, spray tans, garish makeup, etc. I'm sure a significant portion of the male population found women like these highly desirable, but to me they looked like sparkly clowns.

One of the strippers had a strategically messy pile of dark hair on her head that was the largest I'd seen since the late 1980s. On her, somehow it worked. Her eyes raked over me with obvious judgement and a hint of a challenge, like she saw me as competition. Competition for what, I wasn't sure. She sneered, "Who are you?"

I wanted to say, *Was the stethoscope and white lab coat not enough of a giveaway?* But I was a professional and kept it to myself. "I'm the doctor."

"Oh."

"Mind if I see my patient?"

"Whatever," she huffed and turned her back to me.

I squeezed past her into the exam room. More burly men in #TeamLion T-shirts filled the room.

Latisha was right.

One look at the nearly naked man reclining on the hospital bed said it all. He made my favorite firefighters Troy and Rick look like regular Joes. Lion Maxwell was in another league. He was dangerously gorgeous. Emphasis on danger. Thick dark hair and equally dark eyes added a brooding quality. A number of contusions and cuts were scattered over his face and torso, but on him it looked good, like they belonged there. This man was a warrior and he'd obviously been in a fight. Even lying down, he exuded a masculine energy that said *Do not mess with me or I will destroy you.* Add to that his perfect body that was hard and scarred and chiseled in the extreme. Exactly what you would expect from the king of the beasts.

A wave of desire rained down from my head to my toes. I pushed it away. I was here to work, not languish in his good looks.

My eyes focused on his splinted knee. The EMS team had already stabilized the knee joint with orange board splints and stretch bandages. Lion's chart had said dislocation of the joint with possible torn ligaments and/or tibial avulsion fracture, which meant the kneecap tendon contracted so hard it tore off a chunk of bone from the lower leg. The swelling was bad enough it could be any or all of those things. Only an MRI would reveal the full extent of the injury.

"Who ordered the foxy doctor?" Lion said from the bed, relaxed and amused. His voice was deep and slightly gravelly. It shook me out of my diagnostic train of thought and did things to me that were entirely inappropriate.

The men surrounding him all turned to face me like a pack of jackals. All had hungry eyes.

Welcome to the lion's den.

I'd never felt so much testosterone in one room. Most of it came from Lion and made me feel like a piece of meat, the kind that gets hunted down by ravenous carnivores on the plains of the Serengeti.

Lion's dark and dangerous eyes roamed all over me. "Please tell me you're my doctor."

His men chuckled approval. Obviously, Lion was the king of these beasts. But I needed to get this situation under control. Not a problem. I was in my element.

"I'm Dr. Flanagan. What happened to you, Mr. Maxwell?"

"Call me Lion. Everybody does." *That voice.* It oozed confidence and resonated in my chest like he was invading me.

If he kept talking in that sexy voice of his, I was going to be the one doing the oozing. I needed to stay focused. I was a doctor, not a giddy teenager. So I took a moment to collect myself in case I started babbling like one.

Lion smirked at me. A hungry sexy smirk.

I offered a curt smile and swallowed hard. The giddy teenager in me wanted desperately to bat my eyelashes at this gorgeous man.

More chuckles rumbled from Lion's men as they watched me trying to hold it together. One said, "Go easy on her, Lion."

Another: "She looks fragile. You don't wanna spook her."

Spook me? What, like I was some kind of dainty deer wandering through the forest, scared of the big bad mountain Lion? Not even close. I was the opposite of fragile.

Lion said, "What's the matter, Doc? Cat got your tongue?"

I smirked. "Very funny, Mr. Maxwell. I was just taking a moment to ignore your arrogance in hopes that it would go away. But we all know wishful thinking never works."

"Don't worry. I've got more where that came from."

More what, I didn't want to know. Mainly because I was afraid I would like it, whatever it was.

One of the other men said, "Don't mind him. He's always like this with the ladies."

Lion laughed easily. "You trying to make me look bad, Cahill?"

Cahill chortled. "When it comes to looking like a tool, you don't need any help from me."

"But if I did, you'd be the first man I'd ask for lessons."

The men laughed again. Cahill laughed too. Clearly, this group was the best of friends. Or frat brothers. All they needed was a keg and a stack of plastic cups to get this party started.

"So, Mr. Maxwell. About your knee." I said it loud enough to get everyone's attention. "Can you tell me what happened?"

"Busted it up in the cage tonight."

"Championship fight," Cahill added. The nice thing about having an entourage of your own was that they could parade your ego around for you, so you didn't look arrogant. I wasn't fooled. They were on his payroll.

Being polite, I said, "Did you win?"

"Do you have to ask?" Lion cocked his bad boy grin.

Had there been any women in the room, the sound of panties dropping would've been overwhelming. Obviously I was wrong about him needing his men to parade his ego around. He was more than happy to do it himself.

I was over it. "I take it you won. But your knee looks like the biggest loser tonight, Mr. Maxwell."

"You afraid to say my name, Doc?"

"I just did."

Hoots from the men. One said, "She bad, Lion. Watch out she don't bite you."

Lion stared at me, eyes locked on mine. "She can bite me all she wants." He shifted on the bed and let his uninjured knee fall to the side, opening his legs. He wore only skin tight gold lycra shorts. Otherwise, he was entirely naked.

I kept my eyes locked on his. I didn't have to look directly to see he was packing. His huge bulge practically filled the room. Latisha hadn't been exaggerating about him having a python.

"Like what you see, Doc?"

I wasn't taking the bait and I wasn't going to look. But I was going to stare him down.

More muttering from the men as they watched our staring contest.

I was aware that nothing was going to get accomplished if I didn't put my foot down and stop this frat party. In a strong voice I said, "Gentlemen! Do I have to clear the room?!"

They looked shocked.

Lion was as cool as a cat. "You trying to get me alone, Doc?"

"No. I'm just trying to do my job, Mr. Maxwell."

"You don't have to deny it, Doc. I could tell you wanted me the second you *laid* eyes on me,"

Not anymore, I don't. And, could you be any more cocky? I mean, aside from the python in your pants? And did he really think using sexually suggestive words like "laid" was going to work on me? Was that his idea of hypnotism? Did he really think it would make me imagine having sex with him? Hardly.

Hard.

A few of the men started tittering like this was middle school and I was their pushover substitute teacher, the one who didn't know how to herd the class clowns into their pens when they misbehaved.

Wrong.

I clapped my hands together and barked, "That's it! All of you, out! Now! This isn't a locker room. This is my house and we play by my rules! The exit is that way, gentlemen." Like a football referee, I swung both arms around and pointed out the door. Too bad I didn't have a referee whistle to blow in their faces. I hid a smile. *Game, set, and match.*

"Want me to leave too, Doc?" The innocent look on Lion's face was completely fake.

I glared at him. "Are you always this defiant?"

"Always." *And proud of it, no doubt.*

"If you weren't my patient, I would throw you out with the rest of them. Unfortunately, I devoted my life to helping the sick and injured, no matter how annoying they may be."

His men laughed and hooted.

I wheeled on them. "Zip it! All of you! Were you not able to find the door?" Considering the room was twelve by twelve feet, even an earthworm could find its way out. Then again, the average earthworm probably had a higher IQ than all these men combined.

Lion smiled at me, the wheels behind his eyes turning, no doubt wondering what other thing he could do to harass me.

I arched my eyebrows, daring him to speak.

Finally, he chuckled. "Better do what the doctor says, fellas."

Cowed, the men shuffled out of the room, grumbling as they went.

It infuriated me that they obeyed him and not me. Not that it mattered. Mission accomplished. Divide and conquer. Never fight the enemy all at once if you can take them down one at a time.

At least they left.

Order restored, I closed the door, but left it open a crack. Now it was just me trapped in this cage with Lion. *Somebody get me a chair and a whip. Scratch that. Make it a tranquilizer rifle. I swear I'll put this animal down if he tries anything. And someone call the taxidermist. Lion's head is going up on my office wall on a plaque. Which reminds me, I'll need to get a photo of me standing with my shoe on his head to commemorate the kill. The picture can go right next to the taxidermy head.*

I repressed another smile.

"What're you smiling about, Doc?"

"Oh, nothing."

"Anybody ever tell you you got an iron fist?"

I wanted to say, *Yes, and I'll use it on you if you don't behave.* But it was time for me to get to work, so I kept my mouth shut.

"I like that in a woman."

"Is that so?" I was trying to be polite. His taste in women was not my concern, but I was slightly flattered he didn't consider me a bitch. Slightly. I had never been afraid to stand up for myself even if it meant being labelled a bitch.

"Yeah. I can take control all day long. I do every time I step in the cage. I think that's why I like a woman who doesn't take shit from anyone."

"That's me. But I make an exception when asking my patients for stool samples. Then I will take their shit with a straight face." It was a dumb joke. But it just slipped out.

He snorted. "You're clever, Doc."

I was surprised he found that funny.

"You got a man?"

I saw where this was going and I didn't want to encourage him. His injured knee was my focus. I wanted to get the paperwork started for an MRI so I could move on to other patients. So I ignored his question. "Let's get these bandages off so I can get a better idea of what's going on." I started to carefully unwrap the splint.

"You didn't answer my question."

I didn't respond. I wasn't going to get sucked back into flirtation. Since we'd already established that he found my iron fist a turn on, I needed another approach to keep him in line. The next best strategy was re-direction, a tactic that worked well with toddlers. That meant it would probably work well with Lion. "Can you tell me what happened when you injured your knee? What I mean is, did it twist more than normal? Were there any popping noises? Anything you can tell me will help."

"I'll make you a deal, Doc. For every question of yours I answer, you gotta answer one of mine."

I smiled. "No deal."

"Then I'm not talking."

Ahhh, toddlers. They can be so stubborn.

He folded his muscular arms across his equally muscular chest. Everything bulged magnificently, even his bulge, which I was still ignoring. But I couldn't miss his charming grin. It had gone from ferocious to adorably playful.

Sometimes, the best way to let a man down was with a compliment.

"Mr. Maxwell. I'm flattered that you're interested. I mean it. You're a handsome man with a sense of humor. If we'd met under different circumstances, who knows. But we didn't, and I need you to understand one thing."

"What's that?"

"It's against the rules for a doctor to date a patient."

"What rules?"

"The rules set down by the Medical Board of California and this hospital. Dating patients is considered unethical and therefore strictly verboten."

"Who needs rules?"

"Let me ask you something, Mr. Maxwell."

"Shoot."

"You're what, a boxer?"

"Mixed martial arts. Cage fighter."

I ignored the fact that the term cage fighter conjured up all kinds of sexy images of him, me, a gloomy torch-lit cage that vaguely resembled some kind of sexual torture chamber (in a good way), and both of us sweating. A lot. While naked. Him grunting. Me moaning. Excessive amounts of bodily fluids would be exchanged as sexual organs shamelessly filled all relevant orifices with said bodily fluids. The orgasm count would be in the triple digits.

"You okay, Doc?"

"Yes." I cleared my throat, trying to block out the onslaught of images. I needed to re-direct my own giddy teenaged train of thought. What had he just said? Something about rules? Oh yes, rules. "Are you allowed to hit your opponent in the eye or the groin during a cage fight?"

"No. Eye gouges and groin strikes are off limits. If you do it on purpose, you'll get disqualified, automatically lose the fight, and get fined by the judicial board."

I arched an eyebrow. "Imagine that. And, have you ever hit anyone in the groin during a fight? I mean, on purpose?" *Why did I say groin? Groin groin groin.* I pushed the thought away.

"No way. That would be against the—" He stopped short.

"The what?"

He refused to answer, but his adorable grin returned.

"Sounds like you follow the rules, Mr. Maxwell. When it suits you."

The slightest hint of a blush reddened beneath his tan skin. He chuckled. "You got me, Doc."

"Rules, Mr. Maxwell. We all follow them, often when we don't want to."

"So you're saying you would date me if it wasn't against the rules?"

"I said maybe. And we all know maybe means no. Ask any kid, they'll tell you."

He chuckled. "Right."

Why did I feel like I was flirting again? I swear, that wasn't my plan. The truth was, I really was flattered he was interested in me. Men of his caliber rarely spoke to me let alone threw themselves at me. But technically it was too late. I would be remiss if I didn't follow my own rules. The ECU wasn't my own personal singles bar. It was my place of work. As far as I was concerned, every patient who walked through the front doors was off limits, no matter how attracted I was to them or vice versa. "I'm very sorry, Mr. Maxwell. You're my patient. That's not going to change."

"Okay. Then I won't be your patient. You haven't done anything yet so get me another doctor. Please."

I almost bristled at his order. Nobody told me what to do. But the please he added at the end stopped me short. As did his adorable smile. "I did unwrap your bandage. See? It's too late."

"Shit, I coulda unwrapped it. You gonna tell me if you put a Band-Aid on a guy, he's your patient?"

"Yes. If it happens here in the ECU, definitely."

"That's ridiculous."

"That's a rule. And we all know rules are sometimes ridiculous. But most aren't."

"Just get me another doc, Doc."

"I wish I could, Mr. Maxwell. Unfortunately, we're busy tonight and we're short staffed. You would be doing everyone a favor if you just let me treat you."

"I don't know, Doc. Any doctor can fix my knee. But something tells me you're the only doctor in the world who can fix a broken heart." What should have been corny came off charming because he delivered it with such sincerity.

"I wish I could help you, but I'm not a cardio thoracic surgeon."

"Huh?"

"Sorry. Doctor humor. A heart surgeon. I'm orthopedics. I don't do hearts. But I am eminently qualified to fix your knee. So let's focus on that, okay?"

"What's your first name?"

I sighed. "If I tell you my first name, I'll still be your doctor."

"You're too damn smart for you own good, you know that? That's what I like about you, Doc. I mean, Ms. Flanagan." He was looking at my name tag. "Since you're not my doctor anymore, I'll have to call you Ms. Flanagan until I know your first name."

"How do you know I'm not a Mrs.?"

"I don't see a ring."

"Maybe I left it at home."

"Don't see a tan line."

"That's because I'm always here working and don't have time to get one." I had to admit, his persistence was endearing. And he complimented me for being smart, which was the way to my heart. But it wasn't going to work. "Try as you might, Mr. Maxwell, I will not be dating you. I'm sure one of the nice women waiting outside for you would be happy to take on that responsibility." *If they haven't already.* Everything about his demeanor suggested that he was an accomplished manwhore, which likely meant his telling me I was smart was just a trick to get me into bed. I didn't do tricks. I'm sure the strippers outside would be happy to turn all the tricks he could ever want.

"Them? Nah. They're just fight groupies. But you? You're my kind of woman. You're a boss and a badass and smart as hell." *Tricks, more tricks!* "Not to mention your red hair and those mint green eyes make me rock fucking hard."

Tricks, tricks, tricks!!! My eyes aren't even mint green! They were just plain green. Mint. Pfft. He's not fooling anybody. Except... me.

I finally broke down and stole a glance at his cock. He wasn't exaggerating. His python was wide awake and straining against his tight lycra shorts. I could see the shape of the head and the shaft through the fabric. When it pulsed, I almost lost my cool. Almost. There was a reason they called me Dr. Freeze in the ECU. I could deal with rude patients, gunshot wounds, and the chaos of trauma all day long. But this was different and that was one long python...

"You're blushing, Ms. Flanagan."

I was also staring. It was a fact that some snakes hypnotized their prey before going in for the kill. I tore my gaze away before his snake ate me. Or I ate it. If I hadn't been hypnotized, I would've been embarrassed by my utter lack of professionalism. But it was the snake's fault.

"You sure you can't find me another doctor, Irish?"

"How did you know I was Irish?"

"Flanagan is Irish, isn't it?"

"Yes. But don't call me Irish."

"Why not? Is it racist or something?"

"No, just don't call me that." *Nicknaming me makes me sort of like you, so stop.*

"Then tell me your name." His dark eyes smoldered with the promise of forbidden pleasure, the kind of pleasure that took place in his torchlit caveman's cage where I could scream out every orgasm he gave me without worrying about waking the neighbors.

I hadn't had an orgasm with a man in ages. And never with a man this magnificent. Like I said earlier, I wasn't a robot. I had my limits. Apparently, Lion was it. So I caved. I let down my guard and muttered:

"You don't even know me, Mr. Maxwell."

"But I will." Again with that commanding voice. Low and dangerous and oh so delicious.

Ooze.

Latisha had been right about the anti-venom kit. I needed one to break the spell that Lion Maxwell had cast over me. If something didn't break it soon, I was going to make a terrible mistake.

Chapter 2

BRIGID

"I heard you had a knee injury in 109. Sounds like a possible ACL?" The man asking was Dr. Ivan Hackett. He was the Co-Director of Orthopedics, which made him one of my bosses. His voice still had a hint of a British accent from his childhood. The upper-crusty kind with its usual nasal note of smarmy superiority. I'm sure he and the Queen of England would get along just fine. They probably had tea together at Buckingham Palace whenever he was in town.

"Yes. I already had my patient sent up to Radiology for an MRI. I'm waiting on the results."

"If you need a consult, let me know."

"I think I can handle it."

I was never sure if Dr. Hackett was always second guessing me or just a male chauvinist pig. His fine features and classic good looks made him that much more annoying. Although he didn't have the sort of rugged body you would find in a firemen's calendar, he was tall and lean and had a broad-shouldered swimmer's body. I had seen him in a suit and he wore it impeccably well. And he knew it. If there was a sexy doctor's calendar, Dr. Hackett would be *Full of Himself February*.

"Well, if anything else arises, do page me straightaway."

"I will do that." *Sometime in the next century.* I smiled at him.

"Right, then. Off to surgery."

"If you need any help, do page me straightaway."

He smirked. "Cheeky."

"Who you talking to out there, Doc?" Lion hollered from his room. His entourage outside turned to look at me.

Dr. Hackett couldn't resist an opportunity to stick his nose in my business. He waltzed right into Lion's room. I followed. Per my orders, the nurses had already cold packed Lion's knee.

"I'm Dr. Hackett. Is there something I can help you with, sir?"

Lion's eyes danced between me and Hackett. He looked suspicious. "You guys talking about me? I heard something about MRI results. Any word yet?"

I opened my mouth to speak but Hackett beat me to the punch.

"We're still waiting for results from Radiology. Isn't that right, Dr. Flanagan?"

"Yes." I so wanted to throat punch Hackett for doing that.

Hackett ignored me. "I'm sure we'll have the results for you shortly, sir."

Lion said, "Who are you again?"

"I'm Dr. Ivan Hackett. Co-Director of Orthopedics." He loved to tell people his title. Never missed an opportunity. He probably said it to himself every morning in front of the mirror while tying his tie. Double Windsor knot, Royalty approved. He was such a douche. Make that, King Douche V, fifth in a long line of douches.

"So you do knees?"

"Yes, I am specialized in orthopedic surgery, among other things," Hackett grinned.

"Can you do mine?"

Oh, no.

Hackett was taken aback. "Is there a problem with Dr. Flanagan?"

"I don't like women doctors."

Asshole!

"I assure you, Dr. Flanagan is highly qualified in every respect. If I were in need of a proper doctor to perform an orthopedic procedure on my knee, I would ask for her." I was surprised he spoke so highly of me, but then he ruined it by placing both hands on my shoulders in a fatherly way. He was at most five years older than I was.

I wanted to cringe away from his touch, but I didn't want to make a scene.

"Ehh." Lion shrugged. "I still don't like women doctors."

"I completely understand," Dr. Hackett said.

Did he understand that there was a problem with women doctors, or was he just commiserating with Lion? It didn't matter. I felt like a fool either way.

Hackett said, "I would be happy to offer a second opinion once the results are in. From the looks of the swelling, we'll have to wait until it goes down before I can perform any sort of procedure. Dr. Flanagan can walk you through the image results while I'm in surgery, but do have your nurse schedule a proper consult with me before you leave. That is, if you don't mind, Dr. Flanagan?"

Was he being snide? Why was I asking? He was always being snide. If I had a chainsaw handy, I would lop off Hackett's head and hang it on my office wall next to Lion's. These two were unbelievable.

"Dr. Flanagan?" Hackett prompted. "Have we got this sorted?"

I gritted my teeth and smiled. "I guess we do, Dr. Hackett."

"Brilliant." He patted my shoulders in that fatherly way of his, like I was his incompetent daughter. "I'll let you take it from here." He reached over to shake Lion's hand. "Pleasure to meet you, mister…"

"Maxwell. Lion Maxwell."

"Excellent. We'll speak soon. Until then, I assure you, you're in expert hands with Dr. Flanagan."

"That's exactly where I wanna be." His voice was low and dangerous once again. But this time, there was no oozing. Well, not on my part. When Hackett was gone, Lion grinned at me, very much satisfied with himself. "Guess who's not my doctor anymore?"

"Do you have any idea what you just did?" I was pissed.

"Sure do."

I hissed, "If you think after that little stunt that I would ever consider dating a man like you, you're sorely mistaken."

"But you *are* still considering it."

What an ass! Make that a delusional ass! He was an ass who didn't know it.

I turned to go but stopped short at the door. I whirled around and glared at him. "One other thing. I'm still your doctor. Once a patient, always a patient. As I said before, Mr. Maxwell, I don't date my patients."

"Who said anything about dating?" His lascivious grin suggested his interests lay in the gloomy torch lit cage I'd imagined earlier.

"Dating includes whatever filthy thoughts you have in mind, Mr. Maxwell. Those are the rules. And we both know you understand the concept of rules. Some blows are too low to throw. Even for a man like you."

He snickered with cocky self-importance. "I wasn't planning on being the one doing the blowing." He reached down and adjusted his massive erection in his lycra shorts. It hadn't been there when Dr. Hackett and I walked in the room earlier. *Yeah, yeah, yeah, I looked, but only for a second.* Now it was back with a thick veined vengeance.

I fired a finger at his crotch. "Keep that thing in its cage, Mr. Maxwell. Or I will cut it off with a rusty scalpel." I spun around and walked out of the room. Not because I was worried about Lion having the last word, but because I knew I couldn't take my eyes off his cock as long as it was erect and pulsating.

If I'd had any doubts before, they were now completely gone.

I hated men like Lion Maxwell.

The sooner the results came back from Radiology, the sooner I would boot him out of both the ECU and my life for good.

<<<<<<<<<>>>>>>>>

Latisha's eyes popped when she saw me marching toward the nurses station.

"Something wrong?"

Still furious, I hissed, "That man is completely full of himself. Who does he think he is?"

"Who? Dr. Hackett?" Latisha smirked. She knew all about Dr. Hackett's assy attitude.

I sneered. "Him... *and* my patient. Mr. Maxwell."

"Him? What he do?"

"He told Hackett he didn't like women doctors."

"He did?" She was genuinely shocked.

"Yes. And now Dr. Hackett is taking over his care."

Her eyes narrowed and she looked at me thoughtfully. "You like him."

"Who? Dr. Hackett? You're insane."

"No. Your patient. I know you, Bridge. You like him."

"I do not. I hate him."

She leaned back in her chair and snickered. "Right."

"Are you kidding me? That man is rude and crude and acts like a caveman."

"It was that python of his, wasn't it?"

Just then, two random family members of a random patient strolled by the nurses station. Both stared at us. I lowered my voice to a whisper and scoffed. "It's not a python!"

Latisha whispered too. "So you looked." It wasn't a question.

"I didn't look!"

"You looked."

"You're worse than he is!"

"He made a pass at you, didn't he?"

"He made about forty passes."

"And you didn't catch a single one?"

I rolled my eyes. "I couldn't. He's my patient."

"Girl, if a man like that made a pass at me, I'd quit my job on the spot."

"I'm not quitting my job for an animal like him. Who would date a man like that?"

"I would."

"Well, I wouldn't."

She glanced at her monitor. "Looks like Radiology put his images on the server. You need me to page Dr. Hackett for you? Have him go over the results with your caveman?"

I sighed. "No. I'll handle it."

"Make sure you get a good grip."

"That's not what I meant! You're not helping. You know that?"

"Relax, girl. If he gets you all riled up again, just give him your best Dr. Freeze. That always cools 'em down."

"Speaking of freezing, can you get me a bucket of ice? I'm going to pour it down Mr. Maxwell's shorts when I go back in."

She chuckled. "I'll get two. One for him, one for you."

"Is it that obvious?"

"Please, girl."

"I'm acting ridiculous, aren't I?"

"Relax, Bridge. That man is gorgeous. I'm surprised you made it out the exam room without getting pregnant. Take a moment, get yourself together, then go back in there and show him who's boss."

"Thanks, Tisha. I will."

"Any time, girl. And while you in there, tell him I'm off at two." She smiled.

"Sure." I would do no such thing. Why, I couldn't tell you.

I turned and trudged back toward the crowd outside 109.

Time for me to lay down the law.

"A blow job will make you feel better, babe." The feminine voice came from inside 109.

"My dick isn't what's hurting me, Candy," Lion said. "It's my knee."

I knew it.

Manwhore.

Like I said earlier, I hated men like Lion Maxwell.

No, hate was too strong a word. It implied I had feelings for someone I'd met only two hours ago. That was impossible. A better word would be disgust. Mild disgust. That was it. I was very mildly disgusted with Lion Maxwell. But I was also his doctor. I waited in the doorway.

Lion and Candy hadn't noticed me and were still talking because the privacy curtain was pulled partway around the bed and I was behind it.

I cleared my throat. "Mr. Maxwell, should I come back later?" I said it without a hint of bitterness. Well, none that I noticed.

"Candy, would you stop?" Lion grunted and leaned over until he made eye contact with me around the curtain. "The doctor is here."

I glared at him. "Do you need a moment to finish whatever you're doing?" I did my best not to imagine it.

"No, Doc. It's cool. Please come in."

Best to get this over with. I peered around the privacy curtain. On the bed, one of the groupie strippers from his entourage was curled around him. Candy. The one with the big 1980s hair. To my surprise, Lion's shorts weren't around his ankles and he wasn't even erect. Not that I looked (maybe I looked). Candy the Stripper caressed his muscled arm with the backs of her fluorescent nails.

"Candy," Lion said, "would you mind giving us some privacy?"

"Fine." She sulked and slid off the bed and walked out. "Maybe you can have the doctor give you a blowjob."

A slow smile spread across Lion's face when she was gone.

"Don't," I snarled.

"What?" he said innocently.

Men.

Or should I say, dogs.

Because that's what Lion was.

But he was still my patient.

I took a deep breath, trying to relax. Despite his lack of maturity, Lion deserved the same professional conduct I showed everyone else.

I had already reviewed the images from his MRI outside. The damage to his knee was extensive. For an athlete like him, it would mean surgery and at best, a long recovery period of six months to a year before he could return to sport. At worst, he might be facing the end of his career. All I had to do was imagine someone telling me that I could never practice medicine again and it made my natural compassion kick right in. I instantly went from irritated with Lion to worried about how he was going to take it and what his future would hold for him. Breaking bad news was never easy.

"Sorry about Candy."

"I'm sorry, what?"

He smiled. "Candy. She doesn't have the best... what's the word... you know... manners."

"Oh. Okay." I wanted to laugh. Manners? Coming from him that was laughable. It didn't matter. "Anyway. About your knee."

"What'd you find out from the MRI?" His eyes shone with hope. He wasn't making this easy.

"Why don't we take a look on the monitor?" I wheeled the computer from the corner over to his bed and logged in so I could pull up the MRI images. "Do you see here, where the head of the femur attaches to the tibia?"

"Yeah?"

"Your ACL is completely torn. Do you know what the ACL is?"

"Yeah."

"It's no longer attached to the tibia."

"Anything else?"

I couldn't tell if he was playing it cool or in shock or what. "The meniscus on your tibia is also torn and will need to be repaired. There is some cartilage damage as well. All of it will likely need to be addressed through surgery."

"Surgery?" He said it as if he didn't believe me. Denial was a common reaction, especially from a highly competitive athlete. It was the last thing they wanted to hear. Their identity often revolved around their ability to compete at the highest levels. Take that away from them and they lost their sense of self. Some athletes managed to transition to coaching or sports journalism or even sports medicine. As long as they worked with athletes, they were happy. But others fell into depression and never managed to recover. It was too soon to tell which of the paths Lion might take.

"Yes. I'm afraid you'll probably need reconstructive surgery."

"I don't need surgery."

"Actually, you're correct. You don't. But that would mean adjusting your lifestyle to fit within the limits of your compromised knee joint. If you want to continue to compete at the level you're used to, you will definitely need surgery."

He dropped his head back on the pillow and heaved a sigh. All his cockiness was gone. And there was no sign of his adorable grin. He looked thoughtful and a little bit sad. "What are my options? I mean, for surgery?"

"Since Dr. Hackett will be performing your surgery, he'll have to discuss that with you after reviewing your MRIs." It didn't bother me that I would no longer be Lion's doctor. Under the circumstances, I cared far more about his well being than my bruised ego, and I knew he would be in capable hands with Dr. Hackett. "He'll probably suggest a tendon graft of some sort, but I couldn't say which."

A smile played across Lion's face. "You still using zombie grafts?"

"You mean an allograft, like the kind we take from a cadaver?"

"Yeah."

"Not as much as in the past. The current research shows that harvesting the tendon from your body is more effective long term. So Dr. Hackett most likely won't use a zombie graft. Unless you demand one." I smiled, trying to make light of the situation. "But I would strongly advise against it. My understanding is that you might suddenly develop a taste for brains." I winked. "Human brains."

He chuckled. His adorable smile was back. It was good to see.

"You might consider an animal graft." It wasn't a serious suggestion, but I wanted to keep him smiling.

"Do they do that?"

"Believe it or not, researchers experimented with animal tendon grafts in the 80s and 90s."

"No shit?"

"None whatsoever."

"How about a grizzly bear graft? They're badass. Can we do that?"

"If you can find a donor. Know any bears?"

He laughed. "No. Not personally. But I know a lion who would be happy to loan me some of his." It was his turn to wink.

"I bet you do." I was smiling and dangerously close to flirting again.

"Joking aside, what kind of graft will you use?"

"Either a tendon graft, which Dr. Hackett will take from your hamstring, or a bone and tendon graft which he'll take from your kneecap. Both are viable options with a high recovery rate and return to sport. I've done procedures on several athletes who tell me they regained 99.9% functionality."

"Won't taking the graft from my knee weaken it?"

"You would be surprised by how well the patellar tendon attached to your kneecap can regenerate, as well as the surrounding bone."

"Wow. That's incredible. It sounds like I'll be able to go back in the cage as soon as I'm healed."

Sex cage... "I can't make any promises, but it is a possibility. Although you should know that the recovery protocol calls for six to twelve months of rehab."

"No worries." He nodded and his cocky smile returned. "So this is good news."

"I suppose it is." I was impressed by his optimism. Unless it was just denial. It was too soon to tell how he would react when the reality of rehabilitation set in. I wouldn't be treating him, so I would probably never know. But I would be wondering.

"What do we do now?"

"After your discharge papers are processed, you can go home."

"What about my surgery?"

"That won't happen for several weeks. Until then, the goal will be to follow the PRICE protocol."

"What's that?"

"Protection, Rest, Ice, Compression, and Elevation. In other words, be careful with your movement. Take it easy, keep things light and don't over do it. And keep it iced, no more than twenty minutes at a time. You don't want to give yourself frostbite. I'll prescribe painkillers and an anti-inflammatory, and crutches. You'll need them for walking. I'll also prescribe a knee-brace, just in case. Once the swelling and pain have minimized, you'll want to work on getting back as much range of motion into your knee as possible while keeping the muscles strong and flexible. The healthier your knee is going into surgery, the easier the recovery. I'll schedule you for some prehabilitation physical therapy between now and the surgery, and I'll have the nurse give you some pamphlets which will tell you how to care for your knee and follow the PRICE therapy at home. Make sure you read the pamphlets carefully. Oh, and the nurse will also schedule a consult for you with Dr. Hackett."

"Are you gonna be my physical therapist?"

"No. I'm not a physical therapist. I'm an MD."

"Too bad. You would've enjoyed it."

I wanted to laugh, but restrained myself. "I think you meant the other way around."

"Are you kidding? You know you want to run your hands all over me. You just need official permission. Too bad you're not a physical therapist."

I hated that he was right. But rules were rules. "I'm afraid someone else will have that privilege. Well, I think that pretty much covers everything. Unless you have any questions?"

"When do I see you again?"

"Honestly? You probably won't. Your physical therapist and Dr. Hackett will take things from here. I'm not your doctor anymore, remember?"

"That's right. Since you're not, you gotta tell me your first name."

I rolled my eyes. What could it hurt? "Brigid. My name's Brigid." He held out his hand to shake. Being polite, I shook. I wasn't prepared for the warmth or the size of his hand. It engulfed mine like a human cocoon. Something about it was entirely too comforting.

"Brigid." *That voice.*

Ooze.

The heat from his hand was rapidly melting my defenses.

"It suits you."

"What suits me?" I was on the verge of losing all self control.

"Your name. Brigid. It's strong. Unique. Exotic. Just like you."

For a boxing ring bruiser like him, he sure was articulate. I knew I was blushing and about a second away from letting him do anything he wanted with me.

"Now that you're not my doctor, it means you and me can go out on a regular date. How about dinner?"

Reality smacked me in the chest. I reluctantly withdrew my hand from his and shoved it in my lab coat. I cleared my throat.

"You're blushing, Brigid." His eyes darkened and the look of danger returned.

"It's hot in here." I felt the urge to fan my face but I stuffed my free hand in my lab coat pocket instead.

"I was thinking the same thing…"

Ooze.

Damn him.

"Unfortunately, Lion, I mean, Mr. Maxwell, you're still my patient."

One of his dimples appeared. Damn that dimple. It begged to be licked.

Why had I said his name? I cleared my throat again. "As I said, once a patient, always a patient. You should be focused on your knee right now. I can't stress enough how challenging the recovery process can be. So don't get any ideas."

"I've got all kinds of ideas, Brigid. But something tells me my imagination is nothing compared to the reality…"

Why was it that he could simply lay there and be excruciatingly hot? He didn't even have to do anything. If Lion Maxwell had a sexy calendar of his own, the cover would be a picture of him as he looked right now. This image would also be inside as my birthday month: *Sexy as hell September.*

"It was nice meeting you, Mr. Maxwell. Good luck with your knee."

I spun on my heel and rushed out of the exam room before I did something stupid.

"Be seeing you, Brigid."

When I pushed past Lion's entourage outside, I walked as fast as I could to the nearest exit.

I needed fresh air or I was going to burst into flames inside my lab coat.

<<<<<<<<>>>>>>>

The full moon hung low over the hospital.

I stood in front of the main doors of the ECU, staring at the night sky, trying to calm down. Several people stood outside with me, also star gazing. Some of them smoked cigarettes, the tips glowing orange like sluggish fireflies. Smoking wasn't permitted this close to the entrance, but I wasn't going to lecture anybody. They were here because their loved ones were hurt or sick or dying. I didn't want to make things any worse for them than they already were. Sometimes, rules could be bent. For the right reasons.

"You."

Startled, I turned to the sound of the voice.

The woman who'd said it stood in the shadows.

"Were you talking to me?" I couldn't make out her face.

"Yeah." She sounded pissed and projected her irritation in jittery waves I could feel. My defenses immediately went up.

"Can I help you with something?"

"Yeah you can fucking help me." She strutted toward me, her heels sparking off the brick pavers. Her silhouette was tall and curvy and everything was tight-fitting. When she emerged into the light, I recognized her from inside. Candy the bedazzled groupie with the big mane of hair. "You think he'll pick you over me because you're some kind of princess doctor?"

I wasn't about to explain that nobody handed me anything. Paying for college and medical school was all on me and I had the loans to prove it. But that wasn't her business. "Are you talking about Mr. Maxwell?"

"Who else?" she said bitterly.

"I don't want him to pick me. You can have him."

"What, now you're too good for him?"

"No, that's not what I'm saying either. It's Candy, right?"

"Now you making fun of my name, Bitch? Don't think I won't kick your skank ass because you're a doctor."

Was she for real? Was she the kind of woman Lion surrounded himself with? I didn't see how he could think I was his type. "No, I'm not making fun of your name. I was just making sure I remembered it correctly. Your name is Candy, right?"

"Yeah. So?" She searched my eyes, looking for the hidden insult that wasn't there. So defensive, like everyone was out to get her. In her world, maybe they were. It was sad.

"I should tell you...." I stopped to think of how to phrase it so I didn't offend her. "Doctors aren't allowed to date their patients. It's against the law."

"Serious?"

"Yes. Even if I were interested in Mr. Maxwell, which I'm not, I couldn't date him."

"Oh. Want a cigarette?" She pulled a pack and a lighter out of her purse. Did she actually want to be friends now that I was no longer competition?

"Sorry. I don't smoke. But thank you."

She shrugged and lit one for herself. "No matter what I do, Lion won't fuck me."

This was news. Now I was interested in talking to her. "Really?"

"Yeah. He doesn't know what he's missing. I suck good dick. Know what I'm saying?"

"Oh. Yes. Of course."

"Make a man come so hard he turns himself inside out. You ever suck dick like that?"

"Um..."

"Nah." She waved her cigarette in the air, leaving a curling trail of smoke. "You're too uptight for that kind of thing. Am I right? Probably don't even like the taste of dick."

"Actually, I happen to like the taste of dick just fine."

She snorted. "You sure?"

"Yes I'm sure."

"You swallow?"

I wasn't exactly enjoying this conversation, but I wouldn't let her one up me. "Yes, I swallow."

She smirked at me but I was gaining her respect. "When was the last time you sucked a dick? I mean like really sucked it?"

Her crassness was a bit much, but I was perfectly willing to have the discussion if she cleaned up her language. I wasn't holding my breath. "It's been a while. But I did it frequently when I was married."

"You divorced?"

"Sadly, yes."

"Uh huh," she nodded. Somehow, that earned points with her. "He cheat on you? They always cheat. Men are dogs."

"Nope. He didn't cheat."

"That you know of." She said it with such certainty, I had to stop and think about it.

"No, I don't think he did."

She smiled big. "You cheated on him, didn't you? That's my girl!"

"No. I never had time to cheat. That's why he left me. I never had time for him."

"Shoulda sucked his dick more. He woulda stayed."

I tried not to laugh. "You might be right."

"Damn right I'm right. Men don't need much to keep them happy. A good blowjob every week will save any marriage." She had a point, but it was too late to help mine.

"So why are you having trouble with Lion? You're a beautiful woman with plenty of confidence." I had to admit, despite her sandpaper personality, there was a certain animalistic beauty to Candy that made her the perfect woman for a man like Lion Maxwell. All she needed to do was change her name to Lioness. Or Jaguar. Anything except Candy. But she was definitely his type of woman. More so than I would ever be. "So what's the issue?"

She snorted, "He won't let me suck his dick. Don't know what he's missing."

"Oh. Right." I smiled, but found myself wondering if I had the blowjob skills to keep a man like Lion from straying. No, I really just wanted to think about giving him a blowjob. I did like giving them and I did swallow. But Lion's cock was much larger than my ex-husband's. Could I manage a man that large? I repressed a shiver and hoped Candy didn't notice. "Why won't Lion let you give him head?"

"He's probably gay."

"He didn't seem gay to me."

"Did he let you suck his dick?"

"No," I laughed. *But he wanted me to.*

"He's gay. Unless he's in love with somebody else." She gave me a pointed look.

I didn't know how Lion could be in love with me after two hours of knowing me.

She shrugged. "Probably that fucking fiancée of his."

"He's engaged?"

She sniffed in the affirmative.

That explained it. It made perfect sense.

Lion Maxwell was trash. The poster boy for manwhores around the world.

I had been right all along.

Chapter 3

BRIGID

"Good afternoon, Tisha." I was breathless, having just jogged from the staff parking structure to the ECU two days later. Like always, I was barely on time. Traffic between here and Burbank was terrible.

"Hey, Bridge. How was your weekend?"

"Great."

"Go on any dates?"

I scoffed. "No."

"You sure?" She grinned.

"Yes I'm sure."

"That's funny because someone brought something in for you." From under the counter of the nurses station she pulled out a shiny gold box with a black satin bow.

"What is it?"

"You tell me."

"I have no idea." I looked at the card. "It says Dr. Flanagan. Did you see who brought it?"

"Just some delivery guy, I think."

I held the box to my ear.

"What you doing, Bridge?"

"Listening for ticking."

"What, like a bomb?" She looked doubtful.

"Yes."

She folded her arms across her chest. "Girl, you been watching too many old movies. Nobody uses wind-up alarm clocks anymore. It's all electronic these days. You know, 'Don't cut the red wire!' That kind of thing."

"What do you know about defusing bombs?"

"I saw The Hurt Locker," she said confidently.

"I saw Superman but it doesn't mean I can fly."

"Good point."

I shook the box.

"Don't shake it! You might blow up the both of us!" She half meant it.

"This is silly. Who would send me a bomb? My patients love me, right?" Over the years, I had received gifts from patients but it was usually a card or a children's crayon drawing or a plate of cookies or a bouquet of flowers. Not a mysterious gold box. "Maybe it's chocolates? Something fancy like Godiva?"

"They can put bombs in chocolates, you know."

I smirked at her. "*In* the chocolates?"

"You heard a cherry bombs, right? Maybe these are chocolate bombs."

"With or without cherries?"

She rolled her eyes. "Just sayin'."

"Who would send me chocolates?"

"Maybe you got a secret admirer."

"Who?"

"Maybe that jungle man from the other night, Lion what's-his-name."

"I doubt it." I carefully untied the black bow. Tisha winced in anticipation. No boom. The lid was on pretty tight, so I had to cradle it in my arms to peel it off. I angled it away from my face, just in case.

"Don't point that thing at me!"

"Sorry. Here goes nothing." When I finally had the lid off the box, I set both on the counter top.

She leaned forward to look. "I don't see any chocolate."

"Me neither." I dug through the gold tissue paper inside and lifted out a sculpture of a lion. It was minty green with swirls of various pastel greens running through it.

"Is that jade?"

"I don't think so. It's too light. It feels like…"

"What?"

I held the lion up to my nose. "It smells like… Irish Spring."

"You mean like the soap?"

I rubbed my thumb against it. "I think so. Feels like it. Like someone carved a lion out of a bar of Irish Spring. It's about the right size."

"It's really good. Looks like a real lion and everything. Lemme see."

"Wait. I'm not done admiring it. Whoever made this really knows how to carve soap."

"Whoever?" She said sarcastically. "The man's name was Lion. You holding a soap lion in your hands. Please tell me you can connect them two dots."

"Do you really think a man like that knows how to make soap carvings?"

"So he had a friend do it. Or paid somebody. Anything else in the box?"

"There's a card."

"What it say?"

I read it to myself first. I blushed and held the card against my chest.

"Read it to me, girl."

"I can't. It's too dirty."

"Don't make me fight you for it."

I handed the card to her while I continued admiring the detailed sculpture. Even the lion's mane had flowing hair. You could almost see the individual strands.

Latisha started reading out loud. "This pussy smells like Irish Spring. I bet yours smells even better." She snorted a laugh. "He crazy, girl. Now I'm blushing."

I reached for the card. I didn't want her reading any more out loud. "Give me that!"

"Let me finish. It says: In case you want to wash your hands of me forever, rub your hands all over this lion. In case you don't, call me and you can rub your hands all over me." She laughed. "Oh, Lord. That boy is nuts." She turned the card over and frowned. "There's no number."

I frantically searched through the box, checking the underside of the lid, the ribbon, the tissue paper. "I don't see a number anywhere."

Latisha grabbed the sculpture from where I'd set it on the counter.

"Give that back!" Yes, I sounded like a desperate teenager. Yes, Lion's message was crass. But the sculpture was incredible and I was a little bit giddy that he went to the trouble. I wondered if he sculpted it himself? It didn't matter. I was flattered. Nobody had ever carved a sculpture for me. Or had one carved. Either way worked.

"Hold up." She flipped the sculpture over and looked at the bottom. "Here it is. I need a pen so I can write it down."

"Be my guest." I said it sincerely because that was the exact moment I remembered Lion had a fiancée. People said it was the thought that counted, but what good was it when it came from a lying two-timing piece of trash?

"I thought you wanted him all to yourself?"

I sighed, "He has a fiancée."

"You know that for a fact?"

"No. One of his groupies told me."

"You mean one of them ratchet hoochies from the other night?"

"Yes."

"You can't trust what them girls say."

"It doesn't matter because I'm not going to date a patient." I motioned toward the rack of patient records. "Anybody I need to see?"

"There's a man in 106 who took a tumble down a flight of stairs. Possible fracture to the left radius and ulna." She handed me the man's chart.

I turned toward 106.

"Don't forget your lion." She held up the box.

I grimaced. "I don't want it."

"Then it's going in the garbage."

"No!"

"That's what I thought." She smiled and handed me the box.

"I hate you."

"You can thank me later."

One thought hounded me the rest of the day.

Should I or shouldn't I call Lion?

At the very least, I needed to thank him. Then I needed to tell him I wasn't interested.

Chapter 4

LION

"The grand opening of the new dojo is only a few weeks out. Will you be ready to make an appearance by then?" The woman asking was Rhonda Chavez, one of my business partners. She oversaw our chain of dojos. We had six in LA. In a few weeks we were opening a seventh in Burbank and had plans for an eighth in West Covina.

I sat in a lounger beside my pool, my knee up and iced while I worked on my tan. Rhonda sat in a chair under a sun umbrella and looked incredible with her dark skin and her naturally plump lips and long black hair pulled back. In her black fitted business suit and red silk top, she was a knockout.

My short haired black Bombay cat Guenhwyvar was circling her ankles, brushing her tail against Rhonda's calves, trying to get her attention.

Rhonda reached down and scratched the back of Guenhwyvar's head.

"Be careful," I said. "She'll jump in your lap and shed all over your suit if you keep petting her. She thinks you're her mom."

Rhonda smiled. "Since I'm wearing black already, no one will notice." She cooed at Guenhwyvar, "Isn't that right, princess?" She loved my cats. "Where is Tigger?"

Tigger was my insane Savannah cat. He looked like a miniature leopard and could jump like one too. I'd seen him leap eight feet straight up trying to snatch a bird out of the air many times. The birds tended to avoid our yard, but not all of them knew about Tigg. "He's probably busy hunting anything that moves." My backyard was huge and full of trees and bushes and a big lawn that surrounded the pool. Tigger often disappeared into the jungle first thing in the morning and didn't come out until dinner time.

Just then, Aslan, my long-haired Maine Coon came strutting across the pool deck in slow motion.

I smirked, "Someone's jealous. But he won't admit it."

Aslan stopped ten feet away from me and Rhonda. He looked the other way like he wasn't interested in what we were doing. His tail flicked lazily against the cement. *I'm over here, idiots.*

"Aslan! Come here, buddy." I slapped the leg of my lounger.

He stared at me and blinked. *Did you say something, idiot? I'm here, you're there. Get up off your ass and come pet me.*

Rhonda giggled when Guenhwyvar jumped into her lap and settled in.

"I've got a lint roller inside if you need one."

"Thanks. I probably will. So, now that your knee is injured, what are we going to do about the grand opening in Burbank?

"No prob. I'll be there even if I'm in a wheelchair. I'll even teach a demo class."

"In a wheelchair?"

"Hell yeah from a wheelchair. I know a guy with no legs who will kick your ass from his wheelchair. As long as you don't tip him over like a turtle, he's lethal on wheels."

"Why wouldn't someone just tip him over?"

"I've tried. I can't get close enough. Hey, you want anything cold to drink? I'm sweating my ass off out here."

"No thanks. I need to run. I have to get over to City Hall in Pasadena. Apparently there's some road closures coming up because of street construction and they want to close off street access to our parking lot."

"Please tell me you'll handle it. That's the last thing I want to think about right now."

"I'll take care of it." She smiled confidently. Rhonda could cut through red tape like a samurai warrior. "If worse comes to worst, we still have alley access to the lot and I can make warning fliers to pin up and hand out at the dojo so everyone knows." She stood to go.

"You're an angel. By the way, how're Renaldo and the kids?"

"They're good. Just worried about you."

"I'll be fine. Say hi to them for me."

"I will. We should have you over for dinner once your knee heals."

"Why wait? You guys can come over here. I know your kids love the pool."

She smiled. "They do. Maybe next weekend?"

I nodded at my knee. "I got nothing going on."

My phone chimed on the table beside my lounger.

"I should go," Rhonda whispered and grabbed her purse from the table.

"Laters. Oh, hey. The lint roller is in the kitchen in the top drawer beneath the microwave. Let me get it for you." I grabbed my crutches.

"Don't get up. I'll find it." Her heels clicked across the poolside cement as she walked toward the open french doors at the back of the house.

Aslan watched her as she went. *Are you blind? I'm right here. Pet me already!*

My phone chimed again and I picked it up.

Two texts from an unknown number.

Unknown ID: Thank you for the sculpture.

Unknown ID: It's beautiful.

No fucking way. I was starting to think Brigid never got it. I had it delivered days ago. I wanted to bang out a text but I couldn't think of anything to say and suddenly my palms were damp and my heart was pounding. *I can't believe she's texting me.*

Unknown ID: Can I ask a favor?

I took a second to think before responding.

Me: Anything for you, Irish.

Unknown ID: Cute.

Shit. Did I piss her off by calling her Irish?

Unknown ID: Can I ask that you not send me any more gifts at the hospital?

Aw, shit. I did piss her off.

Me: Sorry about that. Won't happen again.

I was back pedaling. I never backpedaled with anybody, not even women. I wanted to throw my phone in the pool out of frustration, but I didn't want to miss another text from her. Think fast. I needed to say something that didn't make me look like a desperate douche.

Me: Tell me where to send things next time.

Unknown ID: Next time?

Me: Yes.

Unknown ID: I think it's better if you don't send me anything else.

Me: Did you not like the surprise?

Unknown ID: I just think it's better if you don't.

Me: Come on. Who doesn't like surprises? You're gonna love what I'm working on now.

Unknown ID: I just realized I made a mistake the night I met you.

Shit. What now?

Unknown ID: I should have given you a CT scan to check for any signs of concussion. Your inflated ego has obviously swollen your head to dangerous proportions.

She was flirting. Now it was on.

Me: Funny you say that. My head is swollen right now. And every time I think about you. I think it's ready to pop.

I took a moment to put her name in my list of contacts. She didn't respond for several minutes. I must've pissed her off. Maybe she was more sensitive than I realized. Or not. She started typing.

Frigid Brigid: Then I suggest you ice it.

I smiled.

Me: Head #1 or Head #2?

Frigid Brigid: Both. But if your balls turn blue, remove the ice immediately.

I chuckled to myself.

Me: They've been blue since I met you.

Frigid Brigid: That was a week ago. You should see a doctor immediately.

Me: My thoughts exactly. What are you doing right now?

Frigid Brigid: I meant someone other than me.

Me: Your loss.

Frigid Brigid: If they're that blue, I'm sure you can take care of it the old fashioned way.

Me: You mean fucking? Sounds like a plan. Wanna come over?

Frigid Brigid: Please. You don't need my help. You have hands.

Me: I promise you, nothing will cure my blue balls better than coming inside you. My hand isn't going to cut it.

Frigid Brigid: Then ask your fiancée. I'm sure she'll be glad to help.

Me: Who told you I had a fiancée?

Frigid Brigid: Your friend Candy.

Me: She's making shit up. Candy doesn't know anything about me.

Frigid Brigid: Is that the truth?

Me: I swear it. Ask anyone who knows me. I don't have a fiancée.

Not anymore I didn't. Damn, it hurt every time I said it, but it was true.

Frigid Brigid: I don't know anyone who knows you.

Me: So get to know me. Then you can ask them.

The dots flashed while she typed. Then they disappeared. They flashed again then stopped. She didn't know what to say. I stared at my phone, waiting for her response. Maybe I shouldn't have been so bold.

I waited.

Frigid Brigid: I don't think that's a good idea. I need to go. Thanks again for the sculpture. Please don't send me anything else.

I knew it. I went too far.

I couldn't decide if she meant not to send her anything else at the hospital or anything else ever. I was afraid to ask. I didn't want to be too pushy and scare her off. A woman like her obviously needed her space. She was jumpy enough as it was.

I waited by the pool for another hour, checking my phone every five minutes for another text from Brigid, but that was the last I heard from her.

I couldn't figure this woman out.

Right then, noise erupted from the bushes in the back of the jungle. A blue jay bulleted into the air, followed a second later by Tigger exploding straight up after it. In mid-air, he swiped at the bird, but it was quicker then he was. He fell to the lawn and landed on all fours, legs spread, eyes wide in disbelief, like he couldn't understand how he hadn't caught that blue jay. It was long gone.

"Got away, didn't it?"

Tigger looked at me, his tail whipping in agitation.

"Don't look at me. Go get it!"

Tigger tore across the lawn and disappeared into the far end of the yard.

"The bird went the other way!"

He didn't care. He was already on to the next thing.

I wasn't.

I checked my phone again.

No texts from Brigid.

Damn.

Chapter 5

What the heck was I thinking?

I just had a highly sexual textual exchange with my recently former patient. And there was a record of it. I deleted the entire conversation with Lion. Why hadn't I just thanked him and asked him not to send me any more gifts and been done with it? But no, I had to start flirting.

Why?

It was driving me nuts. I needed to talk to somebody about it. If I didn't, I was going to do something stupid and talk to Lion about it.

I texted Latisha.

Me: Do you have a minute?

Tisha: About to drive the boys to baseball practice. Can I call you later?

Me: Sure. Have fun.

She didn't respond.

I sighed to myself. Whenever Latisha wasn't at the hospital, she was having fun with her three sons. She always shared pictures of all the things they did together. In every one, she was smiling or her boys were laughing and it looked like a party no matter what the occasion. I knew it wasn't like that all the time. Latisha had told me plenty of stories, but I knew for her, the good times far outweighed the bad. I was jealous she had such a wonderfully full family life outside of work. I didn't. I often felt closer to my work family than my real family. That wasn't the way I wanted things, but it was the way things were.

Welcome to life as a doctor.

I stood up from my couch and trudged to the kitchen. I opened the refrigerator and stared inside. There was food, but nothing I wanted to make. Everything was probably old anyway. I didn't cook nearly as often as I would've liked because of my crazy schedule. It didn't help that I was on call almost every night I wasn't at work. There was nothing more annoying than sticking something in the oven for an hour and getting paged ten minutes later to go in for a consult or emergency surgery.

Since I was on call tonight, that meant takeout.

I wondered what Lion was doing for dinner.

No! Don't wonder that!

At this very minute, he was probably sitting at home eating a TV dinner with his leg propped up on couch cushions, wearing nothing but tight boxers because of the warm weather. Would they be gold like the ones he wore the night he came in? And would his package be clearly defined like I remembered? Would he be hard from thinking about me? I felt myself clench pleasantly and squeezed my thighs together.

Stop picturing him half naked!

But those abs…

I hated those abs. They were trouble.

I tried to distract myself by cleaning the condo. I hadn't so much as dusted in a month. Vacuuming and cleaning both bathrooms took almost two hours. The kitchen could wait until tomorrow. Did I check my phone every ten minutes while I cleaned? Of course. I had to make sure I hadn't been paged by the hospital. I wasn't checking for texts from Lion.

No really, I wasn't.

When I finished cleaning, my stomach was grumbling. Time to go get takeout. There was nothing worse than being called in when you were starving. I grabbed my keys and phone and headed out the door.

My phone jingled.

Loin: You hungry?

For your abs? Yes. As an appetizer. I was thinking sausage for dinner.

I was going crazy. I also noticed that although I had deleted our text conversation, I hadn't deleted him from my contacts yet. That was when I noticed I had misspelled his name. Loin. As in, loins. Geesh. I may as well have entered his name as Rock Hard Cock, or Huge Dick or My Former Patient Who Obviously Wants To Have Sex With Me And I Do Too. Before I could change it or delete it, he texted again.

Loin: I need to get some dinner. You wanna join me?

Me: Right now?

Loin: Yeah.

Loin, loin, loin.

Dick, dick, dick!

If I said yes, I was definitely crossing a line. If I actually met him for dinner, I was crossing so far over the line I would be in another county. Sex Offender County. Newest resident: Dr. Brigid Flanagan.

Me: I'm sorry. I can't.

Loin: Some other time?

I wanted to say yes so badly.

My thumbs hovered over the keys.

A wave of conflicting emotions surged through me. I stopped myself from responding and thought long and hard about what I was doing.

Long and hard.

Wrong choice of words.

DICK!!!!

There was one very good reason I couldn't allow myself to give in to my urges.

Daniel.

He was why I couldn't get dinner with Lion. Or Loin. Or whatever his name was. I had to put a stop to this now.

Me: I can't have dinner with you. Ever. Please don't call or text me again. And don't send any gifts. Forget we met. It's for the best.

I deleted his name and number from my contacts, and all our messages. Then I left my phone on the kitchen counter and ran out my front door. I wanted to get away from my phone in case Lion texted or worse, called. If the hospital paged me, I would be back from getting takeout fast enough that it wouldn't matter. When I pulled the front door shut and turned my key in the dead bolt, my phone rang.

No.

I ran to my car and jumped in.

My head was spinning and my heart was thudding.

Lion.

I hated myself for running away from him.

But I was doing the right thing.

Daniel.

I hated doing the right thing.

It was for the best. For everybody's sake.

Daniel.

I drove to McDonald's and bought Chicken McNuggets with extra sweet and sour sauce, and a vanilla milkshake. I knew it was bad for me but tonight I didn't care. Then I went home and checked my phone. Luckily, the call had been a wrong number. I sat at the kitchen table and cried over my food for two hours while scrolling through photos of Daniel on my phone, and watching videos of us together.

Thank goodness the hospital didn't page me that night.

I was a complete wreck.

Daniel...

I missed him so much I wanted to die.

Chapter 6

LION

I felt like someone had just rammed a telephone pole into my chest. I read the text from Brigid over and over again, thinking I'd misunderstood her meaning.

Nope.

It was pretty clear.

Stay the hell out of my life.

That was the last thing I wanted to do, but it was what I was going to do, no matter how bad it made me feel. If you didn't honor other people's wishes, it meant you didn't give a shit about them. I gave the opposite about Brigid Flanagan. So what if I barely knew her? Call me crazy for trusting my gut.

So much for my gut.

It wasn't always right.

It hadn't been right about my ex-fiancée either, and I loved the hell out of her. Minka loved the hell out of me too. I thought we were gonna go the distance. But three years ago she surprised me and told me she wanted out of our relationship. I begged her to stay. She said she was tired of living the fight life. What was I gonna say? I couldn't force her to stay. It broke my heart to let Minka go, but it was the right thing to do.

People changed and life didn't always go the way you wanted.

Just like with Brigid.

I was suddenly disgusted by the sight of the unfinished basswood carving on my coffee table. When finished, it was going to be a majestic lion and his equally majestic lioness sitting in a bed of four leaf clovers (because Brigid made me feel like the luckiest man alive just by laying eyes on me). The lions' tails curled together behind their backs in the shape of a heart. The clover was mostly finished and just needed detailing. The bodies of the two lions were still rough and needed a ton more work, but they were starting to take shape.

I was sitting on the couch, so I picked one of my crutches up off the floor and swung it awkwardly at the carving. The hunk of wood went sailing through the air along with a bunch of carving tools and sandpaper scraps and wood shavings.

CRASH!!

Everything smashed against the nearest wall and clattered to the hardwood floor.

The cats scattered like a bomb had gone off. Guenhwyvar bolted out from under the coffee table and shot across the room in a black streak before sliding on the floor and making a hard turn into the kitchen, claws clicking every step of the way. Tigger leapt seven feet in the air, launching off the easy chair where he'd been cat napping. If I didn't have sixteen foot ceilings, he literally would've hit the roof. Instead, he ran for the front entry and pounded up the spiral stairs, looking for a place to hide. Aslan was perched on top of the huge twelve foot tall cat tree on the far side of the living room. He was sprawled on the highest shelf, watching like a stone-faced Sphinx, taking it all in like nothing had happened. He stared at me like he thought I was an asshole.

"What?" I grunted.

He blinked once. *Asshole.* Then he bounded down the cat tree and sauntered out of the room.

Cats.

They could be so temperamental. They'd come out of hiding when the dust settled. Or when I put their food out. Whichever came first.

"Sorry, guys," I hollered. "I won't do it again. Danger's over."

The wood carving was in pieces. What would have been the lioness had been snapped off at the base.

So much for that waste of time.

I stared at the rest of it on the floor.

The male lion carving stared back.

Are you gonna give up this easy?

Hell no I wasn't.

I needed to come up with a plan of attack. I'd figure this shit out somehow. I could guess why they had rules about doctors and patients. It was the same reason they had rules about sexual harassment in the workplace. It was so the people on top didn't take advantage of the people on the bottom.

The thing was, I was always the guy on top.

Always.

The only way anyone would ever have power over me was if I let them.

"You're obsessed with getting your way, Lion! Obsessed!" Minka had said that to me the day she left. *"In the cage, in business, in relationships, all you care about is what you want! You don't think about what other people want unless you think it will benefit you. You're selfish! Life isn't about*

getting. It's about giving. It's about learning to take the good with the bad and being okay with it. I hope you figure that out someday. For your sake."

Those were the last words she ever said to me when she left three years ago. They had haunted me to this day.

Kill me now.

Remembering that night made me want to dig a ditch and bury myself in a coffin. Whenever I thought about Minka, I felt half dead anyway. I really fucked things up with her. All because I had to have things my way.

Here I was doing it again, not two minutes after thinking I needed to honor Brigid's wishes and stay out of her life.

I didn't know why she didn't want to date me. If she got to know me, she'd change her mind. I was a good guy.

It doesn't matter why! Minka's voice screamed in my head.

Shit.

She was right.

I needed to leave Brigid alone.

For all I knew, Brigid had a good reason for avoiding me.

Chapter 7

THREE WEEKS LATER

My doorbell rang and I jumped up from the couch.

I tore the door open.

"Daniel!"

"Hey, Mom."

I knelt down and threw my arms around my son. It felt so good to hold him.

"Let go, Mom. You're squashing me."

I pulled away. "Sorry. Did you grow while you were gone?"

"I don't know."

"Well you look taller. You're really shooting up like a weed these days." He was ten going on sixteen.

"I'm not a weed," he groused. Make that ten going on ten.

"I didn't mean it like that." Why was talking to my son always so difficult?

Daniel had gone to Europe with his dad and his dad's parents, Grandma and Grandpa Wright. It was a month long trip. I hadn't been too hot on the idea of him being gone so long, but Grandma and Grandpa insisted on it. They said you needed at least that long to do Europe. There was no way I could take that much time off. The Wrights could. They owned a flourishing insurance business that they'd built from the ground up over the last 35 years. In LA, that made them old money. So it was okay for the boss and the boss' son to take a month off for a family vacation.

Excluding me.

The condo had felt painfully empty with Daniel gone for so long. Normally he was here every other week. A week on, a week off. All I had to keep me company for the past month was work. I was so happy to have him back.

Daniel groaned, "I have to go to the bathroom."

I was still holding his arms. I let go. "Okay. You know where it is."

Outside, his father waited in his black BMW. The glare on the windows hid his face. I couldn't tell if he was watching or not. Donald never came to the door when he dropped off Daniel. It was just as well. Talking to him was always difficult. Like father, like son, I guess.

I waved to be polite.

"Bye, Dad!" Daniel said it with enthusiasm and waved excitedly.

Why was I always such a downer to my son? He wasn't this distant with his father.

The Beemer's horn honked and Donald drove away.

"How was Europe?" When there was no answer, I turned. Daniel was already gone. I heard the bathroom door close. It felt like he wasn't even here. Just the ghost of my son passing through.

Would it be like this forever?

Would my son forget me altogether when he went off to college?

Or would it happen sooner? Would I walk into his bedroom one morning to find an open window with the curtains billowing into the cold empty room and a note on the bed that read *I'd rather live with Dad*.

I fought back tears.

It hurt that my own son wasn't excited to see me anymore. It hurt worse that he was always sad to leave Donald's house when I picked him up. I didn't know what I did to make him so sad. It wasn't like I was a taskmaster or a tyrant. I was nice. Like any parent, I made him do chores and pick up after himself and do his schoolwork, but I made sure he had fun too. Was there some unwritten law that moms were no longer cool once a boy turned ten?

Or was it all my fault because I spent so much time at the hospital?

Nobody ever told me that becoming a doctor so you could save lives and help other people meant you wouldn't have time for your own family.

As much as I loved being a doctor, I often wondered what would've happened if I had chosen a different career path. Would Donald and I still be married? He wasn't a bad man.

That you know of. Candy's words echoed in my mind.

No, I didn't think Donald had cheated on me. He wasn't turning down my offers for sex. It was the opposite. He would literally beg me to have sex. But I was always too tired. Between the ungodly doctor's hours and raising Daniel, I had no energy for sex. I couldn't count the number of times I'd told Donald we would have sex tomorrow or next week, then never did.

I remembered Candy's advice about giving weekly blowjobs to your man. Would that have saved my marriage? Was it really that simple?

Who knew.

It was too late to do anything about it now.

Daniel had finished in the bathroom and gone straight to his bedroom and closed the door. I stared at it. I could open it, but I wanted to respect his privacy. He would come out when he was ready. Or with proper motivation.

"Daniel?" I called through the door. "Are you hungry?"

"No."

"Do you want pizza?"

"No!"

"How about we go out for pizza and get ice cream after?"

"I'm not hungry!" He said it like I was asking him to clean the toilets with his tongue.

I sighed and dragged myself to the kitchen. So much for my fantasy of him telling me all about his trip to Europe over a meal so I could at least share in the fun that way. I'd have to settle for looking at the photo album his Grandma Linda would inevitably post on Facebook when she got around to it.

Maybe someday I would be as close to my son as Latisha was to her three sons. Or as close as I was to Daniel when he was a baby. His first year, which was my last year at UCLA as an undergrad, I had time for him. But after med school started, there was never enough time. Starting my third year, and continuing on into my residency, it was like I was never there. Back then, I questioned my decision to become a doctor every single day, but I stuck with it. I knew some mothers held down three jobs to make ends meet. They didn't have a choice. I knew because I treated them in the ECU and they told me about it. I didn't think I deserved to have it any easier just because I was a doctor.

Now it didn't matter because there was no going back. Daniel wasn't a baby and I was still working more hours than I liked. With all my loans and my mountain of bills, I didn't have a choice. I knew some moms managed to stay close to their sons all their lives. Sadly, it seemed like the trick was simply spending more time with them.

If only I could figure out how.

"I'm hungry, Mom."

I was sitting on the couch with the TV turned down.

Now he was hungry. Two hours had passed since he went and hid in his room. I hadn't eaten anything because I wanted to wait for him. I was well past starving. "Okay. How about pizza? It's your favorite."

"We had pizza in Italy a hundred times." How was it that everything he said made me feel like I was a terrible mother?

"Oh. Okay. I forgot to ask you, where are your bags from the trip?"

"Grandma Linda made me put everything away at her house." The Wright Estate was so large, my ex Donald lived there with his parents, Grandma and Grandpa Wright. Donald had his own wing with a separate entrance. Before the divorce, I had lived there too. It was luxurious to say the least. Yes, Donald still lived with his parents. But it wasn't the same. It was more like living in an apartment complex with your parents, but you were at opposite ends. You didn't know they were there half the time. Donald made more than enough money to buy his own house, but I think his parents liked having him close by and it made it easy for Linda to care for Daniel when the Wright men were at the office.

"Oh. Well, you've got clothes here so you should be okay." Why did it always feel like Grandma Linda was trying to steal my son from me?

"Can we go eat already?"

I barked, "Could you ask nicely?"

He frowned. Just like his father.

I wanted to cry. I couldn't tell my son how he broke my heart when he treated me this way. I tried to calm down. "What's the magic word, Daniel?"

"Please."

"Okay," I sniffed. "What would you like to eat?"

"I don't know."

"How about Mexican? You didn't have Mexican food in Europe, did you?"

"No." The corner of his mouth tugged. Daniel was an ace in geography. He knew the names of every single country, the capitol city, and where they were on the map. He thought for a moment. "Actually, we did have Mexican food in Germany."

"German Mexican food? Was that any good?"

"No." He smiled.

"Then we'll make up for it and get your favorite dish. Huevos Rancheros. For dinner. You still like that, right?" It saddened me that I was doubting how well I knew my own son.

"Yes."

At least I knew that much.

We drove to El Torero's, our favorite Mexican restaurant in Burbank. While we waited for our food to arrive, Daniel wolfed down tortilla chips. I worried he would spoil his appetite. Nope. When our Huevos Rancheros arrived, Daniel wolfed that down too.

"Can we get ice cream now?"

"Maybe you should have some more tortilla chips."

"I want ice cream."

"Okay. But can I finish eating first?"

"Sure. Can I play Candy Crush?"

"Not while we're eating."

He rolled his eyes. "What am I supposed to do?"

"Talk to your mom, silly. Tell me about Europe. What was your favorite thing?"

He looked out the window thoughtfully. Then his eyes lit up. "Did you know they have a real Harry Potter castle in France? I saw it at France Miniature."

"Are you sure?"

"Yeah. It's called Mount Saint Mitchell. It's on a lake and everything."

"Oh! You mean *Mont Saint Michel*." I took French in high school and knew exactly what he was talking about.

"Yeah that." His eyes glimmered. "And there was this place called Asterix Park. They have this roller coaster and you can see Zeus' underwear!"

"What do you mean?"

"You know Zeus? From Greek mythology? He has a roller coaster at Asterix Park. He's all green and he's really tall and he's throwing a lightning bolt at you but you can see up his dress." He was very excited.

"Zeus wears a dress?"

"Yeah! And under it you can see his underwear!"

"You can?" I tried to imagine it.

"Yeah! They're whitey tighties!" Daniel laughed like it was the funniest thing ever.

"Wow. Did you take pictures?"

He shrugged. "Ask Grandma."

It hurt that he'd had all this fun with his dad and his grandparents and I missed all of it. The idea nearly brought me to tears. At least he was happy. I set my utensils down and wiped my hands on my napkin.

"Ready for ice cream?"

"Yeah!"

We drove to the Baskin Robbins nearby. It was in a strip mall. A huge crowd of people were gathered outside the entrance of one of the other stores a few doors down. There were streamers tied to the roof, lots of balloons, and a big GRAND OPENING sign.

"What's that?" Daniel asked.

"I don't know."

"Can we go see?"

"Sure. But don't you want your ice cream first?"

"Oh yeah."

We bought ice cream cones and took them outside to see what the commotion was. Music pumped inside and the people cheered and clapped loudly. The people standing outside crowded around the windows, watching. Daniel looked between their arms and elbows, trying to see.

"It's a karate class, Mom!"

Inside, a bunch of kids and teenagers wearing martial arts uniforms were lined up along the walls while more kids did kicks and punches in unison in the middle of the large space. Blue mats covered the floor from wall to wall. I didn't know much about martial arts, but it looked like they were doing some kind of show. We watched for a while. Daniel was fascinated.

"Mom, can I take karate?"

"Maybe."

"Please, Mom, please?"

"We'll have to talk to your dad."

"If he says yes, can I?"

"I don't know, Daniel. Aren't you busy with soccer?"

"This is different!"

"We should probably go. It's getting late." I didn't know what it was, but something about this situation made me nervous.

"But they're still going. Can't we stay and watch?"

"Fine," I sighed. "But just for a few minutes."

Daniel had never been this excited about soccer. We had to practically drag him to practice. If it wasn't for soccer, I don't think he would've exercised. Just played video games all day. Why did he have to pick fighting as his sport?

Inside, whoever was running things was describing the action on a microphone while high energy music played. Some of the older kids did a routine with metal swords that had sashes on the hilts. They were swinging them at each other so fast and so close, I was worried someone might slice off a finger or a nose, but no one got hurt.

"That was awesome!" Daniel gasped. "I wanna do that, Mom!"

Terrific. Kicks and punches were one thing. Sword fighting was another. I didn't want my son getting beheaded.

"Please! Can I?!"

"We'll have to see what your dad says." I hoped Donald said no. I didn't want to be the bad guy. I was already the bad guy more often than not.

"Give them a round of applause, everybody," the announcer said over the microphone. The boys with the swords took a bow and ran off the blue mats. "Next up is what most of you came for. Lion Maxwell is here tonight to celebrate the grand opening of our newest dojo! Everybody give it up for Lion Maxwell!"

The crowd whistled and cheered.

"Thanks for coming out tonight," Lion said over the microphone.

That voice...

Ooze.

Oh no.

I immediately ducked down below the shoulders of the two men in front of me. "Daniel, we should really go," I hissed.

"But you said we could stay, Mom!"

"Okay, okay." I promised myself I wouldn't be the bad guy. Maybe Lion wouldn't notice me.

Lion rolled into the middle of the big room in a wheelchair.

That was odd. I could see him using crutches, but a wheelchair? Was the injury worse than it appeared on the MRI? Or had he not followed his therapy protocol closely enough? Something told me a rule breaker like Lion had probably done exactly that.

"How're you all doing tonight?" Lion asked through the microphone.

The crowd applauded. A few people whistled.

"I can't tell you how excited I am that we're opening this new dojo here in Burbank. You guys are incredible. Thank you so much for coming out tonight."

More cheering.

"Some of you probably heard I got hurt during my last fight." Murmurs from the crowd. "Nothing to worry about. The doctors said they can fix it. I have surgery in a couple of weeks. Right now, you're probably wondering about the wheelchair. With my knee out of commission, I got to wondering about all the ways you could teach martial arts to people who spend their lives in a wheelchair. Just because they're disabled doesn't mean they're helpless. Martial arts are for everybody. Lemme give you a demonstration. Robert? You mind coming up here a second?"

A tall muscular young man who wore a gold uniform and a black belt and looked about seventeen trotted across the mats toward Lion. He stopped and bowed before dropping into a fighting stance.

"Robert, go ahead and take a shot."

"Sir." Robert nodded and bowed again. Then he danced around on his toes in front of Lion for a moment before throwing a lightning fast punch.

Lion exploded into action—still sitting in the wheelchair—and trapped Robert's arm, yanking him forward. Robert stumbled and Lion twisted the young man's torso so he fell face first into Lion's lap. Lion's elbow arced up and down in a flash, stopping a millimeter from cracking the back of Robert's skull.

Scattered applause from the crowd.

Robert got up and tried again. Every time he threw a punch or a kick, Lion blocked him and subdued him, all while sitting in the wheelchair. After numerous attempts, Robert was breathless. Lion hadn't even broken a sweat.

I was amazed by Lion's ferocity when he took action but also impressed by his restraint. I was also a little bit turned on by his rampant masculinity. Even limited by the wheelchair, he was in total control.

"Thanks, everybody," Lion said, taking the microphone back from one of his uniformed helpers. "Give Robert a hand." People clapped. "As you can see, being in a wheelchair doesn't mean you're helpless."

Someone from the audience asked, "Do you teach wheelchair classes? My nephew is paraplegic."

"We do. Talk to me about it after tonight's demo."

"I will." She seemed pleased.

"Any other questions?"

For the next fifteen minutes, Lion answered whatever the audience asked. There were questions about martial arts in general, about his career, about whether or not he would continue fighting after his knee healed. He answered everything with a sense of humor and humility. There was no sign of the cocky arrogant asshole who came into my ECU several weeks ago. But his playfully adorable grin shone the whole time.

When the Q&A was officially over, Lion thanked everyone and was immediately surrounded by people on the mat. He signed autographs and took pictures with his fans.

"If anybody is interested in taking classes here at the dojo," Lion said, "we'll be having a free intro class this weekend. Grab one of the instructors in a gold uniform if you want to sign up."

"Mom!" Daniel said. "Can I go? Please please please? He said it was free!"

"Why don't we talk to your dad first."

Lion said to everyone, "Please keep in mind, class space is limited. So sign up quick before it fills up."

"Mom!" Daniel begged.

"I don't know, Daniel."

He shook my arm. "Mom! We need to sign up now!"

"Okay! Calm down."

I let Daniel drag me inside. I looked for the nearest instructor. Maybe I could sign Daniel up and get out of here before Lion noticed me. It was pretty crowded. Then Donald could take Daniel to classes, and Lion would never know Daniel was my son because his last name was Wright. I crossed my fingers.

"Brigid?" *That voice.*

Ooze.

Damn fingers. Crossing them never worked.

I ducked my head and hid behind the nearest tall person.

"Dr. Flanagan?"

Ooze.

"Mom!" Daniel whispered. "He's talking to you! The teacher is talking to you!"

"I know, honey."

"Excuse me," Lion said as he wheeled toward me. People made room for him. "Hey, Dr. Flanagan. What are you doing here?"

"How do you know my mom?"

Lion's eyes landed on Daniel. He looked at my son thoughtfully for a long time.

That's when it hit me. The few men I'd dated since the divorce had run for the hills when I told them about Daniel. I put my hands on his shoulders and smiled. "Lion, this is my son Daniel."

"Nice to meet you, bud. You can call me Lion." He held out his hand to shake. He waited. "How long you gonna leave me hangin', Dan the Man?"

Daniel grinned and they shook. I could tell he liked his new nickname and was already looking up to Lion. I imagined most people did. Except me of course.

"What'd you guys think of the demo?"

"It was awesome," Daniel said.

I asked, "How is your knee?"

"Doing good. Still waiting for the surgery. Prehab is great. Been doing all the exercises. My range of motion is almost back to normal."

"That's terrific."

Lion smiled at Daniel. "You gonna come out for our free class?"

Daniel looked at me, "Can I, Mom?"

"We have to talk to your dad." I watched Lion's eyes for a reaction.

Daniel gasped, "But if we wait, we might miss out!"

"Don't worry, Dan the Man. I'll save you a spot." He winked at him.

"Are you sure?" I asked. "I wouldn't want to have some other boy or girl miss out."

"Don't worry, Brigid. I'll make sure no one gets left out."

"That's very generous of you." It wasn't lost on me that Lion was doing everything he could to make room for my son. I also noticed he wasn't flirting. Just trying to help Daniel. That either made Lion the most manipulative man I'd ever met, or a decent human being.

"Excuse me, Mr. Maxwell?" It was a random man with his teenaged boy who wore a gold #TeamLion T-shirt. "Can we get your autograph for my son?"

"Sure," Lion smiled at the man and signed a glossy color photo of himself with a Sharpie pen and handed it to the teenager.

"Thanks," the kid said. He obviously wanted to talk more with Lion.

"We should go," I whispered to Lion. "You're busy."

"If you want to stick around, I'll be here until we close."

"That's okay. I don't want to get in your way."

"Mom," Daniel said, "Can I get an autographed picture too?"

I sighed, "Of course."

Lion signed another one from the stack in his lap and handed it to Daniel while chatting with the teenager in the #TeamLion shirt about his last fight. As soon as Daniel took the photo, I made sure he said thank you and I ushered him out the door.

I didn't want to spend any more time with Lion because I was afraid I might start to like him more than I already did.

And that was far more than a doctor should.

Chapter 8

BRIGID

My phone vibrated in my lab coat pocket several days later while I was at the hospital.

Donald: Can you take Daniel this Saturday? I have a business thing I can't get out of.

Me: On Saturday?

Unlike me, his job was Monday thru Friday and he had relatively normal hours. I depended on his normal hours, especially having his weekends free because mine rarely were.

Donald: Yes. Is that a problem?

Me: I'm on call all day Saturday. You know that.

Saturday was also the only day I had to go grocery shopping, pay bills, do laundry, clean house, etc.

Donald: Can you change your schedule? Just this once?

Me: You know I can't.

Nobody ever wanted to cover a Saturday shift. I was usually the one covering it for everyone else.

Donald: Please don't give me any grief about this. I need to do this business thing.

Me: I'm not giving you grief.

Donald: I don't want to argue about it. Can you please take Daniel tomorrow to his karate thing?

Not surprisingly, Donald had readily agreed to signing Daniel up for classes. He cared about his son, and Daniel desperately wanted to do it. The only thing I didn't like about karate for Daniel was that it kept me tied to Lion Maxwell. If I had to be the one taking Daniel to class, how was I going to avoid the man? There was always my neighbor Heather. She was a stay at home mom who had kids Daniel's age and babysat for me all the time. Maybe she could do it. I hated passing the buck, but I needed to steer clear of Lion.

Me: I'll see if Heather can take him.

Donald: Can you please make it work? For once?

I scowled at my phone. I could hear Donald's haggard tone in my head. It was the tone he used so often toward the end of our marriage.

The one that made me feel like an absentee mother.

Donald: Let me know ASAP. If you can't, I'll ask Mom and Dad to cancel their trip to Palm Springs. I don't want Daniel missing his first day of class.

He wasn't trying to make me feel guilty. His parents Ronald and Linda did more than their fair share of helping with Daniel. They were like second parents and they had made it possible for me to get through four years of medical school and then residency with a young son. So my guilt was genuine and I deserved it.

Me: I said I'd ask Heather.

Donald: Please make it happen. For your son.

Ouch. That stung.

Anyone who ever said women could have it all—a career, a happy marriage, children, and a sex life—were absolute liars. Being Super Mom sounded good in fantasy land, but in reality it was impossible. Someone was always disappointed: your husband, your children, your boss, you, your patients, or your bank account. In my case it was all of the above.

Had someone told me in advance this would happen, I never would've gone to medical school. I absolutely loved Daniel. He was my world. My life. With the help of Ronald and Linda, which had included living with them rent free, becoming a doctor and raising a son had seemed completely doable. Add to that the fact my mother was the primary breadwinner in my family (she was a Nurse Practitioner), and I had wanted to be a doctor since I was six, and getting my MD seemed inevitable. Sadly, I had been in denial about how demanding the hours of med school and residency would be on my marriage. Something always had to give. For me, it had been my marriage. I wasn't able to give it the time it deserved. I thought I had, but Donald thought otherwise. I couldn't really blame him.

I sighed.

This was the life I signed up for. Before the divorce, it had been tolerable and often enjoyable. Whenever I'd had spare time, I spent it with Daniel. He was the brightest light in my busy schedule. I had tried to include Donald in everything we did, but he never seemed satisfied. At least he didn't try to shut me out of Daniel's life after the divorce. Our current relationship was workable and generally polite, and we always put Daniel first. But as always, my time was limited by my schedule. Maybe in a few years, after I gained more experience, I would join a private practice. Then I'd have more time for my son.

Hopefully.

Believe me, I beat myself up every day over my choices.

Again, I blame the Super Mom fantasy.

Me: I'll make it work. Can you bring Daniel to my condo first thing in the morning?

Donald: Would your highness like anything else?

I hated it when he did that.

He was the one who got treated like royalty. For all I knew, his business thing was an early morning golf game at the Beverly Hills Resort with prospective clients and he didn't want to be late to tee off. Me, I didn't have time to exercise. Going to the gym meant that much less time with Daniel. Schmoozing at the golf course was hardly what I'd call work. Clearing an impacted bowel or delousing a patient was work.

Me: If you bring him over first thing in the morning, I'll make sure he gets to karate class. Your parents can go to Palm Springs and you can do your business thing. Then everybody will be happy.

My happiness wasn't part of the equation.

As long as my son was happy, that was good enough for me. Secretly, I dreamed of having a life of my own outside of work.

Experience told me that wasn't a dream I should hold on to.

With any luck, when I brought Daniel to class on Saturday, Lion wouldn't be the one teaching. He was a symbol of the life I wanted but couldn't have.

Hopefully he would have his staff teach for him and I could forget about him for good.

Chapter 9

BRIGID

"Hey! It's Dan the Man!" Lion was greeting everyone as they walked into the dojo late Saturday morning. This time, he was on crutches instead of the wheelchair and had his knee brace on. He wore a gold instructor's karate uniform with black karate pants and a black belt. The top had various embroidered patches that made him look official and authoritative. Not that he needed any help. His physique alone was sufficient. I could see his chest muscles flexing in the V of the uniform top whenever he leaned on the crutches. But there was something about a man in uniform.

Daniel was all smiles when Lion greeted him. "Hey!"

"Hey, Brigid." Lion grinned.

I rolled my eyes, "Hello, Mr. Maxwell."

"Call me Lion."

"Fine. Lion."

"Do I call you Lion too?" Daniel asked.

Lion grinned. "Call me sensei."

"What's that?"

"It means teacher."

"Oh. Cool. Hey, sensei!"

"Hey, bud." Lion smiled at me. "I like this kid."

"Me too."

"You ready for class, Dan the Man?"

"Yeah!"

Lion turned to the young man I recognized from the wheelchair demonstration the other night. "Hey, Robert? Can you and Melanie get Daniel a uniform and help him and the other kids get dressed for class?"

Melanie looked about sixteen and was too cute in her gold instructor's uniform. She and Robert nodded and led the kids into the back, carrying a pile of new white uniforms in plastic wrappers.

There were other supportive parents sitting in chairs near the front windows, but for the moment, Lion and I were relatively alone.

"What do I owe you for the uniform?"

"It's free if Daniel signs up for a regular class."

"Oh."

"Are you planning on signing him up?" He looked hopeful.

"If Daniel likes it, his father and I agreed we would."

Suddenly, Lion sagged and looked slightly sheepish. "I owe you an apology, don't I?"

"Why?" I could think of a hundred reasons why he did, but I honestly couldn't think of a good one.

"You're married." He said it with regret.

"Divorced."

His eyes brightened and that adorable grin of his was back. "Really?"

"Don't get any ideas. Doctor, patient. Patient, doctor." I pointed back and forth between the two of us.

He chuckled. "Right, right. Rules."

"You remember!"

"Course I do. Doesn't mean I like it."

"Remember what I said about rules?"

He smirked. "Sometimes they're ridiculous."

"I'm impressed."

"I'm always impressive."

"That ego of yours is really ballooning out of control. If I had a pin handy, I'd pop it." I pretended to poke the side of his head. "Pop!"

"More like ka-boom."

I giggled. "Are you making fun of your giant ego?"

"Yeah. I never take myself too seriously. You on the other hand…"

"I'm not too serious!"

"Keep on telling yourself that, Einstein."

"Einstein wasn't serious. He was famous for his sense of humor, I'll have you know."

"See what I mean? You sound like a librarian."

"There's nothing wrong with that."

"I'll say." His eyes wandered all over my body. "You look hot in those yoga pants and that hoodie."

His penetrating gaze made me feel naked. "Would you stop? People are watching!" I looked at the parents by the windows, but they were chatting amongst themselves or checking their cell phones. Lion and I stood near the dojo's office, out of earshot and in semi-privacy.

"What can I say, Brigid? I like what I see. A whole hell of a lot."

I whispered, "Stop staring at me you dirty pervert!"

"You like it dirty. Don't deny it." He said it quietly, but that voice of his was still *that voice…*

"I do not!" I was getting turned on in a karate dojo for kids and I felt guilty about it. Was this in any way appropriate? Probably not.

Lion checked to make sure no one was listening, then muttered, "Your denial is code for you love it. For all I know, you work as a dominatrix when you're not at the hospital. Probably got a whole closet of tight black leather outfits and whips at home."

"I do not! I'm a soccer mom when I'm not at work. A plain old soccer mom."

"It's a cover. Admit it. You're hard core dirty behind closed doors."

"How can you say that?" Yes, I was enjoying this. But I wasn't a dominatrix nor had I ever considered being one.

"Because a woman as controlling as you likes to crack the whip in the bedroom as much as she does at work."

My face burned beet red. "I don't even own a whip."

"But you like to tell a man what to do. Tell him what you want. Am I right?"

I wasn't denying it. But my red face was admitting it like crazy. Why were we talking about my sex life or lack thereof? I needed to hide.

"Thing is, you probably don't even know what you want because you don't know what you've been missing."

"Oh? What's that, Mr. Know It All?"

"You want someone to take control of you."

"No I don't." I was about to tell him he could take control of me whenever he wanted.

"You want to know what it would be like to have a man like me pin you down and fuck you senseless. The kind of senseless where you forget everything except how hard you're coming all over my face while I eat you alive."

"I don't want that." My denial was pathetic at best.

"Sure you don't." His eyes drilled into me. "You're probably dripping into your thong right now."

"I'm not wearing a thong." I wasn't. Soccer Mom Surgeons like me wore granny panties. It was the rules. But I was starting to drip.

He grinned lustily. "Mmm. Not wearing anything, Irish? I like the sound of that."

I had completely forgotten where I was. But I was seriously considering dropping my yoga pants and spreading my legs to see if he could live up to his exaggerated claims. In fact, the office next to us had a large desk. If he were to suddenly pick me up, take me into the office, swipe everything off the top of said desk, sit me down on it and go to town, I would probably let him.

One of the parents sitting in the chairs by the front windows coughed, breaking the moment.

"We should…" I muttered, unable to finish my sentence.

Lion's eyes searched mine. "Yeah we should." He was obviously thinking about that desk too.

"Mom!" Daniel ran out of the back in a white karate uniform with a white belt tied around his waist. He looked incredibly cute and was the perfect distraction. "Check it out, Mom! I'm a white belt!"

"You are!" Trying to switch gears, I took a deep breath. Was there a ladies room around here somewhere? I needed a wipe down.

"Sensei, when do we learn how to break a board?"

Lion chuckled and patted Daniel's shoulder, "We'll work up to it. You ready to learn some jiu-jitsu?"

"Yeah!"

"Then line up with the other kids and we'll get this party started."

Daniel ran onto the blue mats and lined up with the other children who ranged in age from about six to twelve.

Lion flashed me the sexiest grin in history. "We can fuck after class."

"What did you just say?"

"I said we can talk after class. About signing Daniel up."

"Oh. Right." I needed a cold shower. Or an orgasm. Since neither was an option I sat down with the other parents to watch class.

For the next hour, Lion wrangled the kids with the help of Robert and Melanie. It was obvious from the start that Lion had worked with children before. Even on crutches, he was a pro at wrangling them and keeping them semi-focused. He also looked ridiculously sweet working with them. Whether on his crutches or in his wheelchair (he switched between both), he instructed them on how to punch and kick and block while Robert and Melanie demonstrated. During group drills, he went from child to child, always encouraging them, always making them laugh, all while correcting them gently and teaching them. The kids loved him.

More importantly, Daniel was having more fun than I'd seen him have since the divorce. All because of Lion Maxwell. The man was melting my heart and he wasn't even trying.

That was when I knew I was in serious trouble.

Why did there have to be a stupid rule about doctors not dating their patients?

When class was over, Daniel ran up to me. "Mom! That was *so* awesome! I can't wait to do it again!" He threw his arms around me. "Thank you so much for taking me today! I love you, Mom!"

To my astonishment, Daniel was once again the happy kid I

remembered, the one who had disappeared into hiding when things between Donald and me had soured. Gone was the perpetual dark cloud that had been hanging over my son's head for too many years.

I hugged my son back as hard as I could.

I was going to cry in front of everybody.

And it was all Lion's fault.

It took an hour for Lion and his staff to sign up the interested families after the free class was over. Daniel insisted we wait around until I signed him up. I didn't mind waiting. I was reluctant to leave. As long as Lion was here, I wanted to be here. There was nothing unethical about me being here. It was for my son. And I intended to enjoy every moment of it.

When Lion finished with the last of the other parents, he came over to me and Daniel and smiled. "I take it you're signing Daniel up."

Daniel looked at me hopefully.

I rubbed his shoulder. "Of course we are."

"Then step into my office." Lion pointed the way and Daniel ran ahead.

Daniel was already sitting in one of the chairs facing the desk, practically bouncing out of it with excitement. I sat next to him and did my best not to remember what I had imagined Lion and I doing on this desk. I might think about it later when I was alone, but not right now.

Lion walked us through the options and suggested I sign Daniel up for a month to month plan, which I did, and paid with a credit card. Lion swiped my card through a machine beside his computer and handed it to me with the receipt for me to sign.

He grinned. "I guess this means I'll be seeing a lot more of you, Brigid. You too, Dan the Man."

Daniel was smiling and kicking his legs up and down in his chair.

My heart swelled. "Looks like it."

Lion finished stapling all the receipts together and handed everything to me.

Robert, the young instructor, stuck his head in the office.

"Everything is cleaned up, Sensei. I'm gonna take off."

"Sounds great, Rob. I'll lock up on my way out."

I watched Robert and Melanie walk out the front doors together. They were laughing at something I couldn't hear and smiling at each other. Were they an item? They sure seemed like it.

Lion caught me watching. He muttered, "Young love," and winked at me.

I felt a sudden rush but pushed it away. "Thank you again, Lion. I think Daniel is really going to love karate class."

He grinned, "It's technically a modified form of jiu-jitsu, but we do include aspects of Shorinji kenpo and traditional Shotokan karate in our curriculum."

"Who's the librarian now," I smirked.

He chuckled. "When it comes to martial arts, yeah, I'm kind of a librarian about it."

Daniel said, "I wanna be a karate librarian!"

"Don't worry, Dan the Man, if you stick with it, you will." Lion stood up. "Well, that's about it."

I stood too. I was reluctant to leave.

Daniel hopped out of his chair and ran to the front doors.

Lion grabbed his crutches from the corner and we made our way toward the doors. "I don't know about you two, but I'm ready for some lunch. Wanna join me?"

"I'm hungry," Daniel said. "Can we go with him, Mom?"

Lion's adorable grin was back. Not the sexy-as-sin grin. "There's a great sandwich shop two blocks from here, and there's a park around the corner. It has a pretty sweet playground."

Daniel gasped, "It's got a playground?!"

"And a climbing wall."

"Mom! Please? Can we?"

I looked at Lion. Was this a mistake? Was I breaking a rule? I wasn't sure. But I knew one thing, lunch wasn't sexual misconduct. It was just lunch.

"Okay. What can it hurt?"

"Cool. I just need to change real quick and we can head out."

Chapter 10

Lion wore a plain white T-shirt, shorts, and flip-flops. He had his knee brace on again. Every inch of him was deeply tanned and muscled. I'd never seen a man look so incredibly handsome in such a simple outfit. I did my best to ignore it while we bought sandwiches, but I may have peeked once or twice.

At the park, the sun was high in the blue sky. A dozen or more kids were playing tag on the colorful playground equipment, running, climbing, jumping, and hollering with happy abandon. Lion, Daniel, and I sat at a cement picnic table eating submarine sandwiches while watching.

Daniel wolfed his down. "I'm finished, Mom. Can I go play now?"

"Okay, but drink the rest of your water first."

He gulped the entire bottle in two seconds and slammed it down on the table with a satisfied *Ahh!*

"You sure powered through that," Lion said with approval.

"Yup," Daniel smiled, obviously enjoying the praise. "Now can I go, Mom?"

"Yes."

He climbed out of the picnic table bench and scampered straight to the playground.

"Cute kid."

"Thanks," I grinned. "I like him."

"Me too. Reminds me of his mom."

"Oh? How?" Daniel didn't have my red hair and green eyes. He had Donald's blond hair and blue eyes.

"Strong and smart. He picked up things today quicker than a lot of kids. He's got a talent for it."

"He probably got that from his father."

"You sure?"

"I'm not very coordinated."

"Aren't you a surgeon? That takes coordination."

"That's different. It's not a sport. I was never the girl on the track team or the volleyball team."

"Then how do you know you're not good at sports?"

"Because I was always picked last in grade school."

"So?"

"Can we change the subject?" Grade school was not my favorite time in life. I was too serious for the other kids and didn't have a lot of friends. It happened when you were obsessed with being a doctor at age six and always had your nose in a book.

"Sure," he smiled. He took a bite of his sandwich and chewed thoughtfully for a while. We both watched Daniel climbing on the playground equipment with the other kids. It looked like he had joined a game of tag and was having fun.

"That's strange," I said thoughtfully.

"What?"

"Daniel usually plays by himself. Part of being an only child, I guess."

"Maybe he's in the mood after working with the other kids at the dojo. He was loving the leapfrog drills."

I smirked. "We already signed up for a month. You don't have to sell me on it."

"Just pointing out the obvious." That adorable grin of his warmed my heart like it did every time I saw it.

"What do you want from me, Lion Maxwell?"

His eyes darkened. "Everything."

That voice. It was dangerous and intoxicating and I wanted to hear it every day for the rest of my life. With all the things I now knew about Lion, my opinion of him had changed drastically. But the reality of how we'd met hadn't.

"You're still my patient." Saying it pained me. I was having so much fun with him, I wished this was a real lunch date. Not a platonic lunch with a friend or whatever we were.

"Seriously, Irish. What is up with you and rules?"

"You mean, why do I want to keep my job? Oh, let's see. I have a mountain of debt. I have a son. I spent literally half my life becoming a doctor and maybe I don't want to throw away all that hard work."

"I can honestly say I'm worth it."

I shook my head, exasperated. "How old are you? Five? The world does not revolve around your giant ego, although it is large enough to attract its own moon. I'm surprised you don't have one or two moons orbiting around your head right now. Oh, wait! There's one!" I pointed over his ear. "I can even see tiny moon men waving at me!" I did a little wave with my fingers. "Hey, guys!"

He chuckled. "There you go again, Einstein."

"Me Einstein? You were karate Einstein today at the school."

"And you loved it."

"I don't love anything about you." I busied myself with my lunch and popped a potato chip into my mouth.

He stared at me while I chewed.

"What?"

"If we weren't in the middle of this park, I'd climb over this picnic table and kiss you until you came."

I gulped and swallowed and tried not to cough. My throat was suddenly dry. I took a sip from my water bottle. "Nobody has an orgasm from kissing."

"You haven't kissed me."

Was that true? Was it even anatomically possible? I'd have to consult the research. Maybe it was. More importantly, what was I doing? Officially, there was no exact rule that said how much time needed to pass before you could safely date a discharged patient, but six months was considered a bare minimum. With Lion, it hadn't even been six weeks. I wasn't going to say any of this to Lion because I didn't want him getting any ideas. He was already finding ways to break the rules. Me having lunch with him was at the very least highly suspicious. If one of my bosses or a hospital administrator saw us together, I'm sure I'd get chewed out about it.

I sighed. "Lion, we can't do this."

"Do what? We're just having lunch."

"Just? Talking about kissing orgasms is just lunch?"

"It's just talk."

"Talk leads to other things."

"Is that a promise?"

"No! It's not. Are you always this irritating?"

"You love it. But I like to think of it as persistent."

"A, we already established I don't love anything about you. B, being persistent and being a pest are very closely related."

"Being persistent is how I give you more orgasms than you can handle. You wouldn't want a lazy lover, would you? A one pump wonder who won't go down on you before sticking it in? No, you want persistence. Trust me."

"Why are we even talking about this?" And why was the idea of him lavishing my lady parts with his mouth so appealing? Perhaps because no one had ever lavished me. Sure, Donald had given me oral sex many times in the early years, but he was never passionate about it. He tried, but he wasn't very good. Not every man was a Don Juan or Casanova. That was probably part of the reason our sex life had dried up long before the divorce. If not for my own fingers, I think my tunnel of love might have dried up and been sealed off and condemned by the city. Thank goodness for sex toys. They kept my river flowing.

"We're talking about this because I want to fuck you, Brigid."

My eyes popped. I looked around at the people in the park. Luckily everyone was too far away to overhear any of this. "Do you kiss your mother with that mouth?"

"Have you ever given a blowjob?"

"What does that have to do with anything?"

"Yes or no?"

"Does it matter?"

"To me it does."

"Why?"

"Because I want to know where your mouth has been."

"That's none of your business."

"Then why did you ask me if I kissed my mother with my mouth?"

"That's different."

"How?"

I thought for a second. "Because we're talking about where *your* mouth has been. Not mine."

"Let's talk about where your mouth has been."

"No."

"Have you ever sucked cock, Brigid?"

"Will you stop asking?"

"If you answer my question I will."

"Fine. Yes. I have."

"Did you like it?"

"I thought you said you'd stop asking."

"It's a different question."

"Which I'm not going to answer." How had he gotten me thinking so much about blowjobs? And not the ones I gave Donald, but the ones I was imagining giving Lion. What would it be like to have his huge cock in my mouth? To feel him throbbing and pulsing as his hot cum shot against the back of my throat?

"You liked it," Lion chuckled.

"How do you know?" I growled.

"Because you're blushing as red as your hair." He picked up his sandwich. "Which do you think is bigger, this sub sandwich, or my dick?"

"You're the one who's about to take a bite out of it, so you tell me."

He laughed and took a bite and chewed. With his mouth full of food, he grinned and said, "My dick. Definitely my dick."

I had to laugh.

"You wanna bite?"

"What, of your sandwich?"

"No, Einstein. My dick."

I laughed again.

No man had ever talked to me like this. This bold, this brazen, this sexual. Donald was not at all cocky. Or funny. Our sex life had been exciting in the beginning because he was the first man I'd gone all the way with. But sex with him wasn't this... charged. Or fun. Nothing naughty or remotely dangerous. Donald was a very conservative and shy lover. Maybe a better word was boring. Bland. But with Lion, his sexuality was in your face and over the top and always on display. From the moment he thrust his erection in my face at the hospital, Lion was strutting his stuff and swinging his dick every chance he got. Was I curious about what it would be like to sleep with a man as bold and cocky (literally) as him? A better word would be dying to find out.

"What's on your mind, Einstein?"

"My exit strategy," I giggled.

"Your what?"

"I was thinking about how I can get Daniel and sneak out of here without you following me." It wasn't what I wanted to do, but it was what I should do.

"I don't need to follow you. I'll see you at Daniel's next class."

"Maybe I'll have his father drive him next time. And every other time."

"We both know you don't want that. You want to see me again as bad as I want to see you."

He was right. With Lion, I felt young and alive and desirable. And for once, like I could have a life beyond work and trying to draw my depressed son out of his permanent post-divorce funk. Lion was good for Daniel. It was obvious. But none of that changed the fact that Lion was still my patient. Time to do the responsible thing. Rules could be ridiculous, but they were still rules.

"Lion, you seem like a really great guy. But I have to be honest with you, I think we're better off as friends."

"Friends with benefits?"

"No benefits. Take it or leave it."

"I plan on taking you every way I can think of."

"Must you always go there?" And why did I want him to keep going there?

"Are you kidding? I live there."

"You're the horniest man I've ever met."

"You say that like it's a bad thing."

"It is. You never stop."

"When I'm eating your pussy and you've come three times all over my face and I just won't fucking stop, are you going to complain then? Are you going to say, 'Lion, I won't accept four orgasms. Three is my limit. Four is just too many.' Is that what you'll tell me?"

"I…" I stared at him. "Do you not realize I'm a mother? How is this talk appropriate? And at a park, no less."

He shrugged. "So you're a mom."

"That's right. I'm a mom."

"And how many kids do you have? I mean, other than Daniel?"

"What's your point?"

"How many kids?"

"Just Daniel. But that doesn't make me any less of a mother," I said defensively. It was my residual guilt over never having enough time for my son.

"I wasn't saying it did. Here's my point. Think about all the people you know who have two or more kids. Do you think Mom and Dad stopped fucking after one kid? No. They kept on fucking."

"Do you have to put it like that?"

"Fine. They made love. They had sex. But they probably fucked a hell of a lot if they were really into each other."

"Okay, I get it."

"The question is, are you getting any?"

None whatsoever. "That's none of your business."

"I'm making it my business."

"Ahem. Just. Friends."

"Friends can talk about sex. It doesn't mean we're fucking."

If he said fucking one more time I was going to… I didn't want to think about it. "What was your point again?"

"Parents keep fucking after their first kid."

"Well, of course. Because they want more kids."

He looked at me thoughtfully. "Your ex-husband never really fucked you, did he?"

I was afraid to answer because I was afraid he was right. Maybe that was why I had always been denying Donald sex. Maybe it was never good. Ever. That was pathetic. Did I not know what good sex was? Perhaps not.

"Anyway. Parents keep on fucking because they're still hot for each other *and* they want more kids. Just because you have Daniel doesn't mean you can't do lots more fucking." His eyes flashed. "And love every dripping wet second of it."

Was it suddenly really hot out here? We were sitting in the shade. So why did I want to squirm on the picnic table bench like it was on fire? It felt like I was melting into it. Or I was more turned on than I ever had been.

"Brigid, you don't have to stop being a woman because you're a mom."

I hadn't had time for either in years. I sighed audibly and folded my arms in my lap, staring off into the distance. My eyes burned. I didn't want to start crying, so I turned away.

"Did I say something wrong?"

"No. It's just... never mind." I hated talking about this. But the last thing I wanted to do was tell Lion to stay out of my life because he wouldn't stop flirting with me. "Look. Lion. We can be friends. That's it. Anything else is off the table. We are just friends. Please respect that."

"Works for me. What do we do next? As friends?"

"If you mean right now, I was planning on spending the day with Daniel. If I don't get called into work, that is."

"Sounds like a plan."

"I meant alone. Just him and me."

"Why? When you can have twice as much fun with me tagging along. I'm betting cash money Daniel won't mind."

I hated that he was right.

No, I loved that he was right.

But that didn't make it a good idea. More time with Lion would likely lead to more problems for me.

"Can we take a rain check?"

"It never rains in LA, so no."

I frowned at him.

"I'm kidding. You can say no."

"What did you have in mind?"

He smiled. "I'm glad you asked."

Chapter 11

BRIGID

"You do realize, I'm the on call physician today. If the hospital pages me, we'll have to leave."

Lion smiled at me, "And?"

"And, I don't want you wasting your money."

"Anything that involves you and your son is not a waste of my money."

How did he manage to say the perfect thing every time?

"Okay. Let's do it. But I warned you."

Lion smiled and turned to the woman in the ticket booth. "Three, please."

"How old is your son?" the woman asked Lion.

He winked at me. "How old is our son, Brigid?"

He was perfect. Simply perfect.

"He's not my dad," Daniel laughed. But he said it like he might actually like the idea. "He's my sensei."

Lion grinned at me like a proud papa. "You hear that?"

"Yes." I grinned and leaned into the ticket window and said to the woman, "He's ten."

She pressed buttons on the touch screen. "That'll be $332.97 for three one day general admission passes."

I winced and looked at Lion. "When did Universal Studios get so expensive?"

"When was the last time you were here?"

"It's been a while." Daniel had been as recently as a year ago. I hadn't gone with him. Donald and Grandma Linda took him. I was too busy working. As always. The one good thing about being a doctor was that I could afford tickets. I pulled my wallet out of my purse. "This is too much for you to pay. I'll pay for me and Daniel."

"Put your money away, Irish. I told you I'd cover it."

"Why did you call my mom Irish?" Daniel asked.

"Because she makes me feel like the luckiest guy on the planet."

Daniel frowned. "I don't get it."

"You will when you're older." Lion looked at me while he said it. His eyes shone with satisfaction.

I knew it. This "just friends" thing was going to be nearly impossible to pull off. I gave myself a 50/50 chance. Not good odds.

We walked through the park gates and stood just inside the park entrance by the big Universal Studios wireframe globe.

"Lion, are you going to be okay on crutches all day? They probably have wheelchairs for this kind of thing."

"I'll be fine. I've got my knee brace. And the crutches are a great arm workout." His T-shirt was tight across his chest and shoulders, and his biceps and triceps bulged beautifully every time he put his weight on the crutches.

I needed to not watch his arms or this was going to be a long and frustrating day. "What do you want to do first, Daniel?"

"Harry Potter!"

Lion snickered, "Did you have to ask?" He bumped his shoulder against mine gently. My entire arm warmed where he had touched it.

I was wrong. This was going to be a long day no matter where I looked.

Since it was after lunch, the park was packed wall to colorful themed wall with people, but the energy was summer vacation fun so it was perfect. Because of the heat and because this was LA, skin was on display everywhere. There were hundreds of young beautiful women in short shorts and tight fitting tank tops. As far as I could tell, Lion wasn't looking at any of them. He was too busy talking to Daniel, pointing out all the cool things and trying to make him feel comfortable. I could tell Daniel enjoyed it.

The line for the Harry Potter rides were insane. Wait time for Harry Potter and the Forbidden Journey was almost an hour. None of us seemed to mind. Daniel and Lion got along like best buds, joking and talking to pass the time. I almost felt left out because they were so busy talking about one thing or another, including video games, which I knew nothing about. At one point, Lion asked Daniel if he had a girlfriend.

"No," Daniel giggled.

"What? Dan the Man doesn't have a girlfriend? I'm not buying it."

Daniel grinned.

"I bet a good looking guy like you has tons of girlfriends." He winked at me. I loved that Lion was boosting Daniel's confidence so casually. He was so good with kids.

Daniel leaned against the railing and buried his face in his arms.

I whispered, "He's still shy around girls."

"No I'm not," Daniel mumbled.

"See? Dan the Man isn't shy around girls. He'll probably have ten girlfriends in no time."

I could see Daniel smiling, but he was still burying his face in his arms. Lion flashed me a grin that Daniel couldn't see. It warmed my heart in a way I hadn't felt in years. Okay, now my odds of remaining just friends with Lion were down to 40/60. When we finally rode Harry Potter and the Forbidden Journey, which was in the dark and had our feet dangling at least ten feet off the ground, I got scared and may have squeezed Lion's hand without realizing it. He squeezed back and leaned against me.

"I got you, Irish." *That voice.*

I felt it dribble down my chest and swirl between my legs like a tingling massage.

He had me, all right. Was it appropriate for me to ooze on a family theme park ride? Because that's exactly what I was doing. Good thing my yoga pants were thick and absorbent. Now my chances were down to 30/70. Things were not looking good. When we walked off the ride, we passed a wall of monitors showing souvenir photos of people riding the ride.

"Where's ours?" Daniel asked.

"There it is," Lion said. "I'm totally buying a copy of that."

"No you're not!" I gasped. Why? Because the photo showed me clutching Lion's hand for dear life and looking scared to death. Not only was it embarrassing, it was also incriminating. It was even dated, making it literally evidence of my inappropriate relationship with Lion. Could I ask Universal Studios to delete the photo from their servers? Or would it be used against me when the state of California called me before their medical ethics committee?

Before I could stop him, Lion had already bought the 8x10 print. Framed. Lion showed it to Daniel.

"Look at Mom," he giggled. "She's really scared."

"This is going on my wall when I get home," Lion chuckled.

"Maybe you should put it in the garbage," I groused.

"Nope. Wall. Got a place for it in my office next to my trophy case."

"Trophy case?"

"From all my fights."

"Oh, because I'm one of your many victories?"

"No. You're the grand prize."

Was it wrong for me to like the ridiculous things he said?

"What are you guys talking about?" Daniel asked.

"Just giving your mom a hard time."

Hard…

Ooze.

The question was, would I be able to resist him giving me a hard time in private at some future date?

The chances of that did not look good.

20/80.

If I was lucky.

Chapter 12

LION

There was no way I was gonna be able to stay friends with Brigid forever. She was too damn sexy to resist.

Good thing I wore my shades to Universal Studios. Whether we were waiting in line for a ride or wandering from place to place in the park, I couldn't stop staring at her. Even with the tinted lenses of my shades, it was so bright out I was worried she'd catch me constantly checking out her ass in her yoga pants.

No matter how hot it got, she never unzipped her hoodie far enough to see any cleavage, but I stared anyway. I didn't think she had any idea how hot she was. She acted like her body was an afterthought. Her torch of red hair was pulled back in a ponytail, but all that did was call attention to her beautiful face. She didn't wear makeup, but I couldn't keep my eyes off her mouth. Every time she laughed or smiled, which she did all day long, all I could think about was kissing that mouth. I had ample opportunity on some of the rides to make a move, but I was going to honor our agreement to stay just friends.

Good thing I had willpower to spare.

I was glad Dan was with us. He was a great distraction from drooling over Brigid. I really liked the kid. It took him a while to warm up to me, but once he did, we were cracking jokes all day. When we walked through the Despicable Me Super Silly Fun Land, we were talking about farts, so I started making fart noises by blowing raspberries into my hand, Dan started busting up.

"Do you have to do that?" Brigid groaned.

"It's funny, Mom," Dan giggled.

"Everyone is staring," she hissed and glared at me.

I pointed at the nearest actor in a yellow Minion costume and said, "It wasn't me. It was that guy." The Minion heard me and pretended to act embarrassed. I made another fart noise and the Minion hopped up in the air like he'd just farted. With the wacky eye goggles and goofy smile permanently fixed on his face, he looked like he was in on the joke too.

Dan laughed so hard he bent over and put his hands on the ground.

"You two are terrible." Brigid laughed, but you could tell she was trying not to, which made me and Dan laugh even more.

"Don't deny it, Irish. You're loving this."

"No I'm not," she laughed.

Damn if that laugh didn't make me want to marry her on the spot every time I heard it. I lifted my shades so she could see my eyes. She locked hers on mine. I felt a jolt go straight to my dick. Seeing her have a good time was a total turn on. She was so damn serious the rest of the time. Watching her let down her guard was better than if she'd unzipped that hoodie and pulled her tits out. Not that I would've complained if she had. But not here with a million people around.

"Hey, aren't you Lion Maxwell?" The guy asking wore a Tapout shirt. He had some woman with him.

"That's him," the woman said. "You're Lion Maxwell."

I smiled at them. I should've worn a ball cap to go with the shades. Today was supposed to be about Brigid and Dan, not me.

"Dude, can we get a picture with you?"

I wasn't gonna be a dick and say no. "Sure."

The guy pulled out his smart phone and turned to Brigid. "Hey, uh, can you take the picture for us?"

"Oh, okay," she said.

The dude and his woman stood on either side of me. I put my arms around their shoulders. "You guys ready?"

"Yeah."

Brigid snapped the photo. "Let me take a couple more, just in case. Say cheese." They didn't but she took more pictures anyway then handed over the phone. "Here you go."

"Thank you so much, man," the dude said. "I'm a huge fan of yours. How's your knee doing?" He eyed my crutches and knee brace.

"Getting better."

"When do you think you'll fight again?"

"Once the doctors fix my ACL. I still need surgery. Then plenty of rehab. Could be a while."

"Man, that happened to my cousin playing soccer. He couldn't play for a year."

I ended up talking to the guy for another five minutes. He knew all about my fight career and my fighting style. Really knowledgable about MMA. When it was obvious his woman was getting bored, I did my best to ease the conversation to a finish. The guy thanked me again for the photos and him and his woman wandered off, both smiling from ear to ear. It was the least I could do to brighten their day.

"Sorry about that," I said to Brigid.

"That's okay. I forget you're a celebrity."

"Not really. Just in the MMA world." I always felt weird when people came up to me. I breathed the same air they did and shit like everybody else. I wasn't special.

After that, I did buy a yellow Minion's baseball cap with a picture of the goggles and the eyes. I got one for Dan and Brigid too. Brigid tried to say no, it was too expensive, but I bought them anyway.

"Now we're all one big happy Minion family." I put the cap on her head and screwed it into place.

Brigid acted like she didn't like it, but she wasn't fooling me.

Dan loved his.

"What do you say, Daniel?" Brigid prompted.

"Thank you so much, sensei! Mom, can I go out and see the carnival games?"

"Go ahead, but don't go too far."

"I won't."

"And stay where you can see me and I can see you. We'll catch up in a minute."

When he ran off, I said, "He's a great kid."

"You're a great big kid. That hat looks adorable on you." She flicked the brim of mine. "Thanks for the hats. Really. You didn't have to do that."

"It was nothing."

"I'm really glad you suggested this. I haven't had this much fun with Daniel in ages."

"You need to get out more. You should be having this much fun every weekend."

"You won't get any argument from me on that subject. I can't believe work hasn't paged me all day." She checked her phone.

"Must be the luck of the Irish."

She rolled her eyes. "Don't jinx me. Now they'll probably call."

"Nah. Good luck always shines on me, Irish." I meant her.

She knew what I meant. The moment was charged for both of us.

I reached up and brushed my knuckle across her chin.

"We should go find Daniel." She broke eye contact and turned her head away.

"Yeah." I backed up a step on my crutches to give her space.

She walked right out of the gift shop without looking back.

Damn.

Did I go too far?

This "friends only" thing was bullshit.

Man, I hated rules.

<<<<<<<<>>>>>>>

We hit up every ride in the park before the day was over.

Revenge of the Mummy. The Jurassic Park water ride. The Simpsons. Transformers 3D. Shrek 4D. The studio tour on the buses where we saw King Kong and Jaws. The WaterWorld show with the stuntmen and the guys riding the WaveRunners in the huge pool and all the explosions. No matter what we did, it always ended up that Dan sat between us. I couldn't figure out if he just wanted to be next to me or if Brigid was putting distance between us.

Either way, it was frustrating.

All I wanted to do was hold her hand or touch her like couples normally did in a place like this. Every time I saw some guy with his hand in his girl's back pocket or the other way around, I was totally jealous.

When I came out of the restrooms and saw Brigid talking with some guy next to the Megatron photo op, I nearly lost my shit. The guy had a muscle shirt on and was pretty built. He was all smiles, trying to charm the pants off of Brigid. I could tell he was a tool from way over here. She laughed at something he said but I couldn't hear what. Time to put a stop to that. I swung toward them on my crutches. I probably looked like an idiot with my crutches and my Minion hat, but I didn't care.

"Hey, guys." I tried to sound friendly but I was pissed. "What are we talking about?"

Muscle Shirt gave me a funny look. "Hey buddy."

"You like my hat, don't you?" I tipped my head, motioning with the hat. I was gripping my crutches so tight I thought I might snap the handles off. I tried to relax.

"Who's this guy?" Muscles chuckled.

"I'm the guy who's with her."

He frowned. "But is she with you?"

He was pissing me off and he was barely trying. I laughed, "Did you not see her matching hat?"

"Bro, half the people here are wearing a hat like that."

"Are you?"

"No, but…" He trailed off, unsure of himself. I was intimidating him. Good.

Brigid made a strange face.

Whoops. Was I out of line? Was I being a jealous dick? Probably. I didn't want to say anything else and end up looking worse than I already did, so I clamped my mouth shut.

Muscles looked back and forth between me and Brigid. He also noticed the size of my arms. Nothing like walking around on crutches all day to keep them pumped. He said to Brigid, "You with this guy?"

Please say yes, please say yes.

"Yeah," she groaned like she regretted it.

What was that about?

Muscles smirked. "You two have fun." He wandered off.

Brigid muttered, "Is everything okay?"

"Uhhh..." I didn't know what to say because I didn't want to sound like any bigger of a tool than I already felt. "Sorry. I was just... sorry."

She smiled. "It's okay."

"Where's Dan the Man?" I needed a distraction.

"He's waiting in line to take a picture with Megatron."

"Oh, right."

The guy in the eight foot tall Megatron suit was making jokes over a PA about all the people standing around watching him. The crowd laughed at his rude humor as he tormented them.

"*A youngling Minion, eh?*" Megatron said in his rumbling robot voice as Dan walked up cautiously and stood in front of him. Megatron stomped his huge robot foot and Dan hopped back, giggling nervously. "*You are obviously an Autobot sympathizer based on that ridiculous hat!*"

Dan laughed.

"Turn around so I can take your picture, Daniel," Brigid said, pointing her phone at him.

Megatron roared, "*Listen to your mother, Minion!*"

I chuckled. This guy was great.

"*Don't dare laugh at me, giant Minion on crutches! I could conquer you and your entire Minion army with my little finger!*" Dan rushed back into the crowd. "*Next victim!*"

Two more kids wandered up for a photo op.

"That was so cool," Dan said. "Lemme see, Mom!"

She showed him her phone.

"Wow! I wanna be Megatron when I grow up!"

"Me too, buddy."

Brigid gave me that strange look again.

I could only hope she was over my bad behavior earlier.

If she was, she wasn't showing it.

It was dark when we left the park.

"That was so much fun, Mom!" Dan said as we walked past the Universal Studios wireframe globe on our way out.

"It sure was." She rubbed his shoulder and looked at me.

Her marry me smile was back. I didn't want the day with them to end. "I don't know about you guys, but I'm starving. What do you think about dinner?"

"I don't know," Brigid said. "It's been a long day."

"Mom, can we get dinner? Please?"

I said, "Since we have to go past all the restaurants in the CityWalk to get to your car, we may as well stop for something to eat, right?" I hoped she said yes.

"Okay. If you insist." That smile.

"I insist. Dan the Man, do you insist?"

"I insist too. Mom? Do you insist?"

"I guess I'm outvoted."

"But do you insist?" I said. "We can't do it if you don't insist."

She grinned at me and Dan. "Okay. If you two insist I insist, then I insist."

Dan frowned, "What does insist mean again?"

"It means we're getting dinner," I chuckled.

We ended up at the Hard Rock Cafe. Dan sat next to me in the booth with Brigid across from us. We all got burgers and milkshakes. Dan and I both sucked our food down. I ended up eating all of Brigid's fries.

"Do you need to order another burger?" she asked.

"Thinking about it."

"Your appetite sure hasn't diminished since your injury."

"I'm still working out like crazy. Mainly upper body and core stuff, but I keep busy."

"It shows."

"Thanks." I wanted to say something flirtatious, but it wasn't the time with Dan next to me. "Who wants dessert?" I picked up the dessert menu.

"I do!" Dan said.

"Haven't you had enough sugar already with your shake?" Brigid asked.

"No!"

I gave Brigid a look, trying to figure if she was cool with Dan having more sugar for dessert. My thought was, when you go all out, you go all out. I never ate sugar when I was training for a fight. But when I was out with a gorgeous woman and her awesome kid at Universal for the whole day, it seemed like the thing to do. I arched my eyebrows at her.

She rolled her eyes. "Okay. We can get dessert. But we should split something."

Dan leaned against my arm as we both looked at the menu.

He said, "I know what I want! Cheesecake with Oreo cookies!"

"That sounds good," Brigid said. "We can split that."

I gave her a sly smile. "I know what I'm getting."

"What?"

"It says here on the menu they have an Irish Kiss." I winked at her. "I'm getting that."

She blushed and stared at me, her eyes twinkling. Damn it, if this was different circumstances, I would lean right over this table and kiss her full on the mouth.

"What do you think, Irish? Should I get the Irish Kiss for dessert?"

"It does not say that!" She reached for the menu.

"Does too." I handed it to her.

She read it out loud. "Jameson Irish Whiskey, Baileys Irish Cream and Monin Spiced Brown Sugar topped with whipped cream, chocolate morsels and chocolate syrup. That sounds really good."

"I want that!" Dan gasped.

She said, "It has alcohol in it, Daniel. You're too young."

"Awww!"

"I'm old enough," I said. "But it sounds pretty rich. You wanna split an Irish Kiss with me, Irish?"

She smirked at me but she was loving this.

"Well?"

"Okay. You get one and I'll just take a sip. One of us has to drive home."

"If you're worried, I can order the alcohol free Irish Kiss."

"I don't see that on the menu," she smirked.

"It's not on the menu." I gave her a pointed look, meaning me.

She knew what I meant. "You're bad," she giggled.

"So they say."

"What are you guys talking about?" Dan asked.

"Just dessert, buddy."

When the waiter returned, we ordered. A few minutes later, he brought out Dan's Cheesecake and one Irish Kiss. Dan attacked his cheesecake with his fork.

"Can I have some?" Brigid asked.

"There's only enough for me," Dan laughed, his mouth full of Oreos.

"Be nice, bud. Your mom didn't order her own dessert. So you and I both have to share with her."

"Okay," Dan groaned.

Brigid forked a bite of the cheesecake and savored it. "That's really good." She set her fork down. "That's enough for me."

I sipped on my Irish Kiss. It crossed my mind that having a public orgasm like in When Harry Met Sally just wasn't the same when a dude did it. Plus Dan was here. But I could still have a foodgasm while I slurped it up. "Oh, man. This Kiss is really good. I mean, really, really good. Wow. Who would've thought an Irish Kiss would be so tripping good?" I never swore in front of kids. "Oops! Got whipped cream all over my lips. Sure is messy. In a good way."

"Would you stop?" Brigid blushed.

"Stop what? I'm just enjoying my Irish Kiss. Bet you want some."

"It can't be that good."

"Best dessert I ever had."

"Oh! I want some!" Dan begged.

"Sorry, buddy. It's got alcohol. When you're older I'll get one for you."

"Do I have to wait?"

"Yup."

"I'm old enough," Brigid said.

"Want some?" I teased.

"Yes."

I smirked at her like I was five and turned away, hooking my whole arm around the glass. "Can't have any."

"Fine," she sneered with a smile. "I don't want any."

I grinned, "Okay, I'll share." I slid the glass across the table.

She tipped the glass up to her face and sipped. "Mmmm, that's really good." When she lowered it, she had whipped cream on her lips, which she licked off.

I would've liked to have been the one to lick it off. I was dying to kiss this woman. She still had a dot of whipped cream on her nose, which she didn't notice. I bumped Dan. "Hey, what's that on your mom's face?"

He snickered around another mouthful of cheesecake. "Mom looks funny."

"What?" She smeared her napkin across her lips. "I already licked it off." She totally missed the dot on her nose.

Dan sniggered harder. "You missed it, Mom!"

She wiped her mouth again. "Did I get it?"

Dan leaned against me, laughing.

"What?!" She glared at me. "Are you guys messing with me?"

She was so damn cute I couldn't take it. I tapped the tip of my nose.

She rolled her eyes. "Oh. You should've said something."

"What, that my whipped cream was all over your face?"

Her eyes popped and she blushed like wine. "Would you stop?"

"Not until I get my Irish kiss," I said suggestively.

Her eyes flicked at Dan. "Not with… Not here."

I played dumb. "I mean this one." I reached across the table and grabbed the glass and took another gulp. "Mmm, mmm. My favorite kind of Irish kiss."

She beamed a blushing smile and silently mouthed the words, *I hate you*.

"The feeling is mutual," I chuckled.

Chapter 13

LION

When we finished eating our desserts, the waiter brought the check, I had to fight Brigid for it.

"Today was my idea, Irish. So was dinner. So I'm paying."

"Okay. But I'm paying next time."

"Next time? Where're we going next time?"

"Disneyland!" Dan blurted.

Brigid laughed. "Daniel, haven't you had enough amusement parks for the summer?"

Dan smiled. "No."

"What he said," I chuckled.

"I'll think about it," Brigid said.

"Next weekend you have free, we're going down to the DL. Ride us some Space Mountain and Indiana Jones, maybe some Pirates of the Caribbean. Right Dan?" I held up my fist for a bump.

He punched it. "Right."

"What do you think, Irish?"

"Maybe," she scowled. But she was still smiling.

It was pretty late when we left the Hard Rock. The CityWalk was still lit up, but the crowds had thinned down to a trickle and the earlier buzz of thousands of people talking and laughing had faded to a soft mutter.

Dan stretched his arms in a huge yawn.

"Goodness," Brigid said. "It's way past your bed time, Daniel. We need to get you home."

"But it's summer, Mom!"

"You still have to sleep."

"I don't want to sleep! I want to go to Disneyland!"

"Look what you did," Brigid said to me.

"It's the sugar," I said. "We just gotta burn it off."

We took the elevators down to the parking garage. When we got off at our level, the elevator next to us was opening too. Three shady looking guys walked out. I didn't think anything of it at the time. There were shady looking people all over LA. It didn't mean they were going to mug you.

Because we had arrived so late, Brigid's car was parked way out in the boonies at the far end of the parking structure.

"That was a nearly perfect day," Brigid sighed as we walked.

"Nearly? What would make it more perfect? I mean, after all was said and done, I had a ton of fun and got my Irish Kiss. What could be better than that?"

She blushed and shrugged. "I don't know."

If it wasn't for the damn crutches, I'd brush my knuckles across the back of her hand to see if she wanted to hold mine. Yeah, it was against the rules. But sometimes you had to say fuck the rules.

Stupid crutches.

We finally found Brigid's four door parked way down at the end of one of the aisles. At this hour, most of the spaces were empty. It had been absolutely packed when we'd arrived. A few of the overhead fluorescent lights were out on this level, giving it a dark and lonely feeling.

Dan was jumping up and down as we walked, still hopped up on sugar and bouncing off the walls. Time to burn it off.

"Hey, Dan. I'll race you to the car."

"But you're on crutches."

"So? I bet I can still smoke you."

"No way."

"Then we're on."

"Okay." He was excited.

"On my count. Ready? On three. One, two—"

He took off running.

"Cheater!" I laughed.

Brigid laughed too. "Better go get him."

I didn't waste any time swinging after Dan. There was no way I was going to beat him, but I could at least catch up. We were both out of breath when we got to the car. He tagged the trunk.

"I win!"

"Yeah you did, Speedy."

Brigid was strolling toward us, but she was halfway back down the aisle. Dan and I leaned against the trunk of the car while we waited, watching her.

The next thing I knew, the shady guys from the elevators were walking up behind Brigid. She turned back and said something to them. I couldn't make anything out because the sound of their voices was muddled by the echoes in the garage. My entire chest tightened. I could tell from Brigid's body language that she was agitated. The shady men kept talking, but I still couldn't make anything out.

"Stay here, Dan." My heart was racing as I crutched toward Brigid and the men.

"Lemme use your phone, lady," one of the guys said when I got close. He had a thin mustache and curly hair like a villain from a drug cartel action movie.

"I don't have a phone," she lied. She'd had it out earlier when we were taking pictures.

"Yeah you do," Curly said, his voice menacing. "Pretty lady like you always has a phone. Lemme use it."

"I said no! So take a hike!" She was in the shadows below where the overhead lights were out. I was in shadows too and Brigid was between me and the men. Maybe they hadn't seen me. If they did, they might back off, so I swung out to the side into view.

"Back the fuck off, buddy!" I barked as I crutched forward like a wobbly wind up toy.

The men slowed, watching me.

"Thank goodness," Brigid muttered as I came up beside her. She stepped behind me, putting me between her and them. "Where's Daniel? Is he safe?"

"Yeah. At the car."

"I better make sure he's okay."

"He's fine. But you should go get him and put both of you in the car."

"What about you?"

"I'll be fine. When you get him in the car, you should drive out of here as fast as you can. I'll meet you down on Universal Studios Boulevard. Where we drove into the parking lot by the 101."

"I'm not leaving you here!" She hissed.

"Can you just go? I'll meet you down by the freeway onramp."

She stared at me, mad.

"Will you go?"

She glared at me before turning toward the car.

I stared at the three guys. They reminded me of the gang bangers I'd grown up with in East LA, which was only a few miles from here. The gangs came out to Universal Studios just as much as anybody else in LA. Everybody loved rollercoasters and theme park rides in a fun and safe family-friendly environment. Sarcasm.

Where the hell was security? Maybe it was late and they'd all gone home. Who knew.

"You got a phone, crip?" Curly asked.

"Crip? What, because of the crutches?" I don't know why he'd be making a gang reference. I wasn't wearing blue anywhere and these guys weren't wearing red or any other colors I recognized. Not that it mattered. Gangs weren't showing like they used to. Not even tattoos. It made it too easy for cops to track them. Nowadays gangs wanted to keep a low profile.

"Lemme use your phone," Curly said. "I know you got one."

"Why don't you and your buddies turn around and head out," I suggested.

"Lemme use your phone and I will."

I knew this drill. It started with harassment and escalated from there, depending on how brave these guys were. Three against one guy on crutches might make them stupidly brave. I had no interest in dealing with them. I considered turning and crutching away, but I wouldn't risk turning my back on them. Too bad I hadn't practiced crutching backward more.

Brigid's car started up in the distance behind me.

"Looks like your lady is leaving you, crip." He looked over my shoulder.

I wasn't going to fall for that by turning to look. I kept my eyes nailed on him.

One of the other guys reached under his baggy T-shirt. It was baggy enough to easily conceal a medium caliber handgun like a 9mm or a .357.

Casually, I swung forward one step on my crutches. I wanted to be in striking range if Baggy had a gun under that shirt of his. You never wanted to be too far away from the guy with the gun unless you had your own. I didn't. Closer was better.

"You reaching for your phone?" I asked. "Thought you said you didn't have one."

Baggy stared at me. "I do. He don't." He nodded toward Curly.

He was lying. Heck, they were both lying.

I said to Curly, "Use his phone."

"He outta minutes."

"Of course he is."

The three of them were sizing me up while they got their courage up. In the shadows, they probably didn't notice my ripped arms. All they noticed were my crutches. This was serious. I could feel the contempt coming off these guys in waves. I was nothing but shit to them. An easy target.

Nothing more.

I knew for a fact people got jumped in this parking lot all the time. One of my students at the dojo told me about their friend getting mugged here a few months ago. Worse, last year, the boyfriend of some woman who worked at the park snuck a gun in and shot himself in front of her while park patrons watched in horror. Lucky he hadn't shot anyone except himself. Two years before that, there was a shooting outside one of the CityWalk nightclubs. Bad shit happened here often enough, no matter what people said.

It didn't take a genius to figure out this was going to be somebody's unlucky day. But it wasn't going to be mine.

"Do I know you?" Curly asked, searching my face. Since it was dark, I wasn't wearing my shades anymore and my Minions hat was in my back pocket.

"Not yet you don't."

"No, I know you. You Lion Maxwell."

I couldn't decide if him recognizing me was a good thing or bad.

"Who the fuck Lion Maxwell?" Baggy asked.

"He that WMAA fighter."

WMAA, meaning the World Martial Arts Association. If they wanted my autograph, I would rather do that then get into a scuffle.

"You undefeated, ain't you?" Curly said.

I didn't like how he said it. "I don't know what you're talking about. My name is Dan Smith." It was the first name that came to mind.

"Nah. You Lion Maxwell. Only you ain't gonna be undefeated after tonight. We gonna beat yo ass,"

The third guy, who had a bald head and a long biker beard and wore a sleeveless Harley Davidson T-shirt cracked his knuckles menacingly. Gothic letters tattooed on his knuckles spelled out LOVE and HATE. Together, this crew looked like a multicultural prison break. The only thing they were missing were the orange jumpsuits.

I had known animals like this. They thought they smelled blood. They all snarled the same tough guy smile. Next they would lick their chops like rabid wolves.

We all knew what happened when a wolf challenged a lion.

The great thing about crutches was that they were made of metal and they added another three feet to my reach. I whipped the first crutch hard against Baggy's shin. I wanted him to forget about whatever he had in his pocket. Sure enough, he doubled over, grabbing at his shin. My other crutch punched Curly in the solar plexus. He folded around it like a meat pillow. I brought the first crutch up and around and sliced it across Baggy's face, nearly tearing his nose off. Then I brought both around and hit Biker Beard high and low at nearly the same time, one to the side of his head and the other to his groin. His nervous system didn't know what to do so he dropped to the cement.

All of this literally took two seconds. I was a whirlwind of aluminum death.

Baggy still had some fight left in him. "Motherfucker done broke my nose!" Blood poured down his face and he covered it with one hand.

I was in full battle mode and went at him again with both crutches. If he had a gun, I didn't want him getting to it. Good thing I had practiced crutch fighting at home for the last four weeks. Beat the shit out of a heavy bag until I tore it open. It was what you did when you spent your life immersed in the fighting arts. Everything had an application as a weapon if you knew what to do with it. I did.

I was so busy making sure Baggy was out of action, I never saw Curly's boot coming for my ribs.

CRACK!!

Sharp pain speared my side.

He probably broke a rib. Or two. I'd thought he was down for the count. I was wrong. Fighting is always messy and unpredictable.

The surprise of Curly's kick threw me off balance and I fell forward onto Baggy. I landed the side of my crutch in his throat and heard something crunch. His problem, not mine. His eyes popped out of his skull and he gagged.

More kicks from Curly rained down on my back. He was aiming for my head. His boot grazed across the top of my head, tearing skin from my scalp and nearly taking my ear off with it. This was too close for comfort. I rolled off Baggy, trying to get some distance. Any second, Biker Beard was going to get up and join Curly in the kicking spree.

This was getting out of hand really fast.

I wasn't a superhero.

But I did have crutches. I whacked one right across Curly's forearm. He wasn't thinking about his arms because he was so busy kicking. He instantly regretted it and screamed, cradling his wrist against his chest.

"Shit! Shit! Shit!" He danced in pain.

I tried to get to my feet, but my bad knee buckled and I went right back down and hit the cement hard. Lucky I had the knee brace. But it didn't stop a nail gun from shooting a thousand nails into my knee from every direction. The crutches had me off balance and I pitched forward and rolled, throwing the crutches down in the process.

This was a disaster.

I landed right next to Biker Beard. His face was inches from mine. His mustache was a gory red mess. Blood was smeared across his teeth. His eyes were sleepy, like he wasn't sure where he was. He must have fallen on his face and knocked himself out.

I didn't have time to think about it.

"See how you like the taste of crutches, *pendejo!*"

I rolled forward just in time to miss getting hit across the back of the head by Curly. He swung one crutch like a baseball bat. I felt the wind as it whirled past. Could've taken my head off. He brought the crutch down again like he was chopping wood. I rolled to the side and tried to hook his ankles with both my legs and trip him, but my knee twisted wrong, making the nails in my knee shoot up to my hip. The pain made me flail the takedown maneuver.

Curly jumped out of the way in time to keep his feet. He might have been right earlier when he'd said he was going to end my winning streak.

Headlights swept across me as a car drove toward us.

I hoped that was fucking security. They were supposed to be the ones to take care of thugs like this, not me. No blue lights came on. I guess it wasn't security.

Curly turned to look, still holding my crutch like a weapon.

This was my chance. I reached across Biker Beard, who was still out, and grabbed my other crutch. I swung it at Curly's Achilles' tendon. His leg buckled and he went down on his ass. I scurried over to him on all fours and got my arms around his neck in a rear naked choke.

The whole time, the car headlights were pinned on us like spotlights. I didn't know who it was. I hoped they were calling 911.

Curly was strong and fought against me. But I was stronger. Nothing wrong with my arms. It didn't take long for him to lose blood flow to his brain. After way too long, he sagged in my arms, out cold.

I was heaving for air and hot as a blast furnace.

The entire fight had taken maybe a minute, two tops, but it felt like an hour.

"Oh my God! Are you okay?" Brigid ran out of the car and knelt beside me. "What did you do?" She sounded horrified.

"What did *I* do? What about them?"

"These men need emergency medical services." She was checking Biker Beard's pulse.

"Fuck these guys. We need to get the hell out of here."

"I'm talking to 911 right now." She held up her smart phone.

I snatched it from her hand and ended the call.

"What did you do that for?"

"I don't want to deal with the cops. We need to vacate before they show up."

"But 911 has my number. They know I called. I gave them my name."

"Did you tell them my name?"

"No."

"Then they don't know it was me."

"What does it matter?"

I glared at her, pissed even though she didn't deserve it. "What matters is I'm a convicted felon with two strikes on my record. If I get locked up for this, I won't be coming out for a long time." I felt like a loser just saying it. Prison time was a badge of honor for some people, but not me. I was ashamed of it.

"Why would you get locked up? They attacked you!"

"You don't know how the system works do you?" I hated talking about this.

"No, I..."

"Trust me, this looks bad."

All three men were on the ground. Curly and Biker Beard were both out cold. Baggy was moaning in this wet gurgly way that had me worried about what I'd done to the hyoid bone in his throat. This was why throat punches were not allowed in the WMAA. You could easily kill someone. And I'd used my crutches, which were deadly weapons by anyone's standards.

"What do you mean it looks bad? You're on crutches. There were three of them. They started it."

"Did you see them start it?"

"No. I was in the car circling around."

"You prepared to lie on the witness stand?"

"Lie? I can't lie."

I smirked at her. "I need to get the hell out of here." I wasn't pissed at her but I didn't have time to explain. I grabbed my crutches and stood up. I patted my pockets, making sure I had my keys, my phone, my wallet. Everything was there. Shit. My sunglasses had been hanging from my T-shirt collar. I looked around for them. Didn't see them. I hoped my fingerprints weren't on the lenses. They were already in the system, so if they were on the glasses, the cops would find me. I didn't have time to search for them. I did find my Minions hat, which was on the ground next to Curly. I stuffed it in my back pocket.

"Okay, I'm out." I started crutching toward the stairwell at the far end of the parking structure.

"Where are you going?" Brigid demanded.

"Away from here." My first thought was the Metro. I could take the subway anyplace else and have someone pick me up. But I didn't want her knowing that if she talked to the cops.

"Get in the car already," she hollered.

"No. 911 knows who you are. They can track your phone."

"I'll turn it off."

"That won't work. You need to take the battery out."

"I don't think you can."

"Then throw away your phone."

"I can't do that. I need it if the hospital calls."

"I need to go." I swung toward the stairwell as fast as I could. I felt like a piece of shit for dragging her into this. The simple solution was to make sure I left her out of it.

The sound of her car door slamming echoed against the cement. She drove up behind me, the headlights cutting across me and casting a long jittery shadow out in front of me. Her car crawled up beside me and she rolled her window down.

"This is ridiculous, Lion. It wasn't your fault."

"That doesn't matter, Brigid. Self defense means you stop after subduing your opponent, not when you finish beating the fuck out of them with an aluminum pipe."

"Let me help you."

"Throw your phone out." I didn't need a kiss, a hug, and a cookie. I needed an escape plan.

"I can't."

"I know," I grunted. This was insane and stupid all at the same time. Dan stared at me from the backseat where he sat behind Brigid. Had he seen me beating on those guys? I hoped not. Unlike martial arts class, real fighting was ugly.

"You're bleeding."

"I'm sure I am." I couldn't tell what was sweat dripping down my head and what was blood. I didn't have time to check with my hands holding the crutches.

"This is crazy. Let me drive you someplace."

My mind was spinning a thousand miles an hour. If I went to prison, who would take care of Aslan, Tigger, and Guenhwyvar? Then there were all the people who depended on me, my business partners who looked to me to call the shots and cut their paychecks every month. My absence would create unnecessary stress and extra work for everyone involved. It might even cost some of them their jobs. Not to mention it would make me look bad in the media, which meant I might lose some or all of my sports endorsements. And nobody wanted to send their kids to a karate chain owned by a three strikes felon sitting in prison. Well, not in some neighborhoods. The original school in East LA would probably get more membership signups because of it. But that was no way to think.

"Please, Lion. Let me help you."

"What did you tell the cops?"

"I told the police that three men attacked my friend here in the parking lot."

"Did you tell them where in the parking lot?"

"I said somewhere in Jurassic Parking."

"Did you say which floor?"

"They didn't ask."

"It's gonna take them a few minutes to find those thugs back there. I think we have time. Gimme a ride down to Cahuenga. Then you take off. Understand?"

"Oh—okay. Are you sure?"

"Yeah." I could probably get an Uber car down on Cahuenga faster than anyone I knew could come pick me up. She stopped the car and I stuffed my crutches into the passenger footwell and climbed in.

Everyone was silent while we drove.

I felt like an idiot for dragging them into this. I also felt blood dripping down my cheek.

Brigid lifted the lid on the center console and handed me a box of tissues. "For your cut."

"Thanks. You okay back there, Dan the Man?"

"Did you beat those guys up?" His voice was small and afraid.

"What did you see?" I was really worried about him. The way things turned out had been pretty gruesome. He didn't need to see that.

"I saw you with your arms around that guy's neck before he fell asleep, and two other guys lying on the ground." Fell asleep. That sounded so much better than the reality. I wasn't going to correct him.

"Did you see anything else?" I gave Brigid a concerned look. She gave me the same one, only on her it looked a bit disgusted. With me.

"No," Dan muttered.

"Good. Dan my man, I need you to understand that fighting is never a good way to solve anything. I only did what I did because you and your mom were in danger. Do you understand?"

"I think so." He didn't sound too sure. "Are the police going to take you to jail?" he asked.

"I hope not." Man, what kind of a role model was I? The worst kind, that's what.

Brigid gave me another long look. She looked about as disappointed in me as I was in myself.

What was I going to say to her after this? Nothing that made any difference, that was for sure.

Because I had just fucked up.

Big time.

So much for our nearly perfect day.

After this, I was pretty sure Brigid would demote me from "just friends" to "just stay out of my son's life, you violent felon."

Chapter 14

"Lion, can I take you back to the dojo in Burbank? That's where your car is, right?"

We were pulled to the side of the road on Cahuenga Boulevard, next to the big Armenian church with the hexagonal pyramid for a roof. I recognized it from whenever I drove by on the 101.

"No. I'm good." He opened the car door and winced when he banged his knee climbing out. Good thing he had that knee brace on.

"Is your knee okay?"

"It's fine," he grunted as he reached in for his crutches.

"Are you sure you don't want me to drive you?"

"Better not." He looked up and down the street nervously. "I don't want to drag you into the mess I made."

"It's our mess."

"Trust me, it's not."

Was he worried about the police? All this was so far outside my wheelhouse, I had no idea what I should do. Then again, I never would've thought he was a convicted felon either. People were full of surprises.

My hands were still shaking with adrenaline. I couldn't believe what had happened, but it had. I didn't know what I was going to say to Daniel when we got home. I would have to tell Donald about it. Daniel was likely to have bad dreams about those men. If not dreams, it would come out some other way down the line. Somehow, Donald would eventually find out.

I hoped Daniel had only seen what he told Lion, namely the man "falling asleep." Not that watching Lion cut off a man's blood supply to his brain until he lost consciousness was a minor thing. Seeing it first hand through the car windshield was traumatic for me, so I could only guess at the effect it would have on my son. I just hoped that was all he'd seen. When we had turned the corner of the parking garage I had yelled at him to close his eyes while I focused on driving. I saw most of the fight, but I hoped Daniel hadn't. But he'd obviously seen more than enough to be frightened.

I was grateful that Lion hadn't been seriously hurt. The laceration on his scalp looked like it needed to be repaired with a few absorbable sutures, but it wasn't life threatening. As for his knee, I hoped he hadn't done any more damage to it. Hopefully the brace had protected it.

"I need to go," Lion said and closed the door. The window was still down and he leaned against the doorframe. "If the cops come looking for you, who are you gonna say I am?"

"My friend."

"They'll ask for my name. What are you gonna say?"

"The truth."

He stared at me for a long time, his eyes intense and haunted. Was he mad at me? I couldn't blame him. I didn't make a good criminal. I wanted to help him any way I could, but I wasn't sure how. He didn't deserve the trouble he was in. And none of this would've happened if I hadn't agreed to Universal Studios. Why hadn't I called it a day after eating lunch in the park? Lunch was bad enough. The rest of the day definitely looked like a date to anyone with half a brain. It was a huge mistake and it was all my fault.

I heaved a sigh. "Do you want me to lie?" It wasn't my preference, but somehow I felt I owed him for protecting me and Daniel. "I'll tell the police you were someone else. I'll tell them it was Donald."

"Who's Donald?"

"My ex-husband."

"What will Donald say to the cops when they ask him how he beat up those three thugs?"

"Oh. Right. Sorry." There was no way I could get Donald to entangle himself in a clumsy web of lies to protect a man he'd never met.

"If the cops come knocking, just tell them it was me. But we'll cross our fingers and hope they don't."

My hand still quivered with adrenalin as I held up my fingers, crossing them. I hoped it did more good than the last time I crossed them.

He smiled. The first one I'd seen since before the fight. What a relief. "Better use every bit of your luck of the Irish on this, Irish."

"I will. I promise."

He turned to go.

"Don't you want your Irish Kiss?"

He stared back at me through the windshield.

I considered hopping out of the car and running to him. Somehow this felt like a goodbye. A permanent one. That was the last thing I wanted. I barely knew this man, and yet I knew he was perfect for me.

The same way he barely knew Daniel and yet they both acted like they'd been best friends forever. Every inch of my being said that Lion Maxwell was a good man. The right man for me. The only thing standing in our way was the Medical Board of California and it's position on doctors dating patients, as well as the identical position held by Los Angeles Central Hospital. There was no way to explain to an ethics committee that the power dynamic that existed between Lion and me was balanced and fair. I had never met a man more powerful than him. The proof was his willingness to risk his life to protect me and Daniel. All I did for him was order an MRI for his knee, which I didn't even do, and prescribe some pills before sending him on his way. I didn't have a hold on him. He had a hold on me. A hold I was afraid would never let go, whether he stayed in my life somehow or left forever.

He saluted me. "See you around, Irish."

Then he turned on his crutches and swung down Cahuenga on the empty night sidewalk. The sight of him making his getaway on crutches in a knee brace bordered on pathetic. My inability to help him made me feel equally pathetic. But what could I really do for him?

"Where is he going, Mom?"

"I don't know, sweetheart."

"When do we see him again?"

"I don't know." My voice was tight and I could barely speak.

Silent tears dribbled down my face as I drove Daniel home.

Chapter 15

LION

A beat up old Cutlass Sierra rolled to a stop beside me. The brakes squeaked so loud I thought the noise would pierce my eardrums. The passenger window wobbled as it rolled down. It needed fixing bad. This late at night, the guy inside the boxy Cutlass could be anybody.

I was about a mile south on Cahuenga from where Brigid had dropped me off. Down in Hollywood where the hookers walked the streets. My armpits were killing me from walking all damn day on these miserable crutches. After landing on my knee in the fight, it was throbbing and I couldn't put any weight on it without it shooting pain. At this point, I was willing to take a ride from anybody. I didn't care who it was as long as I got off these damn crutches. I leaned down and looked in the car.

An old man wearing a flat driving cap and a worn out windbreaker leaned over and grumbled at me in a crunchy voice, "How much for a suck?"

I glared at him, "For you, old man? A million bucks."

"It ain't worth it."

"You don't know what you're missing," I chuckled.

"Get in the car, asshole," he laughed.

I opened the passenger door. "Good to see you too, Coach. Thanks for coming to pick me up so late."

"You better have a damn good reason for dragging me out of bed in the middle of Saturday Night Live."

"You still watch that piece of shit show? It's been a dried out turd ever since Will Ferrell left."

"You still want a ride home, smart ass?"

"Love the show. The new cast is better than ever. Who needs Will Ferrell?"

"Damn right. Get in. And buckle up your seatbelt. I ain't going anywhere until you do."

"Yeah, yeah."

"What in hell you doing gimping around on crutches in the middle of the damn night?"

"Long story."

"Do I wanna know?" He stared at me over the top of the reading glasses he always wore.

I arched an eyebrow.

"I don't wanna know." He shifted the car into drive and pulled into traffic. The muffler farted as he accelerated.

"When are you gonna let me buy you a new car? This thing is falling apart."

"I'm falling apart. You gonna replace me with a newer model?"

"Nah," I chuckled. "Guess I'll have to run you into the ground."

"Heh heh heh." He laughed his usual wheezy laugh. "Where we going, son?"

"My house?"

"You don't sound too sure."

"I'm not."

"Wanna stay at my place? I can put you on the Hide-A-Bed in the living room." Coach had a one bedroom apartment in a fleabag building downtown that should've been condemned years ago. I tried plenty of times to get him to move into my place up in the Hollywood Hills, but he refused. Said the Hills didn't have character.

"You still got those damn hairball cats?"

"Yeah."

"You feed 'em today?"

"Shit. Not since morning."

"Then I'll take you home."

There were two men in my life who gave everything they had to make me a better man. One of them, Jose Chavez, gave his life. The other was Coach, a.k.a. Dean Jackson, the man sitting next to me. Neither one was my biological father. The only thing that sperm donor ever gave me was the name Lion. After that, he disappeared.

The death of Jose Chavez was the reason I went off the rails for a while back when I was eighteen. That was a bad time in my life. Full of bad memories. Broke into a bunch of houses and stole a bunch of shit I didn't need. Ended up getting caught because I didn't care if I did. Pled guilty to two counts of first degree felony burglary and spent two years in prison because of it. I didn't care if I lived or died at that point.

I met Dean Jackson when I was in prison. He was part of an outreach program for the inmates. Teaching them to read. I already knew how, but I needed something to do. Dean took a liking to me right away. The first book he made me read was The Greatest: My Own Story by Muhammad Ali. He eventually told me he used to be a boxing coach. We bonded over our mutual appreciation for the art of hand to hand combat, as men do. He told me if I got out of prison before he died (he was seventy then and almost eighty now), he would teach me everything he knew about fighting in the squared circle.

Fourteen months later, I was out on parole for good behavior. Training with Dean gave me purpose. I even lived in his fleabag apartment until I got a job and found my own place. I never went into boxing like he'd hoped, but I did consider it. At the end of the day, I was a martial artist. Good thing Dean liked the idea of doing something different in his golden years. He was my coach and cornerman for every professional fight I'd ever had. He was family.

Twenty minutes later, we pulled to a stop outside the gate for my house. He knew the code and punched it in on the keypad before driving me up to the front steps. He said, "Do you really need that much damn house?"

"It's a business investment."

"It's a boat anchor, is what it is. Me, I can pack up and leave at the drop of a hat if I need to."

"How long you lived in that rundown building?"

"Fifteen years."

"Good thing you can pack up and leave any time you want. When you planning to do that?"

He snorted. "Whenever the hell I want. You need help getting out?"

"I've got it." I levered myself out of the car with my crutches. My bad knee was throbbing like crazy and felt swollen to the size of a basketball, like it could pop the knee brace open if it got any bigger.

Dean walked me to the door. "You want me to stay and help out?"

"I think I'll be okay. You want some water or whatever before you go?"

"Seeing as how SNL is over," he checked the old Timex on his wrist, "may as well take a load off."

"You can probably watch it on hulu."

"What in hell is a hulu? Is that like a hula-hoop?"

I chuckled. "Never mind."

We walked to the kitchen. Like most of my house, everything in the kitchen was natural woods and stone. Plenty of house plants in every room. Sort of like a jungle. I liked it. So did the cats. There were claw marks all over the place.

The cats trotted into the kitchen, their tails high. They knew Dean well. Aslan circled his legs, wrapping his tail around the man's slacks. They were all meowing for food. Dean helped set out fresh plates. He could bend down better than I could with my knee throbbing. Then I offered him a water bottle from the fridge.

"I know where the tap is. And the glasses." He went to one of the beveled glass kitchen cabinets and pulled out a contoured glass. "You want one?"

"I'm good." I screwed off the top of the water bottle I'd pulled out for myself and took a swallow.

He filled his glass from the sink faucet. "This water is just as good as that. I don't know why you have to waste the plastic."

"I refill it. Stays cold in the fridge."

"Suit yourself." He sipped from his glass. "What's on your mind, son? I can tell something's bothering you."

"I don't know where to begin."

"The beginning is always a good place," he smirked over his reading glasses. "I better sit down. My knees aren't much better than yours."

I pulled out a chair for him from the table in the breakfast nook.

"I'm not a lady. I can get my own damn chair." He pulled out the one opposite.

When I sat down, I felt icepicks stabbing my ribs where Curly had kicked them. I'd had broken ribs before. This was that. Nothing you could do about it except grunt away the pain.

"You okay?"

"I'm fine," I hissed and dug my phone out of my pocket and showed him a picture of me standing with Brigid and Dan at Universal in the Super Silly Fun Land. We all had on our Minions hats and silly grins. Two of the life-size costumed Minions characters stood on either side of us, waving at the camera.

"What the hell are those yellow things?"

"They're called Minions."

"Look like bunions to me."

I snorted a laugh. "Something like that."

"That you in the silly bunion hat?"

"Yup."

"You got a wife and kid I don't know about?" He saw me weekly when I wasn't training, daily when I was. He knew I didn't.

"I wish."

I told him the long version of the entire story of meeting Brigid at the hospital, the whole doctor-patient thing, meeting Dan, all the way through the fight in the parking lot. As I told it, he cleaned up the cut on my scalp and closed it with butterfly bandages and sterile tape. Not only had Dean been my cornerman during my professional fights, he had also been my cutman on occasion, and knew his way around battle wounds. While he worked and I told my story, he said, "Mmm-hmm" and "Hmm" and "Are you crazy?" or "Have you done lost your mind?" numerous times.

"So, what should I do?"

"You in a pickle, son."

"Tell me about it."

"Do you have feelings for this woman?"

"Yeah."

"Strong feelings?"

"I've never felt like this for anyone."

"What about Minka?" Dean had watched me go through the entire relationship with Minka, from perfection in the beginning to disaster at the end. When she left, he helped me get my shit back together so I could keep on fighting in the WMAA. "You have stronger feelings for this new one than you did for Minka?"

"Maybe."

He raised his eyebrows. "Never thought I'd see the day."

"Me neither."

"You love this woman?"

"I just might. But there's this whole doctor-patient thing. And her son. I don't want to mess all that up for her. And now? Shit. She knows I'm a felon. Who knows what'll happen if I get arrested for beating on those guys."

"Mmm. That is a problem."

"After tonight, she probably thinks I'm a bad influence for her kid."

"We both know that ain't true."

"Yeah, but does she?"

"You can always ask her."

"I can't do that."

He chuckled. "Kids. You forget how to talk to each other or something? Call her up tomorrow. Tell her how you feel."

The idea scared me to death. "What if she tells me she doesn't want to see me again?"

"Don't be a pussy, son. Show her you a man. If she don't want you, then take your medicine like a grownup."

"Easy for you to say."

"Damn right it's easy for me to say. I had to do exactly that with my Helen, God rest her soul. You think marrying a white woman in 1965 was easy peasy for me? Hell no. Lucky I wasn't lynched. Or run out of town on a rail. By her own family, no less. They denied my existence for twenty years. But I showed them by standing up for my woman and what I believed in. It wasn't wrong for me and Helen to be together. No matter what them fools said or did." He held up his left hand where he still wore his wedding band.

"That's right."

"You damn right it's right. Now it's your turn to show the world what you're made of. Show everybody how much heart you have. And I know you got a lot of heart, son."

Chapter 16

BRIGID

"Mom? What if I have nightmares?"

I stood in his bedroom doorway, my hand hovering over the light switch. "You can sleep with me if you want."

"No."

"Do you want me to turn on your Spider-Man light?"

"Maybe."

I switched on the colorful red and blue lamp on his night table. It projected a moving picture of Spider-Man on the ceiling. "Spidey will protect you all night long."

"I wish Lion was here instead."

"Me too, sweetheart."

"Is Lion going to jail?"

"No, sweetheart. He's not going to jail." I was spinning lies but Daniel deserved a good night's sleep after such a long and slightly traumatic day.

"What if those men come looking for us?"

"They won't, honey." I sat down on his bed and smoothed back his hair. "Those men will never bother you again. I promise."

"Are you sure?"

"Yes, I'm sure." I wished I believed it as much as I hoped my son did. Daniel was too young to have to worry about these things. "Now go to sleep. I'll leave your door open. Call me if you need anything and I'll come running. If you change your mind and want to sleep with me, that's okay. I love you, sweetheart." I kissed his forehead. "Good night."

I clicked off the overhead light and Spider-Man cast a red and blue glow over the bedroom.

"Are we going to Disneyland with Lion?"

"Maybe." *And we all know maybe means no.* I hoped I was wrong.

"When?"

"I'm not sure. We'll have to wait and see. Now try and get some sleep, okay?"

"Okay."

"Sweet dreams."

I went to my bedroom, changed into my nightgown, washed my face, and brushed my teeth. All I could think about was Lion and what a wonderful day we had with him. I wasn't going to let those three thugs ruin the rest of it. I was a tiny bit concerned that Daniel might mention the fight to Donald. I wasn't the sort of mother who told her son to keep things from his father. In this case, I seriously considered it. There was no telling how Donald would react. Today was the first time I had ever gone out on anything resembling a date with a man *and* my son since the divorce. Would Donald be furious? Would he accuse me of endangering our son? I had no way of knowing. I didn't really want to think about it. I would cross that bridge when and if I came to it.

Still curious about Lion, and a little bit wound up from the excitement of the day, I grabbed my iPad off my dresser and climbed into bed.

Then I Googled Lion Maxwell. There was an hour long documentary about him on YouTube. I put in my earbuds and watched it from beginning to end, riveted. It had one of those dramatic narrators who made everything seem larger than life.

In Lion's case, it was.

There was little information about his past. A few photos of him as a boy with his mom Sharon, who raised him on her own and spent all the spare money she had so Lion could study martial arts and stay off the mean streets of East LA. Smart woman. The man who owned Lion's first dojo was named Jose Chavez. He was a mentor and a father figure to Lion, who credited Jose for instilling in him a love of martial arts and an appreciation for hard work and discipline. Like Sharon had hoped, the martial arts kept Lion out of trouble.

Sadly, both Sharon Maxwell and Jose Chavez's lives were cut tragically short. Sharon lost her fight against breast cancer at the age of 41. Lion was 16. Two years later, Jose was gunned down in cold blood during a drive by shooting outside the dojo that Lion called home. Jose had thrown himself in front of a spray of machine gun fire to protect Lion and a group of fellow karate students. Jose died in Lion's arms that night, bleeding out before paramedics could arrive. Law Enforcement speculated that the shooting was related to Jose Chavez's vocal anti-gang stance in the community.

After losing the two people closest to him, Lion's life understandably went into a tailspin that landed him in prison for felony burglary.

Tears stung my eyes.

I couldn't imagine what Lion had gone through. Both my parents and my brother were still alive. And it was one thing for me as a doctor to lose a stranger on the table in the ECU. Losing a loved one was another thing entirely.

There was so much more to Lion than his cocky first impression.

The rest of the movie focused on his astonishing fight career. He held the record for the most career wins in Mixed Martial Arts without a loss: 28-0. Many considered Lion the greatest fighter in the history of the sport. At the age of twenty nine, he was already a legend.

There was a montage of video clips of him knocking out opponents. He was brutal in action, an unstoppable force. I noticed his trademark gold lycra shorts which he wore for every fight had the slogan FEEL THE BEAST in black letters on his ass. I had missed that part at the hospital.

You have got to be kidding me.

I couldn't decide if those shorts were laughable or a complete turn on. Probably a little of both. He sure looked good in them.

I squeezed my thighs together thinking about it.

The last five minutes of the documentary focused on his philanthropy and how he gave back to the East LA community where he grew up. He still owned a dojo there, the same one he trained at with the late Jose Chavez. It was a haven for kids who wanted an escape from the streets. Thanks to the small fortune Lion had made from his WMAA winnings, the dojo was free if you lived in the neighborhood.

I clicked off my iPad and sighed.

Why did Lion have to be my patient?

I was about to turn off the lights and go to bed when I remembered to charge my phone. I took it out of my purse and found the framed souvenir 8x10 photo of Lion, Daniel, and me on the Harry Potter ride. The one Lion had bought. He'd asked me to carry it because of his crutches. I'd forgotten to give it back when I dropped him off on Cahuenga like a lonely stranger.

In the photo, I was holding his hand and I looked happier than I could remember. That moment had been electric. So natural. I wished he was holding my hand right now.

Or doing other things.

A flood of emotions washed over me. I was extremely attracted to Lion. Who wouldn't be? He had the body of a world class athlete. And, after seeing the way he nurtured Daniel and protected me, I had feelings for the man. What kind, I wasn't sure. But they were very strong feelings. After that documentary I was ready to… I didn't know what. Whatever it was, I knew I wanted a man like him in my life.

Like him.

It just couldn't *be* him.

Frustrated, I hugged the picture to my chest and closed my eyes. True, I couldn't have the real Lion. But I could have the fantasy Lion all night long.

I set the picture on my nightstand and turned the lights off. Then I listened for a few minutes to make sure Daniel was asleep. He was.

The second I closed my eyes, images of Lion poured into my brain: his nearly naked hard body in his tight gold shorts at the hospital. That night, he looked every inch the legend.

Every.

Inch.

I shivered thinking about it.

It.

His python.

Every writhing inch of it.

The residual chemistry still in my body from today, and from our first meeting, flowed through my fingers. It didn't take long for me to shiver my way to orgasm.

After, as I lay in bed breathless, I couldn't get Lion's gorgeous naked body out of my mind. It was like a fever dream and I had it bad.

One orgasm wasn't going to cut it.

But I felt guilty with Daniel in the next room. Maybe I should wait for next week, when he was at his father's. I tried sleeping for nearly an hour, but I kept flopping around in bed. I really needed a release. A good one. Fingers wouldn't get this job done. I slipped out of bed and quietly closed the door until it was only open a crack, then went to my ensuite bathroom.

I wasn't one for clunky vibrators or dildos. Daniel was at that age when he went snooping around the house and was likely to find such things. That's why I preferred discreet vibrators. The kind that weren't veiny pink penises bedazzled with pearls and bunny rabbits and LED lights.

I stifled a laugh as I pictured Daniel running into the living room with just such a vibrator and swinging it around like a sword as he cheered, *Mom! Look at the light saber I found!* Him making light saber noises, *Zzh! Zzh! Zzh!* Me, horrified and shouting, *Put that away! It's not a light saber!* Him, confused, *It sure looks like one.*

Like I said, discreet.

Inside the bathroom vanity drawer next to my hair dryer was my EroTouch Glove Fingertip Vibrator. It wasn't so much a glove as it was a stylish low-profile wristband battery pack with wires leading to the two vibrating pods. I strapped it on my wrist and put the pods on my first two fingers. Something about the design made me feel like I was an electric sex wizard who could shoot orgasms out of her fingertips.

Actually, that was exactly what it did.

The first time I'd used it, I'd timidly pulled it out of the nondescript shipping box, blushing even though I was alone in the house. The second I touched it to my nipples, I knew I needed a second glove. Sure, I waited until after enjoying several clitoral orgasms before ordering another one online.

I pulled the other one out of the drawer and strapped it on before climbing back into bed.

The thing I loved about the gloves was that they were perfect for hitting my g-spot, and with two pairs, I could fry my clit at the same time. Or do both nipples. Mine had always been sensitive, but I'd never believed women who said they could come from just nipple stimulation. Wrong. I'd just never tried EroTouch gloves.

I switched on both gloves and my vibrating fingers slid across my body. My skin lit up wherever I touched it, almost like another person was touching me. With the lights out and my eyes closed, Lion forced his way into my imagination.

He was the one touching me with his electric sex.

Oh, the things Fantasy Lion did to me were undeniably X-rated. I imagined him carrying me through the front door of my condo, my legs wrapped around his trim waist. Already shirtless, he kicked the door closed behind him with the heel of his boot. Fantasy Lion didn't have a torn ACL. He was strong and insistent. He shoved my skirt up to my waist and tore my panties off before sinking his cock inside my wetness.

I wanted to fuck you the second I saw you, Irish.

Yes.

I need your pussy right fucking now.

Yes.

He filled me up. I tightened around him harder and harder with every desperate thrust. We came together, our blinding orgasms crashing through us in perfect harmony.

Your pussy is soaked, Irish. Soaked for me.

Yes.

I had never been fucked against a wall, but Fantasy Lion made me come twice against mine. Of course, the wall changed after the first orgasm to a wall in a tropical hotel somewhere in the Bahamas. In fantasyland, I had all the vacation time a girl could ever want. Then it was sex on the beach with the waves surging around our ankles as we lay in the sand and more orgasms swept over both of us.

When I couldn't possibly come one more time, I lay in my lonely bed, staring at the dark ceiling. I turned off my EroTouch Gloves and took them off.

Why did Lion have to be my patient?

What would my ex-husband say if he knew I let Daniel spend the day with a convicted felon?

If I needed a sign that Lion was not the man for me, despite my attraction to him, tonight had been it. Not because of what he had done to those three men. They deserved what happened to them. They were trouble. I had known it the instant they asked to use my phone. Every hair on the back of my neck had gone up. I felt fortunate Lion had been there to protect me and my son.

But that didn't change anything going forward.

Perhaps I needed to find another martial arts dojo for Daniel. Or have Donald take him to every class so I wouldn't have to see Lion.

Whatever I did, I needed to avoid Lion Maxwell like the plague.

I sighed to myself.

Too bad there wasn't some way to get around the rules.

Chapter 17

LION

"Would you please move?"

I picked Guenhwyvar off the coffee table where my carving tools were. She wouldn't stop walking all over them. I was back on the couch with my knee up and iced.

Working on a new carving.

Like before, it was a lion and lioness with their tails curled into a heart shape behind them, sitting on a bed of four leaf clovers. But I had added an element. A lion cub frolicking in front of them, reaching up to touch a butterfly. The butterfly was attached to his paw, but its wings were spread like it was flying through the air. It was the best I could do without mounting the butterfly on a wire or something.

Since I was off my feet again, carving this was the perfect distraction.

It was also a good excuse not to call Brigid.

I wasn't sure what to say.

Hey, Irish. I know I'm a felon, and I know I beat those guys bloody in front of your son, but do you want to be my girlfriend?

Nope. How about:

Hey, Brigid. Sorry about last night. It'll never happen again. Just don't tell the cops it was me who beat those guys.

What the hell was I going to say?

I could ignore the obvious:

Brigid, since the moment we met, I have wanted to fuck you so bad my balls want to explode. I know you can't date me because you're my doctor, so let's just fuck. A lot. Every position I can think of and then some. Your career? What about it? Oh, you don't want to lose your job? I don't see why that's a problem.

Yeah, right.

Dean had made it sound so easy. *Call her and tell her how you feel.*

Yeah, right.

I felt like an idiot.

I looked up at Aslan. He watched me from the top shelf of the cat tree. *Yeah, you're an idiot.*

"Fuck you too, Azz! If you're not careful, I'll make you go hunt for your food like Tigger."

Aslan blinked. *You won't do that.*

"You think I won't?"

You won't.

He was the cockiest son of a bitch I'd ever met.

But he was right.

Pussy.

"You're the one calling me a pussy? You're the fucking cat!"

Blink. *Asshole.*

"If you blink one more time, I'm throwing you out."

You won't. Blink.

I flipped him off.

He knew what I meant. His tail went swish.

I went back to carving and trying to think of a way to talk to Brigid that didn't make me look like bad news.

Chapter 18

BRIGID

"Can I ask you a personal question, Dr. Whitman?"

"Brigid, I've asked you to stop calling me that for the past five years." He said it with a smile.

"Okay, Brooks. I need your advice."

"Ask away."

I knew Dr. Brooks Whitman from his frequent visits to the hospital. He was a general practitioner with his own private practice in the Eagle Rock area, so he often came into LACH. Even though he was old enough to be my grandfather, he still had a full head of silver hair. I had liked him from the day we met at the start of my residency. He was always trying to mentor me, and I was grateful for it. Someone like him would be invaluable for me to know if I ever took the plunge into private practice.

We sat outside LACH in one of the garden courtyards at a picnic table. It was mid afternoon, so few other people were around and I felt like we were in relative privacy.

I took a deep breath. "Brooks, have you ever dated one of your patients? I mean, before you were married?"

He grinned. "I *married* one of my patients."

"Janet was one of your patients?"

"Indeed she was. Sometimes still is. Usually when I'm brushing my teeth and she wants to know if this or that is cancer."

"I can relate," I grinned. The downside to being a doctor was that you often thought you had every disease or symptom known to modern medical science. It tended to rub off on your family members. "So, Janet was your patient when you started dating her?"

"Oh yes. Definitely."

"Did you date her right away?"

"No. Janet was one of my regular patients. I waited two years before asking her to dinner. Took her to The Brown Derby over on Wilshire before it went out of business. The one that was built to look like a giant brown derby hat."

"But she was your patient for two years before that?"

"That's right."

"Wasn't that unethical? I imagine you knew all kinds of personal details about her. She looked up to you as her doctor. As an authority figure."

He shrugged. "It was a different time. Back then, doctors often married their patients or the nurses they worked with. Nobody thought twice about it. Janet continued as my patient until long after we were married. She didn't find another doctor until much later, when she wanted a second opinion about something or other." He winked. "After we were married, she never took what I said as gospel. Why are you asking about this anyway?"

"Do you really want to know?"

"You don't have to tell me. But I can probably guess. I still have a few functioning brain cells left."

"I'm interested in one of my patients."

"Is he interested in you?"

I laughed. "He has made his interests *abundantly* clear."

"Is he as handsome as I am?" He winked.

"Not by half. But he has a certain charm."

"You do know how to flatter an old man."

I smiled.

"I take it you're worried about the ethical ramifications of dating one of your patients. And the consequences."

"You took the words right out of my mouth."

"I can't endorse it. You know that, right?"

"Of course."

"If you see this man romantically, you'll be taking a risk."

I sagged. "I know. But he was the one who came onto me."

"What did you treat him for?"

"Treat him? All I did was order an MRI when he came into the ECU and prescribe some pills for pain and inflammation. When I told him I couldn't date him, he insisted on being treated by another doctor. It was weeks before I ran into him by accident at a karate event. We've spent time together since then, but it's been totally platonic. We're really just friends."

"That's good news. But it's difficult to say how the Medical Board of California will react. Dating a former patient isn't technically breaking a state law, but it will look bad to the state board. I can't speak for this hospital either. I would imagine for them this is a legal and ethical gray area, one that opens them up to potential lawsuits. But maybe they'll treat yours as a special case."

"Do you think so?"

"I would hope so, but your guess is as good as mine." He shrugged. "Off the record, I don't personally consider your situation an ethical issue. But as I said, things are much stricter than they were in my day. Gosh, when I was doing my residency, you could still smoke in the hospitals. Heck, you could smoke while examining patients."

"Is that true?"

"It most certainly is. We had ashtrays in every exam room. I don't know how we did it. Anyway, back to your point. You'll be taking a risk if you date this man. Have you discharged him as a patient?"

"Yes."

"Good. There's no official time table, but the longer you wait before dating him, the less likely the Medical Board or anyone will care."

"That's what I was thinking."

"But it's always a risk."

"I know." I sighed.

"For what it's worth, Brigid, I know you're a good doctor and a good person. While you'll be taking a professional risk if you see this man romantically, something tells me you wouldn't be taking this risk if you didn't think he was worthwhile."

"He most definitely is."

"Then I wish you the best of luck. But remember, patience is always a virtue."

The only trouble was that I was getting increasingly impatient. I couldn't escape the feeling that some hidden problem was going to blow up in my face.

"Girl, you are not gonna believe what happened Sunday morning while you was off."

"What now?" Suddenly worried, I stared at Latisha as I walked up to the nurses station and set my purse on the counter.

"LAPD brought in three men who were brutally beaten over at Universal CityWalk."

Oh no.

"Allison told me Noah said—"

"You mean Officer Murdock?"

"Yeah, him. She said he said the men said Lion Maxwell attacked them."

"That's a lot of saids." My guts were starting to churn with toxic nausea.

"That's what I said," she smirked. "You know anything about that?" Her tone was worried but intensely concerned. She was smart. She had seen the Irish Springs lion carving and had already put all the pieces together. "You were off Saturday, weren't you?"

"I was on call." I wasn't going to confirm or deny anything. Withholding information wasn't lying, was it?

"Right," she nodded.

"So, what happened to the men? Was anyone seriously hurt?"

"One had a few contusions that needed suturing. The other swallowed a few teeth. The third had a fractured hyoid and a broken nose."

"Did he need surgery?"

"Yeah. His airway was compromised by the hyoid fracture."

"Who did the surgery?"

"Dr. Hackett was assisted by Dr. Foster." Dr. Foster was an Ear Nose & Throat specialist.

"Where is the man now?"

"Up in SIU. Foster wanted him kept overnight for observation."

"Did you see him?"

"No. I was at home when all this went down."

"What about the other two men?"

"Discharged late Sunday."

I stared at her.

"Something you wanna tell me, Bridge?"

I snorted, "No way."

"What are we talking about, ladies?" Dr. Hackett said as he whisked up to the nurses station. "Me, I hope?" He flashed his imitation Hugh Grant smile.

"We always talking about you, Dr. Hackett," Latisha said with fake sincerity that was almost believable. Almost.

Hackett lapped it right up. "Shall I assume good things?"

"Nothing but the best," Latisha smiled.

I tried not to laugh.

"Why thank you, Ms. Brown." Hackett fiddled with his tie. "And how are you today, Brigid? Doing well, I hope?"

"Splendid."

Latisha and I both waited for Hackett to take the hint and wander off.

He sniffed grandly. "Right then. Duty calls." As he strolled off, he tipped an imaginary hat at us. "Ladies."

When he was gone, Latisha mocked him in a snooty British accent.

"Dyoo-ty cawlls." She shook her head. "More like doody calls. Why does that man always walk like he's constipated?"

I laughed. "Because his asshole is so tight he can't pass his stool."

"True that," she snorted.

"And that explains why he has brown eyes."

"You did *not* just go there."

"I believe I did."

She tried to hold in a tickling snicker.

"Go ahead and laugh."

She did.

I didn't.

All I could think about was the ticking time bomb up in the SIU. If I was Nurse Jackie, I would go take care of things myself. Since I wasn't, I would have to wait for the bomb to explode in my face.

Maybe it was a good idea for me to avoid any further interaction with Lion.

No good could come of it.

Chapter 19

LION

A week later, on Saturday, I was lounging out by the pool icing my knee. The fight at Universal hadn't made it any worse that I could tell, but I called Dr. Hackett and told him I tripped and landed on it. He ordered me to come in for an MRI. Turned out it hadn't gotten any worse. I think the knee brace saved it. I also told him about my ribs. An X-Ray confirmed three were cracked, but it wasn't bad. He give me some painkillers and something for the swelling. I didn't bother getting either prescription filled. The pain wasn't that bad. But we did agree to postpone the surgery for several more weeks so I could stabilize.

Tigger trotted out of the house through the open French doors and stared at me.

"Gonna go chase some birds?"

Unlike Aslan, Tigger never said a thing. He just looked at you. What he was thinking was a mystery. I don't think he knew either. He just chased things. That was good enough for him.

My phone played Jump Around by House of Pain.

Brigid.

My heart hammered and I nearly fell off the lounger grabbing for it. My ribs screamed and so did I.

"Fuck!"

Tigger sprinted across the lawn and dove into the jungle behind the pool.

Irish Kiss: I have your Harry Potter picture from Saturday. I should probably give it back.

My world crumbled in the span of fourteen words.

She was done with me.

I knew it.

I wasn't worth the risk.

My body suddenly burned with pure rage. Whoever made the rules about doctors not dating patients needed to die. I pictured a big stone building somewhere with tall columns like a courthouse. I needed to go bomb that building into dust.

Never in my life had an institution stood between me and a woman.

What did an institution know about love? Nothing. This was ridiculous.

What the hell was I gonna do?

Tell her how you feel.

Not over a text.

Me: Can you bring it to my place? My knee is killing me.

It was half true. It didn't hurt, but having it out of commission and laying around icing it all the time drove me nuts.

When she didn't respond immediately, I started freaking out. I could feel her slipping through my fingers. A minute later, she texted.

Irish Kiss: Can I mail it to you?"

Me: I don't want it getting broken.

Irish Kiss: I'll pack it really well.

Me: What if it gets lost at the post office?

Irish Kiss: I'll send it certified.

Me: What if the mailman gets robbed?

I was so scared I sent that before I thought about how lame it sounded.

Irish Kiss: That only happens in the old west.

Me: I live in a bad part of town.

That was a lie and a half and it wasn't going to make her want to come here.

Me: I actually live in the Hollywood Hills. It's not bad at all.

Irish Kiss: That's not what I've heard.

Was she joking? Hinting that I was the bad thing in the Hills or something else? I couldn't tell. I hated texting.

Me: I promise it's safe. My house is gated.

I sounded like a douche because only douches told you their houses were gated. I needed to start thinking before I texted.

Irish Kiss: Do you really want me to drive it over?

Me: If you have time. No rush.

Now I loved texting because I didn't sound as desperate as I felt.

Tigger stalked out of the jungle in a low crouch, pausing in the shadows at the edge of it, ready to shoot off in any direction. He looked as nervous as I felt waiting for Brigid to respond. She could easily change her mind about coming over.

Irish Kiss: Okay, what's your address?

Grinning from ear to ear, I texted it to her.

Irish Kiss: When should I come over?

Right now!!!!

Me: Whenever.

Irish Kiss: How about this afternoon?

Me: That'll work.

Irish Kiss: See you then.

"Hell yeah!" I shouted, excited Brigid was coming over.

Tigger bolted across the lawn and disappeared around the side of the house.

Crazy cat.

I cleaned up all the carving tools and the half finished lions in the living room and put everything in the garage, in case Brigid wanted a tour of the house. I didn't want her seeing the carving before I finished it. The only people who ever wanted to see my garage were the people who wanted to know what kind of car I drove. Brigid didn't strike me as the type, but I put a tarp over the carving just in case.

I paced the house on my crutches until my knee started throbbing. Maybe the brace was too tight. I sat down and loosened it and handled a few business calls, but I finished those quickly.

The only thing left to do was wait.

I played the new Doom game on my PlayStation 4. That got old quick. Too bad Dan wasn't here to play with me. I bought it because he was telling me how awesome it was when we were at Universal.

Tried reading. Couldn't focus on the words because I kept seeing Brigid's face.

I ended up pacing in front of an old Bruce Lee movie on satellite. Enter the Dragon. Couldn't go wrong with that. The movie was in the middle of the fight between Bolo Yeung and John Saxon. Nothing like watching a groin kick bring down a mountain. Saxon destroyed the much larger man. When there were no rules, all bets were off.

The landline portable phone rang. Nobody had the number for it, so it was someone at the gate.

Brigid.

I hoped. My heart skipped a beat anyway.

I was more nervous than the time I lost my virginity, and that was years ago. But I remembered it, and this was ten times worse. I picked up the phone and hit the TALK button.

"Yeah?"

"Hey. It's Brigid."

"I'll buzz you in. Drive up to the front door. You can park anywhere."

I opened the door for her as she was coming up the steps. As always, the sight of her made my dick stir and she wasn't even trying. She looked exactly like the sexy soccer mom she was. Off the shoulder T-shirt and skinny jeans. I could see her bra strap on one side. Did she do that on purpose? Her red hair flowed out behind her like a ball of fire as a soft breeze waved through it. And something I hadn't seen on her before: movie star shades and a hint of lipstick. This was the closest I'd seen her to dressed up.

"You going on a date after this?" I blurted it out. I sounded like a jealous prick.

She frowned. "Why?"

"You're all dressed up."

"This is dressed up?"

"From what I've seen of you, yeah."

"I don't just live in scrubs and yoga pants, you know."

"Good to know. So, are you going on a date or what?" What the hell was wrong with me? I needed to get my game under control or I was going to blow this thing. I didn't even know what this was, but I didn't want to screw it up.

"Wouldn't you like to know." She grinned and lifted her shades off her head. Those minty green Irish Spring eyes of hers just about killed me. Combined with her marry me smile, I could barely keep myself together. She wasn't making this easy. I took a deep breath to relax.

"That's cool. I've got a couple hotties coming over later anyway. We're gonna watch porn then shoot a sex tape after."

"No you're not," she laughed nervously.

"Wouldn't you like to know," I mimicked.

"I don't want to know what you do in your sex mansion."

"You mean besides have lots of sex?"

She smirked. "I brought your picture." She held it up like I was supposed to take it. I didn't want this exchange to end here. I wanted it to last forever. But I'd take an hour if she'd give me that much.

"You wanna come inside? Meet the family?"

She frowned. "You have a family?"

"The four legged feline kind." Women always loved that I had cats. I knew it. And I needed to score as many points with Brigid as I could.

"Oh," she grinned. "Don't tell me you have actual lions and tigers."

"No. I'll leave that to my buddies Siegfried and Roy."

"You don't actually know them, do you?"

"No. I did meet them in Vegas once. After one of my fights. Even went to their house and met all their white tigers. Beautiful animals."

"I bet that was amazing."

"Yeah it was. Also kind of sad. Those cats shouldn't be locked up."

"I know what you mean. Big cats are supposed to run wild and free. They don't like cages and they don't like rules."

I grinned, "You took the words right out of my mouth."

She looked me up and down and smirked. That was a flirt. She was totally checking me out.

Yes, I was wearing a FEEL THE BEAST tank top to show off my arms and shoulders. And shorts so I could wear the brace. And I still had the crutches. Not the studliest look ever, but it was either crutches or limping.

"Should we go meet your cats?"

I motioned inside. "After you."

She held onto the Harry Potter photo like it was hers. Maybe she didn't want to part with it yet. That was a good sign.

We walked through the front entrance and I led her to the living room. I hung back a bit so I could check out her ass. Shouldn't have done that. It made me hard for her every time I saw it.

"Look at that cat tree!" Brigid gasped. "That thing is huge!"

"That's what the ladies always say," I joked.

"Smart ass. Wow! It even has a cat hamster wheel!"

"Tigger loves the wheel. He'll do like five minutes flat out. Never seen a cat with stamina like his."

"Where's Tigger?"

"Probably in the back yard hunting."

"I love that you have tiger stripe carpeting on all the different levels of the cat tree. There's like twenty of them. And it looks like an actual tree. Where did you find it? They don't sell things like this at Petco. It must've cost a fortune."

"Built it myself. It was like two-fifty for the wood, the stain, the carpeting and all the hardware. Labor was free. Did it in the garage where I keep my tools. Took me two full weeks to design and build."

"Really?"

"Yup." I was proud of it.

"The cats must love it."

"Tigger was scared to shit of it when I finished putting it together. Wouldn't come in the living room for a week. Gwen would stare at it from across the room like it might attack at any second. But you shoulda seen Aslan when I finished bolting it together. He climbed straight to the top shelf like he owned the thing. Made it his bitch."

"Is that him sitting on top?"

"Yeah."

Aslan flicked his tail. *What's she doing here?*

"What's his name again?"

"That's Aslan. You can call him Ass-lan."

Ha ha, asshole.

"Why?"

"Look at that smug motherfucker. Why else?"

You're lucky I don't eat you when you're asleep. He turned his head away and stared at the wall.

"He does have that Superior Than Thou thing going. I wonder where he learned it from?" She snickered.

"Not from me," I laughed.

"Uh huh."

"There she is."

Guenhwyvar walked out of the doorway that led to the kitchen and sat down, watching.

"Who's that?"

"That's Guenhwyvar."

"Wait, how do you say it?"

"Gwen-WE-far. Like Guinevere. But you can call her Gwen."

"As in, King Arthur and the Knights of the Round Table Guinevere?"

"Yup. She's the queen of this castle. Ain't that right, Gwen?"

Gwen busied herself licking her paw.

"Should I pet her?"

"Ask her."

Brigid walked over to Gwen, who turned up her head to watch, eyes big. "Hey, Gwen. Mind if I scratch behind your ears?" Brigid bent down and Gwen sat up on her back legs and dipped her head. Brigid went to work. "You love that, don't you?"

I could hear Gwen purring from where I stood. "She loves that. Likes you too." *She's not the only one.*

Brigid smiled at me. "I should give you your picture."

"You can set it on the coffee table."

She did. "Thanks again, Lion. For… everything."

"It's all good." Was that a brush off? I hoped not. "How's Daniel?"

"He's fine. He's at his Dad's."

"Good to hear. He's a great kid. Hey, can I get you something to drink?"

"Oh. Okay."

Why did I feel like this was prom night or whatever and it was my first date ever? I wanted to tear her clothes off. Short of that, I wanted to flirt with her until she was dying to fuck me. But I was walking on eggshells. I would settle for talking.

"Follow me to the kitchen? I can't really carry anything with these crutches."

"Oh, right."

I winced with every step. Damn ribs.

"Are you okay?"

"Yeah. I cracked a couple ribs that night."

"I'm sorry."

"It's fine. Already had them X-Rayed. Nothing serious."

"I'm really sorry, Lion. What happened that day was…"

"Let's not talk about it, okay?" It was a downer. The least we could do was have fun for a few minutes before she left. Forever. "You want some water?"

"As long as it's not bottled."

"What is it with everyone and plastic bottles?"

"They're bad for the environment."

"I reuse the bottles," I groaned.

"I don't want your used bottles," she giggled.

"Fine. How about tap?" I leaned my crutches against the counter and grabbed two glasses from the cabinet.

"Perfect."

I filled a glass. "I hope you like the taste of dirt." LA City water was not the best.

"It's silt. Which is not dirt."

"Then what the hell is dirt?"

"Dirt is soil. You grow plants in it."

"You're such a librarian," I laughed.

"You like it," she smirked.

I did. "Let me get you a chair." I crutched over and pulled one out in the breakfast nook.

"Thank you."

I pushed it in and brought her her water glass and sat down.

"So…" I said.

"So…" She sipped her water.

Damn it. She wanted me. I knew it like I knew my own name. I would take her on my breakfast table if it wasn't for the damn rules.

"I talked to a friend of mine the other day," she said flirtatiously.

"What about?"

"Us."

I liked the sound of that. "Which friend?"

"An old doctor friend of mine. Would you believe he married one of his patients?"

"Just one?"

She snickered. "Yes. Back in the seventies." She had this sexy as hell look on her face. I wanted to kiss it off. My dick started to uncoil in my shorts under the breakfast table.

"What are you saying, Irish?"

"Mmm, I don't know." She shrugged. Her legs were crossed and her top leg bounced like crazy.

"You're blushing, Irish."

"Am I?"

"Yup. I wonder what that means?"

"It means I'm going to fuck you, Lion Maxwell."

I would've choked on my water if I had been drinking any. My dick missiled in my pants. I'm surprised I didn't shoot my load then and there. No woman had ever turned me on as much as she did. I couldn't explain it, but it was a fact.

"Is that a promise, Irish?"

"It's a fucking promise."

"Ho-ho," I laughed. I couldn't believe her boldness. It was quite the turn on. My entire body was sizzling in anticipation of sinking my dick deep inside her wet and willing pussy. "There's only one problem with your logic."

"Oh? What's that, *Lion*?" She said my name like a taunt. A challenge. Her minty green eyes flashed pure sex.

"I'm going to be the one fucking you."

Chapter 20

BRIGID

"Fuck." Lion ran his hand through his tangle of dark hair. "I don't have any condoms." He looked apologetic.

"You don't? You?"

"You say that like I'm a manwhore."

"Aren't you?" I didn't think he was, but it never hurt to ask.

"Not even close. I bet you've had more sex in the past year than I have."

"I doubt that," I snorted.

"Wanna bet?"

"Yes. What are we wagering?"

"How about whoever loses has to give oral to the winner."

"Deal." We shook hands.

"Okay, Irish. We'll both say at the same time how many people we slept with in the past year."

"On the count of three?"

He nodded. "One, two, three! Zero!"

"None!"

We both laughed.

I said, "Wait, Lion. You expect me to believe you haven't had sex in a year?"

"More than a year. I'm officially a born again virgin. I've even been tested. Clean bill of health. How about you?"

"I'm clean too. And born again three times over."

"Wow. That's a long time."

"Don't remind me. So, who won?"

"I think we both did."

"No, I won because it's been three years for me!"

"Sorry, Irish. The bet was sex in the past year. It was a draw. We're both winners. But, since I'm a gentleman, I'll let you go first."

"Wait, what? I'm not blowing you first."

He chuckled. "I meant, you could win first. I'll devour that dripping wet pussy of yours until you scream my name. Then you have to give me the best head I've ever had."

"The best ever?" The idea made me nervous. I wasn't sure if I could measure up to the women he'd been with.

"Don't worry, Irish. Something tells me the second those sweet lips of yours touch my dick, I'm going to lose it. I hope you swallow."

"Yes I swallow." I was confident of that much.

"Good, because I'd hate to give you a facial. Unless you want one."

"Hmm. I've never had one. I'm open to it."

"Serious?"

"Yes, I'm serious."

His eyes darkened. "I knew I liked you the second I laid eyes on you."

"Why is that?"

"Because you're willing to talk about sex. With most women, everyone just goes for it and you hope things work. That works great until they don't. Or, you want to change things up. The only way to do that is talk about it."

"Oh. I'm happy to talk about it. And I'd be happy to have a facial."

"You know what that is, right?"

I rolled my eyes. "I'm not some sheltered virgin. We're not talking about the kind of facial you get at a spa."

"Just checking." He shook his head. "You know, Irish, you are sexy as hell and you're not even trying."

Funny, I thought the same thing about him the day we met. It was hard to believe he felt that way about me, but he'd said it without any prompting. "Thank you."

"So, before I tear your clothes off, what about those condoms?"

"Lucky for you I'm a doctor. I came prepared." I reached into my purse and tossed a box of ten LifeStyles condoms onto the breakfast table. The label read Kyng. "I got the big ones. I saw you in your shorts."

"You only got ten?"

"Isn't ten enough?"

"Not for me it isn't."

"Good. Because I also got these." I tossed a box of 12 Ultra Studded condoms onto the table. "I thought I would give the studs a try." I winked at him.

He grinned that adorable grin of his. "I'm all the stud you'll ever need, Irish."

"Cute." I knew he was right. He was more than enough stud for any ten women, and with that body of his, I imagined he would keep some lucky woman sexually satisfied for a lifetime. But today wasn't about forever. It was a one time thing. To get it out of my system. "I considered getting a third box. Would you believe they now have condoms textured like snakeskin?"

"No shit?"

"They're called Viper condoms."

"Is that the regular size or the large? I ask because you're a doctor and you probably studied biology so you know vipers aren't exactly the biggest snake in the animal kingdom."

"I do know that. But they only have one size. Viper."

"When they come out with Python, we can try that."

"Did you want to get on the phone with customer service and let them know?" I joked.

"It can wait. Right now, my mind is focused on other things..."

I shivered pleasantly as I imagined that huge cock of his filling me up as I came all over him. I could fantasize all day, but the real thing was waiting right in front of me. "So... how are we going to do this? Candles? A little wine? Some romantic music?"

"What chick flick do you live in? I'm going to tear your clothes off and fuck you until forever."

"Oh. Okay. That'll work," I giggled barely above a whisper. "Um, what do I do?"

"Try not to scream." He leaned over and pulled the leg of my chair forcefully, yanking it across the hardwood floor and me with it.

"Oh!" My chest tightened with anticipation. We were knee to knee in our chairs. He leaned forward in his. My heart started to pound as his face neared mine. I caught his scent. Natural, musky, arousing.

"I never got my Irish Kiss," he muttered in that voice of his.

Ooze.

"Me neither," I tittered, suddenly nervous.

This close, Lion's physical presence was overwhelming. He was a very large and muscular man. He hadn't shaved in a day or two, and had the perfect scruff. Or was the word whiskers? What was it that lions had? And why was I comparing him to an actual lion? That was too weird. Maybe it was the sense of danger. Gone was that playful grin of his, replaced by a feral mask that bordered on gorgeously monstrous.

In his YouTube fight videos, I had seen him take on countless men and win every time. Many of the matches were bloody and savage but Lion always emerged victorious. There was an undeniable viciousness to him.

He was literally a very dangerous man.

But he had a softer side I had seen first hand with Daniel. That was why I was giving myself to him. But for some reason, I was still scared.

Probably because I hadn't had sex since Donald. I wasn't sure how I would perform. Was Lion used to women who knew their way around the bedroom? Warrior women like Candy the Stripper groupie? I wasn't sure if I could compete with them, but I would certainly try.

"You scared, Irish?" *That voice.*

"No."

"You sure?"

"Maybe a little."

"Tell me why." His breath was minty. He must've just had a breath mint. He didn't naturally smell like mint, did he? No, that was ridiculous.

"You know why. Because I haven't been with anyone since my husband. And we both know that didn't end well." I didn't tell him that the lack of sex was a huge part of the reason for my divorce. That was embarrassing.

"Don't worry about him, Brigid. You'll forget every man you've ever been with once I'm inside you."

I absolutely believed him. He was that handsome, that virile, that confident, that sexual.

He leaned to my side until we were cheek to cheek. What was he doing? Was he sniffing me? He shifted to my other cheek. Yes, he was sniffing. Like an animal. He buried his nose in my hair and inhaled again, then warm breath blew across my ear, followed by his hot wet tongue flicking against it. Oh my goodness, that was incredibly sexy. I sank in my chair, melting into the seat. He pulled back and licked my cheek experimentally, then down to my jawline. My skin sizzled where his tongue touched it. I felt like he was a beast tasting me before it did… what? Ate me? Or mated with me? I didn't know, but I was so turned on, I decided he could do either.

He fisted my hair and pulled my head back, exposing my neck. Was he going to tear my throat out? Nope. His tongue ran down to the dimple between my collar bones then back up to my chin.

"Nnnh," I moaned.

We hadn't even kissed and I was ready for him. My panties were soaked.

He still had his fist in my hair as his mouth descended on mine. Our lips locked. His tongue speared past my teeth and overpowered my tongue. I tried to fight against it, but he was too strong. All I could do was submit to his powerful kiss.

The intensity of it nearly killed me.

"Nnnnh, nnnnnnnnnnhhhh." My entire body burned with desire that flowed like hot magma down between my legs and to my toes. My vagina clenched over and over, harder and harder, like I was about to come. Maybe I did come. I wasn't sure. Whatever was happening, it felt incredible.

Best. Kiss. Ever.

Strong hands slid up my ribs and massaged my breasts through my bra. He grunted into my mouth as I let his hands have their way with me. Thumbs circled my nipples. Sexual energy spiraled down into my clitoris and spun out of control.

Then I did come.

Hard.

He grunted into my mouth and bit my lip, tugging on it until it popped free of his teeth.

Before I could recover, he lifted me out of my chair and sat my ass on the breakfast table. He grunted in pain. His brace was meant to stabilize the knee laterally and minimize twisting, but that didn't mean it prevented pain during flexion or extension.

Concerned, I gasped, "Is it your knee? We can stop if you want."

"No," he growled, his face aggressive with dark desire. He ripped my shirt over my head and I shimmied my arms out of it. Then he pulled my bra straps off and pushed my bra down without bothering to unhook it.

"Fuck," he hissed as he ogled my breasts.

"They're all yours," I giggled.

He stared at them, rapt, heaving deep breaths. "Fuck, fuck, fuck, fuck!" He lifted his head and pinned me with his eyes.

Suddenly afraid, I was tempted to cover my breasts. I raised my arms half heartedly.

He grabbed both my wrists and forced them down. "This is it."

"What is it?" I was confused.

"There's no going back after this, Brigid."

"That was the plan," I chuckled uncertainly.

"No. I mean, once you and I do this, I... we..."

"What?"

He squeezed my wrists hard.

"Ow, Lion!"

"I'm serious, Brigid. We're about to cross a line. There's no going back." *That voice.* It was all business. Dangerous business. It was thrilling, exciting, a huge risk. He knew it. I knew it. But I was an adult, not a child.

"Yes, I understand. No going back." What was I agreeing to? I was almost afraid to ask. In that moment, I didn't care. I was too turned on, desperate to have him fill me up with his cock and his cum in every way possible.

Still squeezing my wrists, but not quite as hard, his mouth dove for my left nipple. He sucked the hard bud into his mouth and attacked it with his teeth and tongue. One of his hands savaged my right nipple and his other supported my lower back. Good thing, because I almost fell backward as the intense sensations melted every muscle in my body.

My will gave way to his.

I was lost in erotic ecstasy as he laid me gently down on the table. While his mouth lapped at my nipples, both of which were now wet and sore and stinging with need, his hands undid my belt and pulled my skinny jeans down to my knees.

"Wait, my sandals."

He made quick work unbuckling them and they slapped against the wood floor as he dropped each one. My jeans were on the floor a second later.

The heel of his heavy hand suddenly pushed against my mound through my panties and ground across my clit. I jumped. His palm continued up my stomach, which spasmed as he slid it across my skin. My arms were up over my head and I looked at him through sleepy eyes.

His flickered black fire. "I'm going to eat you alive, Irish."

"You better," I moaned.

He sat back down in his chair, between my legs. He winced when he did. His knee must really have been bothering him.

"Do you want to stop? If your knee is hurting we can..."

"No," he barked and grabbed my hips and yanked me to the edge of the table. Hot breath blew across my panties. He inhaled deeply, his nose against the thin material. "You're wearing a thong."

"I told you I came prepared."

"Then I better make you come," he growled savagely. He bit down on the cotton thong and pulled on it. The muscles of his neck corded and he snarled.

"You're not going to—"

Rip!

The cotton panel tore free from the elastic.

Rip, rip, rip!

Like a beast of prey, he pulled with his neck until the panel was dangling down between my legs, exposing my wetness.

"I can't believe you did that," I mumbled.

He glared at me. "Quiet, woman. The only thing I want to hear out of your mouth is moans or my name."

He was so damn hot it was ridiculous.

He inhaled my scent, his nose plowing up and down through my wet folds like he couldn't get enough. Donald had never done that to me before. I'd never even heard of that. It was so fucking hot. His eyes rolled back into his head and he grunted.

Mine did and I grunted too. "Nnnnh!"

His tongue jabbed deep inside me. I was already soaking, my labia engorged with blood. Just as quick, his tip slipped upward and spiraled around my clit.

"Aaaahh!"

He grunted approval.

It didn't take long for his ravenous mouth to bring me to my peak. EroTouch gloves had nothing on the real thing. I was half insane with need for more. Expertly, he would take me to the edge of orgasm then back off, doing it over and over again until I was ready to burst. Finally, I couldn't take any more.

"Please, Lion. Make me come. Please." I was nearly weeping.

He attacked me then and I came hard.

He wouldn't stop.

Just attacked and attacked, drinking me in until everything faded to orgasm.

"I'm going to fuck you right now," he growled.

I noticed his FEEL THE BEAST tank top. That was exactly what I wanted from him. His beast. I wanted to feel it and eat it then let him take me and make me do whatever he wanted. I had recovered just enough to whisper, "What about your blow job?"

"Fuck that. I can't wait." He leaned over me, his massive body pressing against mine, and grabbed a box of condoms. While he weighed down on me, his heavy erection pressed against my stomach and I felt it pulse through his shorts. He sat back down in the chair and peeled his shirt off and dropped it on the table. His body was as magnificent as I remembered. Then he stood and shoved his shorts down over his knee brace and kicked them off.

His cock pointed straight at me like a weapon.

I sat up.

"Lie down," he barked.

"No."

"I'm going to fuck you, Brigid."

"I'm going to blow you, Lion."

"Do it later."

"No!" I glared at him.

He smirked, his eyes glinting. "Fine. Go ahead. Suck my fucking cock, Irish."

I slid off the table and knelt between his legs.

He had a really big dick.

I wasn't going to let that stop me.

I grabbed the base of his shaft hard and tickled around the seam underneath the swollen head with my tongue. There was already a big dribble of pre-cum spilling out and running under the bottom. The taste of it made me moan as I savored it. The taste of sex. Such a turn on. I went to work on the head first to wind him up, squeezing the shaft firmly, but not moving my hand. Something about focusing on the head made men go crazy if you did it right.

"Fuck," he hissed. His cock jumped and his entire body jittered. "You sure know what you're doing, don't you?"

I smirked, looking up at him with the head still in my mouth. I knew what I was doing. Then I released the head and licked downward, releasing my fingers so I could slicken the entire length before giving some love to his balls.

"Nice. Nobody ever bothers with the balls."

He was rock hard, so I pulled his cock down to get a better angle and take him deep into my mouth. My tongue circled languidly around the head, getting it wet. Then I fucked his cock with my mouth, ramming it into the back of my throat, keeping my lips tight around his girth. But not too tight. Just enough. There was no way I could take all of him into my mouth, but I tried. When my gag reflex kicked in, I relaxed it. My eyes watered and drool filled my mouth, turning it into a sopping wet mouth pussy as my tongue cradled the underside of his shaft and stroked the sensitive tip after each thrust.

"Fuck, Irish. Fuck." He slumped in the chair and I planted both my hands on his thighs and pumped up and down with my mouth. His head lolled against the chair back. "Fuck."

I found a rhythm and brought him to the edge over and over, slowing just in time to prevent him from ejaculating, just like he had with me. As long as a man didn't ejaculate, he could have multiple orgasms, just like a woman. It was a fact I had verified through research with Donald in our early days. He may not have fulfilled me sexually, but I knew I did him. Every time we'd had sex, he wanted me to give him a blowjob. Every. Time.

Lion seemed to be enjoying his blowjob just as much. He had already proved his prowess with my pussy, so I was happy to return the favor. I don't know how long I blew him for, but he was a puddle of pleasure and his entire body shook with exquisite abandon while I devoured his cock python.

His eyes were clamped shut and his face was etched into a painful grimace. All he could say was, "F-f-f-f-f-fuuuuhhhh."

I felt him swell in my mouth as I brought him to the edge one last time. I had one hand wrapped around his base, pumping in time with my head. He was going to explode.

"Sssss! Stop! Don't! I'm gonna come! Stop so I can fuck you!"

I chuckled throatily. I didn't care what he wanted at that point. He was coming in my mouth and that was final.

A long low grunt built in his chest as his cock strained to maximum. He sank into the chair, trying to pull away, but I chased after him, keeping him deep. Every muscle in his body popped, veins, tendons, everything bulging and spasming as I pumped and pumped and pumped.

"FUCK!!" He roared.

Semen shot into the back of my throat.

I choked it down, determined to take all of it.

There was more than I anticipated.

I had to gag half of it down, but I did.

I let the last of it spill out from my lips and drip down his shaft. I smeared the hot cum around on his pubis, which was neatly trimmed. I kept sucking and pumping as he emptied himself, gasping for air, his nails digging into the wooden chair like claws.

I licked him clean, loving the salty fresh ocean taste, stroking his shaft lazily, going light with my tongue so I didn't overwhelm him and he could finally relax. As he softened, I slowed my pace until I finally, reluctantly, pulled away.

I gave the tip a kiss. Smiling and looking up the length of his abs up to his sleepy eyes, I whispered, "How was that?"

He smirked at me. "You are a fucking cum guzzler."

"And proud of it."

We both laughed.

"That was the best head I've ever had, Irish. Bar none. I mean it."

"Me too," I smiled shyly.

I was so proud of myself.

I hadn't given into my insecurities.

I am woman, hear ME roar!!!!

<<<<<<<<>>>>>>>

"I hate to be a doctor," I said, "but you have semen all over your cock. And balls. And pelvis."

"What are you talking about? You licked me clean."

"Still. It only takes one microscopic spermatozoa."

"Can't argue with that. Want me to shower?"

"We can do it together."

We both stood, completely naked, except for his brace.

"How's your knee?"

"Workable." He grabbed my arm, pulled it around his neck, and threw me over his shoulders.

"Hey!" I laughed. "Put me down!"

"Shut up."

"Don't forget the condoms!"

He turned so I could grab the boxes off the table, then he walked confidently but carefully out of the kitchen.

All three cats were in the living room.

Staring at us.

"Don't mind them," Lion chuckled.

"Hey, guys!" I waved. "And Gwen."

She blinked.

Lion hefted me up the stairs, taking his time. His strength was not in question, but he did favor his injured knee. The house was gigantic. Upstairs, the hallway branched off in several directions, and skylights illuminated everything with natural light. Double doors at the end of one of the halls revealed a master bedroom.

I laughed. "You do not have a leopard themed bedroom."

"Apparently, I do."

"You are so predictable."

"Based on the size of my cock, do you predict that it will drive you wild?"

"Ummmm… yes."

"So tell me how predictable is bad?"

"In this case, I concede your point. But only in this case."

Unlike the master bedroom, the master bathroom was not leopard themed. It was all slate and stone, almost like a cave, like instead of a shower head it needed a waterfall. The huge mirrors over the sinks reflected our nakedness, him dark and muscled, me pale as a ghost. Dark against light.

The floor of the shower was tiled with river rocks.

"Aren't river rock tiles so last year?"

He set me down and took off his knee brace. "What about me says I give a fuck what other people think about my decoration choices? Was it the leopard print bedspread or the tiger print rug in front of the bed?"

"Those patterns clash, you know."

"I'm a cage fighter. I'm all about clashing."

I laughed.

He turned on the rainfall shower. It wasn't a waterfall, but it evoked a sense of the outdoors all the same. I soaped him down, making sure he was scrubbed extra clean where it counted.

"Be careful you don't give me rug burn."

"I'll do that later when I ride you on that tiger skin rug of yours."

"You are such a bitch in heat, Irish."

"And you love it."

He arched an eyebrow.

"I mean," I giggled nervously, "you like it."

"Like is such a half-assed word, Irish."

I bit my lip. It was best not to use the word love with Lion, no matter what either of us may have felt about the subject. After we finished in the shower and toweled off, he carried me to the bed.

He took the towel draped over his shoulder and twisted it between his hands, ringing it back and forth like a rope. "Hmmm. I wonder what I could do with this?"

"Who cares about a limp towel?" I smirked at him. "I want something hard. Like your dick. It looks ready to kill." Admiring his hard body and equally hard cock had made me wet yet again.

"Be careful what you wish for. The orgasms I give have been known to kill."

"Oh yeah, big talker? Prove it."

He smirked and tossed the towel aside then picked up the box of condoms off the bed and ripped off the top with his teeth.

I laughed.

He grinned and pulled out the roll of condoms, also with his teeth.

His cock was so beautiful it was a shame to sheath it. I wasn't a fan of rubbers, but I wasn't on the pill and I wasn't taking any chances. The last thing I could afford was a baby and a scandal.

He bit the corner of a condom wrapper with his teeth.

For some reason, that gimmick didn't work for me. It was simply too cheesy. In a limburger kind of way. "If you tear that condom package open with your teeth, I promise I will walk right out of this bedroom."

"How do you want me to open it? Using my fingers is too boring."

"You're a man, think of something manly."

"The manliest thing I can think of is to shoot a hole through it with a .44 Magnum."

"That might ruin the condom."

"Melt the package off with a blow torch?"

"That'll melt the latex."

"Chainsaw?"

I laughed.

"Lawn mower? Chipper shredder? Chain it between two Monster Trucks and have them floor it?"

Giggling, I shook my head no to each option.

"I'm running out of ideas. A samurai sword?"

"Do you even have a samurai sword? Wait, I forgot who I was asking."

"I do."

"Of course you do."

"I can go get it."

I laughed again. "Just use your teeth."

He did.

Surprisingly it was sexy the way he did it. Scary and dangerous. I don't know why I doubted him. I really luh—I meant, this Lion Maxwell was a great guy.

"Are you blushing, Irish?"

"No. Put the damn condom on."

He did before climbing on the bed to kiss me. We made out for a while, our passionate kissing as intense as before. He slowly stroked my clit with his fingers the entire time. I was a dripping wet mess when he finally asked, "Hard or soft?"

"You mean the fucking?"

"Yup."

"Both."

"What the hell does that mean?"

"You figure it out."

Boy, did he. He rolled onto me and pushed my thighs open with his good knee and laid his weight on top of me, our eyes locked. His cock pressed against me. He just held it there until I was dying for it. Then he took his time easing inside. Despite me having had a baby, it was a tight fit to say the least. A wonderfully tight fit. He was huge and filled me up completely. Slowly, almost painfully, he withdrew. Painful only because I did not want his cock outside of me. I wanted him deep inside. Deep. Slowly, he eased back in, exactly where I needed him. In.

In, in, in.

He continued to ease in and withdraw again and again until I was writhing beneath him.

"Like that," I moaned. "Yes. Like. That. Ohmygod. Yes. Like... *thaaaaaa...*" My words crumbled into unintelligible moans.

He responded by intensifying his thrusting. With my thighs wrapped around his ass, I clamped down with every thrust. I clawed at his back desperately, wanting more, more, more. I had no nails, which was probably for the best, otherwise I would've left gouges all over his back and shoulders. He wasn't the only animal in the room and his steady thrusting filled me with lust.

"Fuck, Brigid. Your pussy is so fucking tight."

"Nnnnnh." It didn't take long for the pre-orgasmic waves to tighten everything in my body. "Oh, Lion," I whispered in his ear.

He kept pumping and growling, driving deeper and deeper, filling me fuller and fuller.

"I'm going to come, Lion. Ohmygod, I'm going to—"

"Fuck! Come, Brigid! Come! With me! Fucking come!"

I did.

Impossibly, his cock got bigger and he roared, coming inside me at the same time. I pulled him in hard with my ankles, trying to milk him through the condom, trying to pull all of his cum inside me. It was nonsense, but I was thinking it anyway. It felt so good, I suddenly wondered if the condom had somehow broken without either of us realizing it.

I should've been jumping off the bed to frantically check, but I didn't. In fact, that thought never crossed my mind. Instead, I lounged beneath him, content, as he pulsed inside me, gasping for air, his head hanging beside my ear.

I whispered, "Yes, babe. That's it. Give me everything you've got. Every last drop."

Finally, he grunted and groaned and collapsed on top of me, sated.

We lay together for a long time, me caressing his back, kissing his cheek gently, his ear, his forehead. Smothering him with kisses.

I curled my arms around his neck affectionately. "That was so good, babe. So incredibly good." I was completely unaware that I kept calling him babe and never stopped to think how he might be taking it. It just came out. Coming hard did that.

"Mmmmm," he grunted.

Neither of us moved to separate.

Together felt right. Perfect.

Joined.

Union.

I imagined the condom was long gone, nothing but a ring of latex around the base of his cock.

I imagined his cum working its way toward its final destination.

Toward life.

I was so wrong about this being a one time thing.

I was in big trouble.

Chapter 21

LION

"Did you talk to her?" Dean asked me a week later at my place. This was the first chance I'd had to talk with him since.

"You could say that."

"How'd it go?"

"Better than I expected."

"What did I tell you? All you gotta do is tell a woman how you feel, and everything else falls into place. You still working on that wood carving of the lions?"

"Yeah. It's in the garage. I'll show you."

The only problem was that I hadn't told Brigid how I felt about her or us. Not emotionally. It was too soon. But I'd told her over and over how incredible the sex was, and that was every day for the past week. We had sex all over my house, in every room except the garage. I told you, girls never cared about garages.

Anyway, it was the best sex I'd ever had. Period.

Sex with Minka had been incredible. But sex with Brigid was something different. I didn't want to say magical because that sounded fucking lame. But it was, I don't know, more. More intense. More connected. More everything.

I couldn't explain it, but I couldn't deny it either. That's why I knew I had it bad. No, not bad. Worse. I'd known I had it bad for Brigid minutes after we met. Not only was she hot, but she was a damn doctor. I loved her strength and intelligence. And her kid was as cool as she was. But after sex? I was hooked. Addicted. There was no way I could *not* be with Brigid.

No. Way.

The real reason I hadn't told Brigid how I felt about her was because it felt like too much too soon. I felt like I sounded desperate. Nobody wanted desperate.

Standing in the far end of my spacious four car garage where my workshop was, Dean turned the lion carving around in his hands. "That's mighty fine work. Never seen anything like it."

"That's because you don't know shit about wood carving."

"I know how to whup your ass, boy." He threw a half jab with his elbow and we both laughed.

"Don't drop my carving, old man."

"I'll drop you." He carefully set the carving down. "When you gonna show it to her?"

"Soon as it's finished."

"I'm sure she'll love it."

There was that word. Love. "Dean, can I ask you a question? Man to man?"

"Your woman give you the clap?"

"No!" I laughed. "This is serious."

"Fire away."

"Do you think it's possible for a man to, you know…" I wasn't sure how to put it.

"Know what? Do I have to tell you about the birds and the bees, son? You ain't learned that yet? What they teaching you kids in school these days?" He laughed his wheezy laugh.

I rolled my eyes. "Come on, Dean, I'm serious."

"All right, calm down, son. Don't get your panties all up in a bunch. What're you trying to ask?"

"Can a man have… I don't know… really strong feelings? I mean, right away? For, you know, a woman?"

He pursed his lips and nodded. "You love her."

I ran my hand through my hair. "Is that possible after only a few weeks?"

"I knew with Helen in a few minutes."

"I'm sure you knew you wanted to fuck her in a few minutes," I chuckled.

"Naw. We didn't have sex in the old days. The stork brought the babies." He winked at me.

"Yeah, right. I've seen old photos of you and her. She was a fox."

"That she was. Mmm, mmm. I miss that woman every day, God rest her soul." His lips knotted for a moment. "Nobody else like her."

"Yeah." I'd never met Helen, but I'd heard thousands of stories over the years. Dean and I shared a solemn moment. "But you loved her? After only a few minutes?"

"I sure did."

"How did you know?"

"You just feel it, son. I knew she was different the second I set eyes on her. It took a few minutes, but after talking back and forth, I just knew. She was like nobody else."

"That's how I feel. Brigid walked in the room and—BAM!" I

smacked my fist into my palm.

"Then you probably love her."

Hearing him say it made my entire body tingle like it did when I was walking toward the cage before a fight: every nerve lighting up in anticipation of either disaster or victory. "Yeah, maybe I do."

"You tell her that?"

"No."

"Then tell her already."

I just needed to figure out the best way to do it.

Chapter 22

"Are you sleeping with Lion Maxwell?" Donald demanded.

I had no idea how Donald could know about me sleeping with Lion, but I needed a defense strategy. *Play dumb. Quick!* "Who?"

"Your son's karate teacher? Are you sleeping with him?"

Shit. Shit. Shit.

I was terrible at lying on the fly. All I could think about was the truth: I had just spent an amazing week having sex with Lion. More sex than I could remember ever having.

"Well?" Donald pressed. He was here at my condo dropping Daniel off. Normally he never got out of his car. This time he'd come up to the front door with Daniel and asked if he could speak to me outside. I sent Daniel into the house and here we were. Donald stared at me like he was the lawyer and I was on the witness stand. He was good at making me feel like I was the bad guy. "You are, aren't you?" He sounded pleased with himself, and purely furious with me.

"No, I am not!" I barked. It wasn't a lie because I wasn't having sex with Lion at that exact moment. It had been at least eighteen hours ago. Maybe even twenty.

"You are the worst liar I've ever met, Brigid. I've told you that before."

"I'm not lying." *At the moment.*

He shook his head. "I can't believe this. What possessed you to sleep with our son's karate teacher?"

"How do you know I'm sleeping with him?"

"Because you're not denying it. Brigid." He glared at me.

He was right. I was a terrible liar.

He shook his head. "Oh my god, Brigid. Why?"

I growled, "Why not?"

He threw up his arms. "I can think of a million reasons."

Did he know Lion had been my patient? Had Daniel told him? Did Daniel even know Lion was my patient? I didn't remember telling him. Maybe I had. But why would I? Stalling for time, I said, "Name a reason, Donald."

"I don't know. Does the term 'conflict of interest' mean anything to you?"

Shit. *When being attacked, go on the attack.* "He's a karate teacher, Donald," I sneered. "Not a… a…" I didn't want to say my patient. "Not a business associate. Or my lawyer. Or Daniel's fifth grade teacher who I'm trying to woo into giving Daniel a better grade. He's Daniel's karate teacher. They don't even have grades." I was really dancing around the issue. "I don't know what you're worried about. Do you think he'll give Daniel special treatment he doesn't deserve? Cut us a discount on the monthly fee? Advance Daniel to yellow belt sooner than he should? I don't see how any of this is a problem."

Donald flashed his trademarked sneer. The one that said, *Do you know who I am? I'm Donald Wright. THE Donald Wright. Why are you questioning me?* I hated that sneer. I had seen it a million times during our marriage. It was often the reason I was too tired to have sex with him.

"You're not jealous are you, Donald?"

"Fuff," he snorted. "Me? Why would I be jealous of the man you're willing to have sex with? I mean, why have sex with me when your son's karate instructor will do? I was never attracted to you. *Never* wanted to have sex with you. Never even asked." His sarcasm was as subtle as a fist in the face.

"Do you have to go there?" There, as in our ancient history together. I was already thinking there, but he didn't have to go and talk about it. "You were the one who divorced me, remember?"

"Good thing I did. Now you're free to have sex with any Tom, Dick, or Cock that comes along."

"It's Tom, Dick, or Harry. That's what the saying is."

"I know what the saying is," he growled through clenched teeth. "I was being sarcastic."

"You? Sarcastic? I never would've thought." He was always sarcastic when he was pissy.

"Funny, Brigid. Very funny."

"Are we done?"

"The question is, are you?"

"What, with Lion Maxwell?"

"Yes. Him. Your son's karate instructor. The one you're having an affair with."

If he said karate instructor one more time, I was going to punch him in the face. Then kick him softly in the balls. Not too softly, but softly enough not to make him sterile. I wasn't that mad. Yet. "It's only an affair if one of you is married."

"I was trying not to be crude. You want me to be crude? Fine. I'll be crude. I was talking about the man you are *fucking*. The one you spent the day with at Universal Studios with our son. Remember him? Daniel? You do know who I'm talking about, right? Your son?"

I cringed. It had been two weeks since that fateful night in the Universal Studios parking structure. This was the first I'd heard mention of it from Donald. I was surprised he hadn't said something sooner. I'm sure Daniel had mentioned all the fun we'd had on the rides that day, but had he told Donald about seeing Lion fight those men that night? That would be bad.

Donald scanned my face carefully. He sneered, "Yes, that Lion Maxwell."

Did he know about the fight or not?

I waited for him to say more. I knew Donald, and if Daniel had told him about the fight, he was going to tell me right now and tear me a new one. Suddenly, I was overcome by a sensation I could only describe as what it might feel like to grind my own teeth across a chalk board, the kind of feeling that caused my anal sphincter to squeeze tighter than a fist and all the hairs on my body to stand on end like they were trying to jump off my body so they could flee to safety.

Donald arched a superior eyebrow. Apparently, he could tell how tight my sphincter was at that moment. But he didn't say anything, which meant he didn't know.

I sighed. "Donald, we are divorced. I am free, as are you, to date whoever we want. If Lion was a bad person, you might have a point. But he's not." *He's just my patient who I feel only moderately guilty about sleeping with. Forty times in one week.* "So, until there's an actual conflict of interest—" *one that involves our son, not the one where my medical license gets revoked for having sex with my patient* "—I will continue to see who I please, when I please." I may have sucked at lying, but I was pretty good at omitting the truth.

Arms at his sides, he flicked both index fingers repeatedly in that way he did when he was ready to blow his top and that I hated. "Mark my words, Brigid Flanagan. You are going to regret this."

"Is that a threat, Donald Wright?" I smirked.

"No, Brigid. It's a warning. There is something you're not telling me and I know it's going to bite you in the ass. And I don't want your indiscretions spilling over into the life of *my* son."

"He's my son too, Donald."

"Are you sure? Because you're not acting like it." He climbed into his BMW and sped off.

Ouch.

He had played the bad mom card. With me, that card always made for a winning, or should I say losing hand.

Worse, his warning echoed in my mind. Would he find out Lion was a convicted felon? What would he say then? It wasn't so easy to label someone a good person when they'd spent time in prison.

The other pressing problem was keeping my relationship with Lion —if you could call it that—a secret from the people at the hospital. That was critical. My biggest fear was that Donald might tell them. I had no idea whether or not he knew that it was unethical for me to date a patient. The topic had never come up when we were married, so maybe he didn't. But, if he put everything together…

Would he tell on me?

I wasn't sure.

The way he was acting, it was very possible.

Sadly, when we'd given our marriage vows ten years ago, I had thought that the part about loving and honoring each other forever actually meant something. Look how that turned out.

No, I couldn't trust Donald.

Chapter 23

LION

Despite the time I'd spent with Brigid and Daniel, and all the sex I'd had with her (we were at two weeks worth and counting), she and I hadn't had a proper dinner date with just the two of us.

At first, I hadn't thought much about it because Brigid was over at my place all the time and we were having incredible amounts of sex. Brigid was insatiable. I couldn't get enough either. But we'd never gone out to eat. Sure, we'd eat at my house, but it was always food I cooked for her or takeout, which she insisted on paying for.

In the past few days, every time I suggested we actually go out for food, she had an excuse. The truth was, as much as I loved sex with her, I was missing just hanging out with her and Daniel.

Time to mix things up.

I called her up on Monday morning when I knew she was home.

"Lion Maxwell," she purred in a voice that was soft and inviting and unlike her usual brass balls doctor demeanor. "Is this my booty call appointment reminder?"

That sexy voice of hers went straight to my dick and I started to get hard. It never ceased to amaze me how much she turned me on. I chuckled, "I thought we had a standing appointment."

"We do." She did this sexy laugh that made my dick jerk in anticipation of one of her patented ball busting blowjobs. Brigid was fucking perfect.

I snickered, "I know you're usually busy evenings, but how about I trade in one of our booty calls for a dinner date? You know: you, me, some restaurant someplace, good food, great conversation, incredible sex after. If you're pressed for time, we can skip the sex and make up for it the next day." I tried to sound totally casual, but I was kind of nervous.

"Uhhhh... when?" The soft sexy voice was gone. She sounded scared.

Any confidence I had evaporated in an instant. "Ahhhh, I was thinking this weekend?"

"I don't know. I have Daniel this weekend."

"How about Friday? Do you have him then?"

"I work Friday."

"Oh, right. How about next Friday?"

"I don't know. That's a ways out."

"How about this Thursday?"

"Working."

"Wednesday?"

"Then too."

"I'm noticing a trend."

"I'm sorry, Lion," she sighed. "I work nights. You know that."

That was true. All our sex had been either on the weekends or mornings before she went to work, and always at my place. Never at hers. I had told myself it was because she didn't want us having sex with Daniel around, which I totally understood. But she had him one week on, one week off. And when she did have him last week, she left him with a babysitter. I hadn't stopped to think about it. Two weeks later, I could put together the bigger picture.

I took a deep breath. "Can I ask you something?"

"Sure." She sounded like she didn't want to be having this conversation.

If I had been the one who'd pressured her into bed, I might take a hint and back off. But she had opened that door. Now it seemed like she was closing it. If we had nothing in common, it would make sense. That happened all the time. You fucked someone until you got bored then went your separate ways. But this wasn't that. I wasn't bored. Neither was Brigid. I felt like we had perfect chemistry. No matter what we did, we had fun. I loved spending time with her and Daniel. I knew she loved it too. That's why I knew she was hiding something.

"Brigid, this may sound weird, and I feel weird saying it—"

"Then don't say it."

Whoa. She had just put up a wall. We're talking solid granite, ten feet thick. It was clear as day in her voice. I felt like I was one step away from getting dumped. I had to think before I said anything else. Silence hung between us like invisible poison gas. Man, I hated this. What the hell had happened?

"Lion?"

"I'm still here."

"I'm sorry. I'm being rude. What were you going to say?"

I took a deep breath and let it out slow. "Do you not want anyone knowing you're sleeping with me?"

Silence.

Shit.

This was not the way you went about a relationship. Not that this was a relationship, because I knew it wasn't. It was "just friends" with secret benefits. I was cool with that. Or so I thought when this started. After Minka, I was never in a rush to jump into things with anybody, but Brigid had sucked me right in. I didn't think she meant to, but it happened. For me, anyway. I wasn't so sure about her. I knew there was a reason I hadn't told her I loved her. This was it. The least you expected from someone you were fucking was that they were okay with being seen with you in public. Did that make me sound like a chick? Yes. Did I care? No, because I never cared what other people thought.

It's not about you, Lion! Minka's voice, pissed. *You have to learn to take life as it comes, not control every single moment of it. Sometimes you don't get what you want. If you can't make peace with that, you'll go nuts and you'll never be happy.*

When she'd said that, I was used to having everything always go my way. When I went after something, I got it. Being undefeated in the cage added to that sense of entitlement. But that didn't stop the hurt when Minka left me. She was my biggest defeat in life. Her leaving had hurt a thousand times more then tearing my ACL. I didn't want to go through that shit again with anybody, and I didn't want to set myself up for a fall with Brigid. I was ready to pull out and end this. But there was one last thing to ask.

Carefully, I said, "Is it because of the doctor patient thing?"

"Yes." She sighed. "You know I can't be seen with you now that we're..."

A confusion of emotions bounced through my body. Why did I feel like a loser when she confirmed what I already suspected? I grunted, finishing her sentence for her, "Fucking," I wasn't going to say making love or some sappy shit like that. Not now. I was closing down. Time to bail out of this before it got any worse.

"That's right," she snorted and not in a happy way, "fucking."

I squished my palm against my face and cringed. I was glad we were doing this on the phone. "This is my fault, Brigid. I'm sorry. We should have... I mean, I never should have—"

"I'm an adult, Lion. I made my own choices. They may not have been wise ones, but I made them."

That stung. "Do you regret them?" I shouldn't have asked that. I didn't want to know.

"No." Her voice was flat.

I couldn't read her. Not over the phone. "Do you not want to do this anymore?"

"I don't know."

Fuuuuuuuuck.

I leaned back on the couch and shook my head. All I'd wanted to do when I called was take her to dinner. Could I get a do over?

I was about ready to end the call when inspiration hit. I was going to put everything on the line because sometimes you had to put up or shut up. "Do you want to end this, Brigid? Yes or no? If you do, I'll hang up right now and you'll never see me again."

"What? No! I mean yes! I mean, I don't want to end this! Why are you even asking?!"

"Just making sure we're on the same page." My hands were shaking like crazy. I knew things were still on the knife edge of ending, like she might change her mind the second she got off the phone and thought about it. I had to act fast. "Would you have dinner out with me if nobody knew it was us?"

"If you're suggesting we go to a masked ball or something equally Shakespearean, I suppose so." There was humor in her voice and it was a huge relief for me. "But I don't know of any masked balls coming up." She paused. "And don't make any jokes about *your* balls wearing one of those lace masquerade masks."

"One? I would need two. One for each," I chuckled. I loved her sense of humor and I loved she was making jokes. That was a good sign.

"I refuse to picture the image of laughing and crying theater masks on your balls when you pull your pants off." She laughed happily. It was damn good to hear.

"I won't picture it either. But that wasn't what I had in mind."

"What did you have in mind?"

"That's a surprise."

"You have to at least tell me what to wear."

"Irish, you can wear any damn thing and you will always be the hottest woman I've ever seen."

"What if I wear a wooden barrel?"

"Smokin' hot."

"A bear costume?"

"Twice as hot."

"Don't tell me you're one of those furries into costumed animal sex."

"No. I like you *au naturel*. But seeing you in a bear costume would be totally worth it."

She laughed loud and long, totally relaxed.

I was too.

What a relief.

Chapter 24

It was Tuesday night, the night of our secret surprise date.

Thankfully, I wasn't on call. Donald had Daniel, so I was free and clear for the evening. If I so chose, I could spend the night with Lion. I had never done it, but I liked the idea. Maybe tonight was the night.

If everything went well.

I would have to wait and see.

The restaurant was all the way over in West Hollywood, which was quite a drive in traffic. It was tucked away on a side street in an old brick building between a dentist office and an auto mechanic. Odd, but not unusual for this part of town. Red vested valets waited on the sidewalk. One opened my door and I handed him my valet key. He climbed in and drove off. That's when I noticed the name of the restaurant. It was written on the front door in hard to read thin gold script:

Naked Sensations.

What?

When we'd made plans, Lion had only given me the address. When I plugged it into my GPS, it didn't bring up a business name. Just the map location.

Naked Sensations sounded like a sex club.

Was this the sort of thing that would *not* get us noticed together? When the police raided the place and arrested everybody, our mugshots would be all over the internet. The headline would read:

LION MAXWELL ARRESTED IN SEX CLUB WITH DR. BRIGID FLANAGAN!! WHIPS, CHAINS, RED BALL GAG AND SEX SWING INVOLVED! REPORTS OF ASS HAMSTERING UNCONFIRMED. DON'T WORRY FOLKS, HER MEDICAL LICENSE HAS BEEN REVOKED!!

Now I knew why Lion told me to wear something that was easy access. My flowy ruffled Georgette dress with a deep V-neck definitely qualified. It was minty green to match my eyes. I had just bought it this morning at bebe. Now Lion was never going to see it. I couldn't believe he invited me to a sex club!

What was Lion thinking?

What was I thinking?

I needed to get out of here!

I waved at the valet, trying to stop him before he drove off with my car. Too late. He was long gone. I slumped. I'd have to wait until he came back. I folded my arms across my chest.

Did I really want to be standing in front of a sex club where anyone could see me? Nope. I turned to walk up the sidewalk. At least I wore my movie star sunglasses. Hopefully no one would recognize me.

"Brigid? Is that you?"

I cringed and froze in place. I didn't have to turn to recognize the smarmy British accent. Dr. Ivan Hackett.

He walked up behind me. "Brigid?"

I didn't turn around. I wanted to run but I was paralyzed with guilt.

He stepped around in front of me. "It is you. Fancy meeting you here. What brought you round to West Hollywood?"

"Nothing!" *I'm not here for the sex! Or the club!* "Just passing by!"

"I saw you give your car to the valet."

I was a deer caught in headlights. "I'm going to the dentist next door?"

"In that dress?"

"Yes! I always dress up for the dentist! Don't you?"

"Not really." His disbelief was palpable.

"Ha ha ha! Everyone in America dresses up for the dentist! You Brits and your casual ways!"

"Mmm, not so much."

"How would you know? You weren't born here!"

"Lived here ten years."

"Ha ha ha! That doesn't count!" I was insane. Insanely guilty. I needed to run for it before Lion showed up and Ivan caught us together red handed and red faced.

"You're certainly acting very odd this afternoon, Brigid. Is everything all right?"

I shrugged like an insane mime, which meant every mime, because they were all insane. Like me. If you can't picture it, I was slowly tipping sideways like the Leaning Tower of Pisa. Any second I was going to topple to the ground and shatter into a million pieces.

He smirked, "You aren't really going to the dentist, are you?"

Terrible liar that I was, I was in such conflict that I shook my head and nodded it at the same time, making a wobbling circle, all while smiling guiltily.

"So you *did* come for the dentist."

Wobble, wobble, circle, circle.

"Naked Sensations?"

Wobble, circle.

"The dentist."

Wobble.

"Naked Sensations?"

Circle.

"Brigid, are you being cheeky with me?"

Was he talking about my cheeks? Because they ached like crazy from maintaining this goofy guilty smile.

Circle, circle, wobble, wobble.

He chuckled, "Which is it, Brigid?"

"Okay, fine! I'm here for Naked Sensations!" That felt so much better. Guilt hurt and was best avoided. The truth will set you free.

"Shall I presume you're meeting someone? Or going it alone?"

"No! I mean yes!" So much for the truth. It was a nuisance. But that didn't stop me from wanting to shout: *I am meeting my former patient Lion Maxwell at a sex club! Can you guess why? Ha ha ha ha!!!!* Wait, was Hackett here for the sex club too? If he was, then that meant I had some dirt on him. That gave me some relief. Confidently, I said, "I came alone. Alllll alone. Just me. Coming alone." I cringed. Why had I said coming? Or alone? Would he now assume I came here to watch other people while I masturbated? People like him? Gross! Or was I expected to join in the fun? Was that how these sex clubs worked?

"Oh that's bold," he chuckled.

"Is it?" I tittered.

"I'm sure you'll enjoy it." He smiled indulgently. "What they do here is… well, it's indescribable."

"HAHAHA!!" *I'm sure it is!*

He frowned.

"Sorry."

"Anyway, I've been telling my sister about this place for months. Finally convinced her to come and share the experience with me."

Your sister?!?!

Shut the front door!!!!

A beautiful woman walked up in a white lace dress that left nothing to the imagination. She was obviously Ivan's sister based on her eyes and the shape of her face. "There you are, Ivan."

"Nadya, this is my colleague Dr. Brigid Flanagan."

"Pleasure to meet you." Nadya smiled at me. Like Ivan, she was tall, slender, and had dark hair, but his was short and thick while hers was long and luxuriant. Also like him, she belonged on a calendar. In her case, a swimsuit calendar. She would be *Get Freaky with your Sister February*. "Have you been to Naked Sensations before, Brigid?"

"NO!!" *And I'm never going to either!* I sounded insane. "Hahaha. Ha. Ha." My laugh puttered out. "Ha."

Nadya looked slightly confused. "Ivan has been telling me about Naked Sensations for months. Said I simply must try it. I've heard the food is to die for." She hooked her arm around Ivan's elbow. It looked absolutely wrong. In most states, illegal. Most, but not all. Which ones, I wasn't sure, but definitely here in California.

He patted her hand and smiled at her. "Shall we, sis?"

Sis? Oh, goodness. They sure did things differently in the UK!

Nadya smiled seductively, "We shall."

Ivan winked at me, "Make sure you have the dessert. It's the best part."

Dessert? What was dessert? Cherry pie? Cream muff? Cum filled éclairs? Or the old standby: a banana hammock split?

They strolled into Naked Sensations without looking back.

Where was that damn valet?! I needed to leave pronto!

My phone buzzed in my purse.

Lion: Are you there?

I furiously texted back: **Are you crazy?**

Lion: Crazy for you.

Me: What were you thinking inviting me to a sex club?

Lion: It's not a sex club.

Me: The hell it isn't!

Lion: Trust me. It's not a sex club. Go inside like we agreed. I'm parked a few blocks away. I'll be there in fifteen minutes. Make sure you're inside before I arrive.

Me: I'm not going anywhere near that place!

Lion: It's not a sex club. I promise.

Me: What is it then?

Lion: Would you quit worrying and trust me? I would never do anything bad to you. I promise.

I didn't respond. I needed time to process. I hadn't told Lion that I really liked him. I had told him the sex was incredible. But I hadn't gone on to say it was all I could ever want or hope for from sex. And I wanted to have it again and again with him and him alone for a long, long time. But this whole doctor patient thing was a serious problem. We couldn't be seen in public. Certainly not where my boss could see me with my patient!

Me: I can't do this.

Lion: Why not?

Me: Dr. Hackett is here. Your doctor. Remember him?

Lion: I think we'll be okay.

Me: You think?

Lion: Do you want to do this another night? We can if you want.

Me: I don't want to do a sex club any night!

Lion: Irish, it ain't a sex club. And I'm 99% sure you won't have to worry about Hackett. But we can always do this some other time.

How about in six months or a year? When this didn't look nearly as bad? I sighed. I didn't want to do that. I didn't want to be trapped in secrecy with the man I... had strong feelings for.

Me: Do they have private booths?

Lion: Better.

Me: What could be better? Is ours on the moon?

Lion: No. Trust me.

Me: Fine. I'll go inside. But if I see Hackett, I'm leaving.

Lion: Deal. See you in 15.

I stuffed my phone in my purse and took my ladyballs in hand. Nobody was going to tell me how to live my life.

I walked inside the front doors. Just inside was another set of front doors. The ones behind and the ones ahead both had blackout curtains. I pushed through the second set of doors. The inside was very dim, but I could see it was a lobby of some kind. A young woman stood behind a podium, much like a hostess. Maybe it was a restaurant. The woman wore dark glasses. That was odd. Probably so she wouldn't know the identity of the guilty patrons, because there was no way this place was legal.

It is a sex club! Damn you, Lion!

"Good evening," the sex hostess said. "Welcome to Naked Sensations. Do you have a reservation?"

"Uhh..." I was either doing this or I wasn't. "Yes," I sighed.

"Name?"

"Smithsonian." It had been my idea. Lion had suggested Smith, but that was too common.

She ran her fingers over what looked like a regular tablet computer that rested on the podium. Unlike a tablet, it had a row of bumpy dots that clicked along like a scrolling LED sign, except it was little bumps, not lights. That's when I realized it was literally a Braille computer tablet. Above the scrolling Braille dots it also had two sets of four keys that fit the fingers. She typed into it then ran both index fingers across the Braille dots. "Here it is. Smithsonian. Two for seven-thirty?"

"That's us. I mean me. He's running late."

"Would you like to wait?"

"Actually, can you seat me now?" I was still crossing my fingers this wasn't a sex club. I uncrossed my fingers when I remembered how ineffective it was.

"Certainly. Right this way." When she walked around the podium, she kept her hand on it. She didn't grab a menu but offered me her hand. "I'll lead the way."

"Okay." I took her hand.

"Have you been to Naked Sensations before?"

"No."

"Don't worry. I'll go slow. Follow my lead and you'll be fine."

We walked through another set of curtains into complete darkness.

Yup, sex club.

Lion! You ASSHOLE!!!!

The hostess led me around several turns. I had no idea where I was going. It was pitch black in this place. I had to trust that we wouldn't run into any walls. "Here we are. There's a curtain."

I put my hand out in front of me and felt velvet. "Am I going to trip?"

"No. There's nothing on the floor to trip on." She led me into the room and placed my hand on a chair back. "Can you manage the chair?"

"Where's the table?" Being blind wasn't easy.

"Here." She placed my hand on it.

"I think I've got it." I sat down and she helped push my chair up. "Thank you. How do we order? I can't see anything."

"Your waiter will describe the menu to you."

"Oh."

"Don't worry. We have a select menu with only a few choices."

"That's smart."

"We think so." Her voice smiled.

"Um, this may sound odd, but are there any other people in here already?"

She laughed. "No. You have your own private table."

I could hear the faint and muffled sounds of numerous quiet conversations nearby. "Who am I hearing then?"

"Each table is separated by velvet curtains, but there are no walls. So we ask that our patrons keep their voices to a minimum. We think the quiet intensifies the culinary experience."

"That makes perfect sense. So, we'll be sort of alone?"

"As long as you're quiet, yes."

"Okay. I can do that. Thanks."

"Anything else?"

"Nope."

"We also ask that you turn off your cell phone or set it to vibrate."

"Oh. Okay."

I heard the curtain rustle when she left. The first thing I did was point my phone flashlight around the room. I don't know why, but I was expecting racks of sex toys, like a sex armory, but instead of rifles and swords, it would be dildos and whips in every shape, size, and color you could imagine; giant dildos, dildos on spears, cat o' nine, ten or even eleven tails, whips with dildos attached to the ends, that kind of thing. Sure enough, it wasn't. But it was curtained like the waitress had said. Beyond that, there was a table with plates, glasses, and napkins, but no silverware or anything else. No centerpiece or decor on the walls to speak of. But there was a small sign dangling from two gold threads on one side of the room. The writing was so small I had to get up to read it: Please Turn Your Light Off. I noticed a second sign on the opposite side of the curtains. It said the same thing. Oops. Guilty, I sat back down, switched my phone to vibrate, and put it away.

As darkness settled over me, I became aware of every little sound. Although I did hear other people. I couldn't make out any conversations, which was good. And no sounds of sex. That I knew of. A few minutes later, the curtain rustled.

"Is she here?" *That voice.*

"I believe so," the hostess said.

"I'm here," I muttered.

Lion sat down and the hostess told us our waiter would be with us shortly.

I smelled him instantly. He wore cologne. Something musky and feral. In complete darkness, it was an instant turn on.

"What do you think?" Lion said softly, his voice no less sexy. In fact, it was more sexy when it was the only part of him I could focus on other than his scent.

"Not what I was expecting."

"What were you expecting?"

"A sex club."

He chuckled quietly, "I don't know how you got that idea."

"I'll explain later. Have you been here before?"

"No. I heard about it from a friend."

"A female friend?"

"Yes. Are you jealous?"

"It depends how friendly she is."

"She's one of my business partners. Rhonda Chavez. She's married, her husband is a great guy, and her kids are too. You should meet them sometime."

"Not here. I'd like to be able to see them when I meet them."

"Vision isn't everything."

"How would you know?"

"Because the sound of your voice is the sweetest thing I've ever heard. Fuckably sweet."

Ooze. "Okay then." We were whispering, but I was a bit nervous about being overheard. Dr. Hackett and his sister could be in the next curtain over. Oh well. It was a risk I was willing to take. He'd brought his sister here, after all. Who knew what they were doing in the darkness? That's probably why they came. But not to come. To eat. But not each other.

Apparently, the darkness made me extra dirty.

Lion said, "You know what I love about this?"

"What?"

"I could be naked right now."

I was right about the darkness making things dirtier. "You're not naked."

"Are you sure? Maybe I took a detour to the men's room and stripped before I came in here."

I considered shining my phone flashlight on him, but I decided I liked not knowing. "The question is, Mr. Pervert, how do you know I'm not naked?"

He groaned. "Do you have any idea what you're doing to me?"

"Mmm, in the complete dark? No. You'll have to describe it to me."

"My dick is about to punch a hole in my slacks."

"You're wearing slacks? I thought you said you were naked."

"I said I might be naked. Sadly, I'm not. I'm wearing a grass skirt and a coconut bra and a string of flowers in my hair."

I laughed more loudly than I intended. "No you're not."

"I am. And I can serenade you with my ukulele after we eat."

"What are you really wearing?" I giggled.

"A pinstripe tailored shirt and slacks."

"What kind of shoes?"

"Uhhh, brown leather lace ups and a matching belt."

"Are you wearing a chunky watch?"

"Just my Transformers watch. It looks like Megatron."

"You don't have a Transformers watch."

"You're right. It's some fancy brass thing that goes with the belt. Kind of looks like an old-school diving watch."

I moaned. "Why didn't you tell me before? Your outfit sounds even hotter than picturing you naked."

"Don't forget to picture the old school brass diving helmet I'm wearing. My voice doesn't sound echoey because I have the round porthole face-mask open." He chuckled.

"Why do you keep ruining my image of you in a sexy outfit?"

"Because the sound of you laughing makes me happy."

"Oh." That was too sweet for words. "But seriously, why can't you just let me have my mental picture of you in a classy outfit?"

He chuckled. "Women. You don't make any sense. Why would you rather imagine a guy dressed up when you can see him naked? I thought you ladies loved abs and asses."

"We also love the allure of power and the surprise of what might lay underneath. Plus, women love playing dress up."

"Men love playing undress up."

"Shouldn't it be undress down?"

"That's not the way my cock is pointing."

I laughed. "Have you been hard this entire time?"

"Of course. Because I'm picturing you completely naked."

"How do you know I'm not?"

"Be careful, Irish. If you are, I will fuck you right here and now."

"You can't! I'm dressed! In an old school diving suit! You'll never be able to get it off."

"But I bet I can get you off."

"Ahem." It was a third voice.

I nearly jumped out of my chair.

"My name is Pierre and I will be your waiter this evening."

I was silent and extremely embarrassed while Pierre went over the menu in low tones. There were four basic choices: beef, chicken, fish, or vegetarian. He asked if either of us had any allergies to gluten or peanut or anything else. We both said no. He then told us the entrees came with exotic side dishes that would melt in our mouths. He didn't say what kind. My mind raced all over the place in anticipation. Without the distraction of vision, I noticed I was literally drooling. I chose the fish because I was in a deep sea diving mood for some reason. Lion chose the beef and asked to have the chef leave it bloody. Of course.

When Pierre left, I got to thinking about Dr. Hackett, wondering if he might be overhearing all of my dirty talk with Lion. I had told Hackett I was here alone, but if he was listening in, he might ask who I was with when I saw him at work. I could always lie to Hackett, but we all knew how good I was at that. And if Lion used my name, or I his, it wouldn't matter what I said later.

"Mr. Smithsonian, can I ask a favor?"

Lion chuckled, "Anything for you, Mrs. Smithsonian."

"Can you call me Ivy while we're here?"

"Ivy? Why not Irish?"

"That's too obvious. Call me Ivy. And I'll call you... Bob."

"Bob?" He chuckled. "Pick something better."

"You're right. That's too cheesy. How about... Dick. Yes, I like dick." I giggled. "Wait, I didn't mean that."

"I think you did."

I squirmed in my plush chair, already aroused from our earlier flirting. What had I been thinking wearing a thong on a date with Lion? My Georgette dress was as thick as tissue paper. I hoped my thong was extra absorbent. Whatever. You only lived once. Maybe I could sit on my napkin. It was thick linen. "Can I borrow your napkin?"

"Sure. Do you want me to hand it to you?"

"I can get it." I reached over the table, careful not to knock over any water glasses I might have forgotten about, and grabbed it off his plate. I unfolded the triangle and put it under my ass.

"You finished?"

"I'll give it to you later."

"What are you doing with it?"

"Sitting on it."

"Mmmmm." *That voice.* "Iri—I mean, Ivy. You just made my dick hard."

"I thought your *you* was already hard."

He laughed softly. "Now that you mention it."

I giggled. I don't know what it was about Lion, but he brought out my childish side. I really liked that. It was nice to take a break from always being the serious doctor with people's lives in my hands, or the concerned parent at home. I needed some frivolity in my life.

"You know what I'm thinking, Ivy?"

"What?"

"I'm picturing my napkin pressing up against your wet pussy. It's amazing how being blind allows your mind to go all over the place. I'm also picturing wrapping that napkin around my face like an outlaw after you give it back. But only after you've soaked it."

I laughed. "That's disgusting."

"And funny."

I pictured him in the sexy outfit he described earlier, but with the addition of a white linen outlaw mask. "You're right. So, have you always been into sniffing?"

"When it comes to your pussy, absolutely. I can smell it right now."

"No you can't!"

"I beg to differ, Irish. I told you I have a great sense of smell. And I've smelt your pussy many times before and I can smell it now. Not as strongly as I will later when you give me that napkin. But damn, I fucking love it."

"You are so dirty, Dick."

"But I don't have a dirty dick."

"I hope not."

"Your appetizers," Pierre whispered.

Shit. How much of that had he heard? Pierre was too sneaky for his own good. They didn't give you much warning. Probably on purpose. For all we knew, there was a team of people just outside the curtain recording our conversation. Or having a good laugh. Maybe I needed to tone it down tonight. Pierre set the food on the table and left. At least, I assumed he did. I heard the velvet curtain swish, but that wasn't proof. I'd have to trust my sixth sense. Or get my phone out and shine a light. No, that would ruin the ambiance. Besides, I liked the sense of mystery and danger.

Back to the food, which I could smell, and it smelled delicious. I was dying to know what the appetizers were. "Do we use our fingers?"

"I don't see why not."

I felt my food. "What is it?"

"Let's see. It's hot, wet... your pussy?"

"Oh, Dick. You kill me."

"I will later. With my dick."

"Eat your pussy, Dick," I snorted.

"Wow," Lion said after we ate some appetizers. "That is really good. I think it's stuffed mushrooms with spinach."

"I think you're right."

"And it's the best damn stuffed mushrooms I've ever had. Except for yours."

"I don't have a stuffed mushroom."

"Whatever it is you have, I'll be stuffing it later. With my *me*."

I giggled. "Did you just say with your *you*?"

"I did."

When our entrees arrived, we did the same guessing game.

"This is really good beef," Lion said. "I think it's brisket. Mouth watering, I'm telling you."

"Can I have a taste?"

"Sure."

"Should we switch plates?"

"I've got a better idea. Slide your hand out to the middle of the table."

I did.

His covered mine. I felt the warmth before he actually touched me. Before I knew it, he was caressing my hand with his. It was ridiculously sexual.

"Getting wet?"

"I'm sitting on your napkin, aren't I?"

He chuckled. "Right." He continued to caress me. "Do you think if I slid my seat around next to you, I could finger you without anyone noticing?"

"You might confuse Pierre when he returns. We don't want him tripping over you or your chair."

"Then I'll leave my chair where it is."

I heard him stand up and felt a breeze when he came around beside me.

"What about your brisket?"

"I'm gonna give you my brisket."

"Now, Dick," I cautioned. "I meant your meat. Not your *meat* meat."

"I did too."

"Oh my gosh!" I jumped when I felt fingers slide up my ribs. "Is that you?"

"It's me."

"What are you doing?"

"Trying to find your face." His fingers brushed over my boob and hit the nipple.

"That's not my face!"

"I could tell. But I'd really like to kiss it."

Oh, wow. I was so turned on being unable to see.

His hand cupped my breast and massaged it.

"You better stop."

"I'm only stopping because I want you to taste my beef."

"*Your* beef? Or your *beef* beef?"

"I meant the brisket." His hand worked up over my collar bone and up my neck. I shivered wherever he touched. Eventually, his fingers found my jawline, then my lips. "Okay. Smell this."

"Is it your beef?" I giggled. A moment later, I smelled beef. Not man beef. Brisket beef. "Yum." I felt warmth near my lips as he pressed a piece of warm beef against my lips. It wasn't his hard cock like I had secretly hoped, but I put it in my mouth anyway and savored it. "Wow, that's incredible. Did they marinate that for a week and slow cook it for like two days? It's so flavorful."

"What I want to know is, are *you* marinating like you said earlier?"

"Hey!" I felt his hand on my knee. "What are you doing, Dick?" His hand slid up between my thighs.

"I'm going to slow roast you right where you sit."

"I don't think so," I giggled.

"I do. Did you wear something easy access like I asked?"

"Yes, but this muffin is not about to be stuffed."

"I wasn't planning on it. But I would like a taste."

His finger was already prying my thong aside.

This was too hot to stop. I tilted my hips and opened my thighs. Then I gasped. "What if Pierre comes?"

"I wasn't planning on fingering Pierre. And if you come first, we won't have to worry about that, will we?"

I stifled a gasp when I felt his scruffy face push between my legs.

This was crazy.

I was loving every second of it.

And I couldn't see a damn thing.

But I could feel every bit of it. Especially his tongue.

Oh my goodness.

I couldn't begin to describe what it did to my clit.

I don't know if it was the fact that I got turned on every time Lion was near, or the fact that I was so focused on his mesmerizing scent and his seductive voice, or the feel of his hot head between my legs, or whatever magic he was working with his tongue, but I came quickly. I did my best to stay quiet. I hoped no one overheard.

After, he slithered up my body and kissed me deeply.

I tasted myself on his tongue and I liked me just fine.

"I'll return the favor later," I sighed.

"I look forward to it, Ivy."

"By the way, was that my dessert?"

"Why do you ask?"

"I hear the dessert here is to die for."

"Really. What do you suggest?"

"The cherry pie."

We both laughed softly.

Who said Naked Sensations wasn't a sex club?

Chapter 25

BRIGID

We basked in the warm afterglow of incredible sex on Lion's leopard print bed in his wildcat themed bedroom. We had come straight to his place in the Hills after our dinner at Naked Sensations to get naked and to come. Many times each. Our clothes littered a trail from the front entrance to this bed like breadcrumbs of love. I meant breadcrumbs of sex. Not love. Just sex. Numerous condom wrappers were scattered around the bedroom. It turned out that the ultra studded condoms had something going for them. This was our third box of them, despite Lion always complaining about the tight fit.

Sex with him was so easy and so good. Why did it have to be so wrong?

He ran his fingers casually through my messy pile of hair.

"You ever think about having another kid, Mrs. Smithsonian?"

My eyes popped out of my skull. "Uhhhh... Now and then?" I didn't want to hurt his feelings by giving a definitive no or "not with my patient." Not that I thought Lion would make a bad father. He would be a good one. But I couldn't possibly think about the topic of more kids with Lion or anybody else. I barely had time for one. Besides, this was supposed to be a fun fling. It wasn't going to last. We both knew that. Kid talk was not fling appropriate.

"I think about having another kid," Lion said thoughtfully.

Had he said another? I was suddenly uncomfortable. I wasn't sure why. "Um, I thought you said you didn't have a family. Except for your cats."

"I don't have a family. No brothers or sisters. My mom is dead. My dad was a deadbeat and is probably dead in a ditch somewhere. My grandparents are all dead too."

"I'm so sorry, Lion." Three of my four grandparents were still alive and both my wonderful parents were too. So was my younger brother. I was very lucky compared to Lion.

"It's okay. I've got people in my life who are like family. But I think about having another kid." He choked up. "I've always wanted a real family. Of my own."

"What do you mean by another?"

"I had a son named Cali."

"Cali?"

"Yeah. Short for California."

"That's so cute."

"He sure was."

"Can I ask what happened to him?"

"He's dead."

Oh, geez. Lion's life was filled with tragedy. I didn't want to hear any more, for my sake. My heart was breaking for him. The idea of losing my Daniel would kill me. I couldn't bear it if it were to actually happen. I squeezed his hand. "I'm so sorry, Lion." Tears spilled down my cheeks and I sniffed, wiping them away.

"He was ten months old. We put him to bed one night and he didn't wake up the next morning. They said it was SIDS."

"Oh, Lion." I was torn between compassion for him and wanting to ask about the mother. It wasn't the right time. He needed my understanding not my doubt. My heart went out to him. I rolled onto my side and draped my arm and my knee over his naked body. "There's nothing I can say that will make it better," I said softly. "Just know that I... know that I..." I couldn't think of anything that fit within the parameters of a secret fling.

"Thanks. You're a good woman, Brigid. Really good."

"Thank you, Lion. I feel the same way about you."

"Really?"

"Yes. How could you doubt that?"

"I don't know. None of my relationships with women ever worked out. If you include my mom, I lost all the important ones."

I remembered about his mother's breast cancer from the YouTube documentary. She passed when he was 16. So sad. I wondered if the mother of his son had died too. I wasn't going to ask.

"This is gonna sound dumb," he said, "but... it's stupid. Never mind. Forget I said anything."

"What?" I squeezed his arm. "You can tell me."

He turned to me and searched my eyes with his. "Do you want to be my girlfriend?"

His doctor-patient girlfriend? I struggled not to show fear. I had been afraid of this.

"If you don't want to, I'll understand." He didn't sound like he'd understand. He sounded on the verge of heartbreak.

I never imagined Lion would be such a sensitive man underneath has savage exterior. The question was, what did I want out of our relationship? I was so touched that he'd asked about having kids with me. I wanted nothing more than a vibrant family of my own. But I had Daniel and my career to think about. Any unfilled fantasies I had about having the perfect family with the perfect man had to take a backseat to the here and now. This strange and necessarily temporary relationship with Lion was challenging enough. Adding the commitment of being his girlfriend or having a child with him was more than I could deal with at that moment. What happened to this being a fling? That had been my plan. Maybe I should've been more explicit about that. I could kick myself for it, but it wouldn't do any good.

I sighed heavily. "Can I think about it?"

He stared at me, his face unreadable. "Okay."

I felt like an ass. I was hurting him and I knew it.

This was awful.

How had I ended up in this position?

I didn't know when I'd drifted off to sleep in the leopard bed, but I had.

When I woke, it was still dark out.

The bed was also empty.

Had I been in my own house, I might have freaked out, thinking Lion had left. I wasn't sure why, but I would have. Anyway, this was his house. He had to be around here somewhere.

I climbed out of bed and walked into the hallway. I grabbed his black button-down dress shirt off the floor, the one he'd worn to Naked Sensations. I hadn't seen it until after dinner. He looked damn good in a button down shirt and slacks and dress shoes. Very GQ. It was a shame I couldn't show him off around town. Not that I cared. But I cared. Lion Maxwell was a prize in every sense of the word.

But the jury was still out on whether he would ever be my prize.

I buttoned up the black shirt. It hung down to my thighs and the sleeves covered my hands. His scent was all over it and all over me. I needed to put this shirt under my pillow at home. As a souvenir. I needed something to remember him by. Something told me this thing we had was coming to an end sooner than I would've liked.

I walked downstairs, searching the house for him.

The French doors in the living room were open. A warm summer night breeze blew inside. I walked out back and found him reclining on a lounger by the blue glow of the pool. All he wore were black boxers. His knee brace was off. Somehow, he'd managed the whole evening without it. Gwen was curled up in his lap, a fluffy black ball, purring as he stroked her.

"Hey." I sat on the foot of the lounger.

"Hey."

"Couldn't sleep?"

"Guess not."

I pressed my palm to his foot. "I'm sorry for…" I had to stop and think because his abs were distracting me like a flashing neon sign: *SEX! SEX! SEX!*

He waited patiently, focused on stroking Gwen.

"I'm sorry for how difficult this is."

"Yeah," he muttered.

Crickets chirped. It was very quiet this high up in the Hollywood Hills. You wouldn't know we were surrounded by fourteen million people. The only sign was the wind of the constant traffic that twinkled far below.

"Lion, I don't know what to tell you. I want to be your girlfriend. I just can't."

His eyes met mine. "That's something."

"It's more than something. I haven't dated anyone since Donald. Well, not seriously. It was just one date here and there. Nothing ever worked out. I didn't even make out with any of them. Just a few clumsy goodnight kisses that didn't have any sparks. You my friend, are all sparks."

"Like the Allspark?"

"The what?"

"Transformer's reference. Ask Daniel."

I shook my head, grinning. "Right." Why did Lion have to be so incredibly perfect? "You're so good for him."

"Thanks."

Although Lion hadn't been spending much time with Daniel outside of karate class lately, Daniel talked about Lion all the time and was always asking when we were going to Disneyland with him. I was starting to feel bad for Daniel that he wasn't getting any time with Lion lately.

I squeezed his ankle. "Can I ask you something?"

"Anything, Irish."

"Will you wait for me?" I was afraid to say it. I had asked Donald to wait for me just about every day of our marriage for the last several years of it.

"I'll wait for you forever, Brigid." He smiled that adorable boyish smile.

"I appreciate the sentiment. But let me tell you what I mean before you go agreeing to anything."

"Shoot."

"Here are my ground rules. One, no sex."

He winced. "For how long?"

"You said you'd wait forever." I was half joking, but memories of a disappointed Donald stabbed my heart. It wasn't fair to ask any man to wait forever for sex. That wasn't a relationship. Just ask Donald. I was well aware I was asking Lion to do the same thing that had destroyed my marriage. Was I asking too much of him and me? I told myself my connection with Lion was different. With Donald, we had met when I was a naive nineteen year old with very little sexual experience and I had gotten accidentally pregnant right away. At the time, I barely knew who I was as a person. Now I was ten years older and knew myself that much better. Lion and I had a connection I'd never had with Donald. With Lion, everything was always fun and light and felt right. I hoped it was enough. The only way to know was to take the risk. With any luck, things would work out this time.

"Okay," Lion said, "how about five years. I can go five years without fucking you. But that's it. Will that work? Oh, and my ground rule is that in five years, we have to make up for all the sex we missed."

I laughed. "I was thinking more like six months or a year."

"Oh, shit. You shoulda said that. I can do that easy. As long as we make up for it after."

I smiled. "Agreed. The other rule is that we can only be friends. No dinner dates and no lunch dates."

"How about breakfast dates?"

"No. No dating. Just friends. You know what I mean."

He nodded enthusiastically. "I can totally do that, Brigid. If I know you're waiting for me too, I will be your friend for an entire year. And no sex. And I won't be dating or screwing anybody else." He paused for a moment, looking suddenly nervous. "What about you? Will you... you know..." He couldn't finish his sentence but I knew where he was going. I couldn't believe how incredibly sweet this man could be.

"Yes. I will wait for you. Heaven knows I've waited a lifetime for a man like you. I will wait." I meant it with all my heart.

He smiled. "Best news I've heard all day. Make that all year."

I smiled. "Yeah."

He looked at Gwen. "You hear that, girl? Irish wants to be my girlfriend in a year. I can't even believe it." You'd think I'd agreed to have sex with him every day three times a day for forever, or give him daily blowjobs forever, or both, or I didn't know what.

"You're incredible, Lion Maxwell."

"You too, Brigid Flanagan."

Gwen meowed and looked up at him. We both laughed.

He said, "Now all we have to do is wait until the official unofficial amount of time passes, and we'll be free to see each other. In public." There was that adorable boyish grin of his. The one that told me I meant something to him and that everything would be all right.

We could make it. I knew we could.

I believed in Lion.

I believed in us.

Chapter 26

LION

I never thought I'd be able to keep my hands off Brigid after all the crazy sex we'd already had, but I surprised myself.

It wasn't too difficult.

Mainly because she was so damn busy at the hospital. But when she did have time off, we always found something fun to do as a team. Her, Dan, and me. We agreed having Dan around was the easiest way to keep things in the friend zone. It was sure the most fun way I could think of.

I knew Brigid never got out much because of being a doctor, so I made sure everything we did was new for her and exciting.

First place I took them was the climbing gym I used. I'd always loved climbing as a way to develop finesse. Fighting wasn't always about brute force. Neither was climbing. It was also something I could do with my knee still waiting for surgery. Low impact. By that time, my ribs were doing better, but I kept us on the easier routes for their sake and mine. Dan took to the wall like a monkey. Brigid was a lot better than I'd expected. She was super nervous at first, but by the end of our first day, she managed to scale a sustained 5.8 route all the way to the roof of the gym without hanging on the rope. She gave me a huge smile at the top and said, "I did it!" I got the whole climbing gym clapping and cheering by telling the room it was her first day climbing. She blushed. I loved it when she blushed.

Our next day trip was surfing lessons out at Venice Beach. For once, I sucked ass as bad as Brigid and Dan. Surfing was one thing I'd never gotten into. East LA wasn't exactly close to the beach and I didn't have money for a board when I was young. It didn't matter. Learning together made it ten times more fun. My knee did better than I expected. Probably because I spent most of the day paddling out or getting dumped in the water. We had a blast that day. As proof, I had the smiling pictures of the three of us standing in front of our boards with our arms crossed like the Lords Of Dogtown. I had some 8x10s printed and framed. They sat on the bookcase in my office next to the Harry Potter photo from Universal.

Another trip we took was to a gun range. Talking Brigid into that was nearly impossible. Dan was dying to do it. The guy behind the counter told her kids younger than Dan shot at the range all the time. That convinced her and she let Dan fire a .22 revolver. After she knew it wouldn't blow up in his face, I convinced her to let him shoot a .38. He loved it. Damn good shot too.

Probably my favorite thing was hitting up the waterslides out at Blazing Waters in San Dimas. It was crazy fun. Dan was a bit scared of the high speed slides like Tower Falls, which got you going almost forty miles an hour, but I boosted his confidence to the point he went for it. Loved every second of it. The thing I loved most was seeing Brigid in a one-piece. She rocked that simple swimsuit like nobody else. It had been a few weeks since we'd last had sex, so seeing her in a wet bathing suit made it damn hard to honor our deal, but I enjoyed the tease. Half the time I was staring at her ass hanging out just right or her nips poking through the front of the suit. She caught me staring but she liked it. Like I said, it was a long hard day. Really fucking hard. I went home that night and fucked the shit out of my hand three times before I could sleep. Pictured that perfect ass of Brigid's the entire time. Only 49 weeks and 3 more days until I hit that ass again for real. Yeah, I was counting. But I could wait. I already knew what I was missing and I wanted it back real bad.

A couple times, I considered sexting with her, but I didn't want to bend the rules even an inch. Sure, it would've been a great way to blow off steam and blow my load, but I didn't want to tempt either of us.

When I wasn't with her, I was taking it easy at home, waiting for my knee to be ready for surgery. Spent that time putting the finishing touches on the wood carving of the three lions sitting in clover: papa, mama, and the baby. I couldn't decide when to give it to her. At the end of a year? Now?

I'd figure it out.

All the swelling on my knee was completely gone. It was getting time to have my surgery. Yes, I had adapted to the chill life of teaching classes at the dojos all over town, staying home with my wood carving, or hanging with Brigid and Dan. But I was getting antsy thinking about my next fight. People were talking like I'd never fight again. They were wrong. Those who weren't, wanted a shot at my title. Offers were coming in from the WMAA to set me up with various opponents after my rehab. I told them to be patient. The fans wanted a good fight, not one with me limping around the cage. I needed to be fully healed going in. That meant an entire year of rehab after surgery.

By then, Brigid and I would be back to some serious fucking.

I couldn't decide which I wanted more, the fighting or the fucking.

Either way, a year from now, my life was going to be way different from what it was at the moment. Brigid and I would be that much closer, and my knee would be ready to rock.

I was looking forward to it.

Chapter 27

BRIGID

"I did a little digging on your boyfriend Lion Maxwell," Donald said pettily.

"He's not my boyfriend, Donald. We're just friends," I growled.

Not officially. Not even theoretically. Lion was a man I was friends with who I'd once had crazy amounts of incredible sex with. Sure, the sex stopped only a few weeks ago, but it was ancient history as far as I was concerned, almost like it never happened, which absolved me of all guilt. I wished things were different, but I could deal. Although we'd made a commitment to be together a year from now, that didn't mean anything until it actually happened. As far as Donald was concerned, it meant Lion and I were just friends. That was all Donald needed to know. As far as any medical ethics committees went, there was nothing to talk about.

"Did you know that your friend is a two time felon?" Donald expected me to be shocked.

"Yes." I rolled my eyes.

"And you're okay with that?"

At the moment, we were at his parents' house in Beverly Hills in the spacious backyard. I was here to pick up Daniel. The modern Tuscan style house with its columns and brick driveway and red tile roof was large by any standards. By LA standards, it was palatial, a sprawling complex. The Wrights had done well for themselves in the insurance business.

I took a moment to consider my words before responding, and I watched Grandpa Ronald playing tennis with Daniel on the Wright's backyard tennis court. Ronald was lecturing Daniel on how to improve his backhand.

"You're starting your swing too late," Ronald grumbled, exasperated. He had the same annoying tone of superiority and disappointment I'd heard frequently from Donald during our marriage.

"I'm trying," Daniel groaned.

The back and forth exchange of Ronald's complaints and Daniel's frustration had been going on for ten minutes and it was driving me crazy. I wanted to say something, but nobody told Ronald Wright what to do. Every time I had tried in the past, he would smile at me and act like I was speaking a foreign language he couldn't understand. It was a very effective tactic.

Meanwhile, Daniel wasn't having any fun on the tennis court, unlike when Lion taught him things.

Years ago, I'd grown used to Ronald and Donald's annoying know-it-all approach to life and accepted it as the norm. At times like this, I thought of them as Ronald McDonald, the biggest ass-clown in town. I'd also dubbed Donald the Frown Clown because it was his most frequent facial expression. But now, hearing both Wright men parading their arrogance in my face at the same time was suddenly incredibly irritating.

"Well?" Donald said. "Aren't you going to say anything about your felon boyfriend?"

I wanted to say, *Why don't I invite my prison boyfriend to come over here and make you his bitch? While he's at it, he can give your dad lessons in reaming someone. Oh, wait. Your dad is already an expert at that.* I smirked briefly before saying, "It was ten years ago, Donald."

"Once a criminal, always a criminal."

"That's not true. He served his time."

"And you think that didn't have an effect on him?"

"Of course it did. But that doesn't make Lion a bad person. He learned from his mistakes."

"But did you?"

"What's that supposed to mean?" I snarled.

"It's supposed to mean you've probably got your head buried so far in your work you're missing what's in front of your face."

"Oh, what? Like you?" We both knew it was true, but I wouldn't admit it when he was lecturing me.

"No, Brigid. I was thinking about our son. And the influence this criminal is having on him."

"What influence?"

"The one where he took our son to a shooting range? Or were you not there for that? You're not leaving our son alone with the criminal, are you?"

"Stop calling him that, Donald. And, I was there at the shooting range. It was perfectly safe." Once I saw how Lion walked Daniel through all the safety precautions step by step, I was okay with it. Donald was trying to find petty reasons to criticize Lion. "And he's not a criminal. He *was* a criminal."

He sneered, "Is there a difference?"

I sneered back, "Are you a child?"

He frowned his Frown Clown frown. "You don't have to go name calling, Brigid."

"I wasn't. It was a serious question. Are you a child?"

Confused, he chuckled. "I don't see your point."

"Please answer me, Donald," I said calmly. "Are you a child? I should say, are you *still* a child?"

"No. I'm an adult."

"But you were a child. At one point."

"How is that at all relevant?"

"It's relevant because you used to be a child. Now you're not. You're an adult. Lion used to be a criminal. Now he's not."

"It's not the same thing."

"It's not? Prove it."

He opened his mouth to argue, then deflated. "I'm not going to play your logic games, Brigid." One truth in our marriage: I could always out-argue Donald and he knew it.

"It's not a game, Donald. Lion changed. He's not the person he was back then. Look at how many kids he helps for free. I don't see you out in the world donating your time to charity."

He smiled smugly. Donald was generous with his family and friends, but he didn't do anything actually charitable that I knew of. "Charity has nothing to do with the people you're exposing our son to."

"It does when the person in question is charitable and a good person."

He shook his head. "I'm not going to argue with you, Brigid." *Good, because you're already losing.* "But I don't think you should allow our son to spend time around Lion Maxwell. Is that clear?"

"Do you want me to pull him out of karate class?"

"Maybe we should."

On the tennis court, Daniel hit the ball straight into the net. Ronald shook his racket in the air. "No, Daniel! Not like that! You need more wrist! Like this! More! Wrist!"

"I was using my wrist!" Daniel moaned.

I scowled and mumbled to myself, "Maybe we should have your dad teach him karate."

"What did you say?"

"Nothing. You know Daniel loves karate. He's already made so many friends at the school. You know how hard it's been for him to make new friends in the past two years." *Since the divorce, hint, hint.* "And you want to pull him out because of some nonsense concern?

None of the other parents have a problem with Lion."

"Maybe they don't know he's a felon."

Maybe no one knows you're an asshole except me. No, anybody who knows you knows you're an asshole. Except maybe yourself. "That's because it's a non issue to everyone except you, Donald."

"Maybe they don't know."

I suddenly tensed up. "Do you plan on telling them?"

He shrugged but smiled with superior joy.

"You wouldn't."

He smiled even bigger.

"You would sabotage someone's livelihood because you're jealous?"

"I'm not jealous." Denial from an adult was always *so* charming.

"Lion isn't hurting anybody, you know."

"Except for the men he's put in the hospital in his fights."

"Come on, Donald! Every MMA fighter knows what they're signing up for."

"Who said anything about MMA fighters?"

I froze. Did he know about Lion's fight at Universal Studios? If he did, Lion was in big trouble.

His eyes bored into mine. "What aren't you telling me, Brigid?"

I stared back. If I said one wrong thing, he would know I was lying. Time to make something up and lie my heart out, for Lion's sake. I suddenly remembered Lion's YouTube documentary. "All those fights happened when Lion was a teenager." It was possibly true, but I didn't really know one way or the other.

"But they were violent." Was he still talking about Universal Studios or not?

No time to think. Keep attacking. I scowled, "You try growing up with no parents and no mansion and no money and let's see how nice you turn out."

He couldn't argue with that and he didn't.

I wasn't waiting for him to think of a counter argument. "Back to the subject of Daniel and karate class. It would be a mistake to pull him out. If you do, I will make it clear to Daniel that it was your idea. See how you like being the bad guy for a change."

Another Frown Clown frown from Donald. "Fine. Keep Daniel in the felon's class—" I rolled my eyes at his use of the word felon. "—but I don't want Daniel around Lion outside of class. Do you understand, Brigid?"

"So now you're telling me who I can and can't be friends with?"

"If the person in question is a bad influence on our son, I will."

"Oh really. Then I hope you don't have any female friends I might not approve of."

"Why is that, Brigid?" His tone was slightly menacing.

"Because, Donald, if they don't meet my requirements, then I will most certainly be telling you not to be friends with them."

His face soured. "You wouldn't dare."

"Oh, I would," I growled. "So, tell me, Donald. Do you have any women friends I should know about?"

"That's none of your business."

I laughed. "Please, Donald. Don't be so blatantly hypocritical."

"What?"

"We are not going to have a double standard. If you want to run background checks on the people in my life, I will need to run background checks on the people in yours. So you either tell me who you're associating with, or I will hire a private investigator to follow you and find out for me." The nice thing about being a doctor was I did have money for such things, but I immediately regretted saying it. I didn't like to threaten anyone and I was provoking Donald and I knew it. I didn't want to escalate things. I wanted to defuse them. The glory of getting divorced was it meant you didn't have to fight with your spouse unless you chose to. I chose not to.

"Now wait a second, Brigid." He was angry.

I heaved a sigh. "Forget I said that. I'm not going to hire anyone. And I won't tell you who your friends can or can't be. But you won't tell me who my friends can be either. Agreed?" Being mature was usually the most effective solution to any argument.

He grimaced. "You've changed, Brigid. For the worse. You were never this disagreeable."

"Of course I've changed, Donald. You divorced me. Did you think you'd get everything your way afterward? Forget I said that. I'm doing my best to work with you here. When it comes to Daniel, what's best for Daniel comes first. Not what you want and not what I want. But no man is going to tell me how to live my life, especially not my ex-husband."

Donald had nothing to say to that.

Finally.

Chapter 28

BRIGID

"This is better than Disneyland?" Daniel asked doubtfully.

"I was wondering the same thing," I chuckled.

Lion laughed. "Trust me, guys. Yosemite is one of the coolest places on earth. And it's practically in our backyard. By this time tomorrow, you'll be asking me why you didn't go camping here sooner."

I had never been camping before. Neither had Daniel. I had told Lion as much when he suggested it. He'd said that was the perfect reason for us all to go. Since he had been camping and we hadn't, I told him he'd have to figure everything out. True to his word, he showed up at my condo this morning before the sun came up with a car full of camping gear. Daniel and I had piled into his Range Rover, still half asleep.

Five hours later and here we were, driving into Yosemite Valley. The view was breathtaking. Tall majestic mountains climbed up on either side of the valley. Lush green trees in every direction stood tall. So different from the strip mall and asphalt vibe of Los Angeles.

"Where's all the smog?" I joked. "The sky is absolutely blue."

"Clean air and high altitude will do that," Lion said, satisfied.

With the windows rolled down, the fresh scent of the outdoors was intoxicating. "I could get used to this."

We slowed to a stop at a stop sign on the narrow road and Lion looked at me, that adorable grin on his face. "Me too."

I knew he was talking about more than the clean air.

"Me three," Daniel giggled from the backseat.

We parked in the lot for Camp 4, which Lion explained was the heart of the rock climbing world back in the day. Campers and climbers still came here every year to scale the infamous El Capitan, Half Dome, Glacier Point, Church Bowl, Knob Hill, and so many others. They also came to tackle any of the hundreds of bouldering "problems" as they were called.

"What is bouldering again?" Daniel asked.

"That's when you climb on big boulders without ropes," Lion said.

"Are we going to be doing that?"

I said, "Not without ropes, we aren't."

"Don't worry, Brigid. We won't do anything dangerous."

After we parked, we got in line at the campground kiosk to register with the ranger. We lucked out and got one of the last available campsites for the day. Lion suggested we set up camp before we did anything else, so we carried all the gear from his Range Rover to the campsite. Other people were already set up, or in the process of setting up.

Lion unpacked a dome tent and started assembling the pieces. He got Daniel involved with the process. I watched while Lion showed him how it all went together.

"Are we all sleeping in that little thing?" I asked.

"Nah. This is my tent. I brought another one for you guys." He held up the red vinyl bag. He and Daniel set that one up too.

"Do I get my own tent too?" Daniel asked.

Lion smiled at him. "You and your mom are sharing this one, Dan the Man."

He groaned. "Do I have to sleep in the girls tent?"

"You wanna trade, bud? I'll sleep in the girls tent with your mom, you can sleep alone in the guys tent?" Lion winked at me.

Daniel and I both blurted, "No!"

Lion laughed. "Sounds like you two are bunking together."

"But Mom is so boring!"

"I'm not boring!"

Lion chuckled. "Your mom is gonna feel all alone if you make her sleep by herself. Maybe you oughta plan on sleeping with her to protect her."

"From what?"

"From any bears that might attack during the night."

Daniel brightened at the idea. "Bears?"

Was Lion kidding?

Lion nodded seriously. "Yup. There are black bears all over the park. That's why we have to put all our food and toiletries in these metal food lockers." Lion pointed. The lockers were brown painted steel boxes set into the ground and placed all over the campground in rows.

"Bears!" I gasped. "You didn't say anything about bears. Are we going to be safe in these flimsy tents?"

Lion winked at me, "If Daniel protects you, you'll be fine."

"I don't know…" I said, worried.

"Relax, Brigid. The only thing the bears want to eat is our food. They don't want to eat you. The lions on the other hand…" He smirked at me.

"There are lions here?" Daniel gasped, excited. "Where?! I want to see one!"

I smirked back at Lion. "Why don't you explain it to him."

"I was joking, bud. I'm the only lion here."

Daniel grimaced, "That's boring."

I sneered at Lion. "Did you hear that? Lions are boring."

"I wasn't the one who made the rules." He gave me a long look.

For a second I thought he was pouting about our "friends only" agreement, but his playful grin was proof he took it all in stride.

After everything was set up, we had a quick snack. Daniel was antsy to watch the climbers who were on the big boulder in the middle of Camp 4. Lion said it was the Columbia Boulder, which had the world's most famous bouldering problem, a route called Midnight Lightning. The start was marked by a white painted lightning bolt near the bottom of one corner of the big granite rock.

"I wanna do that!" Daniel said while watching some climbers, both men and women, work their way up the rock like it was nothing. "Those guys look like Spider-Man!"

"Pretty much," Lion said.

It was true. To get past the overhanging ledge ten feet off the ground, the climbers all did variations on a difficult move that looked a lot like a Spider-Man pose with legs spread wide.

"I don't know, Daniel. It looks pretty hard." Unlike the climbing gym Lion took us to in Burbank, there were no colorful handholds and no belaying rope. In fact, I couldn't see any handholds at all. Unless you considered a ripple in the rock a handhold.

"Lion, can you do it?" Daniel asked a few minutes later when the other climbers were all resting.

"We'll find out," he grinned and sat down, unzipping a small knapsack and pulling out rock climbing shoes. A minute later, he stood at the base of the boulder.

Earlier, the climbers who'd managed to complete the route finished in a few minutes. It wasn't a long climb. They made it look easy. Those who hadn't finished usually dropped off while attempting the overhang, landing on a big foam pad placed in the dirt below. I knew Lion was a good climber, but I wasn't sure how good, especially with his torn ACL.

"Can you do it with your brace on?" I asked.

"I should probably take it off." He unstrapped it then belted a chalk bag around his waist and went to work. The first attempt, he dropped to the mat after only making it halfway. When he landed, he rolled dramatically right off the landing pad and into the dirt.

"Are you okay?" I rushed up.

"Yeah. Just rolled out of the landing to protect my knee." He didn't look entirely sure.

"Is this really a good idea?"

He grinned. "You doctoring me?"

"No. I'm being a concerned friend."

"Don't worry. I'll be fine." His attitude was exactly what I expected. Times like this made me worry about how he would handle the crushing disappointment that was the reality of rehab for professional athletes. Would he over do it in an attempt to make the process go faster and damage the tendon graft? Or would he accept it for what it was and take his time? I didn't want to think about it.

Lion tried the boulder again. When he got close to the overhang, I held my breath, hoping he wouldn't slip and fall again. If he did, he might not be able to land on his good knee. If he wasn't careful, he could easily land on his head. From ten feet up, such a fall could kill a man or at the very least break his neck and cripple him for life. Lion was clearly unconcerned about falling. As he extended his legs and pulled himself up to the next hold while leaning backward, his arms bulged and started to shake. He was going to lose his grip and fall.

Every muscle in my body was locked tight with fear. I wasn't even breathing. One of Lion's hands suddenly slipped. I gasped. Slowly, he got his fingers back on the hold. At that moment, I swore to myself: if the fall didn't kill him, I would the second he was back safely on the ground.

Lion shifted his bodyweight in a dramatic swing and did his own version of the Spider-Man move, both legs outspread, toes gripping the rock face. He shifted one of his hands to the next higher handhold and hooked one leg over the top of the granite overhang, then used his torso to lever an arm up to the final hold. He grabbed it and pulled himself all the way over, easily finishing the route.

I finally released my breath.

The climbers on the ground all clapped and cheered when he smiled down at them. A few whistled. They'd seen him take off his brace.

Lion climbed down off the rock and gave a bow, which got a laugh from everyone. Thankfully, he put his brace back on.

Daniel wanted to climb too, so Lion took us to some nearby boulders that were easy enough for everybody.

"I brought something for you guys," Lion said. He unzipped his pack and pulled out two new pairs of climbing shoes. "These are the same style and sizes you use at the gym. I even got you guys your own chalk bags."

"You shouldn't have," I smiled.

"Yes he should!" Daniel grinned.

We put our shoes on and belted our chalk bags and climbed until our hands were tired and raw from the granite, which was much more abrasive than the climbing gym. It didn't take long for me and not much longer for Daniel to be done. Lion had stamina to spare, but that was always the case with him.

After, we went hiking and saw many of the sights in the Valley, including the majestic Yosemite Falls, the tallest waterfall in the park at over 2,400 feet. The Lower Falls were framed by redwoods. The view from the approach made me think of a tree lined cathedral. The crowd of visitors added a touristy feel to Mother Nature's church.

"This is so beautiful," I marveled.

"Yeah it is," Lion said. *That voice.* He stared at me.

"The falls are that way." I pointed.

Daniel was busy scampering around on the dry boulders near a bunch of people taking pictures of the crashing white water in the distance, so he was occupied. I looked around, scanning the faces of the various visitors surrounding us. I didn't recognize anyone. We were hours away from LA. It seemed unlikely any of these people could possibly recognize either of us.

I leaned against Lion's side.

He stiffened, surprised. "What are you doing, friend?" He said it with amusement.

"Just hugging my friend." I stood to his side, my arms wrapped around his waist. I nuzzled my cheek against his hard pectoral muscle. "How is your knee doing from all the hiking?"

"Not bad. The brace is helping. It'll probably be a little swollen later, but it's nothing I can't ice out when we get back home."

I wasn't going to lecture him about it. "This place is incredible, Lion. Thank you so much for suggesting this trip."

He grinned. "What are friends for?" His eyes glowed with the reflections of the bright sun off the rocks at the base of the falls.

I closed my eyes and inhaled, taking in his scent. He rarely wore cologne, our trip to Naked Sensations being the rare exception. But his natural smell was always intoxicating. I felt myself quiver as my heart started to pound and my blood raced. I wanted this man so badly I could barely stand it.

"What are you guys doing?" Daniel asked, returning from the boulders.

"Nothing," I said guiltily as I broke my hug with Lion.

We returned to our campsite before the sun went down and made dinner on a small portable gas stove that Lion brought. He cooked. Everything was freeze dried, but once you added hot water, it was surprisingly good.

When it was dark, we sat in folding chairs looking up at the stars. You could actually see them, unlike in LA.

"What do you want to be when you grow up, Dan the Man?" Lion asked.

"Spider-Man."

"Me too, bud. What about you, Brigid?"

"I'm already grown up."

"No you're not. You're only grown up if you say you are. What do you want out of life that you don't already have?"

I smiled at him. "I already have it."

He smiled back. "I was thinking the same thing."

Lion told several ghost stories. They were more funny than scary. Daniel enjoyed all of them. When it was time for bed, we went to our respective tents. Daniel and I got changed into our sweats and unzipped our sleeping bags.

"You guys okay in there?" Lion asked from his tent, which was two feet from ours.

"Yeah," Daniel said.

"If you two need anything, I'm right here."

"What if a bear attacks?"

"Daniel!" I gasped. "Don't say that."

"Don't be such a scaredy cat, Mom."

I rolled my eyes.

"Don't worry, Brigid. All the food and trash is in the food locker. There's nothing for the bears to eat."

"What about the other campers?"

"I'm sure they put all their food where it belongs."

We said our goodnights. It wasn't long before I was drifting off. It had been a long day of hiking and outdoor sun. I felt a little dehydrated, but I didn't want to drink anything right before bed only to end up hunting for the nearby public bathroom in the dark with nothing but a flashlight standing between me and any bears. It could wait.

I knew I fell asleep because I dreamt that Lion unzipped our tent and crawled into my sleeping bag with me. Daniel wasn't in the dream tent. Lion and I did dirty things in my sleeping bag. At the end of the steamy dream, he crawled out of my sleeping bag completely naked and fully erect. In my dreams, my fantasy men always had hard-ons. Always.

"Goodnight, my dream queen," Dream Lion said, "I'll be next door if you want me to fuck you again." He zipped the tent shut.

I lay in my sleeping bag, a satisfied smile on my face.

"One other thing…" He shook the entrance flap of the tent.

"Anything."

He shook the tent flap again, but said nothing. He shook the tent again, hard.

That's when I sat bolt upright, awake.

Had someone just shook the tent, or was that my dream?

My skin started to tingle.

The tent flap bowed inward.

Grunt.

Every hair went up on the back of my neck.

Snort.

The tent shook again.

"Mom?" Daniel said sleepily.

"Shhh!" I threw my arms around him protectively. I was half in my sleeping bag, my legs bound. At least my arms were free.

The tent shook again, followed by a growling grunt.

"Is that a bear?" Daniel whispered.

"I don't know, honey." I really didn't. "Lion? Is that you?"

No answer.

Frantic pawing at the tent flap. The entire tent shook and rattled.

Daniel and I both slid to the back of the tent, frightened.

"Lion!" I called out. "Lion! Help! There's a bear outside our tent!"

"Brigid? Are you okay?" He sounded panicked.

Another low grunt outside. It was definitely a bear.

"Shit!" Lion barked and unzipped his tent.

I saw light shining outside our tent and the silhouette of a bear projected against it. I knew that shadows could play tricks, but this bear shadow looked ten feet long. I screamed. "Lion!"

"Get out of here!" Lion roared outside. Stomping noises. "G'wan! Get out of here, you stupid bear! Go!"

"Don't call him names! You might make him mad!" I shrieked.

Lion roared like a beast. Not words, just animal noises.

The bear shadow flickered dramatically as the flashlight moved around outside. I was barely aware of Daniel cringing and cowering in my arms. The tent suddenly crumpled. Daniel screamed. I couldn't tell what happened outside, but I think the bear backed up into the tent and sat down on the side of it. One of the tent poles snapped with a loud crack.

"Get out of here! Git!" Lion yelled.

More flashlight beams joined Lion's and I heard more human voices outside. Several other people were shooing the bear. Finally, the bear pulled away from the tent and ran. Lion's voice faded as he chased it, screaming and shouting.

I was afraid to move. So was Daniel.

"You okay in there?" a random man's voice asked.

"Yeah, we're fine. Daniel? Are you okay?"

"I'm okay," he mumbled.

"Watch out," Lion said outside, suddenly nearby. The zipper ripped open and he shone his light inside. "You guys okay?" I squinted into the light. "Sorry." He lowered the flashlight. "Are you hurt?" He climbed into the tent.

"No, we're fine."

"Damn bear. Some idiot left food out one row over. Saw a huge mess when I chased the bear off. People are cleaning it up right now. But you're okay, right?"

"Why did the bear want to eat us if there was already food outside?" I asked.

"I don't know. Maybe the scent of shampoo in your hair."

"That would attract a bear?"

He sniffed. "You smell like strawberries."

"Why didn't you say anything?"

"Because I can't think of everything. What matters is you're okay, right?"

I held my hand to my chest. My heart was thudding behind my ribs. "I'm fine. Just a little excited."

"Dan? You okay, buddy?"

"Yeah. Did you see the bear?"

"I did. Chased him off. Or her. I can never tell."

"Was it scary?"

"Yeah it was. But you don't have to worry about it now. It's gone. Too many people around."

Sure enough, outside more people had emerged from their tents to gawk or help clean up. Flashlights danced around. Murmuring as the story passed from one campsite to the next.

"I think we're safe now," Lion sighed. "I doubt he'll come back."

"I don't think I'm going to be able to sleep after that," I laughed morosely. I looked at our tent, which was sagging inward where the bear had broken the tent pole.

"We can go to the Yosemite Valley Lodge and see if they have any rooms. It's a short walk from here. Maybe a quarter mile."

"But there could be bears between here and there," I said seriously.

He smiled. "We'll be okay here, Brigid."

"What about my strawberry hair? It's not like I can wash it right now. It's too cold and too dark."

"You can share my tent. There's room for the three of us. It'll be a tight fit, but we can make it work."

"Yeah!" Daniel beamed. "It'll be like a sleepover!"

"I can't argue with that," I chuckled.

We transferred our sleeping bags into Lion's tent, which was more than snug for three.

"I hate to say this," Lion whispered after zipping the flap shut, "but I'm tallest. I should probably sleep in the middle."

"Oh, okay." He wasn't kidding. There was barely room for me to stretch out. Daniel had enough room, but my only real option was to curl up on my side. Because of the way we were all arranged, that meant staring at Lion all night. When we were settled in, I whispered, "Has anyone ever told you how good you look in a sleeping bag?"

It was zipped up to his neck. He grinned, "I thought it made me look like a mummy, so no."

"Do I look like a mummy too?" Daniel asked.

"No, you look like a man-my, bud."

"Man-my," Daniel giggled. "Hey, why do you think the bear was sniffing around our tent? Was it really because Mom smells like strawberry shampoo?"

"Nah." Lion winked at me, "He probably just smelled a fox."

"I didn't smell any fox," Daniel said. "Do bears eat foxes?"

"No, but lions do," Lion snickered, still staring at me.

"They do?" Daniel asked innocently.

I chuckled. "No, Daniel. They don't. Not here in Yosemite, anyway."

"But they would if they were allowed to," Lion added.

"Lions are pretty big," Daniel said thoughtfully. "And foxes are real small. Lions probably eat foxes all the time."

"What he said," Lion snickered.

At times like this, Daniel's presence was ever so slightly inconvenient. I was happy he was here, but if he wasn't, if Lion and I had been alone in the darkness of Yosemite Valley in this cozy little tent, I was certain that this Lion would be eating my fox. I would do my best to moan quietly so the nearby campers didn't hear. If we were to find ourselves taking our sex play all the way to intercourse, I didn't think I'd worry about our lack of condoms.

I sighed to myself.

It was going to be a long wet night for both the disappointed Lion and the disappointed fox, and I wasn't talking about the mountain dew in the night air.

Best to put it out of my mind.

As I was drifting off, I thought about all the fun the three of us had today, and it occurred to me that I'd been lying when I'd told Donald I wasn't sleeping with Lion Maxwell. He was breathing softly and steadily next to me, passed out. Oh well. We all knew Donald had meant sex, and this wasn't even close to sex.

It was something better.

Donald could suck it.

Chapter 29

BRIGID

"Afternoon, Bridge!" Latisha smiled as I walked into the hospital on Monday afternoon. "You look all refreshed. You have a good weekend?"

"You could say that," I grinned. I hadn't kept her up to date on my time with Lion. Yes, I wanted to gossip with her like crazy, but I knew it would be taking a risk. The fewer people who knew, the better.

"What'd you do? Go to the spa? Pamper yourself? You look fresh faced. You get some sun?"

"A little." Being outside all day had been a bit too much. Even with the hat I'd worn both days, I guess all the sun bouncing off the rocks was enough to get a light sunburn. For someone with my pale porcelain skin, it didn't take much.

"It looks good on you."

"Thanks."

I was also worn out from the drama with the bear and sleeping in a tent in general. I couldn't say I woke refreshed the next morning. I'd dragged the whole day. Even after last night's sleep in my own warm bed, I was still tired. Donald had picked up Daniel after dinner, so I had nothing to distract me and had gone to bed early. The extra rest only half made up for my lack of sleep.

Today was going to be a long day.

By the time evening rolled around, I was already jittering from three cups of coffee. It was the only thing that could keep me focused. I hoped for a slow night and a fast end to my shift.

Nothing out of the ordinary for an ECU happened until about nine o'clock. I was standing at the nurses station at the time, entering info about my last patient into one of the many hospital computers.

Latisha muttered, "Look out, Bridge. Here comes trouble."

I turned and saw Donald marching through the doors into the ECU. He was furious.

"You've gone too far this time, Brigid!" Donald growled as he stalked toward me. "What the hell were you thinking?" He wasn't yelling but he was loud enough to attract the attention of several ECU staffers nearby. They turned their heads to watch Donald.

The first thought to cross my mind was, *What the hell are you doing talking to me this way in front of my co-workers?* What I said was, "What are you talking about?"

"You let our son get attacked by a bear!"

I cringed. I hadn't expected the story to get back to him this quickly. I took a deep breath, trying to remain calm.

The ER staff were now all listening very closely, waiting for me to speak while pretending not to.

"Can we talk about this later?" I hissed.

"No. We're talking about this now. We're talking about how you let our son get attacked by a bear this weekend." Donald knew he had an audience. I think that was the point. He probably figured I'd be less likely to argue.

Wrong.

I grabbed his arm by the bicep and dragged him to the nearest exam room and whipped the door closed. Then I laid into him, "You do *not* walk into my workplace and start throwing around wild accusations! What are *you* thinking?"

"I'm thinking you're not denying it, Brigid. Care to tell me your version of what happened this weekend in Yosemite?"

"Not until we address what you just did. Have I ever walked into your father's offices and chewed you out in front of him, barking like an idiot?"

He sneered.

"Have I?"

He huffed. "No."

"Then show me the same respect. Never do that again. Ever. Do you hear me?"

"Don't get ahead of yourself, Ms. Perfect. You put our son's life at risk. How could you let him get attacked by a God damn *bear?!*"

I was still fuming about the way he'd just tried to embarrass me in front of everybody. Luckily no other doctors or any of my seniors or hospital administrators had witnessed it. That would've been a disaster. I wasn't done reprimanding Donald, but at that moment, the old saying "Pick your battles" flitted through my mind. I needed to focus on the battle about the bear attack. "I didn't let anything happen to Daniel, and he wasn't attacked. The tent was attacked."

"And that's better? You're lucky our son wasn't killed!"

"Killed? He didn't even get scratched. Nobody did. And would you please lower your voice? We're in a hospital, remember?"

"Fine. I will talk in a whisper while I try to drag a believable explanation from you about why you put our son in mortal danger."

"First of all, it wasn't that bad. Second of all, he wasn't in *mortal* danger," I mocked. *He wasn't because Lion was there.* If it had come down to it, I honestly thought Lion could fight off an actual bear. Maybe that was ridiculous, but I wanted to believe it. Especially now.

"What about an actual bear attack isn't dangerous?" He had a point, and it put me on the defensive, which I hated. "Or do you think all bears are friendly and cute like Winnie-the-Pooh? That all they want is to steal your honey? At what point did you realize that the bear who was attacking our son wasn't wearing a red polo shirt and a goofy smile?" How had we gone from me lecturing him to him lecturing me so quickly?

"Go ahead and make jokes, Donald. You weren't there. You don't know what it's like to be woken up in the middle of the night by a hungry bear."

"That's right, Brigid. I don't. And do you know why I don't?"

"Because you never go camping."

That threw him off balance for a moment. "That's... right. So what the hell were you thinking taking *our* son?!"

"Calm down, Donald. It was just camping. There were a hundred other people all over the campground in their tents. It's not like we were out in the wilderness." I was briefly aware that I was now defending everything that had happened, all because Lion suggested we go camping. Was he trouble? Or was this a ridiculous discussion? I didn't have time to process it.

"Are you kidding? Yosemite *is* the wilderness! That's why people who go there sleep in tents and cook on campfires!"

"Geesh, Donald. Would you relax? We. Went. Camp. Ing. No. One. Got. Hurt." Yes, I was irritated. Because he was being completely irrational about this.

"This time."

"Ok, fine. I won't take Daniel camping in Yosemite again." I hated that I was conceding to his demands. But he did have a point.

"I'd prefer it if you didn't take Daniel camping anywhere."

"You're over-reacting. Millions of people go to Yosemite every year and no one has ever been killed by bears."

"Bullshit."

"It's not bullshit. It's a statistical fact. It doesn't happen."

"Who told you that? Lion?"

"No! I looked it up myself."

"And let me guess, Yosemite was his idea, right? Because I don't remember you ever wanting to go camping with me."

"You never suggested it."

"Maybe if you had ever made time to take an entire weekend off, I would have."

"Don't start," I growled.

"You *started* by taking Daniel to bear country without telling me first."

"It was a surprise!"

"A surprise? What kind of person takes a young child camping without telling you where they're going?" He said it like we had taken Daniel murdering or to a live volcano to have a picnic in the crater next to the hot bubbling magma.

"It was camping, Donald. Camping! Boy Scouts and Girl Scouts do it all the time! I'm sure Cub Scouts do it too!" I was losing my cool and I hated it.

He shook his head in disgust. "You know what? I don't want you spending any more time with Lion Maxwell."

I winced each time Donald said Lion's name. I was afraid someone in the hospital might overhear. For all I knew, the ECU staff were standing right outside the exam room door taking notes. Was the head of the hospital standing there too? I could easily get fired if Donald didn't stop. If I said anything to Donald, he might figure out Lion was my patient. I couldn't let that happen either. Damned if I did, damned if I didn't. All I could do was take it like a big girl.

"Did you hear me, Brigid? Or are you too embarrassed by your actions to say anything?"

Donald needed a stabbing. Badly. I considered rifling through the exam room supply cabinets for a fresh scalpel. Sadly it wouldn't do me any good unless I killed him, which I would never do to anybody, not even my ex-husband. I hissed in a dangerous whisper, "Yes I heard you. But we already talked about this. You are not telling me who I can and can't be friends with."

"You're right. I'm telling you who our son can and can't spend time with. From now on, Lion Maxwell is off limits when it comes to Daniel. You can spend every waking minute with the man, but I won't have you taking Daniel on any more trips with him. And that's final." He tore open the exam room door and stormed out.

Despite being surrounded by the familiarity of an ECU exam room, I did not at all feel in my element.

More importantly, how was I going to deal with the fallout from all this Donald drama?

Latisha stood in the doorway, looking concerned. "Are you all right, girl?"

"I'm fine. Thanks. Did you... was anyone listening to all this?"

"No. I kept them away from the door."

"What did you hear?"

"Not much."

"Good."

Donald's little tantrum made me look foolish. He should not come here. He should've been a big boy and let us have our discussion in private.

I was over it.

Sort of.

What worried me was whether or not Donald had put the pieces together and figured out that Lion had been my patient, or how close he might be to discovering the truth. If he were to find out and tell someone here at the hospital, I would be in deep poop. As long as I kept things secret, I would be okay. That's when I realized I was standing in exam room 109. The exact exam room where I had met Lion. Donald had literally been standing at the scene of the semi-crime. He had to know. At this point, it seemed impossible that he didn't. But somehow, I didn't think he knew. Yet. Either way, my secret was getting increasingly hard to keep.

Latisha said, "Was all that true about the bear? Was Daniel really attacked?"

"Not really. There was a bear outside our tent but that's it. It wasn't a big deal." I was bending the truth quite a bit.

"I didn't know you was into camping."

"It was my first time."

"So you just up and went?"

"Ummm... yeah."

"Mmm-hmm." She folded her arms across her chest.

"Yup."

"By your own self? Just you and Daniel? You up and went to Yosemite? Just like that?"

I smiled because I was afraid if I said one more word, she would know I was lying and press for details. Or outright guess that Lion took us. Latisha was smart and had a great memory.

"Okay then." She nodded and turned to walk away. Her words trailed behind her as she went. "By your own self. Just you and your boy. Brave woman, taking a chance like that for no good reason. All out in the wild like that, with the lions and the bears. Lions and bears. Oh. My."

Like I said: Lying and secrets?

Not my thing.

I trusted Latisha without question.

But the truth was doing everything it could to break free, and Lion Maxwell was not the sort of secret that could be caged or kept.

Chapter 30

BRIGID

"Lion, I have to tell you something." We sat on the couch at my condo. "Daniel told Donald about the bear attack."

"Oh, shit." Lion's concern was obvious. "What'd he say?"

"He wasn't happy."

"How not happy?"

"Godzilla attacking Tokyo not happy."

He chuckled.

I was trying to make light of the situation. "I think it might be best if you and I don't plan any more day trips with Daniel. At least for a while."

"What? Because of Donald?"

I nodded.

"Was this your idea or his?" Lion sounded irritated.

"It was mine. But I don't like it any more than you do." I was touched that he cared so much. "I just don't want to give Donald any ammunition."

"This is complete bullshit." He jumped up from the couch and started pacing. "We can't let him do this to us."

He said us. Swoon. My heart blossomed with love. It didn't come as a surprise. I think I had been officially in love with Lion ever since Yosemite. But I wasn't about to tell him. It would only complicate things. I could tell him when our year was over.

"I knew that guy was a douche the second I saw him."

"I wish I had," I chuckled. "I don't mean that. If I had, I wouldn't have Daniel. Question: do you ever talk to Donald when he drops Daniel off at karate class?"

"Huh?" He was distracted, his mind elsewhere. Wherever it was, I hoped he was imagining punching Donald's face in. "No. He always hangs back. Just watches Daniel and frowns."

"So you've met the Frown Clown."

"The what?" Lion laughed.

"I call him the Frown Clown when he gets all pouty."

"He must be pouty 24/7 because that dude is always frowning."

"He's probably jealous that you have me and he doesn't."

Lion grinned. "Of course he is. Want me to beat his ass next time I see him?"

"No!"

"Kidding. But I'll tell you one thing about the Frown Clown."

"What's that?"

He sat down on the couch and squeezed my hand. "That guy is a fucking idiot for leaving you. And I secretly thank him for it every single day."

"Thanks. So... about Daniel. What are we going to do?"

"We?"

"Yes, we."

He smiled his adorable boyish grin. "I know one thing. I don't want to stop hanging around Daniel."

I loved this man so much it hurt. "I know. But... things need to change."

"Do you want me to stop teaching his class? I can if that'll help. Robert and Melanie can handle it. Not that I want to."

"It means so much to me that you care." I squeezed his hand.

Our eyes locked.

I desperately wanted him to kiss me.

He wanted the same thing. It was all over his face.

"I hate this, Brigid."

I love you, Lion.

"But if it's what you need me to do, I'll do it. I hope Dan the Man doesn't take it too hard."

"I think it might be a good idea. At least for now."

He ground his jaw together. "I'll do it for Daniel and for you."

"I think it'll help ease Donald's worries. And you can always teach Daniel when he's here at my condo." I still hadn't taken Daniel to Lion's house. That felt like too big of a risk in the Donald department.

"What about outside your condo?"

"I guess we can do stuff. But nothing death-defying or dangerous."

"Okay." Lion brightened. "We can take him to the library. I've been meaning to get that kid reading. Spends way too much time playing video games."

"Yeah he does. The library it is!"

We both laughed.

Did I have to wait a year to go back to dating Lion?

Couldn't I marry him right now?

It turned out that the timing of Donald's ridiculous demand wasn't a big issue. Lion's ACL reconstruction surgery was only a week away. In preparation, I bought him antibacterial soap to use in his daily showers. He was at my condo again when he unwrapped the gift box I'd put it in.

"Did you carve me a soap lion, Irish?"

"Sort of," I grinned as he pulled it out of the gift box.

"It looks like…"

"A bar of soap."

He laughed, "You really made it look *exactly* like a bar of soap."

I shrugged. "Carving is your specialty. Mine is doctoring. You're supposed to use it to keep your skin clear of bacteria before surgery."

"I might need help washing the hard to reach areas," he winked.

"Your cock is not hard to reach," I smiled.

"What about my knee? It gets pretty stiff when I'm around you."

"Are we talking about your *knee* knee or your *cock* knee?"

"Either or. No, both."

"Tempting… but no. You'll have to do that on your own. For now." I smiled.

"Yeah, yeah. You know, in 46 weeks and 2 days, I'm going to take you up on your promise to make up for all the fucking we haven't been doing."

"Is that a promise?"

"You bet it is." His eyes dipped down to his crotch. He spread his thighs on the couch. I couldn't miss his erection tenting his athletic shorts.

I was sorely tempted to pull them down and give him a blowjob. Or climb on top of his cock.

"You're blushing, Irish."

"So what if I am?" I said coyly.

"You're probably fucking wet too."

"*Fucking* wet?"

"Fucking wet."

How was I supposed to wait eleven more months? A better question was, who would know if Lion and I had sex right now? Daniel wasn't here and he wasn't due back from his father's until tomorrow. Lion and I were all alone in my condo. I squeezed my knees together. We had been so good about not having sex.

Maybe just this once.

He was going into surgery and he was going under general anesthesia. Although general anesthesia was safe, and Lion was strong and healthy, there was always the slight chance that something could go wrong. Did I want to refuse us both the sex we obviously wanted because I had given him an MRI and some anti-inflammatories one time almost three months ago?

No.

I put his gift box and his bar of soap on the coffee table and crawled across the couch like a cat.

"What are you doing, Irish?"

"Whatever I want, Lion."

I pulled his waistband down and his cock popped out.

"You aren't wearing underwear, naughty boy."

"I wasn't expecting an inspection, so no."

"You know what happens to naughty boys?"

"Blowjobs. Worst punishment I can think of."

We both chuckled at that.

His cock was hot when I wrapped my fingers around it and started licking. I could already taste pre-cum on the tip. It drove me wild. I massaged his balls while my tongue went to town. His head fell against the couch cushions and he moaned. It didn't take long before I felt him surge and start spurting into my mouth. I swallowed down every drop lovingly, caressing his extra-sensitive head with my tongue until he couldn't take anymore.

Afterward, I curled up beside him, lazily pumping his slackening shaft.

He wrapped his arm around me. "You didn't have to do that."

"I know. I wanted to."

"Good. I wanted you to too."

I leaned up and we kissed. What was meant to be a quick peck turned into something more. He grabbed my hair and pulled it hard. His tongue pushed into my mouth and I yielded to his forceful passion. The next thing I knew, he was on top of me, pushing me down on the couch and kissing me savagely. My legs wrapped around his waist. I worked his shorts down to his ankles with the heels of my feet. My yoga pants were still on. They did nothing to reduce the friction from the hot rod of fire burning and grinding between my legs. He was fully erect again. He dry fucked me through my yoga pants like he was trying to set them on fire.

I wanted him inside me so badly, I was about to tear my own pants off and demand he fuck me.

He suddenly pushed away. "We shouldn't do this, Brigid."

"Yes we should," I gasped, fisting his T-shirt and pulling his chest against mine.

He resisted, his arms flexing. "What about the rules?"

"Fuck the rules," I hissed while peeling my shirt over my head. When it was halfway up my arms, he grabbed it by the middle and used it to push my arms down on the couch and pin them. Between that and his body weight, I couldn't move.

He kissed me hard.

All I could do was kiss back and squeeze his waist with my thighs. And feel his cock rubbing across my clit through my yoga pants. When my head was spinning, he pulled away.

"You like being tied up, don't you?"

I fought against the T-shirt. With him gripping it, the cotton was as effective as handcuffs. "I'm not tied up."

"Oh yeah?" There was danger in his eyes.

I struggled against the T-shirt. "Are you going to do something or just sit there like an idiot?"

"I'm going to do whatever I want to you. Maybe I'll tie you up. Maybe I won't." He grinned. "But I bet you want me to tie you up, don't you?"

"I want you to shut up and fuck me."

"I thought you'd never ask."

"I wasn't asking."

He forced my yoga pants down hard, taking my panties with them. Then his fingers were sliding through my slippery folds, filling me while his thumb circled my clit. "You are fucking wet, woman."

"What are you going to do about it, caveman?" Somehow, I had managed to lose my mind to the moment. Lion always did that to me.

"This..." He grabbed both my wrists over my head and squeezed them hard, pushing them into the couch cushions. Then he settled his weight between my legs and sunk into me, slow and deep.

I lost it. "Oh, God..." It was like the first time a penis had ever been inside me, but not in a first time sort of way. In the best possible "I haven't had sex with the hottest man on the planet who is also the man I love in weeks and I'm dying for his dick" sort of way.

Every nerve cell in my body, every neuron in my brain, and all the ones running up and down my spinal column were suddenly focused on one thing: Fucking this amazing man. With every thrust, I moaned. He did too. Our mutual pent up sexual energy was enough to light up the city of Los Angeles for an entire week. Every time his cock rubbed across my G-Spot and bottomed out against my cervix, his pelvis ground up against my clit and I grunted. Yes, grunted. There was nothing ladylike about it. I was an animal. A lioness. And my lion was inside me. All my rationality had left the building.

At some point, he tore his shirt off. With my arms free, I ripped my bra off and clawed at his back as he filled me. It was the best sex I'd ever had. It was quick, it was dirty, but it was incredibly hot and more intense than anything I thought possible.

This was the dictionary definition of mind blowing sex, because I had lost mine.

Right when I started to come harder than I'd ever come before, he pulled out.

"What are you—" I looked down between our legs, thinking something had gone wrong.

"FUCK!!" he shouted. Cum fired at my face. The first splotch hit my upper lip. "Shit! Sorry!"

"Shut up," I hissed and grabbed his cock and pumped it as he came again and again.

He pushed up on his arms. The muscles bulged and the veins popped like he was trying to escape. I wasn't letting go. His face was a bright red grimace of pure pleasure.

I kept pumping him until he had spilled every last drop of himself onto my stomach. There was a literal puddle. Drops rolled down my sides and onto the couch cushions. I didn't even think about it.

His head hung between his shoulders. He was breathing hard. "That was… fuck. That was… sorry. Shit. I wasn't wearing a condom. I'm so sorry, Brigid. I wasn't thinking. I should've—"

I pulled him down on top of me.

His stomach smeared the remaining cum against my skin. It was a big sticky mess gluing us together.

Somehow, it felt right.

Extremely dirty and even more right.

Just… right.

Now we were literally stuck together.

Chapter 31

LION

"Can I speak with you for a minute, Mr. Maxwell?" The question came from Donald Wright. He had just dropped Daniel off for class at the dojo. Like Brigid and I agreed, Robert and Melanie were teaching Daniel's class for now.

"Sure." I always thought it weird that Donald never talked to me, but after Brigid told me he'd grilled her about sleeping with me, I wasn't surprised. Who wanted to talk to the guy who was banging your ex-wife? Yeah, he was the one who divorced her, but still.

"Can I call you Lion?" He put one hand on my shoulder and held the other out to shake, waiting. He was glad handing me.

"Sure, Don." I knew a power play when I saw one but I shook anyway. I wasn't worried about whatever he had up his sleeve.

"Lion, is there any way we can speak in private?"

"Yeah. No problem. How about my office?" Class had started and they were making plenty of noise, but I liked the idea of having a closed door between Daniel and whatever bullshit Donald was going to throw at me.

"Sounds good."

We walked into the office and I closed the door.

"Have a seat." I motioned to one of the chairs in front of the desk. It wasn't my office per se. It was the manager's office. Pam Schaefer was in charge of managing the Burbank dojo. I just came in to teach. But I knew this wasn't a Pam issue.

Donald sat down. "I'd like to talk to you about my son."

I smiled. "Daniel is doing great. Really picking things up quickly. Robert and Melanie are always telling me how he's so easy to teach. I wish all my students could stay as focused as he does. He'll be a black belt in no time if he sticks with it."

Donald smiled but it was more of a frowning grimace. "Happy to hear it."

"So, what can I do you for, Don?"

Another grimace. "Lion, I'm a little bit worried about all the time you've been spending with my son." The way he said it you'd think he was accusing me of being a pedophile. The only time I'd ever been with Daniel was with Brigid or in class, so I didn't know what the guy was wound up about.

"Okay. Is there some kind of problem?" I was feeling defensive, but I stayed calm. I didn't get where I was by losing my cool when people took shots at me. The fastest way to get knocked out in the cage was to go into an uncontrollable rage. Part of me wanted to go there, but I knew it was better to wait for Donald to show his hand. Then I could bite it off.

"That's what I wanted to talk to you about."

"So what's the problem?"

Donald smiled, this time for real. But it was an angry smile. He laughed, also angry. His face was red. "You took my son to Yosemite. He was attacked by a bear. You took him to a shooting range. You take him rock climbing. You put his life in danger on a regular basis. What the hell are you thinking? He's my son."

"He's Brigid's son too. I don't make her do anything she doesn't want to. Same with Daniel. He wants to do the stuff we do."

"Are you saying I'm not a good father? Not man enough for my own son?" He was trying to stay calm, but I could tell he was on the edge of losing it. This guy cared about his kid. I could respect that.

"I wasn't saying that. Take a deep breath, Don. You're taking things all wrong."

"Don't tell me what to do."

"I'm not telling you to do anything."

His index fingers were both flicking crazily in his lap. Weird. If I didn't know better, I'd say he wanted to jump over the desk and strangle me. He might try, but he wouldn't succeed. "What you did is unacceptable, Mr. Maxwell."

I was no longer his pal Lion. Now it was Mr. Maxwell. I was okay with that. No reason for me to be uptight too. "Look, Don. About the bear."

"You mean the one that attacked my son?" His teeth clenched and his lips peeled over them in a tight snarl. Man, he was pissed.

I leaned my forearms on the desk. "The bear attacked the tent. Not your son. Anyway, my point is: accidents happen, no matter how careful you are. One of the families here at the dojo just lost their dad. You know how that happened?"

Donald was confused, his brows knit together. He shook his head uncertainly. "No."

"The guy was crossing the street. At the crosswalk. Some knucklehead was texting while driving. Ran the guy over. Died two hours later at the hospital."

"I'm sorry to hear that."

"I was too. The world is a dangerous place. But I would never do anything to put Daniel in danger."

"But you did."

That was when I knew I couldn't change his mind. You can lead a horse to water but you can't make him drink. You can ask people to change or see things differently, but they won't unless they want to.

"Don, I'm really sorry it happened. But I was there. Daniel wasn't in any danger. He wasn't traumatized either. I mean, look at the kid." We both turned to watch Daniel through the glass wall of the office as he jumped around on the mats and laughed with the other kids in uniform. "I've never seen a happier kid, have you?"

I regretted the words the second they left my mouth.

The look on Donald's face said he did too.

I was basically telling him how awesome I made his son's life. He was probably having hate fantasies about offing me any way he could right then and there. I hoped he didn't have a loaded gun in his pocket.

"And what possessed you to take Daniel to a shooting range?" Donald said it like I had taken Daniel to a bomb factory located in forest fire country during dry season at the height of a heatwave. He was looking for reasons to make me the bad guy.

"Don, it's the same thing as Yosemite. I've seen little kids shoot guns safely all the time. Heck, I teach little kids karate. I know how to keep them from hurting themselves and the other kids. I never put anyone in any danger." Except maybe Don. He was obviously worried about losing his status as Dad.

"Mr. Maxwell, I would appreciate it if you did not take Daniel to any more shooting ranges or on any camping trips or anything else that might put him in danger."

"Already done. Brigid and I agreed we wouldn't."

"Oh," he snorted with ill humor. "You and my ex-wife had a discussion about how you were going to raise *my* son?"

"Yeah, Don."

"Isn't that fantastic."

"Don, you gotta believe me. I wouldn't do anything to hurt Daniel. And I'm not trying to take him from you. If I was—" I almost lost it. I almost said, *If I was, there would be nothing you could do to stop me.* I couldn't go there. That was stirring up the hornet's nest.

"What did you say?" He was seething.

"Nothing, Don. Forgot I said anything." Now I was pissed but trying to hold it in.

"No. Tell me. Finish what you were going to say, Mr. Maxwell."

"Forget it." Man, I was dying to punch him in the solar plexus and watch him think he was dying while his body tried to remember how to breathe. But I couldn't do that. Too much was at stake.

Donald's face was knotted into a ball of confused aggression. I hadn't yielded any ground in this discussion, and it drove him nuts. Heck, I would say I'd gained ground and won the day. His index fingers were flicking like crazy. "Let me be as crystal clear as I possibly can, Mr. Maxwell. I would prefer it if you did not take Daniel any place. Ever."

"What are you saying, Don?"

"I want you to stop seeing my son and my wife."

Whoa. My eyes tightened.

His popped. "Sorry. My ex-wife."

Shit. He had said it. *That's* what this was about. I ran my hand through my hair and leaned back in the desk chair. My first urge was to laugh in his face, *You had your fucking chance, dumbass! Brigid is mine now, so back the fuck off or I will bite your fucking face off!* I knew that wouldn't work. Someone had to be the bigger man here. I took a deep breath, nodding, buying time while I thought it through. "Don, Brigid and I are friends."

He snorted, "You sure spend a lot of time with her for someone who is just a friend."

"So what?"

His brows lowered and his eyes were circling nervously. He wanted to look me in the eyes, but he was afraid to. "I know you're sleeping with her."

"No I'm not." It was none of his fucking business.

Donald looked surprised. He stared at me, pulling his head back so his neck flared around his jawline like a bird puffing itself up. He snorted again. "Do you expect me to believe that?"

"Ask Brigid. She'll tell you."

"Ha! That woman won't tell me anything she doesn't want to. And I know she doesn't want to tell me what you and her have been up to behind closed doors. But I can guess. With a man like you, I'm sure she…" He stopped himself and his eyes darted to the side and he ran his hand across his mouth, thinking about something. Suddenly his eyes lit up. "There's something I've been meaning to ask Brigid, but since I'm here, I may as well ask you. Did you meet Brigid at her hospital? Were you one of her patients?"

Oh shit. Time to lie. You learned how to lie with a straight face damn quick growing up on the streets. I had it down to a science. "No."

"Then where did you meet her?"

"Here at the dojo. For the Grand Opening." It was sort of true.

"Uh huh," he nodded. "Daniel said you did a demonstration in a wheelchair. He also told me you were on crutches the night you went to Universal Studios." Shit. This guy knew everything about me. "Tell me, which hospital did you go to?"

"What?"

"When you injured your knee during your last fight?"

How much did this guy know? "Shit, I don't remember."

"You don't." It was a statement, not a question. He didn't believe me.

Why had I said that? Now I was the one struggling to block his attack.

"That's odd, don't you think?"

"Not really. I wasn't paying attention. My ring team drove me there. Anyway, that was months ago."

"Do you think if I asked Daniel, he'd know?" It was a threat.

I was suddenly pissed he was dragging his kid into this. Then again, it was his kid, not mine. Why did that infuriate me? Didn't matter. I couldn't go telling him what to say to his own kid. It's not like Daniel ever pulled me aside to rank on his dad or give me any reason to hate the guy. Whenever the subject of Donald came up, it seemed like Daniel liked him fine. The only saving grace here was that Daniel hadn't been at the hospital when I met Brigid. It's not like the kid asked me and his mom for our "how we met" story. I just sort of appeared in his life and he accepted it without question. Maybe I was safe. And I knew Brigid wouldn't say anything to Donald. I was gonna take a gamble and stick to my lie. In response to Donald's question, I simply shrugged.

"Tell me something, Mr. Maxwell. Who was your doctor at the hospital the night you went in? I know you went to LA Central because I read about it online. I also know Brigid works there. But you probably know that too." He was all smiles, toying with me.

"A guy named Hackett." There was zero hesitation when I said it. I almost said more about Dr. Hackett but I knew that bad liars loved to talk and that's how they tripped themselves up.

"Good to know." He said it like, *Check and mate.*

Whoops. I should've kept it vague. I'd given him a critical clue. He could call Hackett and ask about Brigid's involvement. For all I knew, Donald was friendly with Hackett from before the divorce. If Donald asked, Hackett might say something. This was bad news. I needed to end this discussion before I dropped another golden egg in his lap.

"Anything else, Don?"

He stood up. "I think we're done here, Mr. Maxwell."

I stood too. "Okay. Yeah." I was suddenly burning with nerves. Felt like a million degrees in that office, like someone had just blown up the bomb factory.

He opened the office door before I could open it for him. He suddenly stopped and spun around.

I nearly bumped right into him.

He pointed one of his flicking fingers up at me like a gun. I wanted to grab it and twist it until it broke, which would be incredibly easy to do. I didn't.

He barked, "Let me give you a piece of advice, Mr. Maxwell. Stay away from my son and my—from Brigid." *He almost said wife again.* "Or you will regret it."

My heart skipped a beat.

He spun again and walked out of the dojo and paced outside near the front windows until class was over and Daniel left with him. The whole time I was watching Donald thinking, *That man just beat my ass and he didn't even lay a flicking finger on me.*

It wasn't the first time I'd taken a beat down. When I was young, I got jumped plenty of times. But that was years ago. Now I was an undefeated WMAA cage fighter. But Donald Wright had just owned my ass and wiped the floor with it.

I honestly didn't know what to do next. I didn't have any power in this situation. I wasn't a stepdad. I wasn't even the step-boyfriend. I was the step-friend. Pretty sure that held no weight in family court.

I needed to talk to Brigid.

We needed to figure this out together.

Then again, telling her might freak her out more. It would certainly give her a reason to demote me from friend to stranger. Because let's face it, was she the type of mother who would put me before her son? No. If Donald made legal trouble for her and it was down to picking me over Daniel, would she pick me?

Nope.

I would never expect her to. That didn't mean I had a fucking clue what to do about this mess. But I wasn't going to let Donald Wright boot me out of Brigid and Daniel's lives without some kind of fight. I just needed to figure out a good strategy that didn't involve me disappearing Donald or kicking his ass. It would be so easy, but no.

I needed to do this right.

Chapter 32

BRIGID

"Don't forget your karate gear," Donald said as he dropped Daniel off at my condo.

"Oh, right." Daniel stepped out of the BMW with his back-and-forth backpack on one shoulder, the one he took between here and the Wright house every other week. He opened the backseat passenger door and grabbed his duffel bag, the one that carried his uniform and sparring pads. It amazed me that my little boy was learning karate. I was so proud of him.

"Hey, Daniel," I smiled.

"Hey, Mom. What are we doing this weekend?" His excitement was obvious.

"I'm not sure yet. We'll have to figure that out." I hadn't yet broken the bad news that our fun adventure trips with Lion were on hold for a while.

"Hey, Daniel? Can you run inside so I can talk to your mom?"

"Sure." Daniel walked into the condo, carrying his bags like a little traveler. I often wondered if he would grow up to be a constant wanderer because of how comfortable he was with going from place to place and sleeping wherever he laid his head down.

"So, Donald. What's up?"

"You tell me. What are your weekend plans for Daniel?"

"I hadn't really thought about it."

He smirked self-righteously. "How about bungee jumping? Or hang gliding? Maybe base jumping. Scuba diving with sharks is always fun. Or does Lion prefer swimming with killer whales?"

"Ha ha. Did you spend all day thinking that up?"

He scowled. "No."

"Actually, I was thinking we'd find the nearest freeway and go play in traffic."

He Frown Clowned. "I deserved that." He took a step back and shifted his weight to the other foot. A genuine smile appeared on his face and he shook his head like he was amused by his own behavior. Believe it or not, Donald was a good looking man when he wasn't frowning or scowling. "Sorry. It's just... all this is so... *confusing*, you know?"

"What do you want, Donald?" I really didn't want to talk to him.

"You really have changed since you started seeing this Lion character."

"I know. For the worse, right?"

"Actually, you look different. You're more tan, for one. But I don't know, you're happier. I haven't seen you like this in a long, long time."

"Thank you." We both knew it was true. The last few months with Lion had been the most continuous fun I'd had since before Daniel was born. That was ten years ago. Ten. Sad but true.

"It looks good on you, Bee." He hadn't called me Bee in five years. Or longer. What was going through his head? Whatever it was, I didn't like the looks of him.

"Thank you, Donald." *Don Juan*. His old nickname. I hadn't called him that since forever. There was no way in hell I was calling him that ever again. Now it seemed like a cruel joke. Add our marriage to the list of ones that fell apart when the sex did. Those old memories made me miserable and I wanted to forget them. "I should really go. I need to get ready."

"Is your boyfriend on his way over?"

"Who?" I was playing dumb.

"Your boyfriend. Lion Maxwell."

"He's not my boyfriend. He's my friend."

"Is your *friend* on his way over?"

"Yes, Donald. He is."

"That's too bad." His eyes traveled over my face like he was searching for something. "You really should wear your hair down more. I like it like this." He reached up to touch it and grabbed a few strands.

I pulled away. "What are you doing?"

His eyes glimmered. He slowly lowered his hand. "Why didn't you wear your hair down for me, Brigid?"

"Because I was busy all the time and had a baby and didn't wash my hair often enough and it was too gross to wear it down. Does that answer your question?"

"I never thought you were gross. Or your hair. I always loved your hair. So bright and fiery. Like you, Bee." Donald's eyes were now definitely twinkling with his desire for sex. It was a look I knew very, very well. *Houston, we have a problem.*

"Donald, you should go."

"What if I don't want to go, Bee?" He stepped toward me.

I backed up into the wall beside my front door. "Donald! Stop!"

He pressed his chest against mine. Before I could get my hands up to push him away, he leaned in for a kiss.

Smack!

I slapped him without a second thought.

"Donald! What are you doing?" I pushed him away.

He snarled, his face red and angry. "The same thing I always did, Brigid. Trying to get you to pay attention to me without it working."

Ouch. It was disappointingly true.

Donald wasn't a bad man. Just irritating at times. But who wasn't after eight years of marriage? The only consistently irritating thing he ever did to me was pressure me for sex. He never forced me. But he pestered me, even when I was exhausted from a thirty hour shift at the hospital. In the end, I was the one who withdrew first. Once again, one of the many reasons why trying to be Super Career Woman Mom had hidden downfalls. Everyone was given the same 24 hours in a day. There was only so much one person could do. Anyone with children knew quantity was more important than quality in the long run. Being there for someone day in and day out made all the difference. A present parent who made mistakes was better than a perfect parent who was never there. The same applied to relationships. In the last several years of our marriage, I was barely there. And when I was, I was too tired to engage with my husband. Looking back, I couldn't blame him or hate him for leaving me. You could argue I had left the marriage first, without realizing it. All because I didn't have enough hours in the day for everybody and I put my husband last.

Donald sighed, "I don't know what I was thinking. We both know you aren't interested. I sometimes wonder if you ever were."

I felt bad for him. "That's not true, Donald." Maybe it was, but I didn't want to make him feel worse than I already had during our marriage. He deserved better.

"Tell me something, Bee. What should I have done differently?"

"How about not divorced me," I smirked.

"No, I meant during our marriage. What should I have done to make you more interested?"

"I don't know, Donald."

"Should I have taken up karate?"

"No, Donald."

He sneered and planted his hand against the wall near my head. It was obvious he wasn't completely over me. I sort of felt bad for him. Sort of. He was making too much trouble in my life to deserve my full sympathy.

"Don't, Donald. You're standing too close."

"I'm not going to try to kiss you again. You should know by now that I can control myself when it comes to you."

Way to make me feel guilty. It was depressingly true.

"What the FUCK are you doing?!" Lion roared as he marched up the walk toward us.

A jolt of jagged fright smacked my chest and I jumped.

Donald turned slowly to face Lion, looking totally relaxed. "How are you, Luh—"

Lion slammed a hand into Donald's shoulder and he stumbled backward, catching the heel of his shoe on the door mat. He stumbled into the condo through the open door and landed on his ass. Lion dove through after him and was on top of him a second later. He already had his fist knotted in Donald's polo shirt and his free hand hung in the air, ready to drop like a wrecking ball.

"Lion! Stop!" I shouted as I ran inside.

"Go ahead, Lion!" Donald shouted. "Punch me as hard as you can! Break my nose! Draw some blood! Knock out all my teeth. I'll be sure to file a police report and take plenty of pictures. And I'm sure the judge will love them when I petition the court to give me full custody of Daniel." Donald's eyes were wild and I knew he meant every word.

Lion still held Donald's shirt in one hand and his heavy fist was about to fall on Donald's face like a battering ram.

"Lion Maxwell! You let him go this instant!!!!" I screamed so hard it felt like I tore a vocal chord. I didn't stop to think about it because I was pulling as hard as I could on the shoulders of Lion's shirt. The collar pulled at his neck like a leash.

Lion growled and stood up, which surprised me and sent me stumbling backward. The back of my head was on a straight trajectory for the doorframe, but I managed to turn to the side at the last second. Unfortunately, I landed hard with my hands behind me. Both my wrists exploded with pain. The first panicky thought that shot through my brain: If I broke my wrists, I wouldn't be able to perform surgery with pins and screws in the bones and casts on both forearms. What kind of physical therapy would I need? How long would I be out of work? If the fractures were severe enough, if there was nerve damage... Panic, panic, panic.

"Are you okay?" Lion asked. Rage and concern fought on his face.

Sitting up, I flexed and rotated both hands carefully, trying to sense any pain through the fog of adrenalin blinding my nervous system.

"Brigid? Tell me, are you okay?" Now Lion was panicked. He knelt next to me, his hand on my shoulder. "I'm so sorry. I just... I was..."

I glared at him. I was furious. How could he?

Donald chuckled. "I warned you. I told you something like this would happen."

I didn't know why, but the sound of Donald's voice ate away at my last shred of composure like battery acid. It was probably a combination of all those years of our failed marriage and his recent actions. I growled, "Shut up, Donald."

He shook his head and glared at me.

Lion was clearly worried. "Are you okay, Brigid?"

I flexed my hands some more and circled my wrists. "I think so. Can you help me up?"

He grabbed me carefully by the elbow and hooked my arm around his neck and stood me up.

Donald still lay on the ground. "Look at you two. Like Bonnie and Clyde."

"Shut up, Donald," I hissed. "I didn't make you try and kiss me. You did that."

"*He tried to kiss you?!*" Lion shouted.

"Relax! Both of you!" I glared at both men.

Donald smirked.

Lion was confused but still angry.

I locked eyes with him. "Calm. Down."

Lion was seething. "Fuck!" He whirled and punched a huge hole in my wall.

"What the hell, Lion?! That's my wall!"

"Fuck!" He spun around and strode out the front door and down the walkway. He jumped into his Range Rover and gunned the engine before screeching tires and speeding off.

"Nice guy," Donald chuckled.

"Thanks, Donald! Thank you for that! Thank you very much!" I was just as angry at him as I was at Lion.

He smirked, "I may have been the first man to leave you, but it looks like I won't be the last."

"Get out of here! This is all your fault!" I pointed toward the door. "Go!"

"Mom? Is everything okay?" Daniel stood in the hallway to the living room, peering around the corner like he was scared to come out. "What happened? Was that Lion?" His eyes found the hole in the sheetrock. "Who broke the wall?"

"Your good friend Lion Maxwell," Donald said sarcastically.

I snarled at him. "Go! Now! This mess is ninety percent your fault!"

"Ninety?" He snorted. "Let me see. Who lost his temper? Who

nearly knocked your head into the doorframe? Who nearly broke your wrists? Who punched a hole in the wall? I'll give you a clue. Not. Me."

I wasn't going to fight in front of Daniel. "It's okay, Daniel. Everything is all right. We just had a little misunderstanding." I hoped that's all it was.

Daniel stared at me, wide eyed and speechless.

"Everything is okay, I promise."

He still stared. I didn't think anything like this had ever happened to Daniel before. His father didn't have a temper. None of the Wright family did. They held everything in. I wasn't sure how Daniel would process all this. I wasn't sure how I would either. No one in my family had a temper like Lion's. It was foreign to me.

Donald stood up and smoothed his slacks. "Now you know what kind of a man Lion Maxwell is. I hope he's worth it."

I couldn't decide if Donald wanted me back or just didn't want Lion to have me. Either way, it didn't matter. Donald wasn't getting me. He'd made his choice two years ago.

Now I had a choice to make about Lion Maxwell.

Chapter 33

BRIGID

Daniel and I sat on the couch watching the Minions movie on DVD. It had become a favorite of his after Universal Studios. I wondered if it made him think of Lion. It sure made me think of him. He was all I could think about while we watched the movie.

The last time Daniel and I had watched the movie together, he'd been laughing and talking with me the whole time. This time he was silent. I knew he needed to process the violence of what had happened before he talked about it. What all had he seen? What all had he heard? I didn't know. But I knew that any amount was too much. He shouldn't have had to witness any of it.

I shouldn't have had to either.

Had I just met the real Lion Maxwell? Did he always punch walls when he lost control? Or did he punch people too? How often did he lose control? You never knew in the beginning. It wasn't until you'd been with someone for a long time that all their unappealing qualities came out and you saw the real them.

One thing was for sure: I wasn't going to excuse Lion's behavior. Donald had been right. No one made Lion knock Donald down or knock me down—it didn't matter that it was an accident—or punch a hole in my wall. Lion did or caused all of it. It was unacceptable and inexcusable. His jealousy over Donald's kiss was simply too much. He should've asked what happened first instead of exploding.

I sighed with frustration.

I didn't know if Lion planned to apologize or never talk to me again or what. But he needed to do something or we were through.

An hour into the movie, Daniel asked, "Why did Lion break the wall?"

"Because he was mad at your father."

"Why?"

That was a tough one to answer. All he really needed were the pertinent facts. "Your dad doesn't like Lion very much."

"Why?"

"You know how sometimes when you're at Heather's house

playing with Josh, and Josh's friends from school are there too, and Josh likes to play with them more than he likes to play with you?"

"Yeah?"

"Do you remember how much that hurts your feelings?"

"Yeah," he sighed.

"It's sort of like that. Your dad is scared you want to play with Lion more than you want to play with him."

"Oh. But I do like playing with Dad. Sometimes. Not all the time. But sometimes."

"Think about how it makes you feel when Josh doesn't want to play with you. That's not fun, is it?"

"No."

"How does it make you feel?"

"It makes me sad."

"It makes your dad sad too. When you don't want to play with him as much as you do with Lion, your dad gets sad."

"Oh." Daniel sat quietly for a while. "Does that mean I need to be nicer to Dad?"

I smiled and kissed him on top of the head. "I'm sure your dad would love that. Make sure you tell him that the next time you talk to him."

"I will. So why was Lion mad at dad?"

"For the same reason your dad was. I think Lion is afraid your dad doesn't want you to play with Lion anymore."

"Does he?"

Truthfully, I really thought Donald would be happiest if Lion disappeared forever. But I wouldn't say that to Daniel. "I don't think so, sweetie. I think your dad is confused right now. The best thing you can do to help is tell your dad you love him and be as nice to him as you can."

"Okay. Can I tell Lion the same thing?"

"Yes. Be nice to both of them."

"I will," he smiled. "Can I tell him I love him too?"

"Who, Lion?"

"Yeah."

I suddenly flashed back to Lion's words the first time we'd had sex: *There's no going back after this.* Truer words were never spoken. I was suddenly scared to death. Was I in love with an abusive man and was only now discovering who he really was? That would be horrifying. Worse, what about my son's feelings? Was he getting attached to a man who didn't belong in our lives? The idea made me nauseous. I didn't want things to be hard on Daniel. He didn't deserve more turmoil than he'd already endured because of the divorce.

I looked at my son. His face was pure innocence.

"You can tell Lion the next time you see him." *If you ever see him again*, I added mentally.

For the first time since it all started, I was questioning everything I'd felt for Lion Maxwell.

Daniel and I went back to watching the movie. It didn't take long for him to start laughing like he usually did. I wasn't laughing at all, but at least he was letting go of the drama. I wondered how Lion was doing. Was he letting go too? Or was he building up a head of steam? Was he getting ready to retaliate? Go to war against Donald? Do something dangerous and destructive? I shivered at the thought.

No, I didn't think Lion was like that.

Well, I *hoped* he wasn't like that.

Was I rationalizing? Was I in denial?

I honestly didn't know. My feelings for Lion were getting in the way. That scared me more than anything. Would my love for him blind me to his darker side? A side that was too dark for me or my son?

I tried not to think about it. It was just too awful.

Toward the end of the movie, I considered calling Lion, but I wasn't sure I wanted to talk to him yet or at all. I'm sure he needed to cool off either way. I had no idea how long that would take. But I did know he needed to be the one to call me if this was ever going to work.

When the movie finished, Daniel said, "What do we do now?"

"I'm not really sure."

"I thought we were gonna do something with Lion." His disappointment was obvious.

"I did too. But I think maybe he needs some time to calm down."

"Oh."

"We can do something, if you want."

He shrugged.

That's how I felt. With Lion suddenly out of the picture, I was at a loss for what to do.

My phone buzzed on the counter in the kitchen. I got up from the couch and picked it up.

Lion: Can we talk? I need to apologize big time. I never do shit like that. I feel like an ass. Call me if you want to talk.

I smiled at my phone.

"Daniel?"

"Yeah?"

"I'll be out front talking on the phone for a few minutes. Will you be okay in here?"

"Yeah."

"You can play in your room if you want. Why don't you get your LEGOs out?" Once Daniel started building with his LEGOs, he was totally focused on what he was doing. I wasn't sure how my conversation with Lion would go, so I wanted Daniel distracted, just in case.

"Okay." He got up from the couch and went to his bedroom.

I walked outside, already dialing Lion and feeling hopeful.

"Hey, Brigid," he answered with obvious relief.

"Hey."

"So, I'm sorry. I mean, really *really* sorry. I totally lost my cool. I shouldn't have acted like that."

"But you did."

"That's not me, Brigid. I'm not that guy. You have to understand. I may be a beast in the cage, but I'm not a rageaholic. There's a reason they call me The Calculator. I don't just throw punches around without thinking."

"Then why did you today?"

He heaved a sigh, but said nothing.

"Can you tell me what happened?"

He groaned. "I didn't tell you this, but Don came by the dojo the other day, and we had a talk. Long story short, he doesn't want me seeing you and Daniel anymore."

"He said that?" I was shocked.

"Yes. Point blank. He even... Fuck. He even called you his wife."

"His ex-wife," I corrected.

"No, his wife. I think it was a, what do you call it, a Freudian slip?"

"Like he wants to get back together with me?"

"Exactly. That's why I freaked when I saw him all over you. When you said you kissed him, I saw red. Actual red. That doesn't even happen when I'm in the cage."

"I didn't kiss him. He tried to steal a kiss. I slapped him immediately."

"Oh, wait." He chuckled. "You slapped him?"

"You better believe I did. I made you a promise, Lion. And I keep my promises. I'm not going to date anyone while we wait for a year. That includes my ex-husband."

"So, you don't want to get back together with Don? Not even a little bit?" Lion sounded so innocent asking, so vulnerable.

I smiled at the phone, "Not even a molecular bit. I want to be with you, Lion. No one else." Did I really mean that? I hoped I did. Otherwise, someone else was controlling my mouth and that freaked me out.

"My sentiments exactly."

I felt a sense of relief wash over me. Relief about what, I wasn't sure. It didn't matter.

"Hey, I know I screwed up royally today, but is there any chance you and Daniel want to hang out?"

"As long as it's mellow and relaxing, I'm game."

"How about the beach? I can grab a sun umbrella from my house, and some towels and a cooler full of food and drinks. Bring a frisbee, a volleyball, a football, any kind of ball you want. Oh, and we can stay out of the ocean. Just in case there's sharks."

I laughed. "Okay. We'll have a Jaws-free day at the beach. But bring your bathing suit. We can at least get our feet wet."

"Sounds perfect. Oh, hey. Brigid?"

"Yeah?"

"I..."

"What?"

"I..."

Racing through my head, *I love you Lion I love you Lion I love—*

"Never mind. I'll call you when I have everything packed and ready to go."

"Okay."

Had he almost said he loved me?

I hoped so, because I was loving him more and more every day.

What was I getting myself into?

I hoped this wasn't a huge mistake.

For everybody's sake.

Me, Lion, and Daniel.

Chapter 34

LION

When we were at the beach that afternoon and Daniel was busy throwing my frisbee around with some other kids, I thought about telling Brigid that Donald had guessed I was her patient. She deserved to know so she didn't get blindsided by him if he decided to tell somebody at the hospital. But if she knew, she might decide to cut her losses now and get rid of me before I made things worse. That's why I couldn't bring myself to tell her. It would've ruined the fun we were having in the sand and sun, and we all needed to relax after the shitstorm at her condo. I had no idea if Daniel had seen any of what happened, but he must've heard something. Unless he wasn't at the house? I didn't know and I wasn't going to ask.

I felt like a douche.

"This is nice isn't it?" Brigid sat on the towel under the sun umbrella. She wore her one piece again and looked sexy as hell.

"Yeah." I didn't deserve her. I didn't even deserve to look at her because I was such a fuckup. "How are your wrists?"

"They're fine. I can't believe Donald tried to kiss me."

Was she testing me? I chuckled, "I can." I gave her a look. "I mean, look at you." Meaning, she was gorgeous. But I didn't feel comfortable telling her that right then.

She knew what I meant. She blushed and turned away to look at the waves crashing onto the sand. She was keeping distance between us.

I couldn't blame her.

Why did I have to hit that stupid wall? Blowing up like a baby in front of Donald had made things that much worse.

I was an idiot.

I was also a liability to Brigid.

Maybe Donald wouldn't do anything.

Maybe.

Maybe he would forget what I'd done.

I chuckled to myself. *Not even.*

Maybe he and I would make nice and we'd be pals forever.

Yeah, right.

I was screwed.

I wasn't sure when I'd tell Brigid about what Donald knew. Eventually. Maybe tomorrow. Just not today. For all I knew, he was driving straight to the hospital to tell them everything and today was the last day I would ever spend with Brigid and Daniel.

I wanted to enjoy their company one last time.

I deserved that much.

Not really.

Chapter 35

Everything went well until the day of Lion's surgery, which was today. No more drama from Donald, and no retaliation against him from Lion like I'd feared. I secretly wished all the drama was behind us and Lion really was the man I hoped.

Sadly, I couldn't be there for him at the hospital because it might arouse suspicion. I didn't want Dr. Hackett seeing me. He was the one person most likely to figure out what was going on between me and Lion.

That morning, I wanted to be at Lion's house with him, but I had Daniel. So I told Lion to call me before he went into surgery.

At 7:30am, he did. I was still in my bedroom with the door closed when I picked up the phone to answer.

"Hey."

"Irish." His voice smiled.

"Are you going into surgery?"

"Not quite. But I'm at the hospital and they already got me in a gown and got the IV going. Oh, hey, I showered with the soap you gave me before I left the house, like you said."

"Good. Did you eat or drink anything?"

"Not since midnight. I'm starving and dying of thirst, but I can deal. By the way, my phone battery is about to die. Forgot to charge it and my charger is at home. So if I suddenly cut out, you'll know why."

"Okay. Oh, did you write yes on your knee?" Putting some kind of word or marking on the knee that needed surgery was standard practice. It prevented the doctor from operating on the wrong one.

"Actually, I drew a big arrow and wrote 'fix this one' above it. You can't miss it."

"Great. Who's driving you?"

"I've got a couple people here for me. I'll be fine. You gonna be there smiling at me when I wake up?"

I sighed. "I wish I could. But we both know it's best for me to stay away."

"I know, I know. The rules. You're right."

I needed to change the subject. "Do you have everything set up at home?"

"Yeah. Got the freezer stocked with ice. Fridge stocked with food. My couch is set up like a bed so I'll be close to the kitchen. I'll have people here all week to help out. You're welcome to come by."

That I could do without worry. "I'll be over whenever I'm not working or with Daniel."

"You can bring him. I miss him." Lion hadn't seen Daniel in a week.

"Maybe I will. I'm just worried about him saying something to Donald."

"Fuck that guy."

"Sorry. I shouldn't have mentioned it."

"No, it's cool," he sighed. "He'll always be part of the equation."

I loved how he said always. I also wanted to say I loved him, but I felt shy. Knowing he was going into surgery, I should just say it. But things had been so complicated lately, I just couldn't. For at least a minute, I tried. I really did. But I was so choked up with a confusion of emotions, nothing came out.

"You okay, Irish?"

"Yeah. I'm fine."

"Hey, I want to tell you something. Before surgery, I mean."

"Oh?"

"Yeah. You know there's always a chance something will go wrong when you go under."

"Oh, Lion, don't worry about that. You're young and healthy. You'll be fine."

"Still. You never know. I've seen too many people die way too young. Shit happens."

"It does," I said quietly. "Can we not talk about this?"

"I want you to know, whatever happens, I fucking love you. Okay?" He said it defensively, like he was afraid of what I'd say.

He didn't need to worry.

I was speechless.

I hated that we were having this conversation over the phone. Had we been in the same room, I would've just hugged him and cried tears of joy against his chest.

"Irish? You okay?"

Yes, I mouthed. The word didn't even come out as a whisper.

"Mr. Maxwell? It's time for your sedative," a voice said in the background. It was one of the pre-op nurses.

"Yeah, just a second," Lion said to the nurse. "Hey, Irish? Are you okay? Did I go too far? I'm really sorry. I should've waited. I shouldn't have said anything."

I didn't know if it was the gravity of the moment, my pent up feelings for this man, or some combination of the two, but I literally could not speak. I sobbed silently.

"Irish? I gotta go. My phone battery is almost dead. I'm really sorry for springing that on you, but I just—"

The line suddenly went dead right before I blubbered, "I love you too!"

Something about the dead connection started me wailing. I didn't get myself under control until I heard Daniel mutter through my bedroom door.

"Mom? Are you okay?"

"Yes, sweetheart," I sniffed. "I'm fine."

I was a mess, but I was fine.

The likelihood of Lion dying during surgery was extremely slim. Extremely.

I was a nervous wreck the rest of the morning. I knew the surgery would be quick, but Lion would be groggy long after. I could've called the hospital and had someone check on him, but I didn't want anyone on staff knowing it was me asking. I could've easily gone in and looked for him in recovery, but that was too big a risk.

I really hated these rules.

They weren't mine.

They were the hospital's and the state medical board's.

So I waited.

I took Daniel to the park for a distraction. While he played and ran around, all I thought about was Lion.

I hoped he was all right.

At the rate things were going, I could check his status on the hospital computer when I got to work in the afternoon. Only a few more hours.

While Daniel swung from the jungle gym, my phone rang.

I ripped it out of my purse.

I didn't recognize the number.

Half-panicked, I answered anyway.

"Hello?"

"Hello?" The strange voice was gravelly, an older man I didn't recognize.

"Who is this?"

"Is this Irish?"

"How do you know that name?" I was fully panicked now. The only person who called me Irish was Lion. How did this person know? Unless—

"I'm calling about Lion."

A hurricane of fear surged through me. "Is he all right?"

"He's fine. Little punchy, but he's fine."

"I'm sorry, but who is this?"

"Dean Jackson."

"Coach!" Lion laughed in the background, his voice a blessing. Thank goodness. "Is that my lucky leprechaun?" Lion was loopy, all right. "Gimme the phone, Coach!"

"Hold on a damn minute, I'm talking to the lady."

"She's a leprechaun! She has four leaf clovers coming out her ass!"

"You gonna have my fist coming out your ass in a minute if you don't shut the hell up and let me finish talking."

"Ass fisting!!!!" Lion squealed laughter.

I giggled, my worries gone.

"Sorry about him, ma'am," Dean said. "He's fine. Still waiting to hear from the doctor, but I think it went okay. Lion told me before surgery to call you up after. Set your mind at ease."

"Oh, thank you so much. Are you going to—"

"Gimme that!" Lion cackled.

"Would you get your damn hands off the—"

"Brigid! It's me! Lion! I love you, babe! I love you so much."

I laughed, happy tears running down my cheeks. "I love you too, you stupid idiot."

"She loves me, Coach! Did you hear that? She loves me! Brigid Flanagan loves me!"

"Would you give me the damn phone?!" Rustling noises as the men wrestled for the phone.

"Dr. Ass Gasket!" Lion chuckled. "How is your asshole? Is it gasketed?"

"I'm gonna have to call you back," Dean said. "The doctor is here. Got a couple questions I wanna ask him about taking care of Lion's knee. I'll have Lion call you as soon as the laughing gas or whatever it is wears off."

"Okay, thanks." My heart was pounding.

"Bye now."

The call ended.

One thought ate away at me like a thrashing school of piranhas: Had Dr. Hackett heard Lion shout my name and say that he loved me or not?

My nerves from before the surgery were nothing compared to what they were now.

Chapter 36

LION

I wasn't sure where I was.

My knee was about two miles away.

I couldn't feel it at all. It was someone else's knee.

Voices.

Dean, Cahill, Brigid.

"We should elevate his leg."

"Can you hand me those pillows."

"Should we ice it?"

"Not yet. When he wakes up."

"I'll get a blanket."

"Thanks."

My mom said, *I'm so happy for you, Lion. Brigid is a good woman. Just the kind you need to keep you in line. Don't laugh. It'll be good for you to have someone strong now that I'm not around. So tell me, when do I get a grandson?*

A second later, it was dark outside.

My knee was being stabbed.

Were they still operating?

What the fuck?

STAB!!

Pain! Pain! Pain! Pain!

"Sorry," Brigid whispered.

I opened my eyes. "Irish?" My throat was dry as beach sand.

"You need to take your meds. Your pain block is starting to wear off." She held a glass of water and two pills.

"What is it?" I croaked.

"Vicodin for pain and Toradol for inflammation."

Normally, I wasn't one for medicine of any kind, but I would make an exception for the hole somebody had blown in my knee. I downed both pills and the entire glass of water and fell back into unconsciousness. Some time later, I woke to a strange voice I vaguely recognized.

"JoJo, this is your final rose..."

I blinked my eyes and realized I was in the living room. The TV was on. Brigid sat on the huge couch near my feet.

I grunted, "Are you watching The Bachelorette?"

She smirked at me. "Do you have a problem with that?"

"We are no longer friends," I chuckled.

"I like this show."

"Can I have another pain pill?"

"It's too soon. It's only been two hours since your last one."

"Yeah," I grinned, "but this show is killing me."

"Boo hoo. You big baby. Romance isn't painful."

"This show is. Everyone says the same shit every show. I'm so excited. He's so amazing. I'm so excited. She's so amazing. I've never felt like this before. I feel myself opening up to you. I'm starting to fall for dumbass number one. Dumbass number two showed me a deeper side today. I'm so excited. It's so amazing. I'm so excited. It's so amazingly scripted."

"Wait. Do you watch The Bachelorette?"

"Hell no!"

"Then how do you know so much about it?"

"I don't know shit about it. Except it's shit."

"Liar."

I chuckled. "Maybe."

"Then you won't mind if I turn it up?" The volume was really low.

"Fine. Go ahead. But if I vomit, it's your fault."

"You love it."

And I love you.

I hadn't forgotten that I'd told her before I went into surgery. I didn't remember hearing her say it back. Maybe she felt the same way. Maybe she didn't. No, that wasn't right. I knew she did. I wasn't sure why, but I did.

More importantly, what mattered was she was here.

Everybody knew actions spoke louder than words.

When The Bachelorette was over, I was sleepy and yawned big. "Is Dean still here?"

"No. He went home when you were sleeping."

"What about Cahill?"

"I sent him home too."

"When?"

"Right before The Bachelorette. His wife called. I told him it was okay for him to leave."

"Why'd you do that? He was supposed to stay here tonight in case I needed something."

"I took the night off."

"You did?"

She nodded. Actions, not words.

"Okay then. Hey, I know you met Cahill before, but what'd you think of Dean?"

"I like him," she smiled. "He's really nice. Much nicer than you."

"What?" I laughed. "I'm a saint and you know it."

She squeezed my leg. The one that hadn't been operated on. It wasn't hard to miss. The surgery knee looked mummified.

"You gonna sleep on the couch with me, Irish? It's big enough for two." The couch was shaped like a big L. Both arms were long enough and wide enough to sleep comfortably.

"Yes. I already got blankets from your linen closet."

"I have a linen closet?"

"Do you do anything for yourself?"

"I do everything for myself. But I don't have any linens. Hence, no linen closet."

"What are these then?" She lifted the stack of folded bedsheets from the end of the couch.

"Those are sheets. I'm pretty sure they're made of cotton, not linen."

She smiled. "You never stop fighting, do you?"

"Nope. I hope you don't mind."

"I'd ask you to fight these sheets onto the couch, but I'll let you off this time."

"I can do it." I pushed up on my arms. My knee burst with pain. "Maybe not."

"Sit down and stop fighting already." She whipped open the first sheet and let it billow down onto the couch.

"It's like a sleepover. Are we gonna play spin the bottle or seven minutes in heaven? How about Twister?"

She smiled. "I think you need to rest." She bent over and tucked the sheet into the back of the cushions.

"How can I rest when you have your ass in my face? The most perfect ass I've ever seen, if I might add."

She rolled her eyes at me. Then she shimmed her ass in a circle.

"Don't fucking do that! I'm not gonna be able to sleep if that's the last thing I see before the lights go out."

She finished making her bed with minimal tease. "I better go change."

"You can do it here."

"I thought you said you wouldn't be able to sleep."

"So I'm a masochist."

She picked up her overnight bag. "I'll go change."

"Hey, where are the cats?"

"Around here somewhere. Dean fed them before he left. Aslan is on his cat tree." She walked out to change.

I twisted on the couch until I could see Aslan. As expected, he sat on top, staring down at me.

Sad you're back, asshole.

"Good to see you too, buddy."

His tail went swish.

"Admit it. You missed me."

Swish, swish. He turned away and stared into space.

"You missed me," I chuckled.

He blinked.

A few minutes later, Brigid returned from the downstairs guest bathroom wearing a Wonder Woman night shirt that went down to her thighs.

"Nice."

"Daniel gave it to me last Christmas. You like it?"

"It's appropriate."

"How's that?"

"What about you isn't wonderful, Brigid?"

"I love you too, Lion."

"What?"

"I said, I think so too."

"No you didn't, you said..."

She grinned and flipped off the lights. I heard her crawl under the blankets on her side of the couch.

A few seconds later, something dropped onto my lap. There was just enough light coming in from outside to reveal a small black ball that started purring instantly. "Hey, Gwen. Missed you, girl."

"Where's the other one?"

"You never know with Tigg."

In the darkness, Brigid and I chatted for a few minutes about this and that. While we talked, something rumbled down the hallway upstairs.

"What's that?" Brigid gasped.

"Tigg. If something bites your toes while you're sleeping, it'll be him thinking they're mice. So you might wanna keep 'em covered."

"Good to know." Her sheets rustled as she shifted them around.

"I'm glad you're here, Brigid."

"Me too. You should try and sleep."

"Yeah, okay."

Right when I was drifting off, she screamed.

"Did Tigg bite you?"

"No."

"What happened?"

"Something touched me."

I flipped on the lamp by my head. "What the hell are you doing, Azz?"

He stared at me, squinting because of the light. He sat on the floor near Brigid's head, one paw hovering above the carpet, not sure what his next move was.

"Were you gonna eat her, buddy?"

"Does he bite too?"

"Naw. I think he's trying to get your attention."

He reached his paw up tentatively then lowered it.

She smiled at him, "Do you want something, Aslan?"

He stared at her for a moment then shifted his body weight several times, getting ready to jump.

"What are you doing, bud?" I chuckled.

"Should I be worried?"

"I think he wants to curl up with you."

"He does?" Brigid liked the idea. "You can sleep with me if you want, Aslan." She smiled at him.

"That cat never sleeps with me."

"Probably because you call him Azz. It sounds too much like Ass. Isn't that right, sweetie," she cooed like he was a baby.

"You're gonna make him a pussy talking to him like that."

She made more baby talk, "You're just a big pussy-wussy cat, aren't you Aslan?"

Sure enough, Aslan leapt up gracefully onto the couch and settled in next to her arm. He did a sleepy blink while pretending to ignore me.

"Traitor," I chuckled.

"You sound jealous."

"Not even. He's just getting used to having you around."

I was too.

<<<<<<<<>>>>>>>

The next day, Brigid took off for work.

Dean and Cahill both came over to help out. Rhonda came by too and brought her family. All kinds of people came and went that day. It felt good to have friends who cared.

The next day, Dean drove me to the hospital to get my bandages changed. I was back on crutches and my knee hurt worse than yesterday. That's what happened when they drilled holes in your bones. Good thing I had that Vicodin.

I sat in the waiting area on the third floor with Dean for a while before the nurse called my name. Dean followed as I wobbled back to the exam room on my crutches and waited for the doctor.

There was a knock on the door.

In walked Dr. Hackett.

"Hey, Doc."

"Mr. Maxwell. So good to see you." He turned to Dean. "I don't believe we've met."

"Dean Jackson." They shook hands.

"Dr. Ivan Hackett. The pleasure is all mine."

I couldn't decide if the Vicodin made Hackett seem like more of a douche or less.

"Let's have a look at that knee." Hackett pulled up a stool and started unwrapping the bandages and gauze and padding. I wasn't sure what to expect, but there wasn't much blood and the swelling wasn't too bad. "The incision site looks quite good. How is the pain?"

"Nothing I can't handle."

"Brilliant. Are you icing it?"

"On and off all day. Twenty minutes at a time."

"Very good. Have you been moving your ankles and flexing your quads?"

"Constantly."

Hackett lifted my knee and gently flexed the joint. "You've got a good range of motion already and swelling is minimal. I think you'll be ready to start physical therapy in a few days."

"Can't wait." I meant it. Time to get this show on the road so I could finally get back to serious training.

"I'll have the nurse bandage you up with a lighter dressing. Always a pleasure, Mr. Maxwell." We shook hands and he turned to go then stopped. "One other thing."

"Sure, Doc."

"I was just wondering. If I'm not mistaken, when I stopped by the recovery room after surgery, you said something about Dr. Brigid Flanagan." His eyes drilled into me.

"I did?" After they wheeled me into surgery, I didn't remember much until I woke up back home.

"I do believe you did." He was acting like my pal, but something in his voice put me on edge.

Better to play dumb. "Who is she again?"

"Dr. Flanagan was the doctor who saw you the night you first came to our ECU. You asked me to replace her."

I nodded bashfully. "Right. Her. I almost forgot about her." I tried not to lay it on too thick.

"Did you? How very strange. Because I could swear you said you were in love with her. And she with you."

"No shit?" I played it off expertly. "Why would I have said that? I barely remember her. It doesn't make any sense."

"You see, that's the thing, Mr. Maxwell. It didn't make any sense to me either."

"I was flying pretty high after surgery, Doc. I'm sure I said all kinds of crazy shit." I snorted a laugh and glanced at Dean. He knew the details so he wasn't saying a word. Kept a stone face. Totally inscrutable.

"Indeed." Hackett's eyes were pinned on mine. He was trying to get me to talk.

Wasn't gonna work. I shrugged. "I can't help ya, Doc."

"You and her aren't...." He arched an eyebrow, waiting for me to answer, trying to draw me out. Did this guy think he was Sherlock Holmes or some shit?

I waited him out. *Elementary, my dear Douchebag.*

"You and her aren't perhaps…" He wasn't letting go.

"Aren't what, Doc?" I turned on the mad dog eyes. Just a bit. I didn't want to scare him. But he was making me nervous.

His wheels were turning. "Oh, nothing." He laughed it off. "Just another one of my silly ideas."

Bullshit.

He knew.

Now I was in double trouble. Not only did Donald Wright know, but Sherlock Hackett had somehow figured it out.

Actually, I wasn't the one in trouble. Brigid was. Nothing would happen to me if the hospital found out. But Brigid would get screwed from both ends.

The odds of keeping Brigid in my life just got worse.

When I walked in here an hour ago, I'd thought my knee hurt bad. But that pain was nothing compared to the fear tightening my guts on the way out.

Chapter 37

BRIGID

Over the next several weeks, I was at Lion's house as often as possible. The first few days he needed a lot of help with preparing food, laundry, looking after the cats, etc. I hovered over his wound care like a mother hen, but Dr. Hackett had done good work. The incisions were healing nicely and there was no sign of infection. Within a week, Lion was already starting therapy. I knew the physical therapy protocols for ACL reconstruction, and I grilled Lion about every step. Based on his answers, I was confident his PT knew what they were doing and Lion was in good hands. I would've liked to watch over the process, partially out of interest and partially out of concern, but I didn't want to risk anyone at the hospital finding out, especially not Dr. Hackett.

Lion and I continued our frustrating holding pattern of not dating. His recovery was a good excuse to get away from worrying about it for a while. Rehab was his focus now. For the next few months, everything would be about getting his knee back to what it was before the injury.

For me, life was business as usual. Work and Daniel. His school was starting soon, so I wanted to do as many fun things as we could in the time we had. Sadly, much of our activities were done without Lion.

One of those activities was spending time with Grandma Linda. Unlike Grandpa, Grandma didn't work. She had loads of free time. Ever since Lion came along, she hadn't seen Daniel as much as she was used to. So she suggested a trip to the Will Rogers Polo Club. She wanted Daniel to get some culture.

The day of the trip, I drove to the Wright Estate in Beverly Hills. I still had a remote in my car for the gate, which I used. I parked and knocked on the front door. As always, a maid answered. The Wrights had a full time staff that kept the house up.

"Good morning, Miss Flanagan, I'm so happy to see you." Maria Flores the maid wore a traditional maid's uniform with the white apron. The dress wasn't the standard black because Linda thought black made her home feel like a funeral parlor. Instead it was a bright lemon yellow. Maria had been working for Linda for years. When I had lived here before the divorce, I saw Maria every day. I hadn't seen as much of her in the past several years, but I considered her a friend.

"Good morning, Maria." I hugged her. "Good to see you too. How are the kids?"

"Very good, Miss Flanagan." She was always impeccably polite. Linda demanded it.

"How is Francisco?"

"Very good."

"Is he still doing construction?"

"Yes. Now Alejandro is helping him." Alejandro was her eldest son.

"How old is he now?"

"Eighteen."

"My goodness."

"My little mijo is already a man. Can you believe it?"

"He was eight when I met him. Time sure flies, doesn't it?"

"Yes," she smiled.

I had watched Alejandro and her other children grow up in the photos Maria kept on her phone. On a few occasions, the Flores family had been invited to the estate to celebrate holidays like the Fourth of July or Thanksgiving. But never for Easter or Christmas or any "family" holidays. Linda had distinct opinions about that. I had never heard Linda call Maria or any of the house staff "the help" but she never called them friends either. They were her employees and she treated them as such. Linda wasn't exactly a classist bitch, but she liked to think of herself as above other people. If you worked for her, she was above you. I was grateful that I didn't. As her ex-daughter-in-law, I dealt with other burdens.

"There you are, Brigid!" Linda waltzed out of the kitchen and glided across the intricate Italian marble floor in her flowing white summer suit, complete with an outrageously large white straw hat. Her makeup was perfect, as always. "So good to see you." She air kissed both my cheeks.

"Good to see you too, Linda. Where's Daniel?"

"Probably in his room playing video games. Maria, will you be a dear and go fetch him?"

"Yes, Mrs. Wright." Maria did a quick curtsy before walking upstairs. After all these years, I still couldn't believe Linda's female staff were expected to curtsy for their queen.

"Are you ready to enjoy some sunshine, Brigid?"

"I am."

"Good. I see that for once, you have some color on you. The outdoor look suits you." She meant my tan, but coming from her it sounded vaguely racist. I didn't know why, it just did. She looked me up and down like I was nothing more than a collectible doll she was considering adding to her collection. "The porcelain look never goes out of style, but it is summer." That meant I was supposed to be tan. Like her. *Supposed* to. I didn't know who the invisible judging panel was that graded these things, but Linda obviously knew them personally and cared about what they thought more than I ever did. "Love the outfit, by the way."

"Thank you." Knowing Linda as I did, I had picked out an appropriate outfit in advance. Despite my minimal tan, I wore a short sleeve full length floral print dress to block out the sun, and sandals. I'd even worn a hat. Not as large or outrageous as Linda's, but when was anything as outrageous as she was? Linda meant well, but she was strange. "Is Ronald coming with?"

She waved her hand. "You know Ronald. It's Saturday morning, so he's at the country club. Probably starting a second round of golf as we speak."

"Of course."

Daniel thudded down the stairs. "Hey, Mom!"

"Don't run, Daniel," Linda chastised. "Life isn't a horse race."

"Sorry," Daniel said and slowed to a walk. When he reached the bottom of the stairs, he gave me a side hug. He'd been doing that a lot lately. Slowly turning from a boy to a man.

"Shall we?" Linda asked.

Outside, we all climbed into Linda's Mercedes. The one thing everyone in LA did, no matter how rich they were, was drive themselves. It was a point of pride. When Linda went anywhere, she *always* drove. Nobody took the wheel in Linda Wright's game of life except Linda. Not even Ronald. He may have run their insurance company, but Linda ran the show the rest of the time.

Linda took the scenic route along Sunset Boulevard. When we passed the UCLA campus, Linda said, "It seems like just yesterday that you and Donald were students at the university. Those were good times."

They were. But that was a long time ago.

"What's UCLA?" Daniel asked.

"That's where your mother and your father went to college," Linda said. "It's also where you were conceived."

"What's conceived?"

Linda smiled at me. She prided herself on being progressive. "I'll let your mother answer that."

Gee, thanks. I was a doctor, so I didn't beat around the bush where the birds and the bees lived. I talked about ovum and spermatozoa and fertilization. Daniel was perplexed.

"Here we are!" Linda cheered as we parked at the Will Rogers State Park in the Pacific Palisades. The 200 acre polo field was part of Will Rogers' ranch. His widow Betty had willed their home, the stables, the field, and the surrounding land to the State of California on her death in 1944.

We toured the grounds and had lunch before the first polo match. Quite a few of the spectators attending were in period dress. The men wore classic seersucker suits and the women wore summer dresses and extravagant hats as ridiculous as Linda's. Before the match began, a rider from each of the opposing teams explained the basic rules of the game, and likened it to playing golf during an earthquake. The game itself was intensely exciting. The horses and riders in their colorful uniforms thundered up and down the field chasing after the ball. They routinely bumped into each other while fighting to gain control of it. I was constantly in fear that the horses would trip over each other and someone would break their neck or a horse would break its leg, but nothing like that happened today. There were a few falls, but nothing the horse and rider couldn't shake off moments later. Daniel and I both cheered for whoever had the ball. One of the teams won, but it didn't really matter which because we'd never heard of either.

Between games, everyone took to the field for the classic divot stomp. The kids loved it and the adults helped too. Daniel ran ahead of me and Linda, stomping as many divots as he could back into place. Linda and I trailed behind. Linda did not stomp a single divot. I wanted to make a joke by asking her if she considered it beneath her, but I didn't want to offend her. She didn't know how to joke. As we walked, she sipped champagne while I turned a few divots over with my sandaled toe.

"Daniel is getting so tall," Linda said. "I remember when he was a helpless little infant. It seems like just yesterday."

"I know," I sighed. "I feel like I blink and he's an inch taller."

"It doesn't help that you work so much." This was a constant saw between Linda and I. She never told me outright to quit being a doctor, but she was always reminding me of the toll it took on motherhood. I couldn't argue with her. I just wished she'd drop it after all these years.

I said, "I've been spending a lot of time with Daniel lately. Probably more than I have since the divorce." *Take that.* Linda knew Donald divorced me and not the other way around. When Donald first announced it, I had gone to Linda for advice. She sided with her son, of course, but she had been encouraging at the time. I didn't think she wanted the divorce any more than I did, but it wasn't her choice. Or mine.

"So I've heard. I've also heard you've been spending a lot of time with a new man. Is that right?"

"Sort of," I said cautiously. Linda could be a venomous viper, often striking without warning. Always with proper decorum and refinement, but she attacked without mercy all the same.

"What is the young man's name?"

"Lion Maxwell." I'm sure she knew more than she was letting on. Donald told her quite a bit, especially when it involved Daniel.

"What kind of a name is Lion anyway?" She said it with polite disdain.

"A good one," I smiled.

She smirked. "Are the two of you dating?"

"No. We're just friends."

"That's not the impression I got from Daniel."

"Oh? What impression did he give you?"

"He said this Tarzan character was your boyfriend." The way she said Tarzan was not meant as a compliment.

I brushed it off. "I can see how Daniel would think that. Lion and I have a lot of fun every time the three of us are together."

"There was a time when you said that about Donald." Was she jabbing at me, or just mourning her son's divorce? Considering Linda had been married to Ronald Wright for nearly forty years, it was possibly just that. She believed in commitment. "But that is neither here nor there. What concerns me is the relationship Daniel has with this boyfriend of yours, whom I have not met, by the way. Daniel talks about the man incessantly. Sen-say this and sen-say that. I don't even know what a sen-say is."

"It's sensei. Lion is Daniel's karate teacher. And he's not my boyfriend." Was she trying to trip me up?

"I gathered that. But the way Daniel talks about the man, you'd think this Lion character was living with you," she chuffed.

"He's not living with me." Suddenly I was irritated. "Where is this coming from, Linda?"

She sipped her champagne and left lipstick on the rim of the glass. "Oh, I'm just a concerned grandmother looking out for her grandson. You know Daniel is like a second son to me."

"Yes. And thank you for all that you did to help raise him over the years." I owed Linda in ways I could never repay and we both knew it. "But I promise, Daniel's well being is my top priority and—"

"Are you sure?" She smiled when she said it, crocodile style. Red lipstick splotched her teeth. Despite her fading beauty, the stain looked terrible and brought out her conniving side.

"Yes I'm sure. I think Lion is a good influence on Daniel."

"So is Donald."

"What are you saying, Linda?" I suddenly wondered if Donald had told her about his kissing me. For all I knew, he and Linda were scheming up ways for him to win me back. I cringed at the thought. After two years, I had thought Donald was completely done with me. But I wouldn't put it past him to start sniffing around now that Lion was making a claim. It wasn't like Donald spent his spare time chasing women around. In fact, I wasn't aware of him dating anybody seriously. Maybe he did want me back. I hoped not. But if he did, that would complicate things for me and Lion.

Linda shrugged like we were discussing recipes. "All I'm saying is that young Daniel already has a strong father figure in his own father. He doesn't need another one."

"Linda, I'm not trying to replace Donald. Not as far as Daniel is concerned. Anyway, how could I? Donald has Daniel every other week. He would have him every week if he hadn't divorced me. But he did." *Suck on that.* "And I'm not going to stay single forever. Sooner or later, there will be other men in my life. That's all there is to it. It could be Lion or it could be someone else. Who knows." I said that just to put her off the scent. "But you and Donald need to get used to it."

"So you *are* dating this Tarzan, or whatever his name is?" She was baiting me. Clever snake.

I was so irritated with her, I almost said, *Yes and we're fucking and it's so much better than it was with your son. Not that you would know. When was the last time you gave Ronald a blowjob? Or do you have the maid do it for you, you rich bitch cunt?* "Lion is just a friend, Linda." I said it through clenched teeth.

"Is he?" Linda's eyes searched mine, glinting victory.

"Yes, Linda." I was practically growling.

"Then I suggest you keep it that way. For your own good."

She knew something.

But what? And how much? Were her and Donald now both conspiring against me?

"Hey, Grandma!" Daniel shouted as he came running toward us. "I stomped a hundred divots!"

"You did? That's wonderful sweetheart." Linda tossed me a look that said, *Did you notice how your son came to me first?*

At that moment, I wanted nothing more than to stomp Grandma Linda's head into the nearest divot.

Chapter 38

BRIGID

Everything blew up in my face two weeks later while I was at work.

It started with an email from Human Resources. The head of HR wanted to meet with me. The reason was vague. I set up an appointment time to meet that Wednesday after lunch, which meant I had to get to the hospital before my shift.

I did my best not to panic as I walked from the parking structure to the circular administration building across from the main hospital. I was shaking by the time I made it up to the third floor. When the receptionist asked me to wait, I was glad for the extra time to collect myself.

Why was I so jittery?

The reason was obvious.

Somebody here knew about me and Lion. There was no other possible explanation. The only question was, who told them? Donald or Linda?

I had known all along it was only a matter of time before this day came. What I didn't know was what I'd been thinking when I'd agreed to see Lion in the first place. Everyone knew bad girls got punished, especially the ones who fucked the bad boys. I wasn't above the law. Bad people got caught.

So much for collecting myself.

"Dr. Flanagan?" The receptionist asked.

"Yes?"

"Director Badhoff will see you now."

I stood slowly, suddenly light headed. It was fitting. I felt like I was walking to the chopping block. My head was about to roll, and my career would roll right along with it.

The director of Human Resources was a woman named Cynthia P. Badhoff. Fittingly ironic. The only thing that would've been more ironic was if her name was Sinthia P. Badgirl. Middle name Punishes. Cynthia was in her forties and attractive with platinum blonde hair pulled back in a barrette and a fitted business suit.

"Have a seat, Dr. Flanagan."

I nearly fell face first into her desk when I caught my toe on her carpet. I wasn't even wearing heels and I could barely put one foot in front of the other without collapsing. Somehow, I managed to sit down.

This was it.

The beginning of the end.

She folded her hands in front of her on the desk. "Do you know why I called you here today?"

Yes! I'm dating one of my patients! "No. I'm afraid not."

"Are you aware of the sexual misconduct policy here at LACH, and the sexual misconduct policies set forth by the Medical Board of California?"

"Yes." *Because I've been violating them daily for months!*

"And are you aware that both the hospital and the Medical Board take those policies very seriously?"

"I am." *But I sure don't!* I was literally nauseous with guilt. I didn't know why I hadn't spilled my guts yet, but I was well on my way.

"And did you know that sexual intercourse with a patient is a violation of the state's professional code of conduct, and therefore a public offense punishable by disciplinary action?"

"Yes." *Go ahead and lock me up! My red hair and green eyes will go great with an orange jumpsuit! Ha ha ha ha!*

"Uh huh," she said strangely, like maybe I wasn't taking this seriously. "And were you aware of the sexual misconduct lawsuit filed against LACH three years ago?"

"I was." Everybody who worked here knew about it. A few years ago, a woman sued LACH because she had sex with her doctor, Dr. Sonny Gilbert. He was her gynecologist. She accused him of abusing the power dynamic and taking advantage of her by having sex with her during an appointment here in the hospital. He denied it, and the woman didn't have any proof beyond her version of events, but he probably did it. Dr. Gilbert had a reputation for being a flirt, and prior to the lawsuit, he'd been reprimanded and put on probation twice for alleged instances of sexual harassment involving some of our female staff. The woman suing Dr. Gilbert won her lawsuit. He lost his job at LACH and his medical license was suspended for three years. The hospital had to pay a huge settlement. The amount was secret, but I'd heard it was in the low seven figures. As in $2 to $4 million dollars. After it happened, all the staff had to attend ethical conduct seminars so everyone was aware of what was acceptable and what was not. I had gone. They were a repeat of what I'd learned in medical school and I'd been married at the time, so I didn't exactly take notes on the part about sex with patients. I was faithful to Donald. But maybe I should've listened more closely. To be fair, I never once imagined Lion suing the hospital because I slept with him. He would have been far more likely to sue the hospital if I had *not* slept with him. And, my situation was far different from Dr. Gilbert's. I wasn't a flirt and Lion was the one sexually harassing me. So what if I liked it?

"You attended the ethical conduct seminars, if I'm not mistaken, Dr. Flanagan?"

"I did."

"So you're aware that the hospital takes any accusation of sexual misconduct extremely seriously?"

"I am." *But I don't care!* Actually, I did. I cared so much my stomach was in knots. In fact, I felt seasick. A hot flash burned across my brow and my stomach did a backflip.

She looked at me. "Then perhaps you need a refresher course."

I tried not to scowl. "I'm well aware of the rules." My stomach did a front flip and hot bile shot up the back of my throat. I gulped it down.

"Are you sure?" She wasn't accusing me of anything. But she was hinting like crazy.

"Yes I'm sure." I wanted to ask her why she was asking. I needed to know who my accuser was and what accusations had been made. She obviously knew something because she wouldn't have called this meeting otherwise. But if I asked, I would give myself away or at the very least make her more suspicious than she already was.

"Then you can imagine my concern when—"

"Excuse me," I covered my mouth as more bile bubbled up my throat. I could taste it. Nasty. I swallowed hard, forcing it down, and burped again. "Sorry." Still covering my mouth, I burped a third time. "I'm really sorry."

Cynthia frowned and waited a moment before continuing, "Then you can imagine my concern when it was brought to my attention that —"

Without warning I leaned forward and threw up all over her desk. Luckily, I'd had a light lunch. But you couldn't miss the chunks of kale from the salad I'd eaten. You also couldn't miss the splatter of vomit on Cynthia's suit.

"Oh!" She shot to her feet, disgusted.

"Sorry," I gurgled helplessly.

She swiped tissues from a box she kept on a low cabinet behind her desk and handed them to me. "Are you all right, Dr. Flanagan?"

I retched again and clamped my hand over my mouth. This time, I was able to contain the spew because most of it was already on Cynthia's desk. And her suit. The spew I could not contain dribbled between my fingers and onto the carpet.

"I think I need to see a doctor," I said with sweaty mirth.

This situation was so horrifying, all I could do was make light of it. Cynthia was revolted and ready to be done.

"We should plan on continuing this discussion when you're feeling better, Dr. Flanagan."

"Great idea!" I croaked wetly and a fresh spasm clamped down on my stomach. Another blast was on its way up the pipe. I hunched over and hurried out of her office.

She called after me. "How about next week?"

Something told me nine months would be a better fit for both our schedules.

I gave myself a pregnancy test that night after my shift.

Not a blood test at the hospital. I didn't want them knowing just yet. I bought a home pregnancy test kit from Walgreens.

Surprise!

I was pregnant.

This was a disaster.

What was I going to do?

Once I started to show, people at work would start asking questions. The most obvious: who is the father.

I could lie, but we all knew I was terrible at lying.

As a doctor, I was a staunch supporter of a woman's right to choose. But I would never choose to terminate Lion's baby. My baby. *Our* baby. I couldn't do that to him or me or our child. He'd already lost his son Cali. I wouldn't let him lose another.

I was going to have this baby. There was no question.

Once the names went on the birth certificate, everyone would know my patient had impregnated me shortly after we met.

This was going to kill my career.

Would I get fired from LACH?

Would I lose my medical license?

Would I ever work as a doctor again?

If that happened, how would I support my new baby? Donald would make sure Daniel had everything he needed, but I doubt he'd want to help pay for Lion's child.

If I didn't get fired, who was going to raise my baby? I'd barely had time for Daniel when he was born, and I'd had the help of the entire Wright family, especially Linda. But I barely had time for Daniel now. How was I going to make time for two kids, one of them a newborn infant?

Worse, would Donald use this as an excuse to take Daniel away from me?

These and a thousand other frightful questions raced through my head for the next week.

The most painful of all:

How was I going to tell Lion?

Chapter 39

LION

Rehab was kicking my ass.

It didn't matter that I had access to the best sports rehab center in LA. And the best physical therapists in sports. My knee was a long way from what it once was.

After a few weeks of therapy, I could walk without crutches, but I was light years from getting back in the cage. My leg was weak and my balance was shot. The range of motion was nothing like it was going into surgery. I had to baby my leg with every step I took. My PT guy was all over me not to baby it because he wanted me to get back full extension. He was right. I sucked up the painful exercises and the sound assisted soft tissue mobilizer he used to rape the back of my knee after every session.

I was used to pain, but this was a different kind. This was the pain of wondering whether or not I'd ever return to the cage. I didn't tell anybody about it because it freaked me the fuck out.

Some days I regretted getting the surgery. My knee hadn't been this bad leading up to it. Before surgery, once the initial swelling had gone down, I'd managed fine. Sure, I wasn't training for a fight, but I was active. I knew some people with ACL injuries didn't go for reconstruction like I did. Even some athletes. They lived their whole lives without it. But I didn't know any cage fighters who still competed with a torn ACL.

So every day I told myself I'd made the right decision.

I didn't always believe it.

I had to stop watching fight videos, which was something I did all the time. Normally, I watched them with Dean. We would analyze my opponents and look for weaknesses or re-watch my old fights and look for areas where I could improve. But Dean's brother suddenly died a week ago, so he had to fly back to St. Louis for a month to help his brother's widow deal with the aftermath. Between that and my knee, I couldn't bring myself to watch the videos.

It didn't help that I hadn't talked to Brigid in almost two weeks. I would call, but she never answered, so I left messages. She'd text back one word texts like **busy** or **working**. She was avoiding me. Something was wrong. I could feel it.

I knew it had something to do with the hospital.

Either Dr. Hackett or Donald had said something to somebody.

That meant any plans I'd had to stop them were now useless. If it hadn't been for my damn operation, maybe I could've done something sooner. No, I knew that was bullshit. I couldn't have bribed Dr. Hackett or Donald Wright without admitting guilt. I couldn't kill them because I wasn't a murderer. And I wasn't going to kidnap them or even intimidate them into silence because they could still talk to the cops or the hospital, I'd end up in prison, and Brigid would still get screwed. I even considered begging them not to say anything, but that too would be admitting guilt. I wouldn't take that risk for Brigid's sake. Protecting a secret that was out was impossible. This situation had me boxed in from the start. I was used to fighting my opponents, trading hit for hit. But this wasn't that. This was some bizarre game where hitting your opponent meant you lost. Sad to say, I had been completely out of my element from the beginning. That made me feel like an even bigger loser.

The final outcome was that Donald had won and Brigid was in serious trouble. She had probably decided I had fucked up her life and wanted to distance herself before I made it worse. At least she still had something to live for.

Without Brigid to give me something else to focus on, I was hating life.

I felt completely broken.

I hadn't been this down on myself since I'd lost Cali and then Minka shortly after.

I tried to distract myself from worrying about Brigid by focusing on business issues, because there was always something to be done with the dojos. Despite all the people working for me, the business didn't run itself. But all of it left me feeling empty.

It all came down to Brigid.

I needed her back in my life.

Without her, and without Daniel, nothing else mattered.

I didn't even have Dean around to bust my balls and whip me into shape. I called him several times in St. Louis, but he didn't always have access to a phone and he refused to carry a cell phone.

I was on my own.

On the days when my knee was at its worst and it seemed like I might never fight again, I thought to myself that I wouldn't care as long as I could keep Brigid and Daniel in my life. When we were together, everything was perfect. Without them, all I had was fighting and the businesses. If I couldn't fight, I wasn't sure if I had anything.

Living a life alone wasn't worth living.

I wouldn't be the first athlete to off himself after a career ending injury. I knew things were bad when I started looking at handgun prices online.

Just when I thought I couldn't sink any lower, I got a text from Brigid that just about killed me.

Irish Kiss: We need to talk.

My heart stopped when I read it.

Translation: I'm breaking up with you.

When she didn't text anything else, I knew I was right. Best to get it over with.

Me: Tell me where and when.

An hour later, she replied.

Irish Kiss: How about your house?

She wasn't suggesting her house because she wanted a quick escape if I started punching things. I couldn't blame her.

We set up a time for the next morning.

I didn't sleep all night. I had never been this nervous before any of my fights. This was ten times worse because I knew I was going to get slaughtered tomorrow no matter what I did to prepare.

Chapter 40

BRIGID

I stood outside Lion's front door. My nerves were getting to me. I wasn't sure I could go through with this. Right when I started to turn to leave, the door opened.

"Hey," he mumbled. Dark circles shadowed his eyes.

"Are you all right? You look like you haven't been sleeping well."

"I haven't."

"That makes two of us."

"I'm sure." He sounded so cold, so distant.

I couldn't decide if that would make things easier or more difficult. "Can I come in?"

"Yeah. I guess," he grunted.

Okaaaay. He wasn't doing a good job of making me feel welcome. Maybe I should leave and do this some other time. No. He needed to know. The longer I waited, the harder it would be. I trudged up the steps and he closed the door behind me. I followed as he walked slowly to the living room. His knee was stiff and appeared to bother him.

His living room was a mess. It had been a while since I'd been here, but he'd never left the place this dirty.

"What happened?"

"Huh? You mean the mess? I told the maid to stop coming."

"Why?"

He shrugged. When he sat down on the couch he was extra careful with his knee, moving like an old man.

"Is everything all right with you, Lion? I'm a little worried."

"You tell me." His eyes were haunted.

I took a deep breath. "Someone at the hospital knows about us."

"Figures."

That wasn't the reaction I was expecting. I wasn't sure what I was expecting, but total apathy was not it. Now I really wanted to leave. But I couldn't run away from this no matter how far I went. "Read this." I handed him the letter I'd brought with me.

"What's this?"

"This is the letter that the head of human resources at LACH personally handed to me yesterday."

He scanned it and started reading out loud. "This letter is a summons for Brigid R. Flanagan, MD, to appear before the Los Angeles Central Hospital Ethics Committee for an investigative hearing to gather information and review charges against her for ethical and sexual misconduct in her role as attending physician to her patient, Lion Michael Maxwell. The doctor is charged with sustaining an ongoing sexual relationship with her patient in violation of California Business and Professional Code, Article 10.5 Unprofessional Conduct section 726(a) and (b) and 729(a), the LACH Conduct Code, section 5-909(a) and (b), Doctor-Patient Conduct. This will be a closed hearing consisting of Dr. Flanagan and the LACH ethics committee, and representatives from the Medical Board of California only. The doctor is free to seek legal counsel in advance of the hearing. Approved counsel will be allowed to accompany the doctor during the hearing, per hospital guidelines. The outcome of the hearing will determine whether or not Dr. Flanagan's actions shall be reviewed in full by the Medical Board, and what punitive actions will be taken. This may include suspension or revocation of Dr. Flanagan's medical license. This investigative hearing will take place on Friday, August 31st at 10:00am in the LACH Administrative Building, 4th floor, Sequoia Meeting Room."

He shrugged and handed me back the letter. "We knew it was gonna happen, right?"

"Don't you care?"

"What do you want me to say, Brigid?"

"I don't know! Anything!"

"You said yourself I didn't force you into anything."

"How can you be so callous about this?"

"I'm not the one forcing you out of this."

"Out? Out of what? What are you talking about, Lion?"

"You came here to break up with me, didn't you?"

I laughed. "Is that what you think this is about?"

"Pretty much."

I dropped onto the couch next to him. "Lion, I didn't come here to break up with you. The opposite. I came to show you this letter and—" I couldn't bring myself to say it.

"And what?"

"Nothing."

"So, you're not breaking up with me?" He sounded like a frightened child.

"Not a chance." I kissed his cheek. "I made a promise to you. I will keep it. So stop worrying. What we need to worry about is this letter."

"Lemme see it again." He took it and read it over. "Sounds like you need a lawyer."

"I'll say," I chuckled morosely. "Do you know any good ones?"

"Not any who do medical stuff."

"Me neither. But I can ask around." I sighed. "Who do you think tattled on us?"

"Your ex. Or Dr. Hackett."

"Him?"

"He was asking me some weird questions when I went in after my surgery to have my bandages changed."

"Huh. Did you tell him something?"

"No. But he tried to drag it out of me."

"That's weird. And here I thought it was Donald."

"Maybe it was both of them."

I shook my head. "It doesn't really matter at this point."

"So what do we do about your investigative hearing?"

"There's not much you can do. It's all on me, really."

"It doesn't have to be."

"What do you mean?"

"We could say I forced you."

"What, like you raped me? No. I would never do that to you. This is my fault and I have to take the blame."

"We could always deny it. I mean, what does your ex-husband know? Other than what Daniel told him?"

"Nothing. You and I were always so careful." My stomach flopped at that thought. Mostly true, except for that one time.

"Exactly. Nobody knows anything and I'm not gonna admit to anything against the rules. You don't have to either. We're just friends, right?"

"Right. But how do we explain all our time together? It looks suspicious."

"Easy. Like you said. We don't have to explain it. They don't know we were sleeping together."

"They will."

He looked surprised. "Why, are you gonna tell them?"

"No. But I'm pregnant."

"What?" His voice was flat. "Hold up. What did you just say?"

"I'm pregnant." I winced in anticipation of how he might react.

"Is it mine?"

I smacked his arm. "Of course it's yours, asshole! What kind of woman do you think I am?"

His face started to oscillate through a hundred different emotions. "Are you sure? I mean, sure you're pregnant?"

"I'm a doctor. I'm sure."

His eyebrows climbed and the adorable boyish grin glowed with pure happiness, the first time I'd seen it today, and the first time I'd seen it in weeks. I didn't realize how badly I'd missed it until right then. He gasped, "I'm gonna be a dad?"

"You're already a dad. I mean, were, I mean, sorry. I didn't mean..." I was thinking about his son Cali. I was going to cry. "Yes. I'm going to have your child, Lion. Our child."

"Hell yes!" He jumped up off the couch and shouted with joy. When he landed, he grimaced and sat down suddenly. "Fuck, my knee."

"Are you okay?" I reached out to check it.

His face twisted in pain. "I shouldn't have done that. Hurts like a bitch. Rehab is going way slower than I expected." He leaned forward, cradling his knee with both hands. "Fuck. Ow, ow, ow!"

"Oh, Lion. I'm so sorry. I should've warned you."

After a minute of choking back silent pain, he started laughing. "We're gonna have a kid! I can't believe it! What are we gonna name him?"

"How do you know it's a him?" I giggled.

"Her, I don't care. As long as it's got two arms and two legs and calls me Daddy, that's all I care about."

I started crying and threw my arms around him. "I love you Lion. I love you so much."

He showered me with kisses. "I love you too, Brigid. I can't believe we're having a baby!" His happiness washed over me. But it wasn't enough to silence my fears.

"We won't be able to deny our sexual relationship. You realize that, right?"

"Oh, man..." His face struggled between elation and fear.

"People are going to ask who the father is. Word will get around. When our child is born, we'll have to fill out the birth certificate. Then everyone will know. It'll be official."

"I told you, I hate these fucking ridiculous rules."

"Me too."

"I've got one more rule for you, Brigid."

"Oh?"

"No matter what happens, I'll take care of you. If you lose your job, you can live with me. Daniel can live with me. You need money to pay an attorney? I'll give you whatever you need. I love you Brigid, and I'm not going to let some bullshit rule bring you down. You got that?"

With Lion on my side, I felt like we could get through this. It was my turn to kiss him all over. One thing led to another and we were kissing passionately and deeply. His hands were all over my breasts, squeezing and kneading them desperately.

"Careful. They're extra sensitive."

"Just how I like them," he grinned, but relaxed his touch and was much more gentle with them.

It occurred to me that we hadn't had sex since before his surgery. It had felt like an unnecessary and artificial abstinence, one based purely on those ridiculous rules that neither one of us wanted to follow anymore. Now we were free to express our love for each other without doubt or hesitation.

Within minutes, all our clothes were off.

We sat on the couch side by side, completely naked. His cock was fully erect.

"Stand up and let me see that amazing ass, Irish. I've missed it so bad."

"It's not that amazing."

"To me it is. Stand up and give me a spin."

I did.

"Damn, you look good." His eyes were all over me.

"You too. Is, um, is your knee up for this?"

"Forget about my knee. All I want you thinking about is my cock. And it's more than up for this. It's straight up for this." It was. That huge throbbing cock pulsed with need.

He reached out and pulled me toward where he sat on the couch.

"Lion!" I fell forward and sat down on his thighs clumsily. His cock stood at attention between my legs. "Mmm... I've missed this."

"Me too." He wrapped his arms around me and turned us both, pulling me down on top of him on the couch. Then he grabbed my thighs and pulled upward.

"What are you doing?"

"I've missed this." He pulled my pelvis straight up to his face.

I would've tumbled off the end of the couch if I hadn't stopped myself by planting my hands on the armrest. I was on all fours. I looked down between my legs. He was on his back, his eyes gazing up at my vagina.

"Sit down."

I did.

His tongue went straight to work.

"Oh!" I gasped and watched him devour me. His face and nose

were instantly slick with me. I was already good and wet. His tongue felt incredible, hitting everything just right. Pure pleasure exploded inside me and I came so quickly I surprised myself. When I caught my breath, I turned over and around, lying across him in a classic 69 position so I could focus on his cock, which stood tall and proud. When I started licking, he did too. At first, feeling him eat me while I sucked him was distracting. It felt so good I could barely concentrate on his blowjob, but I did my best. At some point, my pleasure leveled off to the point where I could thoroughly enjoy it but still focus on fucking his cock with my mouth. Then out of nowhere, I exploded with another powerful orgasm, better than the first.

He chuckled, "You like that?" The words were muffled and wet. *Slurp, slurp, slurp.* He was still busy eating me. His insistent licking made me gasp for air and quiver all over and the orgasm just kept on going. "You are soaked, woman," *slurp* "I can feel your pussy pulsing around my nose," *slurp* "You're still coming, aren't you?" *Slurp.*

I was. I felt myself clenching hard over and over again as he licked my clit and his nose worked my wet entrance. I couldn't speak to answer him. It felt too damn good. All I could do was ride the orgasm to conclusion.

"Damn, I do love the smell of you."

I could tell because his cock was twitching in my mouth and I could taste pre-cum dripping out.

When he finally stopped and the waves finally faded, I whispered, "I've never done sixty-nine before."

"Now you have."

"What do we do about you?"

"You mean, what do you do about me? My knee is all busted, remember?"

"Would you like me to ride you?"

"Go for it, cowgirl. But be careful, this lion bucks and fucks like a bronco."

"Is your knee okay to buck?"

"I don't need to use it when I'm on my back. Now climb on. I'm dying to come inside you."

"Yes, Master," I giggled as I turned and slowly lowered myself onto his girth, feeling him filling me to the hilt as I slid down and ground my clit against him. "Oh, fuck. I like this."

I leaned my hands against his muscled chest and started to thrust and tilt my pelvis in a hypnotic rhythm that took both of us out of our bodies and into each other's. We rocked and moaned in perfect unison, riding wave after wave of multiple orgasms together. Somehow, he never seemed to lose his erection. I just kept riding him. When he finally ejaculated inside me, I felt that we had melted together, become one.

Become love.

At last.

No rule could ever take that away from us.

Us.

Chapter 41

BRIGID

My doorbell rang on the morning of the investigative hearing ten days later.

I was in the bathroom in front of the mirror, still getting ready and in the middle of tying my hair up in a simple chignon.

The doorbell rang again.

"Coming!" I opened it without a thought. "Holy shit!"

Lion stood there in the slickest navy blue suit I'd ever seen.

He grinned. "You like?"

"You look incredible."

He really did. I never imagined a man with so many muscles could wear a suit this well. He had one hand in the front pocket of his slacks and stood with his weight on one leg. The jacket was unbuttoned, revealing a vest underneath. His sapphire blue tie matched the scarf in the breast pocket, and the silver tie tack matched his silver cufflinks. Low profile black leather lace-up shoes completed the perfect outfit.

"Do we have to go to my hearing? Maybe you can whisk me away on a private jet to Paris or something."

He chuckled, "I would like nothing more."

"Wait, you don't have a private jet, do you?"

"No. But I can charter one. Anywhere you want to go. The world is your oyster."

"Let's get through the hearing first."

"Can I jump you first? Because your black lace bra is begging to be torn off."

"Oh." I looked down. All I had on was the bra, my suit skirt, and black hose.

"Why are you wearing sexy underwear for the hearing? No one is going to see it."

"It makes me feel more confident knowing it's there."

"Smart. You wearing panties under that skirt?" He tugged on it.

"Stop!" I laughed.

He grinned. "I should probably check."

"No you shouldn't."

"Yes I should." He walked inside and closed the front door. Then he stalked toward me.

I backed up into the couch. Nowhere to go. "What are you doing?"

"I'm going to fuck you before your hearing."

"No! I need to stay focused and I need to get dressed!"

"You need to relax."

He had a point. And we had time.

He spun me around and pushed me down so my chest folded over the back of the couch. Then he hiked up my skirt.

I was instantly wet. It was probably my anxiety. I had that feeling of "One last fuck before the end of the world" going on. I was game.

"What the hell are these?"

"You mean my garter socks?"

"Yeah. They're the hottest thing I've ever seen."

"I thought you might like them." The garter socks were black lace and they rose up to my inseam. Each had a strap at the top that criss-crossed my body, making an X below my navel in front and an X above my ass in back. The whole effect looked like skin tight lace chaps that did a perfect job of highlighting my naughty parts. I knew because I'd admired them in my bathroom mirror before putting my skirt on.

"You said you wore them to feel more confident, but it looks to me like you wore them to make me fucking crazy."

Still leaning against the couch with my ass in the air, I looked over my shoulder and said, "I did. So go *fucking* crazy."

"With pleasure. Now I'm going to attack that hot wet pussy of yours. But first this thong has to go." He ripped it apart and threw it across the room. Strong hands pushed my pelvis forward and I felt myself exposed to him. He dropped to his good knee behind me and buried his hot tongue in my waiting wetness then licked all over my clit.

It wasn't long before I was moaning. He stood up and slapped my ass.

"Hey!"

"You like it."

I heard him unbuckle his belt and drop his slacks. I wasn't going anywhere.

"This is what we do to rule breakers." The hard hot head of his cock pressed against my soft wet heat.

I was into it. "I'm so sorry, Mr. Maxwell. I didn't mean to spill your morning coffee all over your important papers."

"Too bad. You fucked up royally, Ms. Flanagan. Now you get royally fucked."

"I've never been fucked by royalty before," I gasped.

"I *am* the king of the beasts," he chuckled and pushed himself in slowly.

"Nnnnn," It was all I could manage to say.

"Fuck, Brigid. You feel so fucking good."

While I gripped the top of the couch, he gripped my hips and pumped me slowly from behind. There was an authoritative quality to his thrusting that I loved.

He groaned, "I could do this all damn day." He reached around and massaged my clit with his fingers. Lightning zinged through my entire body.

"Me too," I moaned, squeezing my eyes shut while he filled me up. I stood up on my tip toes and arched my back, pushing my ass back in time with his thrusts.

"Yeah, like that. You should see the view from back here. Incredible."

I was too overwhelmed with sexual pleasure to respond. Whatever he was doing to my clit was making me insane.

"As much as I like it, I want to see your face when you come." He pulled out and spun me around. His cock throbbed between us, slick with my wetness. A swollen pearl of pre cum expanded on the tip. He grabbed my ass and jerked me forward. His cock bumped against my navel and slid upward, smearing that hot pearlescent bead up my stomach. "Get on my dick, woman. I am going to put all my seed inside you."

He lifted my ass and I hopped up and wrapped my thighs around his waist. He said, "Put it in."

I reached down and positioned his cock.

Slowly, he eased me down.

"Stay right there." He turned and walked me up against the nearest wall until my back pressed against it. He started slow, but it wasn't long until he had a steady rhythm going. Most of his weight was on his good leg, which was more than strong enough. It didn't take long for me to start screaming. Every time he thrust all the way in, I screamed. We were nose to nose when we came together, both of us snarling like beasts, eyes locked, foreheads pressed together, me screaming, him grunting, both of us sounding like we were dying painful but intensely pleasurable deaths. I felt him explode inside of me over and over again.

"Take my cum, Brigid," he hissed. "Take all of it."

"Nnnnh," I moaned, squeezing my thighs as tight as I could, trying to pull all of him into me, clenching him with my pussy, one hand around his neck clawing at the shoulders of his suit jacket, the other knotting his tie in my fist like it was a silk dick.

As the throes of our orgasms faded, a passing thought whisked through my mind. *Is that what ties are? Silken symbols of hanging dicks? Whoever thought of the silk tie is a genius.* I snickered to myself.

He sagged into me, pressing me into the wall, breathless and heaving for air. "Feel better?"

"Yes," I purred.

"Mission accomplished."

I could already feel his cum leaking out of me. "I better go drain before I drip all over your slacks." They were still around his ankles.

"No."

"What?"

"Shut up." He pulled out and lowered me.

I let my feet touch the floor. He pushed me against the wall and squatted down in front of me. "What are you doing?"

"Cleaning you up." He squeezed my ass and pulled my hips into his face while his mouth ravaged my dripping cum-filled vagina.

I couldn't decide if this was too kinky for my tastes, but he was the one doing the tasting, so I let it ride and stopped caring when I felt another orgasm begin to build. I leaned my weight back against the wall. His tongue dug deep into my folds and hit my clit just right while both his hands reached up and massaged my breasts. Total stimulation. As my orgasm started to peak, I ran my fingers through his thick hair and gripped it hard as I came.

After, when he finally pulled away, he grunted, "The taste of you and me together is something else."

I giggled, "I thought the same thing the first time I blew you."

"You relaxed now?"

I smirked. "Like I wasn't after the first orgasm?"

"Did I give you too many?"

"No," I chuckled.

"So, are you relaxed or do you need one more?"

"Considering, I feel like syrup from head to toe, what do you think?"

"Sounds tasty. I think I need another fuck."

"Okay, now we're going to be late if I don't get dressed. And if I get any more relaxed, I'll fall asleep right here and now."

"Sounds like a plan. Then after we wake up, I can charter that private jet."

I rolled my eyes. "Just come with me to this hearing. That's all I need."

Reluctantly, he pulled up his boxers and slacks and belted them. "If you insist. But I will be fucking you afterward whether we do it here or on that jet to Paris."

"Is that a promise?"

He brushed my cheek softly with his thumb and kissed me gently. "You should know, Brigid, your wish is always my command."

Although I was nervous about the ethics hearing, I knew I was in good hands with Lion by my side.

No matter what happened.

Lion drove me to the hospital in his Range Rover. Traffic on the 5 south was still heavy because of the morning commute, but we had enough time.

Lion signaled and changed lanes. He reached over and grabbed my hand and held it.

"Is your attorney meeting you at the hospital?"

"Yes," I said. "She texted that she's already there."

"Excellent." He squeezed my hand. "I have a good feeling about today. Things are going to work out. I can feel it."

"That makes one of us," I chuckled with no humor.

He glanced over and smiled. "Don't you know love conquers all, my love?"

"That's only in the movies."

"This isn't a movie."

I hoped he was right.

We parked in the hospital parking structure with time to spare, then made our way to the administration building. On the fourth floor, there was a waiting area across from the Sequoia Meeting Room. It was called that because it was named after the gigantic redwood trees found in California. These trees lived for hundreds of years, some as long as a thousand. Sequoia redwoods had an eternal quality that was the exact opposite of my career, which was minutes away from being cut down long before its time.

The double doors of the meeting room were closed, so I couldn't see inside. Who knew what fate awaited me behind those doors?

A firing squad, possibly.

Or insane crazy-eyed lumberjacks with chainsaws ready to cut down my career.

Take your pick.

My attorney Vikki Baxter stood up from one of the waiting area seats and walked over to us wearing a charcoal gray skirt suit. I had already met with her two weeks ago at her office in Pasadena. I'd liked her immediately. She exuded calm confidence, but also a lightness and a sense of humor. She was very charming, and exactly the sort of counsel I wanted for something as serious as this. We both agreed my case was a human issue. It was about love, not breaking the rules. Hopefully we could make the committee see that.

"Good to see you, Brigid." Vikki turned to Lion and offered her hand. "Vikki Baxter. And you are?"

"The patient." He shook her hand. "Lion Maxwell."

"So you're the indiscretion," she grinned.

Lion chuckled. "You could say that."

Vikki winked at me, "I would say he was worth it." She took a step back and looked us both over. "Did you two pick matching outfits on purpose?"

I looked down at my navy skirt suit and then at Lion's navy blue suit. "Oh, no! What was I thinking? Why didn't you say anything, Lion?" I guess I'd been too distracted by our sex and the rush out the door afterward to notice.

Lion chuckled, "I kind of like it. We look like a team."

I grimaced at Vikki. "What should I do?"

She smiled reassuringly. "I think Lion's right. You do look like a team. It might even work in your favor. I think it's kind of cute. A show of solidarity."

"I hope so," I sighed.

Lion rubbed my back. "I agree with Vikki."

The three of us sat down and reviewed our strategy. Let the committee present their case. Answer honestly but say as little as possible. We didn't know what the committee would ask and Vikki had never handled a case exactly like ours.

She'd done quite a bit of research after we'd met, but she wasn't able to find any cases similar enough to ours to use for guidance. Every case she found involved male doctors dating female patients, cases which often had the stink of prostitution (trading prescription drugs for sex with a patient who didn't need the drugs for any medical reason) or coercion on the doctor's part (abusing the power dynamic, especially during breast and pelvic exams). My situation was nothing like any of those, so we were essentially flying blind. Not my preferred way to operate, but we didn't have a choice.

After Vikki and I finished, Lion said, "Brigid, remember, they need to know that we didn't do anything wrong. This isn't a scandal. It's love."

"I wish it were that simple."

He frowned, "It is that fucking simple."

Vikki arched her eyebrows but said nothing.

"Would you keep your voice down?" I hissed. "And watch your language please?"

"Sorry." He squeezed my hand and muttered to himself, "It is that simple."

How could he be so sure? I knew I had broken the rules. He knew it too. We'd had a discussion about rules the night we met. The entire time we'd been dating, we'd been taking a huge risk and we knew it. We were both complicit. That was the simple part.

I knew I needed to stay positive, so I tried to push my negative thoughts away. It didn't help. My nerves were threatening to get the best of me. I took a deep breath and tried to relax. At the very least, I needed to stay calm if I wanted to get through the investigative hearing successfully.

The door to the meeting room opened and a women I recognized from HR named Michelle stuck her head out. "They're ready for you, Dr. Flanagan."

"Okay."

We all stood up and walked toward the door.

Michelle looked at Lion and Vikki and said, "Are both of you Dr. Flanagan's attorneys?"

Lion didn't say anything, just looked at me hopefully.

I sighed. I wanted him in there with me, but I knew he wasn't allowed. "No. He's my boyfriend."

He smiled when I said it. "Damn right I am."

Michelle frowned. Did she know the details of the hearing? Or was she just offended by his language? "He can't be in here."

"Yeah, yeah," Lion said. He took my hands.

My eyes darted between Vikki and Michelle who were both watching me and making this moment more uncomfortable than it should've been.

He rubbed his thumbs on the backs of my hands. "Just remember, it's love." He raised both my hands and kissed the backs of each one.

That made me feel better. I smiled at Lion, on the verge of tears. "Okay."

"Awww," Vikki said.

Michelle scowled impatiently.

Vikki said softly, "We should probably go in now."

"Yeah, okay," I sniffed.

Reluctantly, I released Lion's hands and walked through the doors.
Time to face the firing squad.

Or the crazy lumberjacks with their revving chainsaws.

The meeting room was set up with a line of tables near the windows. Behind them sat a row of people I recognized.

Sidney Copeland, MD, the Chief of Staff at LACH.

Cynthia Badhoff, the Head of Human Resources.

Marina Davis, MD, the Chief Medical Officer of LACH.

Randolph Tanaka, MD, the Chairman of Orthopedic Surgery and the head of my department.

Ivan Hackett, Major Dick and one of the assholes who probably told on me.

There were two women I didn't recognize, but I knew both were representatives from the Medical Board of California.

The only dick who wasn't here was Donald. Maybe that meant Hackett was the tattler? Or would someone on the committee read a prepared statement from Donald accusing me of breaking the rules?

I'm sure I would find out.

Michelle from HR led us toward the two empty seats facing the committee, then sat down at the tables with the rest of the firing squad. The only thing they were missing were rifles and chainsaws. I'm sure both would be brought in at the end of the hearing so each committee member could pick their weapon of choice.

Vikki and I both sat down. We didn't have a table for her briefcase, which was rude. I didn't bring one so I didn't need the table, but I felt like we were hanging out in the open without one. If the committee decided to pull out their rifles, Vikki and I could always kick the table over and hide behind it for cover. That was probably why the committee hadn't provided one. I hoped Vikki didn't get caught in any crossfire.

Cynthia Badhoff spoke first. She made an official preamble noting the time, the purpose of the hearing, blah blah blah.

My eyes glazed over as Dr. Sidney Copeland read a prepared speech from several sheets of paper, periodically glancing up to meet my eyes. He droned on about things like "my grievous disregard for the ethical policy of the hospital and the Medical Board of California" and "the likelihood of irreparable and monumental financial consequences" and "punitive action commensurate to the numerous instances of sexual misconduct in question."

In so many words, he was telling me that my career would be over shortly.

I was nauseous in the extreme. I didn't know if it was my hormones from the pregnancy or my fear. Probably both. I'm sure I was scaring the baby. Well, my fetus. He or she probably wasn't enjoying this either.

When Dr. Copeland finished his speech, he set his papers down and folded his hands together on the table. "Dr. Flanagan, how would you like to respond to these allegations?"

I wanted to shout, *Who's the asshole who told on me?!* I felt like jumping across the table and strangling Dr. Hackett, who looked suspiciously guilty and had not looked at me once during Copeland's prepared speech. I restrained myself just in case it wasn't him. It easily could have been Donald who tattled. But I didn't know either way because *they had not fucking told me!*

"Dr. Flanagan," Copeland said. "Are you or are you not engaged in a sexual-romantic relationship with Lion M. Maxwell?"

YES!!!

I hated this. I didn't want to say it out loud.

Vikki nudged me gently, "Brigid? Are you okay?"

"I—I'm fine." But I wasn't fine. I was furious and scared and didn't know what to do. They had me dead to rights. I had broken the rules. I had known I was breaking them, but I'd kept right on going like I didn't give a shit, which was partially true. Once I knew Lion had good intentions and was a good person, I didn't really care about the rules.

Why couldn't I be bold at a time like this? Why couldn't I stand up and flip everyone off and shout, *Your rules are fucking stupid! I love him! He loves me! We're having a baby! What's the fucking problem?!*

I bet Lion would do something like that. But the truth was, I knew that kind of behavior would backfire in my face. I needed to calmly explain my side of things and hope the committee understood.

I took a deep breath before opening my mouth to speak.

The door behind me banged open loudly.

I gasped and jumped out of my seat.

Vikki gasped too and everyone behind the tables stared over my shoulder.

"Okay, fuck all this bullshit," Lion growled in a commanding voice. "You all need to listen to what I have to say."

Chapter 42

LION

Everyone stared at me.

I set my bag down just inside the door. I was breathless from fast walking down to my car to get it.

Vikki the lawyer and Brigid were twisted around in their seats. Brigid hissed, "What the hell do you think you're doing?"

I walked up behind her. "Trust me. I've got this."

"You need to get the hell out, is what you need to do!"

I placed my hands on her shoulders and leaned down, kissing the top of her head. "I told you, Irish. I've got this."

I walked up in front of the tables and started pacing while I talked. "I know you guys got a bunch of rules about doctors dating patients. I also know those rules are there so doctors don't take advantage of patients because of their authority. Here's the thing. Dr. Flanagan wasn't the one who took advantage of me. I took advantage of her." There were a few women on the committee sitting behind the tables. I focused on them. "I mean, look at me. What woman in her right mind could resist me? Can I wear a fucking suit or what?"

One of the women rolled her eyes. Another grimaced. The third? I could tell I was getting to her. So I turned to the two who weren't convinced.

"Don't give me that eye roll bullshit, ladies. You would both fuck me and you know it."

One of them grimaced.

The other blushed.

"And you guys," I pointed at the men. "You know I can pull ass anytime, anywhere. You all hate me for it too. I'm sure you have plenty of doctor money and you get your fair share of hot gold diggers. But that isn't how things work for Lion Maxwell. That's me, by the way. I'm an MMA legend. Undefeated champion. Never. Lost. A. Fight." I nodded for emphasis. "You wanna know what my reality is? Women throw themselves at me all the time. Hot women." I singled out the platinum blonde, the one who'd blushed and was pretty cute. I winked at her. "Yeah, I see you looking." She snorted a laugh. I turned to the men. "Guys, I've had naked women waiting for me in the locker room after a fight plenty of times. No bullshit. Can you picture that? Once, there were three. Three. It was like walking into a strip joint filled with naked hotties and all those strippers make a beeline for your dick, but they don't want your money. They just want your dick. Correction. My dick. That's my life, guys. And that's a fact."

The men glared at me.

They hated me.

Good.

"Yeah, yeah, yeah. I'm a fucking dick. I know it. And that is my point, gentlemen. And ladies. Because Dr. Brigid Flanagan knew it too. She knew I was an asshole from the moment I laid eyes on her and I tried to get her to suck my dick in the emergency room. No, seriously. I tried to get her to suck my cock in the exam room. That's how I roll."

Brigid was horrified.

But the three women on the committee? Their gears were turning. I was wearing them down. They were wondering what it would be like to get plowed by a cocky motherfucker like me.

"But you know what, people? Brigid didn't play that. She wasn't having any of my bullshit. So I chased her. Chased her hard. I've never wanted a woman so bad in my life, and I went after her with a vengeance." That wasn't entirely true. We both wanted it and it was the easiest relationship I'd ever had. That's why I knew it was for real. But I was making my case. "I wore her down, people. At no time did she ever take advantage of me. Truth be told, I think I took advantage of her. When I want something, I get it. And I got her. And I plan on keeping her. No matter what you decide." I looked each of them in the eyes, one after the other. "And there you have it, ladies and gentlemen. I put a spell on Dr. Brigid Flanagan. It wasn't the other way around. I rest my case."

I hoped that worked.

I walked to the wall and sat down in an empty chair and folded my arms across my chest. I half stood from the chair, "Oh yeah. Brigid is a kick ass doctor and the only reason I wanted Dr. Hackett to do my knee surgery was so I could date Brigid." I sat down. Then stood up and muttered, "So let her keep being a doctor. She's a damn good one."

Finally, I dropped into the chair.

The room was dead silent.

The doctors stared at me, stone faced.

Vikki stared at me, her eyes a mile wide.

Brigid stared at her lap.

She was either pleased or incredibly pissed off.

It didn't matter which. Somebody needed to do something drastic today, and I was always the go-to guy for drastic when the situation called for it. I could take drastic all the way to the final bell.

But.

They kept on staring.

Had I pushed it too far?

The head guy in the middle of the table cleared his throat and said, "Mr. Maxwell, are you aware that your consent is not a defense against the charges of sexual misconduct?"

Shit.

Chapter 43

The committee was silent.

Oh. No.

The entire time Lion had been giving his speech, I'd felt hope that his passion and honesty would sway them and save the day. But I hadn't realized that it wouldn't make any difference. The rules were the rules.

Lion said to Sidney Copeland, "Yeah, I know my consent isn't a defense. But you gotta understand, when it comes to women, I don't consent to anything. I take what I want. If I didn't want Brigid, I wouldn't have gone after her in the first place."

I felt renewed hope. That was absolutely true. The sexual misconduct rules always seemed geared more toward male doctors. This was different.

Copeland said, "Her consent is not a defense either, Mr. Maxwell. This is a question of professional responsibility. Dr. Flanagan's role is as a caregiver only. She violated that role when she consented to a sexual-romantic relationship with you."

This is what I'd feared all along. Dating Lion was against the rules, plain and simple. They were black and white and I'd foolishly broken them with blatant disregard and now it was time to pay the price for my transgressions.

"Yeah," Lion said, "but, don't forget I dumped her as my doctor right away. We didn't start dating until after we bumped into each other by chance at my dojo. More importantly, if I'm not mistaken, according to section 726(b) of the Business and Professional Code of California, none of the rules about no sex with patients apply to a doctor married to her patient."

I leaned against Vikki and whispered, "Is that true?"

She flipped through a bunch of papers she had in her lap. "I believe it is. He really did his research."

"But we're not married," I hissed.

Lion stood up from his chair by the wall and walked over to me and knelt down with a grunt. "Shit. Sorry. Still in rehab for the knee. Brigid,

I wanted to do this afterward, but these guys aren't taking no for an answer. I won't either." He reached into the pocket of his suit jacket and pulled out a velvet box and opened it. "Brigid Flanagan, I have only one thing left to say."

I hissed barely above a whisper, "Are you insane?"

"Yes," he chuckled. "Insanely in love with you. Brigid, from the moment I first saw you, I knew you were the woman for me. I've been asking myself every day, how did I get so fucking lucky? How? I don't know the answer to that, but I do know that after all the time we've spent together, I was right all along about you. You're the only woman for me. The only woman I'll ever want and the only woman I'll ever need. And I want to marry you, Brigid. Marry the fuck out of you. I want to make a family with you and Daniel and our baby." Lion turned to the panel, "That's right. She's pregnant with my kid. Can you guys believe it?" He was exuberantly happy.

I cringed, scared out of my mind. He'd just made things worse by telling them that.

"Brigid Flanagan, will you marry me?"

My heart raced.

I saw my career crumbling before my eyes.

I also saw the one man who would do anything to help me, staring up at me with that adorably boyish grin of his. Despite the gravity of the situation, despite the rules, and despite my fear that Lion's crude speech had just made everything ten times worse, I knew with absolute certainty that I loved this man.

"Yes," I whispered as tears blurred my vision.

Amazingly, his boyish grin got a little bit wider and a little bit brighter. "Are you sure?" His eyes were wet too.

"Yes I'm sure, you idiot." I leaned over and kissed him, holding his cheeks in my palms. The kiss was so powerful, so loving, so totally encompassing, I completely forgot where I was.

"I need to put the ring on."

"Oh. Right."

He slid it on my shaking finger.

I wasn't sure what the brownish-gold stone was, but the intricate design was clear as day. A roaring lion head holding the stone in its toothy maw. I tried not to laugh at how garish it was. But, as cheesy as it was, I absolutely loved it.

"The stone is Tiger's Eye because they don't make a Lion's eye. But you get the idea. It's so everyone will know you're with me. I know it's a cheap stone, but the sentiment is priceless."

"I love you so much, you priceless idiot," I laughed softly and kissed his forehead.

"There's one other thing." He stood up, pushing down on his bad knee to help him stand. He walked over to the door and picked up a brown paper bag he'd set down when he first came in. He walked past me and put the bag on the table in front of Chief Medical Officer Sidney Copeland. The bag rumpled loudly as he opened it and reached inside. "A little visual aid for you guys. Take a look and pass this down the line."

I was far enough away that I couldn't see the details, but the thing from Lion's bag was some kind of wood carving.

"In case you guys think I'm full of shit," Lion said, "take a look at this carving I made for Brigid. I've been working on this since I met her. Took months. You can all see that it's three lions. A papa lion, a mama lion, and a baby lion cub."

The members of the committee leaned over to better see the carving held by Dr. Copeland. I was dying to jump out of my seat so I could see it too, but I didn't want to ruin the moment. I felt like the second I moved, I'd wake up and realize all this was a dream and Lion wasn't really here and I was one second away from losing my job.

Lion said, "If you can't figure it out, the papa lion is me, Brigid is the mama, and the cub is her kid, Daniel Wright. Great kid, by the way. The only problem is, I didn't know Brigid was pregnant when I started carving this months ago. Shit, I hadn't even gone on a date with her, let alone had sex with her. But I knew, you guys. I knew. That's why I started carving it way back then. Anyway, now there should be four lions on here instead of three because we're having a baby." He turned and flashed an excited smile at me.

Now that everything was out on the table, there was no going back from this.

Lion continued, "I wanted you guys to see this so you'd realize I've been serious about Brigid since day one. This isn't some bullshit scam we cooked up yesterday. This is the real deal. This is true love. The shit poets write poems about. Brigid Flanagan is carrying my child. I'm going to be a father. Brigid and I are building a family together. How is that wrong? How is that breaking any rules? Do you guys think I didn't know what I was doing when I put my dick in her? I wasn't just fucking her. I was falling in love with my future wife. What do you say, Irish?" He held out his hand. "Wanna go down to the courthouse and tie the knot right now? Make it official?"

I looked between Lion and the committee. "I don't know. Can we?" It was crazy to ask, but I had to. Maybe my boldness was as important as his. I looked right at Sidney Copeland who was glaring back. "After we're through here, of course. But I am going to marry Lion Maxwell as soon as we get to the courthouse and I sign the papers."

Lion gently squeezed my hands in his. "Forget them, Brigid. Do you want to go make this official? The worst they can do is take away your medical license, but they can never take you away from me. They can never take away our love."

I was shocked by his naked honesty and his boldness. No one had ever stood up for me like this before. But I didn't want to lose my medical license. I wanted to keep it and keep working here at LACH *and* be married to Lion. Could I have both? I looked to the members of the committee.

They stared back at us.

This was it.

This was the moment they decided the fate of my career.

Dr. Copeland turned and whispered back and forth with Cynthia Badhoff and the representatives from the Medical Board. All were frowning and serious and intent. I couldn't make out a word they were saying. When they finished, Dr. Copeland spoke directly to me.

"Dr. Flanagan, does Mr. Maxwell's description of events match yours?"

I took a deep breath because I was shaking like crazy. "Yes." I gave them a brief rundown of the events starting with the night I met Lion, his request for a different doctor, my discharging him, and finally bumping into him by chance weeks later at the grand opening of his karate school.

Lion said, "Don't forget, guys, once we bumped into each other at my dojo, I wouldn't leave her alone."

Dr. Tanaka, the Chairman of Orthopedics, said very seriously, "Dr. Flanagan, is this a case of sexual harassment on the part of Mr. Maxwell?"

I chuckled, "Oh, goodness no. I wanted him to pursue me. I just don't think either of us wanted to wait six or twelve months."

Lion smirked, "Hell no I didn't want to wait. I mean, look at this red hot bombshell. She's a fucking fox. My fucking fox." He grinned his adorable grin and brushed a lock of hair behind my ear.

Next to me, Vikki Baxter stifled a snicker.

No one else on the committee said anything, but their faces were unreadable.

I said, "Oh, and I'm only six weeks pregnant. So you can see from the timeline that we didn't start having sex until long after—"

"Thank you, Dr. Flanagan," Copeland grumbled. "That's enough."

"Sorry," I muttered.

He leaned over and chatted with Cynthia and the Medical Board representatives. After almost two minutes of whispering back and forth, he said to me, "I believe the committee needs a few minutes to confer in private. If you would be so kind as to wait outside with your attorney and Mr. Maxwell."

"Yes, of course." I stood.

Vikki stood too.

Lion pointed at his carving on the committee table, "Be careful with that. It's my wedding present to my wife and it's one of a kind, just like her."

My heart melted when he said that.

The three of us walked outside and closed the doors to the meeting room.

"My goodness, Mr. Maxwell," Vikki said, "you sure put on quite a show."

"You should see me in the cage," he chuckled. He rubbed my back. "And the bedroom."

My eyes popped.

Vikki looked away, grinning with embarrassment.

Theatrics were fine for a professional fight, but I didn't know if they'd work for an ethics committee.

The three of us were still sitting in the waiting area an hour later. Well, Vikki and I were. Lion had paced the entire time despite his knee.

"They've got to give this to you," he said. "If they don't, they're heartless bottom feeding maggots."

Michelle from HR opened the door, surprising all of us. She said, "The maggots will see you now."

I leaned over to Vikki and whispered, "Did she just say maggots?"

"I heard committee."

"I am losing my mind."

She patted my hand. "Relax. I think we're good."

We all filed toward the doors.

Lion stopped and asked Michelle, "Can I come in too?"

"Um…" she turned into the room. "Can Mr. Maxwell come in?"

Mumbling from inside.

I couldn't hear anything.

Michelle nodded to the committee then said to Lion, "That would be fine, Mr. Maxwell. But the committee asks that you not say anything else or interrupt in any way."

Vikki and I both glared at Lion.

"What? I can keep my mouth shut."

We all filed into the room. Vikki sat down.

I said, "Lion, do you want my chair? For your knee?"

"You sit. You're the pregnant one."

I smiled. I wasn't going to argue. I sat down and he stood behind me and placed his hands on my shoulders. I reached up and squeezed one for comfort.

Sidney Copeland said, "Mr. Maxwell, do you need a chair?"

"I'm good. I'll stand. Behind my wife. The woman I love. The mother of my child. The best mother—"

Copeland cleared his throat. "That's enough, Mr. Maxwell. We get the idea."

"Right. Sorry."

"Dr. Flanagan," Copeland said, "you have tread very close to crossing over the limits of professional responsibility and propriety in this situation. The bond between doctor and patient is a sacred one not to be taken lightly. It requires the utmost care and respect. Without that respect, we as physicians do a disservice to our patients and the community at large. Their care must always come first. In light of recent circumstances involving your fiancé, and in consideration of Dr. Hackett's confirmation that you did indeed discharge Mr. Maxwell at his own request while in the presence of Dr. Hackett, and due to the fact that Mr. Maxwell has made no allegations against you, we the committee have decided…"

I leaned forward on the edge of my seat.

So did Vikki.

"…that your actions do not constitute a violation of the ethical standards or codes of conduct of either the hospital or the state medical board, and that your actions and intentions ultimately fell within the bounds of your professional responsibility toward your patient."

Silence settled over the room.

Lion leaned down and whispered in my ear, "What the fuck did he just say?" The room was so quiet, everybody could hear him.

Dr. Hackett cleared his throat. "Dr. Copeland just said that Brigid is off the hook." He smiled at me, then Lion. "Brilliant wood carving by the way, Mr. Maxwell. I never would've pegged you for an artist."

"Hell yeah!" Lion cheered and pumped a fist in the air.

Relief.

<<<<<<<>>>>>>>

"Mind if I have a word?" Dr. Hackett called from behind as we waited outside the meeting room by the elevators.

Lion had his arm around my shoulders and Vikki stood beside me. I was busy admiring Lion's wood carving of the three lions. It was incredible, just like the man who made it.

The elevator dinged and we all stepped inside. When the doors closed, Hackett said, "Brigid, I hope you don't think I was the one who brought your relationship with Lion to the attention of human resources."

"Did you?" Lion asked bluntly.

"I did not," he said confidently.

I believed him. "Do you know who did? I thought I was supposed to know who my accuser was."

He put his hands on his waist and craned his neck. "That I do not. Would you believe someone called HR and left an anonymous tip?"

Lion looked at me and we both said at the same time, "Donald."

"Asshole," I muttered.

"Fuckin-A right," Lion grumbled.

"Your ex?" Hackett asked. He had met Donald before the divorce more than once.

"Yes. But it doesn't matter. I already knew my ex-husband was worthless."

Lion said, "You could always sue Donald for defamation of character. Send him a message not to try anything like this again."

"But everything the committee said we did, we did. There was no defamation."

"She's right," Vikki said. "For defamation to apply, Donald would've had to make a false statement about Brigid. But he didn't. And we don't have any proof it was actually him who said something to the hospital."

Lion sighed, "I guess you're right. I just don't want him getting away with anything."

I smiled, "He didn't. So forget about him. I got what I wanted." I wrapped my arm around Lion's elbow and we smiled at each other.

"Me too," he said.

"Right," Hackett grinned at both of us. "I'm so very sorry you had to go through all that, Brigid."

"Thanks."

"Hey, Doc," Lion said to Hackett, "Since it wasn't you who told, why were you asking me all those questions about Brigid when I saw you at your office?"

Hackett smiled. "Simple. I had my suspicions from the beginning about you two, and I merely wanted to warn you, Mr. Maxwell, that dating one's doctor is against the rules, as you so eloquently pointed out. But most male patients aren't aware of this fact, and not all doctors are quick to tell them. For Brigid's sake, I thought it best you know, Mr. Maxwell. But you were so adamant about your disinterest in her, I decided against it. No reason for me to tempt fate."

Dr. Hackett may have had pompous tendencies, but he was a good man.

"So," he grinned, "do you two need a proper chauffeur to drive you to the courthouse? It's the least I can do under the circumstances."

"I can handle it," Lion chuckled. "Irish, did you mean what you said? Do you really want to drive to the courthouse right now?" He smiled his boyish grin once again.

I looked into his eyes.

His darted nervously. "Well?"

"Yes. I would love nothing more."

Lion leaned down and kissed me passionately.

Vikki cooed, "I think I'm going to cry."

Hackett clapped softly. "Bravo, you two."

The elevator dinged when we arrived on the first floor.

The doors opened and sunshine poured inside.

Hand in hand, Lion and I both turned and walked out into our bright new future together.

Epilogue

LION

EIGHTEEN MONTHS LATER

"Knock him out!" The shrill scream came from Daniel, who sat ringside with Brigid. I could barely hear him over the roar of the crowd, but I was right up against the cage fence as I rained elbows on the head of my opponent Carey Bennett. We were well into the fifth and last round. I was running out of gas but Bennett wasn't giving up. He was a professional badass. The kind of man who the proverbial mugger you wouldn't wanna meet in a dark alley wouldn't wanna meet either.

But Carey Bennett didn't scare me.

He tried to buck me off his chest, but I wouldn't let him and finally landed an elbow on his nose. Like that, his arms dropped.

He was out.

I was still swinging, but the ref pushed me off Bennett before I did any serious damage. I rolled backward onto my ass. The ref called the fight, scissoring his arms in front of me, keeping himself between me and Bennett. I jumped up and ran around the cage, my arms in the air. My corner team poured inside and everyone started grabbing me.

"I knew you could do it, son!" Dean Jackson said, slapping my back and hugging me.

"Couldn't've done it without you, old man!"

Cahill was jumping up and down, giggling like a girl. "The come back kid! You did it, brother!"

Two minutes later, Carey Bennett stumbled up to me, still wobbly after getting his ticket punched. His nose was pulped and dripping blood. I threw my arms around him in a bear hug. I talked in his ear, "You were a beast out there, Bennett. You almost had me in round four."

Bennett was still groggy, but he hugged me back. "I can't believe you knocked me out."

"Me neither, brother. Me neither."

"Nobody has ever knocked me out."

"You're still a total badass in my book. You had me on points and would've won if I hadn't."

"Lucky you knocked me out, Maxwell," he chuckled and slapped my back with his gloves. "You owe me a rematch."

"Name the time and place. But give me at least six months to recover."

"Yeah," he laughed. "Me too."

Cameras were flashing and the ring filled up with people. The ref stood between me and Bennett and held our wrists at our sides as the announcer read the official decision over the PA.

"Winner by knockout, the undefeated and undisputed reigning WMAA cruiserweight champion of the woooorld, the King of the Ring, Lion Maaaaaaaax-weeeeeelllllll!"

The ref threw my arm in the air and the crowd went nuts, filling the arena with a collective roar as loud as a thousand lions. A chant started up, everyone joining in. "LI-ON! LI-ON! LI-ON!"

It was overwhelming. I almost cried. Almost.

It was damn good to be back.

I waved at them for two minutes straight while the chanting continued.

"LI-ON! LI-ON! LI-ON!"

Okay, I did cry. But only a little.

When the chanting faded to a dull roar, the guy from ESPN held a mic in front of my mouth and his cameraman pointed a lens at my face. I was still hot from the fight and pouring sweat.

"Lion, how does it feel to be back on top?" His amplified words echoed around the arena on the PA system while the crowd continued cheering.

I leaned down to the mic. "Like I never left." *Which was true.* People had talked smack about me being washed up for the past year. I was plenty sick of it.

The ESPN guy chuckled at that. "Everyone wants to know, how is your knee?"

"Solid. Didn't give me any trouble."

He asked me more questions and I answered everything, giving the fans what they wanted. When he was finishing up, I grabbed the mic. "Hey! Everybody! I want you all to know that I couldn't have done any of this without my family. Brigid? Daniel? Where are you guys? Come on up here!" I searched for them in the crowd.

Brigid waved back and made her way to the ring with Daniel. He was starry eyed being inside the cage for the first time. In the past year, he and I had watched a lot of MMA fights on TV, YouTube, and even live. Now that Brigid and I were officially married, I saw him all the time. She had sold the condo and moved in with me not long after the wedding. We did get hitched at city hall the day of the investigation hearing, but we also had a fancy ceremony a few months later. Brigid said we didn't have to, but I'd never been married and she deserved some pampering after all the bullshit she'd been through.

To my surprise, Donald Wright had learned to like me. I didn't care if he was the one who told the hospital about me and Brigid. In the end, I got what I wanted and he did too. I think the only thing he was worried about was losing his son. Daniel still spent every other week with his dad. I wasn't going to take Daniel away from him. He loved him, and I respected that.

When Brigid stepped into the cage, she was as beautiful as ever. She looked slightly unsure of herself as she carried our son Panther over to me. She didn't want to bring him to the fight, but I insisted. I think she was afraid I might get killed out here tonight, but I knew that wouldn't happen. I wasn't about to let my family down, especially not while they were watching. They gave me strength.

"Come here, guys." I put my arms around Daniel and Brigid. "Say hi to the world." Daniel waved shyly at the camera. Brigid lifted Panther's arm and waved for him. "Would you look at this kid of mine? Show him to the camera, Brigid."

She bounced little Panther in her arms. He wore a plush black panther jumpsuit. It had a little hood with ears and a panther face with whiskers on top. Even had a long tail. Brigid said it was ridiculous, I said that was why he had to wear it.

I was so proud of my son and my family.

They meant the world to me. Having them with me for this victory made everything perfect.

It didn't get any better than this.

No, that wasn't true.

After the excitement of winning faded, after we left the Staples Center where the fight was held and drove home to our house, after we put Panther in his crib in his bedroom, Daniel, Brigid and I sat and talked quietly in the sitting room just across the hall. Eventually, Gwen made her way into the room and jumped in my lap. Aslan climbed into Brigid's. Tigger sat outside the door and watched. Daniel went and picked him up and Tigger melted into his arms and started purring instantly. Tigg was definitely Daniel's cat and missed the heck out of him whenever he was at Donald's.

While we sat with the cats, we talked about the future and the past. We talked about our hopes and our dreams. We talked about what mattered and what didn't, and we all agreed it was right there in our house.

That was when I knew everything in my life was absolutely perfect.

Yes, I had won my fight tonight, and my record was now 29-0.

But the biggest victory was the love in this room.

BRIGID

I took a leave of absence after Panther was born. I got to be with him every single day, all day. Lion was also there with me every step of the way. To my pleasant surprise, despite his busy rehab schedule, followed by his busy training schedule, he always made time for us. In one year of marriage to Lion, I felt like I spent more time with my husband and my infant son than I had in eight years with Donald and Daniel.

Did I regret all the time I'd missed with Daniel when he was an infant? Of course I did. But I couldn't take back the past.

Thanks to Lion, I now spent more time with Daniel than I ever had. Daniel loved his role as big brother to Panther. He even knew how to change diapers because Lion showed him how.

Whenever I saw my three men together, I knew that my future would be the one I had always dreamed of but never thought I'd get. That is, not until Lion Maxwell barged his way into my life.

I had finally found love, true love, and a happy family, all because a broken man had refused to follow the rules.

Sometimes, the rules needed a little breaking too.

.

End

.

Want to find out about my next book before everyone else and get free novellas not available anywhere else? Then sign up for my mailing list!

Sign up here and get a FREE novella now!!

http://eepurl.com/B7crf

Personal thanks from Devon Hartford:

Thank you so much for taking the time to live with Lion and Brigid and their families for a while. If you enjoyed *Broken Lion*, please leave a review wherever you purchased this ebook, on Goodreads, or any book blogs you frequent. Be sure to tell your friends about it!

Connect with me on my Facebook fan group:

Devon Hartford's Heartbreakers

If you're not on Facebook, visit me at:

devonhartford.com

ABOUT THE AUTHOR

Devon Hartford spent most of his life in Southern California frequenting many of the locations in Cover Model. Devon is an artist and musician, and drew upon his experiences with both while writing his previous romance series The Story of Samantha Smith and The Story of Victory Payne.

OTHER BOOKS BY DEVON HARTFORD:

ROMANTIC COLLEGE COMEDY
Fearless (The Story of Samantha Smith #1)
Reckless (The Story of Samantha Smith #2)
Painless (The Story of Samantha Smith #3)

ROMANTIC NEW ADULT COMEDY
Cover Model
Stealing Chastity

ADULT ROMANCE
Broken Lion
Taking Back Beautiful

ROMANTIC HIGH SCHOOL COMEDY
Stepbrother Obsessed

BILLIONAIRE ROMANCE
ONE YEAR LOVE - Part One
ONE YEAR LOVE - Part Two
ONE YEAR LOVE - Part Three
ONE YEAR LOVE - Part Four
ONE YEAR LOVE - Collected Edition (Parts 1-4)

ROCKER ROMANCE
Victory RUN 1 (The Story of Victory Payne)
Victory RUN 2 (The Story of Victory Payne)
Victory RUN 3 (The Story of Victory Payne)
Victory RUN 1-2-3 (The Story of Victory Payne - Collecting Parts 1-2-3)

ACKNOWLEDGMENTS

A HUGE thanks to:

Jackie Barnett for her usual genius

Bethanie "The Typo Hammer" Melander for killing those typos

Her Highness Samantha Sheeley, Queen of All Typos and Ouster of Oopsies!

An even HUGER thanks to all my passionate and fantastic beta readers:

The REAL Julie England, Elizabeth Pawelczyk, Sandy England, Neicy Cassidy, Stephanie Svajgl, Michelle Crane, Maria Combee, Renee Julian, Mylinda Abraham-Powell, Always Handy Mandy Jamerson, Jordan Bault, Sarah Frost, Megan C Christmas, Tania Clark, Rosanne Triegaardt, and The Ever Special Mel Bushell for invaluable feedback and encouragement! You guys rock the typo sauce!

Jessie Duchannes for her awesome reviews and Sailor Moon.

Kelsey Burns for always backing my play.

Hayley Picknell for slick Brit Pimpin' and awesome reviews everywhere!

Michele McKenzie for equally all-star pimpin' and typo-snyping.

Amy Cossio for always rocking the Awesome Saucio.

And last but not least, for last minute typo-snyping of the highest order and in the face of great personal danger, I award a Typo Heart to **Colonel Melanie Starr**, the one and only **Comma Bomber**, who saved this mission from certain disaster at the 11th hour, but not without significant personal sacrifice on her part. Colonel, I salute you!

Thanks to everybody else who has helped make this book a reality!

www.ingramcontent.com/pod-product-compliance
Lightning Source LLC
Chambersburg PA
CBHW021952170626
46808CB00001B/120